MW00940971

Books by Alina

The Frost Brothers

Eating Her Christmas Cookies
Tasting Her Christmas Cookies
Frosting Her Christmas Cookies
Licking Her Christmas Cookies

The Manhattan Svensson Brothers

The Hate Date
I Hate, I Bake, and I Don't Date!
Hating and Dating Your Boss with Style!
Yeah, I Hate-Ate Your Cupcake!
Love, Hate, and Terrible Dates
The Worst Dates Bring Chocolate Cake

The Svensson Brothers

After His Peonies
In Her Candy Jar
On His Paintbrush
In Her Pumpkin Patch
Between Her Biscuits
After Her Fake Fiancé
In Her Jam Jar
After Her Flower Petals

Check my website for the latest news:
http://alinajacobs.com/books.html

Resting GRINCH FACE

Resting Grinch Face

A Holiday Revenge Romantic Comedy

ALINA JACOBS

Summary: Oliver doesn't deserve a quaint small-town Christmas or a fancy Christmas tree from my family's farm. This billionaire should be haunted like Ebenezer Scrooge by the Ghost of Christmas Past. Or at least the Ghost of Hookups Past. But will he even remember me or how he ruined my life?

To Netflix for giving Hallmark a run for their money this Christmas. That new Lindsay Lohan movie, amiright?

You're a mean one,
Mr. Grinch

CHAPTER 1

"Toasted white chocolate peppermint mocha with chestnut praline whipped cream, an extra shot of espresso, and extra, *extra* Christmas cheer sprinkles!"

I took a deep breath of the cold winter air and let it out.

"So a number six with an extra shot of espresso?" I said slowly to Elsa, trying not to completely lose it and scare the tourists.

"Nooo," she said, her eyes manic from the lack of sleep and all the caffeine. "It has extra, *extra* Christmas cheer sprinkles."

It was the day after Thanksgiving and I already knew, in my shriveled black heart, that I would not survive this holiday season.

The espresso machine whirred while I mixed the sugary concoction like a Christmas witch.

Really more like a Christmas bitch, I thought nastily. I dumped two handfuls of the holiday sugar sparkles and crispy white pearls that made up the Christmas cheer sprinkles on top of the mountain of whipped cream.

I was getting a migraine from the nonstop Christmas carols the band played in the gazebo in the middle of the Harrogate town square. Sure, it added to the quaint small-town atmosphere in the picturesque Christmas market—until you'd been trapped in said market for the last ten hours, hearing the same five songs over and over and over again. Not to mention all the warring smells from the Christmas stalls—the *Glühwein*, the gingerbread, the roasted chestnuts—were nauseating me.

I glared out over the line of people waiting at the Naughty Claus coffee stand as I started on the next ridiculous order.

You need the money, I reminded myself.

"Noelle!" My mom's friend Deborah waved to me.

All I want for Christmas is for Santa to end this madness in a fiery explosion.

"I didn't expect you to be here slinging coffee like you were still in high school." She laughed like she was just making a joke. Mean girls never changed.

"I thought you had gone back to Harvard to give it another try," she said, pretending to do a boxing move with her Chanel fur-lined leather gloves.

"I'm doing it remotely," I replied as I made the peppermint mocha mechanically.

Deborah shook her head slowly. "It's such a shame. We all thought you were going to go off and do great things. See, Stacey?" she said to her daughter, who was busy texting on her smartphone. "This is why you can't just slack off when you get to college. You'll flunk out and be a huge embarrassment."

Deborah took her coffee and dropped two quarters into the tip jar.

"Buy your mom something nice for Christmas! Poor woman."

"Don't let Deborah get you down," Elsa whispered to me as she reached around me for two reindeer cake pops. "She's just jealous."

"Of what?" I hissed. "Having a daughter who's a failure and a college dropout?"

"Don't sell yourself short. Your tits look very nice in your elf uniform!"

Just take it one day at a time. Everyone moves at their own pace. But repeating my father's words did nothing to dampen the shame that was now exposed to everyone at the Christmas market.

"Do you work for Santa?" a little boy demanded.

I glanced down at him. "No. What's your order?" I barked.

"Um..."

"Do you want the hot chocolate or—ooh, look!" His mom pointed. "They have reindeer cake pops."

People standing in line behind the woman started grumbling.

"If you don't know your order," I said loudly, "please go to the back of the line."

"Someone needs a little Christmas cheer in her life," the woman huffed.

Elsa kicked me.

But I was done. Done with the holidays, done with this itchy uniform, and done with listening to the amateur jazz rendition of "All I Want for Christmas Is You" for the tenth time that day.

"Lady," I said, "you have been standing in line for the last thirty minutes. To facilitate the coffee-buying experience, I have, for your convenience, placed several menus along the queuing area. With photos. How do you not know your order?"

"This is not the type of customer service I expect at the Christmas market," she complained. "I want to speak to your manager."

"We're called naughty for a reason." I pointed up at the sign.

The little boy started to cry. "I'm telling Santa that you're a mean elf."

"Oh really?" I said, crossing my arms. Was I seriously about to get in an argument with a five-year-old? You betcha.

"Can you even read and write? How are you even going to lodge this complaint?"

"Santa's on Twitter." The kid stuck his tongue out at me.

St. Nick help me.

"Will he have me sent off to elf reeducation camp?" I demanded. "Am I going to be tied down on a gingerbread table and waterboarded with royal icing until I sing Christmas carols?"

Several people had their phones out.

"What are you even filming? Do you want me to flash my tits?" I shrieked at the crowd.

Did I mention I had been under a lot of stress lately?

"Don't let the mean elf ruin your holiday spirits."

I froze as the deep voice washed over me.

A tall man in an expensive wool coat stepped out of the crowd, leather shoes crunching lightly on the freshly fallen snow. His ice-blue eyes swept over me. He nodded to the little boy's mother then gracefully knelt in front of the kid.

He smiled a familiar, easy smile, and the boy stopped crying.

"Why don't I help you order?" the tall man offered.

The kid hiccupped and nodded.

"I'm partial to the snowman cookie. And to drink?" He glanced up at the menu, his eyes sliding over me again while I stood there pinned like a stocking on a mantel.

"Let's do a Blue Christmas hot chocolate. For Mom, maybe an eggnog latte." He stood up. "I'll just have the drip coffee, black."

"No cookie?" the little boy asked, grabbing the hem of the man's coat.

Snowflakes rested softly on the man's platinum white hair—hair that had washed like moonlight over my hands when I had run my fingers through it.

"You know what?" he said with that same easy smile. "It's Christmas. Why not?" He pulled out his wallet.

My stomach flip-flopped, and I tried not to lose my own Christmas cookies.

"How much do I owe you?" the boy's mom asked me.

"Don't worry about it. I've got it," the man practically purred. "Merry Christmas."

"Merry Christmas to you too." The little boy's mom practically drooled as the handsome man handed me his credit card. The heavy metal card was cold in my hand as I swiped it.

He signed his name with the signature of a man used to signing his name on the line of billion-dollar contracts. Then he slid the receipt over to me.

His eyes met mine. I waited for him to say something, to ask me what I was doing there—anything to show he recognized me, that he remembered me, remembered the night we spent together...and the day after when he'd ruined my life.

But all he said was, "Could I have a copy of that receipt?"

Like a puppet, I pressed the button on the cash register. I handed him his coffee, feeling numb.

He gave me a bland smile then waved to the little boy.

"Wait," I croaked out.

He turned.

"You forgot..."

Me.

"You forgot your cookie." I handed him the little paper sack with the frosted snowman shortbread cookie I had baked with my mom into the wee hours of the morning. "It's homemade."

"Thanks," he said, saluting me with his steaming paper cup. "Happy holidays."

I stared after him, his broad shoulders cutting a path through the crowd.

I felt like crying.

"Was that..." Elsa trailed off.

"Yep."

"And he didn't..."

"Nope."

"Maybe he was just feeling awkward after what he did to you," Elsa chattered.

"He wasn't feeling awkward." The sadness turned into rage. "He literally had no idea who I was." My voice was taking on a screeching tone. "He looked right at me and didn't even remember me."

"You have, er, changed a little bit."

"I didn't gain that much weight."

"I just meant you went back to your natural hair color and aren't wearing your fake glasses," Elsa said delicately.

"Yeah, sue me. I wanted to look the part of a Harvard girl. In truth, I will always be a messy small-town girl at heart. Probably why I meant nothing to Oliver. I'm just the help. An elf in a sea of worker elves."

"We're getting philosophical, and it's not even lunchtime yet."

"How dare Oliver not even remember me? How dare he ruin my life and just walk off with barely a 'happy holidays'?" I was breathing hard, my breath clouding around me like I was an angry, cookie-addicted, Christmas-hating dragon. "How dare he enjoy the Christmas market? Oliver doesn't deserve to have a nice Christmas. He doesn't deserve to have a nice life. He ruined mine. He deserves the same treatment."

"Oliver Frost is a billionaire," Elsa hissed, shoving two more cups of coffee across the counter. "You live with your parents and share a bedroom with your niece and your grandmother. You will never get revenge. Sometimes life's not fair."

"It should be." Anger settled deep in my chest. "Men like him shouldn't just get to wander around the Christmas market in my small town, paying for people's coffee like they're Christmas superheroes." I wiped at my eyes, smearing the heavy makeup. "Someone has to right the scales."

I picked up the large metal tanks of Snowman Surprise, a nasty concoction of leftover hot chocolate and extra syrups that blended until it was frothy then was topped with whipped cream and glittery red and blue sprinkles. It was served on ice.

People who'd been around the Christmas market block called it elf vomit. Tourists, and especially their kids, loved it.

I picked up a stack of cups for plausible deniability.

"So, this is your Christmas villain origin story," Elsa remarked.

"Damn right."

CHAPTER 2

Oliver

My older sister didn't smile when I stepped up beside her.

Her bare arms were crossed and not from the cold. Across the Christmas market, her ex was on the phone while his little sisters raced around him, chasing the snow flurries.

"I got you a coffee, Belle." I shoved it in her hand. "And a cookie."

She turned to me. "A cookie?"

"It's a happy snowman. See?"

I handed her the bag. My oldest brother, Owen, glared at me.

"Belle, he's being mean to me," I said automatically.

"You can't be out here trying to get people to invest in your company if you're just going to run and hide behind your sister whenever anyone looks at you funny," my next oldest brother, Jack, scoffed.

"He can't help it," Matt, who was one Frost brother too many, ruffled my hair. "He's the runt of the litter."

"Now, Belle." Jonathan, the classic middle child, rubbed her shoulders. "We're all here to cheer you up."

"I don't need cheering up," Belle said slowly, still staring at her ex. She bit the head off the snowman. *Crunch.*

"Yikes." Jonathan stepped back from her.

"Guess this isn't going to be a merry Christmas," Jack muttered.

I needed it to be.

Last year was miserable. I had barely managed to graduate from Harvard because I was so concerned about my sister. I had always loved Christmas, mainly because my sister had always made it special. She would always have the house decorated, presents under the tree, and a nice meal cooked, even when my parents couldn't be bothered. We would all have a merry Christmas this year, even if it killed us.

Out of the corner of my eye, I saw a young woman in an elf costume creeping around through the crowd.

It's a Christmas market. Who cares?

I'd had a stressful few months, working on building my company, running my hedge fund, and trying to keep my family from falling apart. I just needed to keep it together through the holidays.

I wanted this Christmas to be nice for my sister. She had given up so much for me to be able to go to school. I had to show her that her struggles had been worth it.

If I didn't, I was afraid she would leave again.

The elf girl was closer to us.

I felt twitchy with paranoia. I recognized her from somewhere. Maybe she was a corporate spy?

She's probably just making a delivery.

"I can punch Greg in the face for you," Owen offered.

"I'm not bailing any of you out of jail this Christmas," Belle warned, glaring at each of us in the eye. All my siblings had the same coloring—silvery white hair and ice-blue eyes. Backdropped against the falling snow, my sister resembled a *Game of Thrones* character.

I shifted my weight on my feet.

You're about to make a huge capital outlay for your new company, I reminded myself. *Your investments just peaked over a billion. Act like it.*

But my older sister was terrifying.

Her ex looked over at us. His little sisters waved.

After a moment, I suggested, "Maybe we should go say hello?"

Belle's eyes narrowed.

"Or not."

The elf girl, lugging a large silver canister on wheels, slipped and slid through the snow toward us.

"Snowman Surprise," she called. "Five dollars!"

"Yes! My favorite," Jonathan whooped. "I have a ten." He waved the bill at my siblings and me. "Who wants a cup?"

"That stuff is toxic." Owen scowled.

"It's a Christmas tradition," Jonathan replied cheerfully.

I trailed Jonathan over to where Greg's little sisters were lining up for a cup.

"You are not each buying one," Greg scolded them. "You can split one amongst yourselves."

"Hey," I said as the elf ladled out the frothy liquid that smelled sickly sweet, "I know you, don't I?"

She froze and looked up at me with big brown eyes. Her lips parted.

"Wait," I said, eyes narrowing, "You're the Christmas-hating elf from the café. Are you seriously stalking me?"

"Stalking you?" she screeched. "How dare you? I'm trying to make an honest living."

"Selling toxic waste?"

I was met with protests from Jonathan and the gaggle of little girls.

"This is a small-town tradition. I'm sorry that you and your Manhattan ego can't appreciate Snowman Surprise," the young woman snapped.

"Isn't this that elf vomit stuff?" I asked Jonathan. He'd tried to convince me to drink it last year.

"The one and only." He handed his ten-dollar bill to the elf. "Load me up."

She gave me a dark look then hefted the stainless-steel container.

"Bottoms up!"

"Why don't you just use the—fuck!" I yelled as her arms jerked and the sticky sweet drink splashed all over my bespoke suit and expensive coat.

"You did that on purpose!" I roared at her.

She stood her ground, looking defiant.

"It was an accident," she said, blinking up at me innocently.

"Are you insane?" I sputtered. The frothy drink dripped from my hair, soaking my suit. My wool coat was covered in clouds of whipped cream and slowly dissolving red and green sprinkles. "I have a meeting."

"Guess you better go change, then." She spun on her elf boot and started to head back to her stall.

I rushed after her and grabbed her arm, my feet squelching in my shoes.

"So that's it? You're just going to run off after you ruined my suit and probably my meeting?"

"It sure does suck when someone ruins your life, doesn't it," she muttered, jerking her arm out of my grasp.

"What?" I demanded.

She whirled around, expression angry.

Something about her fury felt familiar, but I brushed it off. I hadn't been sleeping well. Besides, I would, of course, remember someone like this woman. She was a holy terror.

"You need to at least pay for my stuff that you ruined."

"Pay for your stuff?" she snapped, the ribbons on the elf hat bobbing. "Screw you. This isn't the North Pole. You don't get to just demand that people give you free stuff."

"No, but I can have you replace the items you ruined."

"You were standing in the danger zone. You should have moved," she argued, stabbing me in the chest with one slightly chipped red and green nail.

The townspeople, ready for holiday drama, had gathered around us, recording with their phones and hoping for the next viral video.

I slowly stepped back from the elf. The last thing my company needed was for its CEO to be the target of an online witch hunt.

"Not only did you ruin my afternoon with my family at the Christmas market, but you tried to ruin that poor little boy's Christmas. Something tells me that you're not a cheerful, Christmas-loving elf."

"Got that right, buddy," she muttered, rubbing her arm where I'd left a sticky handprint.

Before I could get in one more parting shot, an irate middle-aged woman stomped over.

"Noelle Wynter," she raged, "I'm not paying you to abandon your post during the lunch rush. This is coming out of your tips."

"Worth it," Noelle said under her breath.

The older woman paused and looked at me, the Snowman Surprise having started to freeze and congeal on my clothes. Then she turned her gaze to the empty stainless-steel canister.

"Did you waste Snowman Surprise?" She was horrified, like Noelle had just flushed holy water down the toilet.

Noelle flicked her eyes back to me then to her boss. "Oops. I can make some more. It's just—"

"It's a secret family recipe," her boss harrumphed. "Now get back to your post; there is a line."

Noelle, dragging the canister behind her as she followed her boss, looked over her shoulder and blew me a kiss.

The wind blew, and I caught a whiff of how I smelled. "I'm just going to burn this suit."

"Elf vomit indeed," Belle said dryly as she shoved her way through the milling onlookers.

At least she was smiling. That was worth getting doused.

"Should be illegal to sell that," Owen said gruffly. "He smells flammable."

That earned us a small laugh from Belle. Normally I would be elated, and I was.

But a mystery consumed part of me.

I stared back through the crowd in the direction Noelle had disappeared.

Why was she so obsessed with me?

CHAPTER 3

"I literally cannot believe you did that!" Elsa crowed as I drove down the long winding road that led through the woods to my family's Christmas tree farm. "Gosh, Oliver must have been so pissed."

"He was furious!" I whooped over the Christmas carols that Elsa insisted on blaring.

Sure, for the rest of the shifts, Olga had kept a watchful eye and snapped at me whenever she thought I was going too slow or not displaying enough Christmas cheer, but it had been worth it to finally have the upper hand on Oliver for once.

"You're my spirit animal," Elsa sighed. She was my best friend and cousin and had been with me every torturous step of the way since I'd met Oliver.

"You did what every girl dreams of—get revenge on the walking penis who wronged her." Elsa rolled down the window of the old Chevy truck and screamed, "Girl power!"

"It barely counts as revenge," I complained.

"You ruined his expensive suit and gorgeous hair," Elsa said reverently.

I clenched my hands on the steering wheel. I was not going to think about how it felt to run my fingers through said hair.

"Wealthy guys like him don't care about ruined clothes."

"When he eventually remembers you," Elsa said as I pulled up and parked by the wood pile, "then he'll put two and two together and see that his own actions led to his public humiliation."

"If he does remember me—which, honestly, he probably never will because he's a sociopath and a player—he'll just play it off like, 'Oh, my dick's so magical that it drives women crazy,'" I snapped, turning off the car.

"To be fair, it did make you a little bit crazy," Elsa said, kicking the passenger door open with her boot.

"No, that was the aftermath of..." I blew out a breath. "Never mind."

I needed to go into the holiday war zone with a clear head, not with eighty percent of my brain occupied by Oliver Frost.

"Maybe your mom will be in a good mood today," Elsa said, wincing.

I paused, my hand on the wobbly front door handle.

"And maybe my sister finally got some emotional maturity and is acting like an adult."

I opened the door and ducked as my mom's calico cat, Gingersnap, flew past me, chased by Max, a chunky, still untrained corgi who was last year's Christmas present.

"Someone stop that dog!" my mother hollered, waving a rolling pin, apron strings flying as she ran out of the kitchen. "He tipped over my last bottle of wine."

Elsa raced after the animals.

My mom wavered on her feet. "It was my last bottle."

"I'll make you some tea instead," I said delicately, taking the rolling pin.

"Don't judge me," my mom insisted as I herded her back to the kitchen and past my brother. He was sitting in the living room, playing a fantasy video game on his laptop while my grandmother yelled obscenities at the rerun of last year's *Great Christmas Bake Off* that blared on the small TV.

My mom picked up the empty wine bottle and shook the last few drops into her glass.

"Don't judge me." She pursed her lips. "It's the holidays. I'm allowed to drink during Christmas."

"No judgments," I promised. I turned on the kettle and pulled the latest batch of snowmen cookies out of the 1950s oven.

"All your baked goods sold out," I told her, tugging a mug out of the pile of dirty dishes in the sink and washing it. "The reindeer cake pops are a huge hit."

My mother slumped down at the kitchen table and buried her head in her hands.

When you get preggo at fourteen and marry a Christmas tree farmer, everyone says the silver lining is that you get to be kid-free in your thirties and enjoy your life. That is, unless your children follow in your footsteps and make you a grandma when you're thirty.

My two littlest nieces raced screaming into the kitchen, melted candy smeared all over their faces. "Gramma!" they shrieked.

"Let's give Granny some alone time," I said to the little girls.

They wailed as I wiped at the candy cane-flavored drool on their faces.

"God, where is your sister? Where is your brother? Why will no one raise their own children? Dove. Dove!" my mother yelled at the top of her voice.

My eldest niece slumped into the ancient galley kitchen.

"What?" she snapped with all the ire of an eleven-year-old being asked to do anything.

"Would you mind," I asked Dove as I picked up the two wailing little girls, "taking them outside, maybe? I need to help your grandmother get the rest of the baked goods ready for delivery tomorrow. The Christmas market never sleeps."

"Sure," she said, rolling her eyes. "I'll just take care of other people's children."

"Yes you will," my mom barked, "because we're family, and that's what we do."

I winced. "Thanks, Dove," I said, making a heart with my hands. "Elsa's probably still out there with the dog. I bet she'd help you all build a snow fort."

Dove stomped out of the kitchen.

"Don't tip that cheesecake over!" Gran hollered from the living room.

"What are today's numbers, Mom? Were you able to make extra M&M holiday sugar cookies? I don't know why people don't want to just make them at home. They're so easy to do," I chattered, trying to lift her mood.

"What am I doing with my life?" my mother groaned.

"You're baking," I reminded her as I took inventory of all the cookies, cakes, and miniature pies. "And you and I will have an existential crisis on January second when the Christmas market closes."

The side door opened, and my father filled the doorway. He grinned at me as he unwound his scarf.

"There's my retirement plan," Dad crowed.

When you were born to a sixteen-year-old dad, you became used to him always being an energetic young man. But lately he seemed tired and worn down, even though he wasn't even forty.

My dad hugged me, some of the snow from his clothes sliding down my collar.

I felt horribly guilty. My parents had sacrificed so much so I could go to Harvard and earn a fancy degree. I was supposed to land a good job so I could finally buy my mom the house she had always wanted and let my dad finally put his feet up instead of working eighteen hours a day in the elements.

I had failed.

I was supposed to be the one who broke the cycle and let my mom prove to Deborah and the other mean girls she had gone to high school with that teen moms could be good parents.

But I failed that too.

Now I was back in my small town, trying to tread water as fast as possible so that I wouldn't be a burden on my parents.

And it was all Oliver's fault, I fumed as I stacked the boxes up so they'd be ready to take to the truck early the next morning.

Screw him. Dumping elf vomit all over him didn't come close to making him repay his debt to me. But Elsa was right. What could I even do about it?

"Hey, Jimmy," my dad called into the living room. "Why don't you come out and help me cut down a few more Christmas trees to sell tonight?"

My brother yelled obscenities into his headset.

"Jimmy?" my dad called again.

"I'm busy, Dad," he said, still staring at his game. "I have to babysit. Krystal dropped off Destiny. Her mom has to work double shifts the next few weeks."

"I could really use your help..." Dad trailed off.

"I'll help, Dad," I offered, grabbing my mittens. "We'll pick some really nice trees."

Elsa was playing with the little girls and had even coaxed Dove into pretending to be an ice princess.

"Bless her for coming for the Christmas season," my dad said. "I don't know what we would have done. I just wish I could get your brother interested in the Christmas-tree business."

"Speaking of," I told him, pulling out my phone, "can we please go over the numbers for the business soon? I've inputted the expenses and revenue and made a few projections." I showed him on the app I had coded to ideally, finally, get my parents to be conscientious about the states of their various businesses. It had bright colors and little icons to make finance fun.

It didn't seem to work on my dad.

"Don't worry about the money, Candy Cane," my dad assured me. "It's Christmas. It will all work out."

I ground my teeth. "I can't make accurate projections or even finish a business plan unless I see the full financial picture. I need all the paperwork related to the Christmas tree farm. Just because I didn't graduate from Harvard doesn't mean I don't know the basics of accounting and how to run a business."

"You haven't graduated *yet*," my dad said kindly. "You're working on it. Everyone moves at their own pace."

I was afraid my pace would be too slow to ensure financial stability for my parents for the next two decades while I ideally got my life together enough to take care of them in their old age.

"Oh, this is such a lovely tree," my dad said as we stopped in front of a Frasier fir. The bushy dark green branches were dusted with a light powdering of snow. "Some family will be very happy to have that tree in their living room."

It was a big tree. When I was a little girl, I had dreamed of having a big house with twelve-foot-tall ceilings that could fit a tree like this one.

"It's almost too pretty to cut," my father said wistfully. He was a Christmas romantic.

And I was the Krampus.

"Lots of new residents have bought up all those old Victorian houses and renovated them," I reminded him. "They're from Manhattan, and they would totally shell out a hundred bucks for a tree like this."

"We are not charging anyone that much." My father was horrified.

"Yes we are, Dad," I said, hating how mean I sounded. "We run a Christmas tree farm. That means we have been operating in the red the entire year and need to make it up. Christmastime is money-making time, so let's go."

"Don't be such a grinch," my dad coaxed, wrapping his arm around me. "You used to love Christmas when you were a little girl."

Past tense. *Had* loved Christmas. But someone had to be the adult in this father-daughter relationship, and it certainly wasn't going to be my dad.

I revved up my chain saw, carefully cutting the tree as close to the base as possible, perpendicular to the trunk. My father caught the tree gently to not damage any of the branches.

Then I chose several more trees, and we cut them down too.

After we had them all lined up in the trailer attached to my father's rickety pickup truck, he crowed, "Fran's not going to have trees as nice as these."

Inside the house, my mom was mixing up frosting, working on a catering order for a holiday party.

"Santa Baby" blared from the radio, listing out all the things my father and his Christmas tree farm had never been able to give her. Things I had never been able to give her.

"We're leaving," I called as Elsa and I picked up the boxes of cookies earmarked to be sold at the Christmas tree lot.

My dad picked up the container of hot chocolate. "Noelle, you've been working since five this morning. You can't go back to work."

"It's fine, Dad," I said firmly as my mom stacked another box on my pile.

"Totally, Uncle James," Elsa said. "We've been sucking coffee all day. We are totally pumped to sell Christmas trees."

"Your siblings could—"

"I highly doubt that," I said, shoving my dad out the door while my brother yelled at the computer screen. "Have you even seen Azalea today?"

"She woke up around two," my dad said defensively as we all crowded into the cab of the truck. "She just had a baby, so it's been hard for her."

"She had that baby fourteen months ago but sure."

"Don't leave without me," Gran hollered.

I jumped out of the cab and ran and grabbed her before she could slide on the snowy driveway.

"I've been running naked through the snow longer than you've been alive," Gran yelled, throwing me off. "Here. If you want to help, put that in the back." She shoved a large sports thermos at me. "It's a Holly Jolly Christmas citrus cocktail. Trust me," she said, squishing into the back of the cab with Elsa, "once word gets around that Jolly Elf Christmas Trees has booze, we'll be selling out in no time!"

CHAPTER 4

Oliver

"Why is your hair green and red?"

I forced my expression to remain neutral. Had none of them listened to my pitch?

Tristan's brother Beck didn't look up from where he was making notes on the slide printout in front of him.

His brother, Walker, who ran Quantum Cyber with my brother Owen, was the one who asked the off-topic question.

"He had a mishap with an elf," Tristan explained.

"An elf? Was she cute?" A grin spread over Walker's face. "Did she slip something into your hot chocolate?"

"Tristan, you need to watch out for your friend." Greg frowned. "People are insane during the holidays."

"Don't you dare sit there and act like you give a shit about my little brother," Belle exploded at Greg.

Yes, they did in fact both work at the same investment firm now. Hence, I had barely graduated from Harvard—it was the stress of the situation. Also because I was in the middle of trying to get my company off the ground.

"My hair color isn't important," I said, trying to keep the irritation out of my voice. I was also forcing my hands to stay down by my side and not reach up to pull at my hair, which was streaked with green and red dye.

"I just don't know if we in good conscience can invest in a company run by someone with multicolored hair," Hunter Svensson stated.

"Fine," I said, about to lose it. "We'll have Evan Harrington, Chris Winchester, or one of the Richmond brothers invest."

Hunter just laughed. "Sure you will."

His daughter toddled past me.

"My wife is the mayor in this town, so good luck building a microprocessor factory here without Svensson Investment to help grease the wheels."

I rubbed my jaw. "I'll put it somewhere else."

"We don't want to get into threats and ruining business relationships," Tristan said, jumping into the fray. "Harrogate is perfect for the micro-processing factory. It's going to create high-skilled jobs. As you can see on this presentation, the microprocessor factory needs to be located somewhere cold and on the train line. Harrogate is an ideal location. Not to mention, it's close enough to Manhattan that if we go to war with Russia, they won't dare bomb the city because it would ruin the processing plant."

I flipped to the next slide, which showed a site inventory map.

"All of the potential locations are far out from town. Option A is the old county expo site. It's a brownfield, but we can get tax credits to clean it up. It's on the train line and on a state highway. Option B is by the bridge over the river. It's not a brownfield but does need a bit of site work. One plus is that it's by water."

I clicked to the next slide.

"Option C is an old Christmas tree farm that's failing. The good thing about the Christmas tree farm site is that it's a little closer to town and on an old rail line that's mostly intact," Tristan explained.

"I have the capital to purchase the land," I said, "and I will leverage my hedge fund to secure a loan for the construction of the factory. We're going to get some Defense Department money, since they're trying to invest in American infrastructure to develop microprocessors and we anticipate a steady client for the next hundred years, but we're probably going to be operating at a big loss the first five years, and we need Svensson Investment to cover some of that."

"It is an intriguing investment," Greg said, leaning back in his chair. "Belle, why don't you and I go discuss—"

"I'm not going anywhere to discuss anything with you," she snapped. "Svensson Investment will give you the money."

"Score! Love having your sister at the company," Tristan said, elbowing me.

"But I'll have to think about the terms," Belle added. "I need better projections of how much loss we're talking about."

"I have a chart." I pointed at the presentation.

"This chart is bullshit," Belle said. "Crunch better numbers. Also, we need to know exactly which property you're going to purchase. Depending on the parcel, we may be able to couple the factory with additional manufacturing, research and development, or high-security office space to offset the loss. I need to think about it."

Belle stood up and grabbed her briefcase.

Greg jumped up too.

"Alone. I am thinking about it alone, Greg." My sister was built like a Norse goddess and in her heels was almost as tall as her ex.

"Man, you're not having any kind of Christmas," Walker said cheerfully.

"Thanks for the productive meeting, everyone," Tristan said, scooping up his niece.

"Belle," I said, catching up to my sister before she left. "Why don't we do something fun, you know, get in the Christmas spirit." I lightly punched her in the arm.

"I can tell Owen to throw him in a river if he's bothering you, Belle," Walker called to her.

I scowled at him.

"We just had a lot of Christmas cheer this morning," she reminded me. "In fact, you were covered head to toe in it."

"I was thinking more along the lines of getting a Christmas tree for my new house. You haven't even seen it yet. It's an old Victorian. I know how much you like a historic house."

She raised an eyebrow.

I gave her a pained smile. "Nothing says home like a Christmas tree."

CHAPTER 5

Noelle

"Do you think her firs are bigger than ours?" my dad whispered to me as we unloaded the last of the Christmas trees.

I stepped out of Jolly Elf Christmas Trees and peered down the street at Fran's Christmas tree lot.

"Who the fuck cares how big her trees are?" Gran said loudly. "It's all in how you use 'em."

"Mom," my dad begged, "this is a family-friendly enterprise. Please, let's use child-friendly language."

Elsa and I shared a glance.

My dad didn't know it yet, but Elsa and I had something decidedly family unfriendly planned to sell Christmas trees.

Elsa reached into my bag, pulled out the custom price tags she and I had letterpressed by hand, and started tagging the trees.

"No, no," my dad said to Elsa, picking the tag off the tree. "This is the priciest tag. It needs to go on the ten-foot trees."

"Dad," I said firmly, grabbing the tag back and retying it onto the tree, "we are raising prices."

My dad's mouth dropped open. "We haven't raised prices in... in... since ever."

"Carpe le Christmas season." I whipped out my app. It was customizable. I had made one account for my mom's baking business and one for my dad's Christmas tree business. The dashboard for the Jolly Elf even had a little dancing tree emoji. My mom had been passing the app around the Christmas tree market like a regifted craft set, and it actually had a fair number of users.

"See?" I said, showing him the chart with the cost projections. "This is what you get on December twenty-fifth if you keep the current prices, and this"—I hit the compare button—"is what you earn if you raise the prices to what I set."

My dad's eyes bugged out. "I've never made that much money." He lowered his voice. "Are you sure we can sell trees for this much? That's a lot of money for a Christmas tree. I don't think Fran is charging that much."

"Fran looks like a horse, and she's in her fifties," Gran said. "We've got two hot twenty-somethings."

Gran picked up a cowbell, stood in the middle of the closed-off Main Street, and began ringing it and yelling loudly, "If you want to get sold a Christmas tree by a hot girl, stop on by!"

Elsa and I removed our overcoats to reveal extremely skimpy Mrs. Claus outfits.

I adjusted the belt under my boobs, which felt like they were about to fall out of the low-cut jacket.

My horrified dad covered his face with his hands.

"Hot girls!" Gran yelled.

"I know this is a nasty surprise, Dad," I said, patting his hand, "but I have to do something to keep us in the black. Sex sells." I knew enough about accounting to see that business wasn't good. I had failed to get my big break at Harvard, so we were going to resort to the time-honored traditions to keep my dad afloat.

"Trust her, Uncle James," Elsa trilled. "Noelle went to Harvard!"

"Dad, go sit in the truck. I have hot chocolate and bourbon for you."

I snapped pictures of Elsa and me making duck faces at the camera while we reached and stretched to place the tags on the Christmas trees.

"My Christmas trees bring all the boys to the yard!" I captioned the photo, added hashtags, then let the algorithm do its work.

Gran continued to ring the big bell.

I tried not to breathe in too deeply as we waited at the front for customers.

"What if this doesn't work?" I chewed on my lip. "What if there was a reason I flamed out of Harvard? Maybe I just suck at business."

Though I had wanted to study English, I had majored in business with a minor in computer science, thinking it would be the ticket to big money on easy street.

How wrong I was.

A business degree was useless unless you came from a wealthy family with the right connections. Like Oliver did.

"It's a very merry Christmas after all!" Elsa crowed, shoving her phone in my face. "We have so many likes!"

Gran had switched her pitch to "Booze! Buy a Christmas tree and get drunk."

People wandering through the Christmas market were excited about that. I started pouring cups of the strong-smelling holiday cocktails while Elsa swiped credit cards.

"Guess we didn't need to freeze our tits off after all."

"Or not," I said, pointing.

Svenssons PharmaTech's workers were just now leaving the office, and all the young men with tons of disposable income were flocking to the Christmas tree lot.

"Hey, Mrs. Claus," one of them hooted at me, "why don't you give us a little Christmas cheer?"

"Looking is free if you buy a tree," Elsa called out.

"Yes, ma'am," one pimply-faced guy said in a cracking voice. He must have just graduated.

The guys all crushed into the lot.

"Just give me your most expensive tree," one of them said.

"I don't know if you can handle it." I blew him a kiss.

"I have a big house!" another one of them hollered.

Of course he did. Probably had one of those old Victorian mansions that he totally did not appreciate.

"I want to take my Tinder picture in front of a decorated tree," another young guy was saying to his friend. "Andy just adopted a corgi, and he said we could borrow it."

Elsa and I did a little jig while Christmas carols played over the loudspeaker.

My dad finally had enough bourbon in him that he could carry the Christmas trees to the bagger then help load them onto customers' cars.

"You need a wreath to go with that tree," Gran insisted to one man as he was trying to make his purchase.

I picked up the wreath and did a shimmy with it.

The guy's eyes about fell out of his head.

The things I do for money.

"I'll take two," he said.

"Good boy!"

"I added an extra zero on the wreaths," Gran whispered to me. "Best thing to do while drinking is make a wreath. I have enough to buy a body." She gave me a shot of whiskey.

Then Elsa and I jumped up on a table while customers sang along as we lip-synced Christmas carols.

Through the crowd floated a deep voice. "The markup on these wreaths is insane."

"Ho ho ho fuck no," I said, almost crashing into Elsa as she spun around and I didn't.

"*Oliver.*"

I felt a nasty bit of glee that his hair had a faint green and red tie-dye effect.

"Is he seriously here buying a tree?" Elsa hissed as Oliver's mesmerizing blue eyes swept over the drunken holiday party vibe at our Christmas tree stand.

"Bet they're going to buy a ton of trees and put them in the manor house they stole from our family." Elsa's cat-winged eyes narrowed. If anyone hated the Frost brothers more than me, Elsa did.

Matt Frost had bought the old Wynter estate out from under the nose of Elsa's brothers.

To be fair, Elsa's brothers had money that was all tied up in their businesses that they thought would make it big one day. Maybe. Not to mention the house had been in an extreme state of disrepair. And as we had seen with the state of my parent's finances and mine, we had a snowman's chance in hell of purchasing it.

"He doesn't deserve one of our trees," I fumed. "And he definitely doesn't deserve to stare at my tits again."

CHAPTER 6

Oliver

"So that was why you wanted to come here to buy a Christmas tree."

"What I—no, no, that is not why we're here," I told my sister.

She raised an eyebrow.

"We're here to find a nice large Christmas tree for my living room. Then we're going to decorate it all together as a family."

I snuck a glance at Noelle, who was doing a little dance up on a table that made her tits jiggle in a very distracting manner.

"Isn't the Christmas market supposed to be family friendly anyway?" I added, irritated that all I wanted to do was stare at her. Thanks to her thigh-high black boots, the wide belt cinched at her waist, and her ridiculously short skirt, I was feeling uncomfortably warm, and I wasn't even wearing a jacket.

"They're serving booze and overpriced wreaths," Belle said dryly, handing over her credit card for a cup of the holiday-themed cocktail. "I saw someone advertising a pop-up Christmas bar. I don't think this small town is all that family friendly after dark."

A brown-haired man in a ski cap came over to me. He had Noelle's eyes.

"Are you looking for a tree?" he croaked. He seemed a bit shellshocked, which was an understandable reaction if your daughter was using softcore porn to sell Christmas trees.

I snuck another glance at Noelle. The whole scene was a collage of all my favorite fantasies.

Please keep it together.

She's crazy. You don't want anything to do with her. Once you get your company on the right track, you can find a nice girl from a good family.

Unfortunately, part of me was a little too interested in the messy girl who hucked sugary coffees and ran her hands under her boobs to sell Christmas trees.

I swallowed.

"Do you have any ten-foot-tall trees left?" I asked Noelle's father. His name tag read James.

"Of course we do," he said, leading us through the crowded lot. The trees were flying off the racks.

"I love a good businesswoman," Belle said.

James's shoulders sagged slightly. "This is not how we normally operate."

"You have to change with the times," Belle assured him, patting him on the shoulder.

"How about this one? It's a Fraser fir, cut just a few hours ago." James pointed.

"It's nice. I think we can—"

"Or," James interjected, "this one is a blue spruce. It'll smell divine in your house, and if you keep it well watered, you can repurpose it as a Christmas Valentine's Day tree."

"That one's nice too."

"Or," James said, ushering us to another large bushy tree, "this Douglas fir is—"

"Dad," Noelle barked out from behind a tree. "We are not selling him a Christmas tree." She slapped my hand away from the Douglas fir. "You can go buy a tree from Fran."

"*Noelle*." Her father was appalled. "Please excuse my daughter," he told me. "We are happy to be a part of your family's Christmas tradition."

"Uh, no we aren't. You don't deserve one of these trees. These trees are for nice people."

"I'll take the Frasier fir, sir," I said to James.

"Excellent choice. And I'm so sorry about my daughter's rudeness," he said pointedly at Noelle, who did not break her death glare on me. "Please accept a free wreath with your purchase."

Noelle squawked indignantly and kicked her dad in the shin.

"No discounts. I swear to God, Dad." She pulled out a pen, clicked the top, crossed out the price on the tree, and doubled it.

"*Noelle*," her father hissed. "You can have the normal price," he told me, shaking his head at Noelle. He easily picked up the tree.

"Absolutely not," she told her father, taking off after him.

I grabbed her wrist, pulling her back to me.

"Why do you hate me? You don't even know me."

"You just look like an Ebenezer Scrooge," Noelle insisted, crossing her arms.

I kept my eyes firmly on her brown ones. I was not going to let her see me even thinking about looking at her tits.

"You have resting bi—er, grinch face," I amended. "You hate Christmas. You're like a holiday energy vampire, just trying to ruin everyone else's Christmas spirit."

"Well, you just want to walk around here swinging your dick and flinging money everywhere to make other people feel bad that they're not as rich and privileged as you are," she snapped back.

"And here I thought you'd be grateful that I was here buying one of your little Christmas trees," I said mockingly.

"You don't have to buy one," Noelle replied hotly. "This is not a charity. We don't need your money."

"You sure were working hard to sell them." My eyes finally lost the battle and flicked down to her tits then quickly back up to her face.

"Guess I have to buy a tree now," I said, before she could hit me with a cutting remark.

"You're so"—she sputtered—"*awful*."

"Merry Christmas," I called, turning to head up to the front where Belle was paying for a tree and a wreath.

Dammit, I was going to pay.

My sister had gotten into a habit of always paying for my stuff. I had vowed to stop letting her do it. It was my turn to take care of her. My brothers were dimwitted and oblivious to her pain, but I wasn't.

"Hey!" Noelle yelped behind me.

I whirled around, fists clenched.

A guy was looming over her.

"What did you do?" I snarled.

The guy held up his hands as I advanced on him.

"It was a mistake, honest. I didn't mean—"

"One hundred dollars," Noelle ordered, spots of color on her cheeks.

"I, uh—" The man balked.

I looked between her and the man.

"Touch my tits, it's one hundred dollars."

"You did what?" I snarled at the man. I had zero tolerance for that type of behavior.

"Go away," Noelle snapped at me.

"I don't have the money," the guy whined.

Noelle pulled out a Taser from under her short skirt and clicked the button. Out popped an arc of electricity.

"I suggest you find it." She blew me a kiss. "As I said, I don't need you."

CHAPTER 7

"Oh my gosh, maybe his soul recognizes you after all," Elsa breathed as I drove the car down the dark windy country road, snowflakes reflecting on the headlights of the truck.

Dad and Gran were snoring softly in the back seat.

I yawned and chugged coffee from the thermos.

Vintage Christmas carols tinkled softly on the car radio.

"I think maybe his dick remembered me might be more accurate," I fumed as I thought about Oliver and his purchase of that magnificent tree. "I bet he's at his fancy-schmancy house, done up for Christmas with all the best decorations money can buy. It's so unfair. I wish I had a huge house where I could put an expensive Christmas tree."

"I thought you didn't like Christmas," Elsa reminded me.

"I hate it. But it's the principle of the thing."

Gran woke up with a snort, smacking her lips. She said sleepily, "You've been doing all the driving. Why don't you let me drive?"

"Absolutely not," I said as Gran fell back asleep.

"That would probably solve all your money problems," Elsa said with a snicker.

"Solve? More like end with a fiery explosion." I carefully navigated down the snowy road to the one-lane gravel drive that led to the small cabin.

Built in the 1850s, it had one bathroom and used wood heating, and ice formed on the single-paned windows during even a hint of cold weather.

It did look cozy when we pulled up, thanks to the snow-covered Christmas trees that dotted the landscape, the smoke wafting out from the chimney, and the firelight flickering through the small window.

Inside, the house was anything but calm.

"This is so unfair," my sister was wailing when we all trooped into the house.

My mother was drinking straight whiskey, while my grown-ass adult sister threw a tantrum in the living room.

"I have to work. I'm trying to work. I'm trying to get a job and build a better life for my kids and me." Azalea was really turning on the waterworks. It was a lot for three in the morning.

"I have to bake tarts and cookies," my mom slurred angrily at Azalea, "and a thousand reindeer cake pops."

"You were a teen mom just like me. Have some sympathy, you hypocrite."

"Azalea," my father begged, "don't speak to your mother that way, please."

"None of you are being supportive," Azalea wailed, juggling the crying baby on her hip. "We all had the same circumstances, and you all are judging me."

"No one is judging you, sweetheart."

"I'm judging," Dove called out from the hallway.

"Dove, go to bed," my mother snapped.

My niece stomped up the stairs.

My dad dished up scoops of the seafood casserole that was perched on the stove. He handed plates to Elsa and me.

I headed into the kitchen, undoing the cinched belt.

My mother finally got a good look at me.

"What in God's name are you wearing? James, did you let them go out in public like that? Oh my god, you're both going to end up pregnant, and I'm going to be taking care of children until I die."

Gran shuffled around the kitchen.

"Sex sells," she said, pouring my mom the last glass of the cocktail. "Noelle learned it in business school."

"What if someone saw you?" My mother pressed a hand to her forehead.

"I think everyone saw everything." Gran patted my mom's hand. "Don't worry, everyone knows you two made some mistakes in your youth. I didn't hear anyone talking smack about you."

I took a bite of the casserole. It was a little cold, but the microwave broke in August, and we didn't have the money to replace it, so I soldiered on.

"We sold out of the trees, Mom," I told her.

"And the wreaths and all the baked goods," Elsa chirped. "Plus, we made tons in tips."

My dad paused, the fork hovering below his mouth. "You were collecting tips from people?"

"She let some guy touch her boobs for a Benny," Gran crowed.

"Not helping, Gran."

"I'm a failure as a parent," Mom said, gulping her whiskey.

"It's just business." I pulled out my phone and showed them the app. "Look how much money you all made tonight. And we don't even have all the cash numbers inputted."

"I don't want our daughter out there with her boobs hanging out anymore," my mother said stubbornly.

"Yes," my dad said. "Noelle, we appreciate the help, but you need to concentrate on finishing your project so you can graduate and get a good job. Your mom and I have been doing all right on our own."

"Have you?" Azalea said snidely.

I clamped my mouth shut as my mother and Azalea restarted their argument.

My parents were delusional. You couldn't support a family of nine selling Christmas trees and cakes from your kitchen. That wasn't how the world worked. Not to mention that my dad refused to give me a full picture of the financial state of the Christmas tree farm, which did not inspire confidence.

I yawned as I stood in line for the single tiny bathroom. Elsa knocked politely on the door.

Dove wrenched it open and screamed, "Why can't we have more than one bathroom in this house?" She slammed the door and locked it.

"I have to pee," Elsa complained.

"The outhouse is perfectly serviceable," my dad said.

"When I was in the military," Gran recalled, "I knew this gal who could pee in a beer bottle."

"I'm just going to hold it and sleep in my makeup." I yawned.

My mother was appalled. "People will think you spent the night with a boy."

"Yeah, because she's your last chance for a good child."

"Don't say that, Azalea. Your mom and I love you very much," Dad begged.

"See you in three hours," Elsa told me as I ascended the tiny staircase to the attic bedroom I shared with her, Gran, and Dove. I climbed into my rickety bunk bed and watched the frost form on the windows.

Spent the night with a boy.

As if.

My parents had drilled into me since the moment I started school that having sex with a boy would ruin my life.

I had thought, once I had made it to my senior year in college, that I was finally out of the danger zone and could have a normal youthful experience before entering the rat race.

However, my mom had been right. Sleeping with a guy had ruined my life.

Fuck you, Oliver, I mouthed.

I would find a way to make him pay.

Somehow.

CHAPTER 8

Oliver

The sun reflected off the freshly fallen snow as I milled around with the other small-town locals. The filming of the first episode of *The Great Christmas Bake Off* was about to start. This year, they had Chloe, my brother Jack's girlfriend, and Holly, my brother Owen's wife, as judges. I waved to them.

My company was sponsoring the kickoff event in town. Since I would have to go before the community at the next town hall meeting and convince them to let me build my microprocessor factory outside of town, I needed all the goodwill I could get.

Sure, you would think that no one in town would care about my company building a factory, since it wasn't like I planned to put it smack dab in the middle of historic Main Street. But if one of the small-town busybodies decided that they were bored or felt like I had slighted the town in some way, they could cut my investment off at the knees.

"Great turnout." My best friend and business partner clapped me on the shoulder as we surveyed all the happy townsfolk eating pastries and sipping steaming cups of coffee and hot chocolate.

"I hired a local café to pass out drinks," Tristan added, "and I also paid some of the elderly to slip people a little bourbon in their hot chocolate if they wanted it."

"Who's drinking at ten in the morning?" I frowned.

"Free hot chocolate! Free coffee courtesy of Mithril Tech."

I think I will take that bourbon.

"Why did you hire her?" I hissed at Tristan.

"What? She's smoking hot in that reindeer costume."

"She was the one who ruined my suit."

"Yikes," Tristan said as Noelle crisscrossed through the crowd. She had a large tank strapped on her back that had a hose and dispenser attached and was handing out freshly poured hot chocolate or coffee. She looked like a Christmas reindeer from outer space in that getup. It was a good thing she wasn't because she would have blasted me with a ray gun when she saw me.

"Don't even think I'm giving you a cup of coffee," she declared, holstering the coffee gun.

"Are you the coffee gatekeeper now?" I asked.

"Only one of us is lactating caffeine currently, so I guess I am," she shot back.

Do not look at her tits, I ordered myself.

"You're supposed to be giving anyone who wants one a coffee."

"Dealer's discretion," she scoffed. "I highly doubt that the company who paid for all of this is going to want someone like you getting free drinks."

"Actually," I leaned in, saying in a low voice, "Mithril is my company, and I'm paying for the drinks. But we appreciate your dedication to upholding our brand's good name."

Her eyes, encircled by slightly smudged makeup, widened. Then she pressed her mouth together in a thin line and pulled out a cup from the stack.

"Fine, have a coffee," she huffed, squeezing the handle of the coffee gun and sending brown liquid spraying all over my shoes. She handed me the dripping paper cup.

"Oops. Think this thing needs a refill."

I pulled out a handkerchief and wiped my hands.

"That's not any way to talk to the man signing your paycheck."

"Ah," Noelle said, "the mating call of a billionaire who's never had to work a day in his life and spends his time bumbling around town, forcing performative gestures of Christmas charity upon innocent townsfolk."

"Who doesn't like free coffee and pastries?" I took a sip of my drink.

"Don't act all innocent, Mr. Frost." She gestured to one of the seniors Tristan had paid off, who was tipping a bottle of bourbon into the cups of townspeople wanting a little extra zing in their coffee. "If a company is sponsoring free food in a town that finds any excuse for a snack and booze, they're trying to pay people off. Why? Who knows? Probably for some nefarious, Scrooge-y purpose."

"That isn't a word."

"It is in this Christmas town," she countered. "Now get out of my way. Some of us are actually working."

Noelle was going to be a problem, I decided. But I had full confidence in my ability to handle a seasonal retail worker. Somehow. It would take more than a cookie and a free drink to get her off my case.

At least the townspeople were happy about the snacks and drinks. Several people saw me and waved, pointing me out to their friends.

If it wasn't for Noelle, I'd have this development in the bag.

Something had to make her tick. Until I figured it out, I would continue to play the Christmas-loving billionaire.

A tween girl in a Mithril Tech T-shirt over a baggy black hoodie was passing out pastries. She was trying not to look upset and angry as her friend, another tween girl in a designer coat, talked rapidly to her. I wondered if Noelle had said something to her. I couldn't have them all bad-mouthing my company.

As I approached them, I caught the tail end of their conversation.

"...but what I am saying, Dove, is you're probably going to end up a teen mom just like your mother and your grandmother. Honestly, it's a good thing the Frosts and the Svenssons are raising the bar in this town. Otherwise, your family would be dragging this place down."

Damn.

Tween girls really were vicious. I'd rather be punched in the face.

I smiled at Dove.

She glared up at me. "What do you want, creep?"

Glad she's standing up for herself.

"Oh my gosh!" Her friend pushed her way in front of me, adjusting the fur-lined hat on her head. "I am so sorry, Mr. Frost," she stage-whispered to me. "Dove has a difficult home life and wasn't really parented all that well. Thank you so much for sponsoring *The Great Christmas Bake Off*. It really is becoming a small-town tradition."

"Of course. Dove," I said to the girl in the T-shirt, "I just wanted to thank you for standing out in the cold and handing out pastries and putting out the good word for my company."

She shrugged but gave me a small smile. "Noelle's paying me."

"As she should."

Dove shuffled on her feet in the snow then pulled out a fistful of cash and stuck her hand out to me.

"Do you want the tip money back?"

I grinned at her. "You cleaned up. You keep it. Don't tell Noelle, though. She might take it."

"She wouldn't; she's my aunt, and she's really nice."

Before I could stop myself, I said, "She wasn't very nice to me."

"Probably because she thinks you're hot."

"*Stacey*." Dove kicked her friend.

And we're backing away slowly...

"Oliver." Belle strode over.

Dove and Stacey waved to me then disappeared back into the crowd.

"I thought your company was passing out free coffee. I need the caffeine."

"It's being refilled," I told her, gazing in Noelle's direction.

"You better not piss off anyone in town," Belle warned me. "If you don't want to have your project killed for Christmas, you better turn the charm up to a thousand."

Somehow, I thought even that might not be enough to get Noelle on my side.

Maybe I needed to think of a different tactic.

CHAPTER 9

"Oh, thank God. I'm swamped," Elsa said when I swung the Platinum Provisions drink dispenser onto the table behind the serving counter.

"I'm here for a refill."

"Just help me clear out some of these orders," Elsa begged.

"Sure." I probably needed a moment to defuse the anger I felt over Oliver.

I wouldn't have made Elsa hand out coffee if I'd known it was for *his* company. Oliver totally had some angle.

I set the canisters under the coffee and hot chocolate pots to slowly refill. Then I waved up the next woman in line.

"I need a cozy cookie almond milk latte, and Jayden wants a Santa Claus Is Coming to Town latte. Large."

"Would you like whipped cream on that?" I asked the older man standing slightly behind her.

"I'm not with them," he clarified, stepping back.

I looked down to see a little boy with gelled-down hair blink up at me.

"Yeah. I want extra whipped cream," he snapped.

I slid the orders across the counter. "That will be—"

"Excuse me," the lady said, tapping her gloved finger on the counter.

"Why aren't there any sprinkles on his latte?"

"Yeah!" her son screamed. "I paid for sprinkles."

Actually, he didn't pay for them at all.

"This particular drink doesn't come with them," I explained.

"I want sprinkles!" the little boy screamed.

"It's okay, Jayden. Mommy will make it right. Honestly, what kind of customer service do you all have at this venue?"

I pulled out the shaker with the Christmas cheer sprinkles and dusted the top of the whipped cream of the giant cup.

"Here you go." I ground my teeth into a smile.

"More!" the kid yelled then screamed like a pterodactyl.

I gave him another liberal shake of sprinkles.

His mom lovingly handed him the sugary coffee, which was about as big as his head.

"Here you go, sweetie. You don't want to have too much sugar."

The kid took a swig from the coffee like he was a thirty-year-old lawyer, not a five-year-old.

"Blech!" he yelled, then threw the drink at me.

I shrieked and stood there as it dripped down the front of my reindeer costume.

"Son of a—" I bit my tongue.

"I wanted two shots of espresso in this," the child demanded. "It just tastes like milk. You're trying to rip people off."

My boss hurried out.

"Don't worry," she said to the woman and her son. "We will comp your drinks. It's Christmas, and we want everyone to be happy."

"Seriously?"

"This is coming out of your pay," she hissed at me.

Once Olga was out of earshot, I complained, "Is it even legal to give your kindergartener that much caffeine, or really any caffeine at all?"

"My brothers used to knock back a six-pack of Mountain Dew, one after the other," Elsa said, scrubbing at me with a wet rag.

"Your brothers are crazy."

"Also true. I could call them up here and let them have at Oliver," she offered.

"Tempting, but they'd probably just get thrown in jail, and we are not going to be able to sell enough Christmas trees and reindeer cake pops to bail them out."

I scowled and tried to ignore the soaking-wet sexy reindeer uniform that was slowly freezing to my chest while we rang up the rest of the customers. Then everyone headed over to watch *The Great Christmas Bake Off*.

"Screw Christmas and screw Oliver," I cursed as I slammed the lid on the now-full canister. "It's unfair and humiliating. I have to go out there and pass out free coffee and tell everyone how great Oliver and his company are."

"I can go do it, and you can stay here." Elsa held out her hands.

"I'll probably go off on a tourist if I do that." I grimaced.

"You reek of coffee and candy cane syrup," she said flatly. "Dove can watch the stand. Dove!"

Elsa whistled and waved to my niece, who sighed and shuffled over. "Can you manage the counter while I go pass out coffee?"

"My mom wants me to watch my siblings," Dove said, her tone conveying her unhappiness about it.

"Why does she need you to watch them?" I asked, "Azalea isn't working."

"She wants to watch the bake-off with him." Dove jerked her thumb to where Azalea and an older man were waiting in line for the bake-off entry.

"Oh my gosh," Elsa whispered, "I think that guy is, like, married. I saw him at the Christmas tree lot last night with his wife and kids."

"Maybe they're just being friendly," I said dubiously

"I saw her put her hand on his junk," Dove said flatly.

"Yikes."

"Whoops, there it goes again," Elsa said as we watched my sister, mom of three children with three different guys, going hard for her apparent fourth baby daddy.

I pulled out my phone and snapped a picture.

"Cheaters are the worst." Elsa scowled.

"Maybe I'll make an app called Cheaters, and you just post photos of people cheating and call their behinds out."

"Yes! You'll get rich like Oliver, and we can all move to a house that has a microwave and a water heater big enough that everyone can have a hot shower." Dove jumped up and down in excitement.

"Your parents are, er... well, your grandparents are doing the best that they can," Elsa assured her.

I tested the hoses. Elsa handed Dove the apron.

"Noelle will be back in a couple of hours. I'm going to go spread the gospel of the greatness of Oliver Frost to the masses," my cousin said as I helped her into the canister backpack.

"He needs to go down," I said as I followed Elsa out of the stall.

My cousin rolled her eyes.

"I'm serious," I insisted. "I know I can't ruin his business, but I've decided to ruin his Christmas. The stockings are off. All-in, full-on grinch. And it starts tonight."

CHAPTER 10

Oliver

The smell of freshly cut pine wafted over me as I stepped inside the foyer of the old Victorian mansion I'd just bought.

The town of Harrogate was founded before the Revolutionary War, but growth didn't take off until the industrial scions of old had pumped their profits into the town. There were blocks and blocks of stately Victorian homes, which were popular houses with all the employees working at the nearby medical tech and pharmaceutical companies. These businesses had recently set up shop in the small town, leading to its revitalization.

Sure, it was probably more house than one person needed, but I'd mainly bought it because I had a whole plan that my siblings and I would decorate the tree, make cookies, and forget about all the ugly Christmases past with my parents. And then maybe one day I'd have my own wife and kids to live here with me.

The decorators I'd hired had done an excellent job.

Real pine garland interspersed with twinkling lights wound its way up the curving mahogany banister.

The house still had the original gas lighting, and the crystal globes twinkled.

My siblings and their significant others—minus Belle's ex, of course—were all scheduled to be there that evening.

But first...

A horn honked from the street.

I quickly slipped off my dress shoes and pulled on steel-toed boots.

"What time is your family coming into town?" Tristan asked as I jumped into the front seat of his SUV.

"Not until six thirty. There should be plenty of time to hit these properties."

Christmas carols blared on the radio.

After spending the last four years in Harvard then in Manhattan fundraising, I was in awe at the beauty of the countryside.

The fluffy white snow clung to the huge trees that lined the winding country road as we headed out of town.

"First stop, the expo center," Tristan said.

The now-defunct expo site was an hour or so outside of town. I hadn't been out there yet, and I pulled up the schematic architectural and site plans for reference as we walked the property.

"It's already flat and has infrastructure running to the site," I said as we walked.

"But it's a brownfield. The soil's pretty contaminated," Tristan said, "from when this used to be a factory before they turned it into the expo center."

"It's a historic building, though," I said, studying the site plan, "so we're going to have to put in some additional money to rehab the building."

"We can always turn it into R and D space and lease it out like your sister suggested."

I scowled. "I can't believe Greg screwed her over like that."

Tristan blew out a breath. It clouded around his face. "They seem to be coexisting relatively peacefully."

He looked away. "I know you and your brothers are mad."

"It's going to ruin the next few Christmases."

"Maybe you can find Belle a new boyfriend."

"Or maybe your brother can stop being such an asshole," I snapped at him.

Tristan grimaced. "I'd bet money on you and your coffee elf stalker getting married before I bet on Greg changing."

"Talk about ruining Christmas. Is everyone in this town as crazy as her? I might need to rethink moving here."

"Who would get rich and become a partner in power in the defense industry?" Tristan exclaimed, throwing his arm around my shoulder.

"I'm not sure this site is going to do it for us, though," I said, scrubbing my toe in the hard dirt. Cleaning up this site was going to take a lot.

The land by the river wasn't all that much better. This whole portion of the State of New York had been subjected to a century and a half of industry.

"The microprocessors need cleanliness," I reminded Tristan as we strolled along the icy river.

"This is clean, mostly. It's a little far from town, though. And I know you think the Christmas tree farm is the best site, but we're going to have to run utilities to it."

I mapped out the amount of sewer and water we would need on the drive back to town and to the Christmas tree farm.

Because it bordered my brother Matt's property, we just parked there, grabbed two of his horses, and rode out through the snowy woods.

The scenery was pretty as the horses picked their way through the fallen snow, their hoof falls muffled.

"It's not that hard to bring a sewer here. I can run it through Matt's land," I told him, showing him the sketch I'd made on the tablet while the horse shook its mane, flicking off the snow that had fallen on its muzzle. "It's worth the cost. There's nothing like a green field development."

"Yeah, nothing like paying for water, sewer, electricity, gas, and broadband. Not to mention the townspeople freaking out when we tell them we're going to bulldoze a forest."

"The positives outweigh any negatives," I argued. "We don't need that much space for the factory." I showed him the overlay diagram. "We just have to run a road through here, and we need a small pad for the factory. Installing a high-security facility here with a fence around it will protect the forest better than if your brothers bought up this place and turned it into houses. We'll spin it that it's about preservation."

Clearly, no one was using most of this land for farming, Christmas trees or otherwise. Maybe they had at one point—based on the pattern of the forest, someone must have planted the firs and spruces in neat rows decades ago—but they were tall and overgrown now.

"I can ask the Naughty Claus to cater the town hall. We can serve Christmas tree cookies to sweeten the deal."

I scowled. "No. You need to use a different company. I don't want that girl Noelle anywhere near my business again."

The holiday season was already spiraling. I didn't need Noelle making it worse.

No matter how good she looked in that outfit.

CHAPTER 11

"You need Santa to bring you a man to turn that frown upside down!"

Gran and her friend Ida were waiting for me when I walked up to the Naughty Claus coffee stand.

"One of the elves at the Santa Claus meet and greets is single," Ida told me. "He's a little on the short side, but he's on winter break from Yale. You guys would be cute together."

"Thanks but no thanks. I already have enough men in my life," I said, thinking about Oliver and his entitlement.

"Then you need to convince one of them to give you an engagement ring for Christmas," Gran insisted.

"Or I could, you know, make my own money."

"That was plan A," Gran reminded me, "but it didn't work out, so we have to pivot. Isn't that the word you all use in business? I've been watching YouTube videos so I can be on the up and up with all you young entrepreneurs."

"Nothing more entrepreneurial than catching a man," Ida said.

"If you get preggers by a rich one, then we'll all be set for life," Gran agreed.

"How about I just finish my degree," I said, cutting off that line of thinking.

My niece was glowering in our direction as she stacked up more of the holiday-themed coffee cups by the espresso machine.

"Thanks, Dove," I told her as she wordlessly handed me the Santa apron she'd been wearing. "Why don't you and your friends go enjoy the Christmas market?" I slipped her a five-dollar bill.

She glanced over to where the pack of stylishly dressed tweens cooed over a literal reindeer someone was walking through the Christmas market.

"This town gets crazier every year."

Dove handed me the bill back. "My mom will probably just take it."

Azalea was storming through the Christmas market in our direction, a screaming toddler and a crying baby under each arm.

"Dove!" she yelled.

Dove shrank into herself as Stacey and the other girls from her school looked over, clearly whispering and giggling to one another behind their mittened hands.

"I cannot believe I raised such an ungrateful daughter. Why are you here helping your aunt? I need you to babysit. You didn't even answer that phone I bought you," Azalea raged.

"You mean the phone *Noelle* bought me." Dove glowered again.

"Oh, shut up," Azalea yelled at the girls, who were doing that scream-gasping thing middle-school girls did when they saw something horrifying but worthy of gossip.

Guess what the studies say is true—if you have a baby at fourteen, you never mature past that age.

"Azalea," I snapped at my sister, "Dove was helping work the coffee cart. It wasn't like she was—"

"I don't care." Azalea cut me off. "She's *my* daughter, not yours." She grabbed Dove by the arm. "I'm the one who had to deal with a horrible baby daddy. I'm the one who carried her for nine months and pushed her out of my vagina. You can't have her." She dragged Dove off.

Ida silently took out a flask of whiskey and poured us all a shot.

I downed mine and coughed at the burning in my throat.

"I am so going to make that app. Maybe with any luck, I'll catch Oliver cheating on someone too," I decided.

"Oliver Frost? He's so hot. If only I were fifty years younger." Ida sighed. "But I'll just leave the field wide open for you, Noelle!"

As if I would pursue Oliver Frost for a relationship or even sex. There was no way in Christmas hell I would ever entertain sleeping with him, I fumed later that day.

The sun had just disappeared behind the tree line, and I was sneaking through the shadows around his house, a large Victorian mansion.

I really should have put on a stealth elf outfit, I thought, fingers clamped firmly around the bells on my elf uniform.

I ducked behind a herd of metal reindeer staked out in Oliver's yard. I recognized the pieces. They were expensive because they were made by a local artist, and he had a whole fucking family of them in his yard.

What a prick, an entitled rich prick.

The first two windows I tested didn't open, but one around the back did. I slowly lifted it. I figured Oliver was at work or, more likely, at a bar, pretending to make business deals with his other douche-bro finance friends and harassing waitresses.

I put my hands on the windowsill and hoisted myself up, attempting to avoid making too much noise as I huffed and puffed and tried to wiggle my way through the opening.

Previously, I had thought I was going to look like Ana de Armas in *The Gray Man*, but really, I was more like Winnie the Pooh after he'd binge eaten honey in Rabbit's home.

"Oof!" I gasped as I fell through the window and crashed in a heap on the pristine hardwood floor.

I lay there for a moment, staring up at the ornate plasterwork on the ceiling.

No wonder Oliver hadn't recognized me. I was twenty—okay, maybe twenty-five—pounds heavier, and while I had been helping my dad with the Christmas tree farm, it was not enough to counteract my mom's cake, cookies, and hearty casseroles.

Wheezing, I hauled myself upright and wandered into Oliver's house, looking for some way to ruin his Christmas.

"Inspire me."

Thoughts of revenge flew out of my head when I walked out of the small laundry room and into the formal part of the house.

The area was like a Victorian postcard. It was pure Christmas. Garlands with dried oranges, cranberries, and spices wound up the graceful mahogany railing on the curved stair.

Snowflakes and mistletoe hung from the gleaming chandelier in the middle of the foyer. Every window had a wreath and a candle. Each richly stained doorframe was decorated with an arch of garland.

In the living room, more garlands framed the fireplace, from which handmade stockings were strung up and in which wood lay ready for a fire.

On the tables and on the antique grand piano were little Christmas touches—here a small toy train in a snowy Christmas village, there a lush poinsettia and winter fruit arrangement.

The crown jewel, the Christmas tree I'd sold him, presided over the homey holiday scene, waiting for a cheerful family tree-trimming evening.

I wandered through the house almost in shock. It wasn't just the foyer and living room. The dining room had been laid out with antique Christmas-themed china. Fresh flowers and pomegranates crowned the table, ready for a family feast. Even the bathrooms had been decorated for Christmas.

I furiously wiped at the tears that threatened to ruin my makeup.

My mother loved Christmas. She had always strived to make it special, but it had never come close to anything like Oliver's house.

"This isn't fair." My voice echoed off the high ceilings.

It wasn't right that Oliver, a single straight man with no family and no children, got to have the perfect Christmas house, like a little dollhouse, where he could just wait for a jolly Santa to come down the chimney and give him everything his heart desired.

"I bet his parents never sat him down when he was eight and told him Santa wasn't real," I muttered to myself as I stomped toward the kitchen, unsure what I was looking for.

When I was still a very little girl, I had loved Christmas—the magic, the anticipation of wondering what would be underneath the tree on Christmas morning.

I had been so proud that my dad grew Christmas trees. That was, until the year the last forestry company in town had closed and my dad lost his job. In school, the teacher had had everyone make a list for Santa, and I had written down every American Girl doll that I had wanted.

Of course, nothing on my list had appeared under the tree. I had received socks with corgis on them. I recognized them from the local dollar store, but I had written a thank-you letter to Santa all the same.

The first day back from Christmas break, the other girls had teased me, showing me all the nice presents Santa had given them and asking me why Santa didn't like me.

"She must have been bad if she didn't get any presents."

When my dad picked me up from school, I immediately started crying in the car, wondering what I'd done wrong. Then he spilled the beans.

I never asked for anything for Christmas ever again.

Now men like Oliver just had a perfect Christmas vomited all over their house.

Or rather, they paid someone to give it to them.

I scowled at the decorator's notes on the large white kitchen island, with instructions for keeping the garland pristine for the rest of December.

"Cheater," I muttered. I opened the fridge and saw trays of food waiting.

Maybe he was having a dinner party.

I made myself a napkin full of cheese and crackers while I spun around on the stool at his kitchen island, daydreaming about what it would be like to own a house like this.

I could move my parents here. My brother could live in the carriage house in the back, and my sister could stand in the middle of the street and screech about how I wasn't being a loving family member by allowing her to live in my fancy house and enabling her bad behavior. I'd have a guest room where Elsa could live, and Dove could have her own room. It would be perfect.

"Damn, this is good cheese." I cut off another piece of Brie and rearranged the cheese platter so it looked like that wedge of Brie had been that small to begin with.

I checked my phone. I'd probably already been here too long. Oliver might be back any minute.

How was I even going to ruin his Christmas?

Sure, I could trash his house, but that seemed sacrilegious. Also, I expected he wouldn't even care. He'd probably just call the police then pay the decorator extra to redo everything.

No, I needed to do something subtle and nefarious.

On the kitchen island was an artful Pinterest-worthy basket of cookie supplies, ready for a cozy evening of Christmas baking—not because you had to get up at four the next morning to sell them so you could buy groceries that week but just because making cookies was fun and relaxing.

I eyed the twin sugar and salt canisters.

Well, it would be relaxing if the cookies didn't taste like garbage.

I cackled evilly as I carefully dumped out the sugar into a large mixing bowl then switched it with the salt.

The lock on the front door turned right as I was carefully placing the two canisters back where I'd found them.

I tiptoed to the window and hoisted myself through, muffling my pained grunt when I banged my hip on a birdbath.

Several voices echoed through the house as I eased the window closed.

Guess he was having a dinner party, I thought as I rubbed my hip.

I texted Gran that I was going to be late. My family was supposed to decorate our much smaller tree tonight, but I felt like I had earned watching Oliver choke on a Christmas cookie.

CHAPTER 12

Oliver

Just be cool, I told myself as my brothers and their significant others filed into my house.

I'd hired a decorator from Manhattan. It was worth it.

"This is amazing!" Owen's wife, Holly, exclaimed. She had her hands clasped around her hugely pregnant belly.

"Do you want to sit down?" Owen asked in concern.

"No, I want cookies."

"You should have some more energy tea, not processed sugar," Morticia, Jonathan's girlfriend, said. She hated Christmas as much as he loved it, though she tolerated it for his sake.

The goth woman was wearing dark sunglasses and long black gloves. She pulled a literal cauldron out of her bag and set it on the stove in the expansive kitchen. She filled the cauldron with the pot filler and added a handful of herbs.

"You all right there, Matt?" Merrie, Matt's girlfriend, asked, patting his hand. "You look a little woozy."

"What is in that tea?" he wheezed as the cauldron let off a belch and a green vapor.

I opened one of the windows in the kitchen and turned on a fan.

"This is probably the most action your kitchen has seen in forever," Jack joked.

"I can cook," I protested.

Owen scowled. "Can you?"

I opened my mouth to answer then paused at what sounded like someone giggling outside.

"Did you hear that?"

Morticia pulled an ancient revolver out of her bag. "I bet it's a squirrel. We'll eat it for dinner."

"She's just grumpy because it's another ten months until Halloween," Jonathan said cheerily, taking the revolver from her.

"Eleven months," she snapped and stirred the cauldron.

It let off a bang, and we jumped.

Holly groaned. "I don't want any of that; the baby wants cookies."

"I have buttercream frosting," Merrie offered.

"Gimmie." Holly made a grabbing motion with her hands.

"And I have actual cookies," Chloe, Jack's girlfriend, said, handing her a bag. "They're made with almond flour, so they probably have a little bit more nutritional value."

"Oliver wants to bake cookies," Jack said mildly as Holly stuffed the entire snowflake cookie into her mouth.

Before she could grab another, Morticia snatched the bag from her. "Drink this." She slid a frothy, noxious-smelling mug in front of Holly, who gagged.

"The baby doesn't like this."

"It's good for your humors," Morticia replied in a monotone.

"Just knock it back," Jonathan said cheerfully.

"Once the cauldron is empty," Morticia told Belle in a low voice, "I'm happy to whip up a poison for your ex."

"Please don't kill Greg," I begged. "I need Svensson Investment to give me, like, two billion dollars for my microprocessor factory. They won't give it to me if you kill their brother."

"I don't have to make one that kills," Morticia offered. "We can just make him so ill he'll wish he was dead."

"Tempting," Belle said dryly.

I set the cheese and hors d'oeuvre trays out for everyone.

"All right, people. Holly, drink your tea," Chloe said. "I'm ready to bake cookies."

"Didn't you spend all day baking?" Merrie asked, taking the plastic wrap off the trays.

"Nope, I was in meetings all day. The joys of being a small bakery owner."

Holly screwed up her face then gulped down the frothy mug in one go.

After a moment, Owen said, "I don't know if I'm alarmed or impressed that you know how to do that."

"Crap, that's nasty," Holly rasped, wiping her mouth.

In the distance, I thought I heard the first few bars of a ringtone.

"There *is* someone out there," I growled, throwing open the side door and storming out into the dark yard.

My family gaped at me from the window.

I poked at the dark bushes. "If you're in there, come out."

I didn't see anyone, and I felt a little foolish standing outside yelling at the plants in the garden.

"He's been spending too much time with the Svenssons," Jonathan said when I stormed back inside, shaking the snow off my shoes. "Oliver sounds paranoid and crazy."

"He needs some alcohol."

"I'm so glad Oliver's finally old enough to drink," Jack said, pouring me a bourbon. "It makes you way more interesting."

I grabbed the canisters of salt, sugar, and flour and spread out the recipe.

"Mom's sugar cookies," Merrie read over my shoulder.

"Is this your family cookie recipe?" she asked.

"Hardly," Belle said. "Our mother liked to make macarons because they were much more difficult and therefore more impressive to friends and guests."

The atmosphere turned tense.

"You were like a macaroon machine," Jonathan joked as Jack and Owen exchanged concerned looks. "If you get tired of Greg, you could just open up a bakery..." He trailed off under her withering gaze.

"These cookies are supposed to be foolproof and child friendly," I said.

"And Mom isn't here to scream at us if the cookies turn out less than perfect," Matt added darkly.

Belle downed her drink.

I hastily flung the ingredients into a large mixing bowl and turned on the stand mixer. Admittedly, it took me longer to figure out than someone with a nine-figure net worth and college degree had any right to.

Morticia forced Holly to drink the rest of the tea then repurposed the cauldron to make a booze-laden grog. By then, the cookies were in the oven, and the tension had eased.

My brothers were swapping stories about the most insane things the Svensson brothers had convinced them to do.

"What was he even going to do with that many llamas?" Chloe asked in confusion.

I used a metal spatula to scoop the hot cookies onto a cooling rack.

"Guess I don't need to make any frosting," I said to Merrie, "since you brought some."

"Whoops!" Holly exclaimed, looking down at the empty frosting bowl.

"It's not hard to make buttercream," Chloe assured me.

"I have a recipe." I showed her the card the caterer had left.

Chloe read it and scowled. "If you make this, you're going to make everyone sick." She tossed the card in the trash.

"I've been on an Italian buttercream frosting kick lately. You start by making a simple syrup." She handed me a saucepan and pulled out eggs. "Add equal parts water and sugar in that while I separate these eggs."

Morticia handed out her grog while I methodically dissolved sugar into the water.

I wasn't really sure what I was looking for.

"It's still clear," I told Chloe.

"It's supposed to be." She held out the bowl of egg whites. "Light 'er up."

"Are we setting something on fire?" Morticia perked up.

"We'll burn the Christmas trees on the twelfth day of Christmas. Don't worry. You'll have your bonfire," Jonathan said, patting her head.

"Are you sure that's what it's supposed to look like?" Belle asked dubiously as we stared at the frothy white mess in the bowl.

"Who cares?" Holly said, trying to reach across the island, though her belly was in the way.

I frosted a cookie for her then one for myself.

"Merry Christmas!" Holly said, toasting my cookie. "Eat up, Owen. I like my men covered in frosting."

He gingerly took a bite of the cookie she held out and immediately spat it out.

"That's disgusting. Don't eat that, Holly."

"It can't be that bad," I said. After taking a bite, I immediately gagged. I looked around wildly for somewhere to spit out the bitter, salty cookie.

Belle laughed into her drink as Owen and I fought over who was going to wash their mouth out at the sink.

"I'm older than you," Owen growled, pushing me aside.

"This is my house."

"Figures Oliver doesn't know how to cook." Jonathan laughed.

"I can," I sputtered under the spray from the sink.

I could swear I thought I heard someone outside the window snickering.

"I double-checked that I scooped the sugar from the sugar container." I opened it and tasted a few of the sugar crystals. "It's salt."

I glared out the open window.

"Sounds like operator error," Jonathan joked. "I highly doubt an elf broke into your house and swapped out your sugar and salt."

"Yeah," I said dubiously, still staring out the window. "Sounds highly unlikely."

CHAPTER 13

I stifled the laughter as I watched Oliver gag on the cookie.

Freezing half to death in the rose bushes was so worth it.

I stumbled through the dark garden, my leg still half-asleep, and stifled a curse as I tripped over one of the metal reindeer yard sculptures.

"You know what?" I whispered in the dark. "Screw you, Oliver. I'm liberating some of these reindeer."

I pulled up the closest two and tried not to let them clank against each other as I carried them awkwardly down the street to my car.

Even though I was weighed down by the steel sculptures, I felt the lightest I had in months.

I was finally getting back at Oliver, and the salt in the cookies was just the beginning.

Once I was back in front of my parents' house, I turned off the old pickup truck. After making sure it wasn't leaking oil, I stuck the reindeer on either side of the drive to greet anyone who pulled up to the house. These sculptures were my first revenge trophies.

"Merry Christmas!" I called, walking into the house and unwinding my scarf. "Sorry I'm late."

"We still have plenty of ornaments to hang on the tree," my mother said happily, hugging me when she saw me.

"Ida gave me a few bottles of good wine," Gran whispered to me. She handed me a glass while my mother handed me a box of Christmas ornaments.

I stared up at the tree. My dad was hanging paper cutout snowflakes my siblings and I had made in elementary school over the doorframe that led into the narrow kitchen. Gran had put a few small wreaths in the windows. It wasn't anything like the Christmas scene at Oliver's house, but it was comforting and familiar.

The light from the fire danced on the low ceiling. The cat was snoozing on the windowsill while Max the corgi raced around the room, chewing on the tissue paper that had wrapped the Christmas ornaments my family was placing on the tree.

"Oh!" my mother gasped, holding her hand to her chest and looking at the little handprint. She held up the homemade Christmas ornament. Created from my handprint, which I'd traced on construction paper then painted and added on googly eyes so it would look like a reindeer, the ornament had seen many a Christmas.

"Give it a nice spot on the tree," my dad boomed, hopping down off the ladder.

"Let's just put this one in the back," I joked.

"Put it next to the Harvard Christmas tree ornament," my father insisted. "Then everyone can see how far Noelle has come." He proudly held up the glass ornament with the silver and crimson Harvard logo visible inside. That senior year, I had worked extra shifts at the Christmas market to surprise my parents after I'd received the letter stating I'd been accepted as early decision to the Ivy League university.

They had been ecstatic, and it had been one of the happiest Christmases ever.

And this one was the worst.

My sister gave me a dirty look. "She's not a Harvard grad. You shouldn't put up that ornament; she's a fraud."

My brother, who had put on a T-shirt for the occasion but, of course, no pants, grabbed one of the homemade cookies from the plate on the rickety coffee table.

"At least she got in. You didn't even graduate from high school."

"Kids," my dad begged, "let's try and have a nice family Christmas evening."

"You didn't either!" Azalea screeched at Jimmy.

"No one in this family graduated from high school," Gran piped up. "GEDs all the way down."

"Except me," I said under my breath.

"Everyone graduated from sixth grade," my mother said, a hysterical edge to her voice. "And look at all these adorable Christmas ornaments you all made."

"Let's put some of these silver ones on the tree," my dad said, handing a box to Dove, who was slumped on the couch texting one of her friends.

"No phones during tree decorating," my sister screamed at Dove, her own phone firmly clutched in her hand.

Dove sighed and loudly rolled her eyes.

"You can put the angel on top of the tree," I told her.

"No, let one of the little ones do it," my mother said, making kissy faces at the babies, who were playing in the corner of the living room. "It will be such a cute picture."

My brother's daughter toddled over to my mom.

"Come to Grandma!"

Azalea's daughter made a rush for the fragile ornaments.

"Azalea!" Elsa called.

"What? She wants to help."

The toddler screamed when I picked up the breakable glass balls from the coffee table. The noise set off the cat, who raced up and perched on the highest branch of the Christmas tree. "Down, Gingersnap," I called to her.

She meowed furiously at me.

Max, thinking it was playtime, raced across the living room and launched his stocky corgi body into the tree to join the fun.

The corgi had, like the rest of us, been consuming a steady diet of casseroles and baked goods. The tree didn't stand a chance. As it crashed to the floor, ornaments cascaded everywhere. Gingersnap bolted out of the tree, and Max gave chase. Knocking into the coffee table, he spilled the plate of cookies on the floor and tipped over the bottle of wine. My mother raced after him while my dad tried to right the Christmas tree. The whole room was covered in pine needles and broken ornaments.

I scooped up the dog and dumped him outside, where he barked furiously.

"That damn dog," my mother raged.

"I, uh," my dad said, "I think I should probably get going over to the Christmas tree stall."

"Same," Elsa and I chorused hastily.

"You're not going out to the Christmas market with your tits hanging out." My mother wagged her finger.

"Definitely not," Elsa and I lied.

"Just leave all this mess, honey," my dad said with a grimace. "I'll clean it up when I get back."

"Or you could, you know, have the other two adults that live here clean it up," I muttered to Elsa as we shrugged on our coats and headed out into the snow.

"Why can't I just have a nice Christmas for once?" my mom seethed as I quietly closed the front door.

You and me both.

CHAPTER 14

Oliver

"Looks like you're missing some reindeer." Mrs. Horvat, my elderly neighbor, pointed at the Christmas yard ornaments when I was out to get my mail the next morning. "You had ten yesterday. Now you only have eight."

"Oh no," I said, "what a shame." I didn't really care that a couple of reindeer were missing. "It's probably just kids."

"It's all those tourists," her husband insisted. "Transients. This town has gone downhill since the Christmas market became so popular. Back in my day, there wasn't so much insanity. Let me tell you."

"Come inside, Oliver, dear," his wife insisted. "I have a streusel in the oven. We can have coffee, and I'll show you pictures of how the town used to be."

"I actually have to get to work," I said desperately.

Everyone in this town was insane.

I needed a coffee. My siblings had stayed up late last night drinking, and I needed my brain at full capacity to work on nailing down the numbers on Mithril Tech's profitability timetable. The splitting headache wasn't helping much.

For once, no one was waiting in line at the Naughty Claus.

I frowned. "Weird."

You don't actually have to go to this coffee stall, you know, I reminded myself.

True. There was another stand, run by a kindly old woman who was trying to convince me to date her granddaughter. At another stall, across the square, the guy kept trying to rope me into investing in his business.

The Naughty Claus was the logical choice.

Stop lying to yourself; you just want to see Noelle in that skimpy costume.

"Hello?" I called into the empty stall. The espresso machine was on, and there were receipts in the receipt holder.

A roar rose from a crowd of people near the bandstand.

I walked over to see what was going on just in time to witness an elf slug another elf in the belly.

"Ooh," the crowd yelled.

"What the fuck?" I said aloud. "Is there a fight in the middle of the Christmas market?"

"I'm taking bets," one elderly woman yelled above the noise.

The elf that had just been punched blew her hair out of her face and lunged at the other elf.

"Noelle?" I said in shock as the elves went down on the ground and rolled around in the snow.

Fucking small towns, I swear to God.

"You slut!" the other elf screeched. "You're bouncing your tits all over the place and poaching our customers." She threw a punch at Noelle.

"Fuck you, Madison!" Noelle yelled.

"Keep your hands up," one of the elderly town residents hollered, swinging his fists.

Noelle blocked the punch and grabbed the elf by her long red braid. The elf yelped in pain, and Noelle shoved her and jumped up.

The elf came at her swinging and caught Noelle with a mean right hook.

"This is insanity."

"Don't get in the middle of them, boy," a wrinkled old man in a fur-lined aviator hat said gravely. "You have to let nature take its course."

"They're fighting in the middle of the town square," I said firmly. "Someone has to put a stop to this."

I reached out to grab the two women to try to separate them...

And was promptly slugged in the ribs.

"Dammit," I wheezed.

The elf grabbed Noelle's hair and threw her to the ground.

"You're in my way, Oliver!" she screeched at me and kicked me in the shin with her boot.

"You were going to lose this fight anyway," Madison hollered.

"Protect your head. Don't mind it if she hits you in the tits," an older woman shouted. "They're big; they can take it."

Noelle grunted as the two girls slugged each other. She blocked a punch but didn't block the next one.

I cringed as Madison hit her square in the nose. Blood spurted out. Madison tackled her to the ground.

Several people in the crowd groaned.

"Stay off my aunt's Christmas tree turf," the elf yelled at her just before jumping off and flouncing away.

Noelle wheezed and slowly rolled over on her side.

Around me, money was changing hands.

Was no one going to help Noelle up?

Ignoring the twinge in my ribs, I knelt beside her.

"Don't sit up," I told Noelle, gingerly peeling some of her tangled curls off her bloody nose.

"I would have won if you hadn't gotten in the way," she said, her voice sounding nasally.

"Let me take you to urgent care. I think your nose is broken."

"S'fine," she said, grabbing onto my shoulder and hauling herself upright. She pitched forward, and I cursed, reaching out to catch her before she could pass out.

Noelle batted me off. "You're such a privileged city boy," she said, grabbing up a fistful of snow. "Haven't you ever been in a fight?"

"We had boxing in private school, and I do mixed martial arts. Plus I have four brothers. So yes, I have been in a fight."

Noelle scoffed. "I meant a real fight, not in an air-conditioned gym."

"Don't put that on your face," I protested as she held the fistful of snow to her bruised nose. "It's filthy."

"It's good for the immune system," she said, clambering to her feet.

"That's not how that works," I said, trying to herd her as she stumbled through the Christmas market back to the coffee stall.

"You don't know anything."

"I know better than to get in a fight in the middle of the town square."

"Madison started it," Noelle said, hand still clamped on her nose.

The slushy pink snow was sliding down her face.

I made a disgusted noise and pulled her behind the coffee stall counter, where a line had already started to form.

"Can I get a—" A woman started when she saw me.

"Ma'am, if you could please give us a moment," I insisted.

I turned on the tap at the small sink, wetted a paper towel, and held it to Noelle's nose.

"You might want to wash your hands off," I told her.

She seemed a little bit dazed as she ran the water at the sink.

I gently applied pressure to her nose. It didn't feel broken. My brothers and I had whaled on one another often enough that I knew what a broken nose felt like.

"Are you sure you don't have a concussion?"

Noelle glowered. One of her eyes was swelling up.

"I don't need you to pretend to be the billionaire who saves Christmas. Lame. Now get out of my stall."

CHAPTER 15

Noelle

"Your poor face!" My mother hurried over to me.

"We need to start you on hand-to-hand combat training," Gran declared as my mother rushed to the freezer and filled up a bag of ice. "I hear you lost Ida a lot of money this morning."

"Honestly," my mother tsked as she dabbed at my face.

Gran held up a bottle of vodka to my mouth. "Unfortunately, it runs in the family; your dad lost his share of fights too."

"Lovely." I took the ice from my mom.

"Get out of that dress," she scolded. "I need to wash it before the bloodstains set."

I thought about Oliver as I peeled off the stained elf outfit in the bathroom. Why had he been so nice—kind and helpful—to me earlier?

"It was performative," I told myself as I ran the dress under the faucet and stepped into the shower. The hot water was out. I shivered as I scrubbed off under the cold spray.

That was the problem with small towns. You always ran into the people you least wanted to see. What was more annoying was that Oliver hadn't seemed to even care that I had ruined his Christmas evening with his family the night before.

I stepped out of the shower and wrapped myself in a threadbare robe.

Why would he care? If the cookies were bad, he could just order new ones and have them delivered. I had run his credit card at the Naughty Claus. It was one of those fancy ones that had an annual fee the cost of a tuition payment and came with a concierge you could call up any time of the day for any request, no matter how stupid.

"Oliver's just an out-of-touch billionaire who's playing like he's a good person," I told myself as I tried to tame my tangled hair.

Dove stomped up the stairs into the shared tiny attic bedroom as I stabbed myself with a bobby pin.

"How was school?" I asked her.

"I hate school," she said sourly.

"At least you're going to be on winter break next week."

"Yeah, but then it starts all over again in January."

I gave her a hug.

"I know school is hard, but if you keep your nose down, you can earn a scholarship and go to a good university," I reminded her.

"Then I'll leave this horrible town and never come back," she said vehemently.

I winced. That had been my original life plan. I was going to be the rich aunt that breezed in, dumped presents, and peaced out.

"If that's your dream, just hold it in your mind and do everything you can to achieve it. Don't get distracted by the minor things that don't matter and—"

"I know, and stay away from boys. They'll ruin your life," she finished.

"*Exactamente*." I grabbed my niece's hand. "Come on. We're going to do round two of the tree-trimming before we have to go open up the Christmas tree stall."

The tree had been righted since the misfortune last night. Minus several of the less-hardy ornaments, we were ready to trim it.

"Could you please pause that game for thirty minutes while we try to do something as a family?" my mother begged my brother.

"I can't pause the game, Mom," Jimmy said, staring at the screen. "I'm in the middle of a mission."

"He doesn't care about this family," Azalea sneered. She then giggled like a lovesick teenager when several messages chimed on her phone.

My sister ignored her toddler, who was trying to climb on her lap using her baby brother as a handhold.

I ran over and scooped the little girl up before she could pull the infant onto the floor.

"Azalea," I snapped at her.

"Don't judge me," my sister raged, snatching the little girl back from me. "Being a mom is hard."

I was sure my mother could agree.

She poured herself more wine. "Dove, can you entertain the children? *Please*," she added forcefully before Dove could start huffing.

I picked up a box of ornaments.

"Where do you want me to put this one?" I asked my mom, holding up a photo of my parents' wedding picture. They were standing in the middle of the snowy forest of Christmas trees. They looked so young. My mom's pregnant belly was just showing, and she was wearing a long white dress. She and my father were beaming at each other.

"Aww, look, James." She held up the photo to my father.

"That was such a wonderful day. You were the most beautiful bride, Sarah." They smiled softly at each other and kissed.

When I had been younger and more naïve, I had wanted to find love like my parents had. The type of love that conquered all.

But love didn't pay the bills, and as I got older, I had decided that it would be better to spend all my wishes on economic stability.

Until that horrible night with Oliver when I had almost thought I could have it all.

Stupid, stupid, stupid, I told myself as I jammed ornaments on the tree.

"Here, Dove." I handed my niece a clay Christmas pigeon hanging from a red ribbon before the toddlers could grab it with sticky fingers. "Why don't you find somewhere high up so that Max doesn't accidentally jostle it."

The calico cat jumped up into the tree. I grabbed hold of it and looked around wildly for Max, bracing for impact.

When I didn't hear the chubby little corgi barking, I asked, "Is he locked up?"

"Who?" my mother asked. She and my dad were cooing over the baby-picture ornaments.

"Max," I said slowly as the calico cat batted at one of the large colored lightbulbs on the tree. "The dog that has been living in this house since last Christmas."

"I got rid of him," Azalea said.

"You what?" I choked out.

"See?" she said, smiling and looking up from her phone. "I am a good daughter. Mom has been tired of taking care of that dog, a dog she didn't even want. So I made her life easier and got rid of him."

What the literal fuck?

"So that's where we're at?" I demanded. "We're just throwing people out into the cold? Some family we are. Really getting in the Christmas spirit, tossing out a poor helpless little dog with the trash."

To their credit, my parents did look guilty.

"You found a nice family for him, didn't you, Azalea?" my mom urged.

"Hm?" Azalea said, focused on her phone again.

I bet she was texting with that married man.

"Oh, I didn't have time to make a post on Facebook Marketplace. I just left him at that trailhead a few miles down the road. There are lots of tourists that come through there. Someone will pick him up."

"I tried to convince your mom to leave you at a trailhead and let the universe have at it, but she refused," Gran said, shaking her head.

"Why are you all judging me?" Azalea screeched. "None of you ever cared for the dog."

"It was a dog *you* bought with money *you* didn't have," I argued.

"I bought it for Kayleigh."

"Who is a three-year-old," I reminded her. "She was never going to take care of that dog."

"It's a dog," Azalea said in annoyance, "it's not a big deal. I swear, no good deed goes unpunished."

"I didn't know she was throwing him out on the street," my mother said in a small voice.

"We can't really afford the dog anyway, Candy Cane..." my dad said then trailed off at the anger on my face.

I grabbed my coat, wrenched the door open, and stomped out into the falling snow.

CHAPTER 16

Oliver

"I heard you lost a fight with an elf," Tristan said with a smirk.

"I—what? None of that is true."

"It's all over the Harrogate Facebook group. Ergo, it must be true," Tristan said, waving his phone in my face.

While I looked less than stellar in the photo, Noelle looked like she had been hit by a truck.

"We need to call the lawyers and have this photo taken down," I insisted. "Noelle probably had a concussion, and while I don't think her nose was broken, I'm not a doctor. But I told her I didn't think it was broken, and I know she didn't go to an urgent care. What if she's horribly disfigured and sues me for practicing medicine without a license?" I opened a new email window to compose a message to the lawyers. "We need to get ahead of this. It's going to be a disaster. It's going to ruin our company. It's—"

"You know what you need?" Tristan said, closing the laptop. "You need to go on a holidate. You are way too high-strung, and you have been for the last year."

"How is that different from a regular date?" I asked dubiously.

"It's holiday themed," he explained. "Take it from someone with double-digit numbers of drama-llama brothers—you can't let your siblings' issues hijack your life."

"My sister's not—"

"Relax. Belle can hold her own," Tristan said, cutting off my complaints. "You are a newly minted billionaire, and you haven't even enjoyed the spoils of being at the top of the food chain. Where are the fawning groupies? You should be fending off gold diggers with a Swiffer, not rolling in the snow with a demented elf."

An elf costume that was way more revealing than it had any right to be at ten in the morning.

"When was the last time you had a little stress relief?" my friend asked, digging his hands into my shoulders.

"That is a very personal question."

"You held my head when I puked in your bed after losing the donut-eating contest," Tristan reminded me lightly. "We are already inappropriately close."

I sighed.

The truth was I didn't remember the last time I'd been with a girl. At least a year.

At Harvard I had dated, sort of, but never had time for anything serious. There was no shortage of pretty, intelligent college girls who had wanted to hook up.

The shock of Greg grinding my sister's company into dust, the fallout among my brothers, and the worry that she might leave again, this time for good, meant that I had just been going through the motions. I barely remembered what classes I had been in during my last semester at Harvard, let alone who I had slept with after getting blackout drunk.

It had been a miracle I'd even graduated. It felt like I had been sleepwalking through the whole semester. The terror of being left behind gripping my chest. The stress and anxiety making it impossible to sleep. Texting my sister asking if she was okay, lying there in the dark for hours, drinking and calling her over and over again. Only for her to answer annoyed and sleepy, wanting to know what was wrong.

You need to get it together.

"I don't need a relationship," I said, throwing off Tristan. "I need to go for a run."

The cold air was bracing as I raced down the trail. I felt more clearheaded and alive as my feet pounded through the soft snow. I wore only a thin long-sleeved T-shirt, and the cold made me feel alive.

As I ran, my thoughts wandered from my business to my hedge fund's market positions then finally to Noelle.

"Not because I think she's attractive or anything," I said aloud, my breath clouding in front of me.

I breezed through the cloud, sending the smoky tendrils swirling in the winter air. It had stopped snowing, and the sky was a brilliant blue streaked with the last of the clouds.

No, even if I did want to date anyone right now, Noelle was not the type of girl I would date.

Bet you would sleep with her.

"Bet not." I pushed myself to increase the pace.

Noelle was going to be a problem. It was obvious that she was a local small-town girl, not a transplant working at one of the big tech companies in town. She was brash, assertive. Probably would be CEO material in another life.

As it was, she would have no problem whipping up the townspeople in her misguided vendetta against me.

"Maybe I should look at another town for my factory."

Other towns wouldn't have the quality of employees, or offer locations this desirable.

There has to be some way to get her off of my case, I thought as I ran down the trail.

As I pounded over a wooden bridge, I heard a small animal cry out. I paused, listening.

Birds chirped; the stream burbled against the ice.

I heard another whimper.

"It's probably a wild animal, or maybe a bobcat left their cub somewhere," I told myself as I looked around.

However, it wasn't the season for bobcat kittens.

I whistled as I cut my way through the snow-covered underbrush, carefully, just in case the noise came from an injured wild animal.

"Hm," I said when I pulled back a bush and saw what had been making the noise, "I don't think corgis are native to New York." I pulled the Styrofoam cup off the dog's head.

The small tan and white furball let out another howl now that he was able to open his mouth.

"All right, it's okay," I crooned to the dog in a soft voice, scratching him behind the ears. "You're free now."

The dog struggled but didn't come out of the bush.

"Or not." I pulled out a knife and cut the fur that was tangled in the thorny vines.

It was slow going. I really needed a pair of scissors. The dog had thick fur that was matted with dirt.

"How long have you been out here, buddy?"

The dog barked then panted.

My brother owned a big estate out in the country a few miles outside of town, and people were constantly dumping animals on the road or at his front gate.

I bet someone threw this dog out to make way for a brand-new furry Christmas present that was going to be unceremoniously dumped this time next year.

"People are the worst," I said to the dog when I finally had him free. The stocky, short-legged dog did a few half-hearted zoomies then flopped down on the snow in front of me.

I picked thorns out of my shirtsleeves then hefted him up.

"You need a bath and a hot meal."

He whimpered quietly as I carried him out of the woods and down the trail back to where I had parked my car.

I heard the other runner before I saw them. Well, *runner* was probably a generous term. It sounded like a walrus crashing through the woods.

I stepped to the side of the path as a girl in a tattered red plaid coat approached.

"Good afternoon," I said, then tried to keep my expression neutral when I met a familiar pair of brown eyes.

"That's my dog," Noelle said, pointing.

"Yes, it is lovely weather," I drawled. "Glad to hear you're enjoying your walk in this magnificent countryside."

"I should have known an entitled billionaire would be a dog thief."

"Dog thief?" I snarled, shifting the corgi under one arm.

"Max belongs to me," Noelle said hotly. "So put him down." She stomped over to me, mittens clenched into fists.

I ignored her and peered down at her.

She craned her neck up and stared at me.

"I don't believe you," I said. "I think you just want a free corgi. You're probably going to sell him online."

"I'm taking him home to his family."

"Some family, letting your pet wander around outside." She reached for him.

"Do you know this girl?" I asked the dog. He wasn't acting ecstatic to see his owner.

I bet she's just fucking with me, I decided.

"I think you have the wrong corgi."

"Max," she begged the dog.

I set the corgi down. "We'll do a little test."

"Max. Max!" Noelle whistled and clapped her hands. "Max, come! Come here, Max."

The corgi ignored her and sniffed around at a nearby tree. He gave no indication that Max was even his name.

"Max, come on, don't you want some casserole?"

"Casserole? You're feeding this dog tuna casserole?" I asked, appalled. "No wonder he's so overweight."

"Ha! So you do admit he's my dog."

"No collar," I said, "so I can't say for sure. I'll take him to a vet and have his microchip checked."

She looked guilty.

"Is he microchipped?"

"We couldn't afford it."

"Huh." I leveled my gaze at her. "How did he escape and end up all the way out here?"

Noelle shuffled her feet and mumbled something.

"What was that?" I asked sharply.

"My sister dumped him out here last night," she admitted. "But she didn't tell any of us she was doing it."

I felt rage ignite in me. People dumping their pets in the woods was absolutely the hill I was prepared to die on.

"I found him stuck in a bush with a Styrofoam cup over his head," I roared at her. "He could have died."

She shrank under my anger.

"You don't deserve this dog; your life is a mess. You make horrible decisions. You live in a hovel and can't even afford pet food. The dog isn't trained; he doesn't even know his own name. You're neglecting this animal. Good thing you don't have kids. I hate to think how your poor niece is treated," I added snidely.

"You take that back," Noelle cried. "Dove is very happy."

"Max's condition gives me little confidence," I said, scooping up the dog in my arms and brushing past her.

"Fine!" she screamed after me. "Keep the dog. You'll be sorry!"

CHAPTER 17

Noelle

"God, I hate that man," I fumed, slamming the car door.

I kicked one of the stolen reindeer as I headed across the snow to the cabin.

"I need to borrow your shotgun," I announced to my dad, as I shoved the front door open.

My mom was sewing his Christmas-tree-selling sweater, which had a light-up reindeer on it.

"You're not using it on Fran's niece, are you?" Dad asked uncertainly. "You can't come sell Christmas trees if you're going to just pick fights with people."

"Madison started that fight," I insisted.

"Give her that shotgun so she can finish it," Gran slurred drunkenly from her spot in front of the flickering TV, where *The Great Christmas Bake Off* was blaring. "Ooh, why do they always do ice cream? You don't have enough time to make an ice cream; you're going to lose. Someone help this poor boy."

"Someone stole Max," I fumed.

"Who? It's not a puppy mill, is it?" my dad asked in concern.

"It was Oliver Frost, and I'm going to shoot his balls off."

"So Max found a good home, then," Dove said with a small smile.

"Change the baby," her mother interrupted. "He needs to be changed, and you need to use more diaper cream; you didn't use enough last time."

"I'll do it, Azalea." I grabbed the baby from her. "Dove, why don't you put on a Christmas outfit and come sell trees with us tonight. Maybe some of your friends will be there, and you can take a few breaks to have fun in the Christmas market."

"She needs to help babysit," Azalea snapped at me. "You can't just undermine my parenting, Noelle. Dove is *my* daughter."

When we got back from selling Christmas trees, my sister was still in the same spot on the couch, still texting and giggling and FaceTiming with some guy that was totally the married guy from the Christmas market.

"I bought you some Christmas snacks, Dove." I waved a box at her.

"Ugh, you're buying her food? You're going to make her fat, and she'll never get a boyfriend," Azalea complained.

"Maybe that's a good idea considering how well boyfriends worked for you," Gran said tartly.

Dove looked sad.

I seethed.

I'd had a very difficult Christmas, and we were barely into the first week of December.

If only Oliver hadn't freaking ruined my life, I could have had a nice high-paying job by now and my own apartment, and I wouldn't have to be stuck in this house with my freaking sister.

The anger gave way to the memories of Oliver. The sight of him today had been startling. I had longed to run my hands over his chest, slide them along the ridges of muscle there that I still occasionally had dreams about but would never admit to my nonexistent therapist.

I had only seen Oliver in his bespoke suits at the Christmas market. It was almost enough to lie to myself that I had just imagined the muscular torso under that suit, that the feeling of his hard naked body against my own was a figment of my imagination, that I'd made up how he had gritted his teeth and nipped my mouth when I'd touched him.

"I have first dibs on the bathroom," Azalea shouted, sprinting past me and running into the bathroom.

"The audacity of this bitch," Elsa said, shaking her head.

I pounded on the door. "Azalea, you've been in this house all freaking day."

"I'm breastfeeding."

"Not in the bathroom you're not." I rattled the handle.

"I have a headache," my mother screamed at us.

"That's it," I fumed, pulling out my laptop and opening my code editor. "Dump a dog, be mean to my niece, but the bathroom is the last straw."

I had a good rough draft code for the Moi Cheaters app by the time my alarm went off to let me know it was time for another day in the Christmas salt mines.

"Minimum viable product, here we come," I said as I compiled my code.

I prodded my feelings as I finally stood under the shower. The water was lukewarm, but that was better than freezing cold. It was good enough to wash my hair, anyway.

I was still furious at Azalea and even more furious at Oliver.

As I stood in front of the mirror, trying to detangle my ornery curls, I recalled a similar scene last year, when I had stood in front of the mirror in my dorm room, happy that I'd found a man who'd said he liked me.

Not.

With the code compiled, I loaded the app onto the app store.

"Fuck cheaters." Then I uploaded the picture of Azalea and the married guy onto the app and posted it with a pithy caption.

I texted Gran a link. She and her senior-citizen friends could find a flaw in an app like no one's business.

Now if only I had an app that would shove Oliver's face in a vat of frosting...

CHAPTER 18

Oliver

"Come, Max," I ordered the dog.

The corgi flopped over on his back and sank his teeth into the leash. I dragged him a couple of feet on his back then stopped.

The dog refused to walk. In fact, he refused to do anything.

He was not trained. At all.

Noelle and her family must have let the corgi run absolutely wild.

As soon as we'd arrived home yesterday, he drank all the water in the Christmas tree stand then promptly puked it all over the carpet. Then he somehow got into the fridge and ate a wheel of Brie. Not to mention he was only halfway housebroken.

He still did not know his own name.

I knelt in front of the dog. He panted up at me forlornly.

"You and I?" I told the dog. "We need to come to some sort of an understanding."

My brothers had dogs. Jack's husky, Milo, was extremely intelligent and very well trained.

"Do dogs train other dogs?" I mused as I prodded and poked the corgi to walk with me.

He perked up as soon as he smelled the food in the Christmas market.

The stocky dog practically dragged me through the market toward a familiar stall.

A line of people stood waiting for a coffee where smoke wafted up.

"Breakfast sausage! Made from locally sourced deer, aged for three months," Noelle called from behind a grill.

Max situated his furry bottom right under the grill and flopped his head back, his mouth open.

I might have been a little too harsh on Noelle. This dog clearly had a food addiction.

Noelle saw me. "Dog thieves go to the back of the line."

"I'm not here for your sausage."

"Just my frothed milk?"

I opened my mouth and closed it.

"Are you... *lactating*?" I asked, lowering my voice. "I didn't realize you were pregnant. I'm so sorry. No wonder you're acting like such a... uh, grinch."

"You're pregnant, Noelle?" a middle-aged woman standing in line exclaimed.

Excited murmurs rose from the crowd.

"Who's the father?" someone called.

"I'm not pregnant!" Noelle shrieked.

She grabbed me by the tie, yanked me down, and hissed, "This is a small town. You could power half of Manhattan with the gossip mill here. You need to watch what you say. Got it?"

She released me. "Poor Max, did the big bad man not feed you at all?" She cut off a piece of the sizzling sausage and dropped it down for the drooling dog.

"Are you even allowed to cook outside?"

"Yes, because this is a small town, so fa la la la la, fuck off." She handed the next person in line a blistered skin sausage in a fresh baked roll.

The food did smell good.

"Don't even think you're getting one after you stole Max." She clapped the tongs at me.

"Ms. Wynter." A cop in a dark blue overcoat marched over.

Noelle cursed.

"Do you have a license to sell meat?" the stern woman demanded, pulling out her ticket book.

"Er..."

So much for anything going in a small town. Fortunately, one of us had actually read the legal ordinances. It was best practice when you were going to open a business in an unfamiliar town.

"Ms. Wynter isn't selling these for human consumption," I said smoothly to the cop, turning my head slightly so the sun bathed my face. I knew women went apeshit for my blue eyes.

The cop wasn't so easily swayed.

"Oh really?" She frowned.

"Yes, these are for dogs," Noelle said firmly.

"Everyone here is buying for their dog?" the cop asked.

"Of course," I said with a sweep of my arm. "Many of the businesses in the area allow pets."

The crowd gave murmurs of agreement.

The cop scowled.

I gave her a dazzling smile.

She softened. "I do like dogs. Is that your corgi?"

"Yes," Noelle and I said automatically.

Her eyes flashed as they briefly met mine.

"Hm." The cop pursed her lips.

Max panted at her.

"I guess that's good practice for when you two have a baby. Carry on." The cop slapped a sausage in a roll, exchanged it for a five-dollar bill, and trudged off through the snow.

"So..." the next woman in line said slowly when she took the sausage, "you two are pregnant..."

"No!" Noelle yelled. "I am not and will never be pregnant with this candy-cane-sucking moron's baby."

"Your insults need a little bit of work," I told her, grabbing the tongs from her and loading up a sausage in a roll. I added some sauerkraut and mustard from the containers she had on a nearby table.

"You need to pay for that." Noelle was aghast.

I ignored her.

"Can I just have a black coffee?" I asked her friend, who was working behind the counter.

Noelle sputtered in anger.

I took a bite of the sausage. "I just saved your little illegal operation. Like you said, I'm a soulless businessman. I'm just taking my cut." I winked at her.

"You... you..."

I grinned to myself as I turned and cut through the Christmas market. Max trotted next to me, hoping I would drop a morsel for him.

Tristan was arriving at the office when I walked up. He immediately zeroed in on the food.

"Sharing is caring."

"Buy your own food."

"You said you didn't even like the girl at the coffee stall," he complained, following me inside the historic building on Main Street that we were leasing for our office space.

"I don't like her," I told him, sitting down on my desk.

"Good, because I have your big reentry into society planned tonight."

Max flopped on Tristan's feet, begging for a bite of food.

"I'm busy."

"Dude, you just adopted an overweight corgi. You are clearly desperate for a relationship. You might as well have slapped a sign that said, 'Marry Me—I'm Free' on yourself."

"I can't leave Max home alone," I said, which was true. I did not trust the dog in the house by himself.

"Lucky for you, the venue I picked is dog friendly."

I scowled and took a sip of my coffee. A marshmallow Santa floated in it.

"That was not what I ordered."

"It's a sign," Tristan insisted. "You need to get back out there. The place we're going is super Christmas themed and serves cheap alcohol." He showed me a photo of servers in sexy Mrs. Claus outfits blowing kisses at the camera.

"We're going to a Christmas-themed strip club?"

"No, that's illegal. It's like a Hooters but with reindeer instead of owls."

Christmas music with filthy lyrics was blaring out of the alley when Tristan, Max, and I headed down the narrow way. At the far end were two tricked-out food trucks on either side of the alley, framing a seating area with small tables and chairs.

It was packed.

"Do you have a reservation?" an elderly woman in an extremely short skirt and crop top demanded. Her eyes were highlighted by sparkly red and green eye shadow.

"Do we really need a reservation, Ida?" Tristan gave the elderly woman a brilliant smile.

He nudged me.

"We have a corgi," I added, picking up Max and pressing his furry face to mine.

"Good-looking guys are good for business," Ida said, unclipping the velvet rope behind her. "You can come in, but it will cost you a selfie."

The flash on her phone was blinding, throwing stars in my eyes. The lights faded as my eyes adjusted to the low candlelight.

The waitresses in the skimpy Santa Claus outfits navigated their way through the crowd. One of the Mrs. Clauses looked sickeningly familiar.

"Dang," Tristan said. "I was hoping to get your mind off of her."

"I am not attracted to her at all," I forced out

Tristan gave me an odd look. "I meant more like you were getting a little obsessed with her potentially tanking Mithril Tech, but hi, Oliver's subconscious. Guess you do secretly want a relationship after all."

"No, I want to break someone's face," I snarled, because a few tables away was some disgusting drunk man with his hand practically up Noelle's skirt.

CHAPTER 19

Noelle

"So tell me, sweetheart," the drunken besuited man, who was about three elf-nogs into his evening drinking, slurred at me.

I held out a foot to shove him back into his chair before he could topple off and hit his head.

"I only answer questions for tips," I told him tartly.

"Yes, Mrs. Claus." He pulled out a twenty-dollar-bill and waved it at me. I shifted the heavy tray of drinks and let him slide the bill into the band of my belt.

His friends all hooted.

I smiled tightly, trying to keep the irritation off my face. I was tired and wrung out, and Christmas was weeks away. My mood wasn't helped by the lack of sleep I'd had last night.

"Aw, come on," the guy whined. "It's twenty dollars. At least let me stick it in your garter."

If only Oliver hadn't rocked my world then thrown me off a cliff, I could be at a cushy white-collar job right now, not being slobbered on.

I saw the guy's hand going under my skirt. Unfortunately, I couldn't slap it because I was carrying a tray of alcoholic drinks.

I took a step back away from him, glancing at the drinks to make sure none of them were in danger of spilling before I decided whether to kick the guy in the shins or the balls.

Before I could, the guy screamed. I couldn't get a good read on what was happening because a man in a deep navy-blue suit had stepped in front of me, blocking me from the handsy patron.

"Don't touch her," he warned in a dangerously soft voice.

The man blasted obscenities and tried to buck him off. Oliver was thrown slightly off-balance enough to jostle the glasses on the tray. I cursed as one of them spilled.

"I was handling it," I shrieked at him.

He turned, the sleazy guy's hand twisted behind his back.

"No you weren't." His eyes were freezing cold.

I gulped.

Part of me was screaming in delight.

Maybe Oliver had remembered me after all and was here to rescue me and whisk me away as my knight in shining armor.

"She is just trying to do her job; she is not here for your amusement," Oliver snarled to the rude patron.

"But she's wearing—"

Oliver twisted his arm, and the patron groaned.

"I think they'd like their bill, Noelle," Oliver said, voice shards of ice.

"Oh, um..."

The spilled drink on the tray was dripping over the side. A familiar overweight corgi started licking at the drops on my shoe.

Just what this evening needs, a drunk animal.

I did the quick calculation in my head for the table's total. Since this establishment was not quite legal, we weren't charging tax.

"Sixty-five fifty," I told the men.

"What a rip-off," one of them muttered.

"What did you say?" Oliver asked softly, releasing his hostage and shoving him into the table. He took a step toward the guy's friends.

The two men at the table babbled, and one of them emptied his wallet on the table.

"Thank you for generously tipping your waitress. Merry Christmas." Oliver gave them a toothy smile.

They fled.

Oliver picked up the bills with an elegant gesture and smoothed them out. He handed them to me.

"Can you just, er..." I said, my hands still full. "No, not on the tray. It's wet. I need to clean it."

"Your pocket, then?"

Actually, can you put it in between my tits?

"Yeah," I croaked, "pocket is good."

He stepped up close to me.

I inhaled the familiar masculine scent—woodsy and fresh, like all those expensive cologne companies were trying to go for but always failed and made gross teen-boy smells. I wanted Oliver to wrap his arms around me so I could breathe in his scent, mountain air on a snowy morning.

There was the barest bit of pressure at my hip as he slid the bills into the pocket on my skirt.

I had personally sewn that pocket in there, and I was kicking myself now.

If you didn't have a pocket, he would have had *to put those bills in your cleavage, right?*

Oliver cleared his throat.

"Who are you taking the drinks to?" he asked, extending his arm.

I was still mesmerized by his eyes, the same eyes I had been obsessing about before they had imploded my life.

"I'm not taking them anywhere." I said, unable to think clearly.

"So you're just wandering around with drinks no one ordered?"

Crap.

"Yes, someone ordered them," I said, mentally slapping myself.

Get it together, Noelle. This man is your sworn enemy. Don't let his hotness carry you off into the land of sugarplums and orgasms.

But damn, being with him had been amazing.

Yes—and life ruining.

"All right," I said abruptly, turning away, "I'm going to get back to work."

Oliver followed me as I navigated through the crowded pop-up bar to a group of twenty-somethings.

"I just wanted to apologize on Noelle's behalf," he said before I could hand out the drinks. "Unfortunately, I seem to have spilled one of your cocktails. I hope you'll forgive me."

"It's okay," one girl drawled. "They ordered it for me." She smiled at him, showing off a dimple.

Madison.

I hated that Oliver seemed very interested in that smile and the rest of her.

She was wearing overalls, but they didn't make her look dumpy. They made her look cool and accessible, like the low-maintenance yet pretty girl all the guys said they wanted.

Madison also had the upper arm tone of someone who had enough leisure time to work out and didn't stuff down half a casserole in between running to her multiple jobs. She was the perfect small-town girl fantasy.

I bet they all go have a bonfire on her dad's property and drink spiked cider after this.

Oliver gazed at Madison like he'd just found his soul mate.

Then he glanced quickly back at me. It was horrible *déjà vu*. Except this time, he did recognize me.

"Is that the girl you were in a fight with?" he asked. Then he caught himself.

Madison and her friends giggled.

"I see you covered up most of your black eye with makeup, Noelle." She smirked at me.

"Small-town girls really are something else." He shook his head.

"You got that right." She hooked two fingers into Oliver's belt. "You should see what else we can do." Then she laughed like she was just making a casual joke and not offering a roll in the hay.

I was crushed.

"Since that table is free, why don't we all grab it?" Madison suggested, linking her arm with Oliver's.

She looked down her nose at me. "Bring the drinks over."

I slunk behind the crowd of well-rested, happy people out enjoying their youth. They probably didn't have to bunk up with half their family when they went home either.

I felt ten inches tall as I set out the drinks on the table.

"I'll go put that order in for a replacement cocktail," I said to Madison, taking away the dirty tray and empty cup.

She ignored me, instead laughing loudly at some joke Oliver's friend, one of the Svensson brothers—Adrian, maybe? Or was it Tristan?—was telling.

I practically ran into the food truck that served as a bar and bent over, trying to calm down.

Elsa paused the loud shaking of an elf-tini. "Was that Oliver?"

I dumped my tray into the sink and slumped down on the floor.

"Guess so." She set the shaker down.

The live band ended their jazz rendition of "Sleigh Ride." Then the accordion started wailing a slow holiday tune.

I pulled out the bills from my pocket and transferred them to my wallet.

"His hands touched these."

"You have a problem."

"He was all over Madison. It was like I didn't even exist, like I was just the help."

"That's how rich guys are," Elsa reminded me. "You always complained about how oblivious and entitled they were. What happened to your revenge kink?"

I speared three olives, stuck them in a martini glass, and handed it to her. She poured the toxic green martini into the cup.

"It is not a kink," I countered.

"Dark obsession, then."

I gazed out over the crowd. Madison was sitting on Oliver's lap. Another of her friends was on Tristan's. Both billionaires looked like they were having the time of their lives.

I had a horrible thought.

My worst nightmare had been that Oliver was going to end up with some preppy Ivy League girl from a good family and that I would occasionally cyberstalk their perfect life. I had never considered he might marry a small-town girl. I would have to see him every Christmas for the rest of my life.

I wasn't going to survive.

"Here's your mistletoe Negroni," Elsa said, sliding the drink across the counter. Then she handed me a shot of eggnog vodka.

I downed it. "That's disgusting," I rasped. I put the cocktail on the tray and headed out into the crowd.

The accordionist's wailing transitioned into a heartfelt if slightly off-key version of "Feliz Navidad," which, after working in the Christmas market, the Christmas tree stand, and now the pop-up bar, I had heard, oh, only thirty-eight times today.

"If you can't play anything else," I screeched at him, "then just leave so we can all sit here and nurse our misery in peace."

The accordion let out a sad wheeze, and the crowd went silent for a moment.

"You're a real grinch, lady," the accordionist said, shaking his head.

"Anyone who had to listen to the same five freaking Christmas songs over and over and over again," I railed while in the background Elsa slowly shook her head, "would hate this holiday."

"Some people just don't have any Christmas spirit."

CHAPTER 20

Oliver

Noelle stomped over to our table and slammed the drink down.

"Do you want to close your tab or keep it open?" she asked, voice harsh. She was pointedly not looking at me.

I wondered if I shouldn't have put the money in her pocket. My brain would not let me forget how warm her body was.

She asked me to put it there.

Madison draped her arm around my neck for leverage as she reached for the drink. She shifted on my lap as I pulled out my wallet and handed Noelle my card.

"You can just put this all on mine."

She glared at me.

"So generous," Madison cooed.

"Sure, I guess if you're just used to guys whose idea of a dream date is to show you their pickup truck that they've been trying to refurbish for the last three years," Noelle snapped.

"You would have low standards," Madison scoffed. "I work at Svensson PharmaTech, you know. I'm not some college dropout. I just happen to still be in touch with my small-town roots."

Noelle gave her a dark look and snatched the card from my hand.

After Noelle left, Madison said, "Her whole family is trashy." She sipped her drink.

"Did you see her sister all over the Moi Cheaters app?" another girl asked. "There were new pictures posted of her with Andelle Maxwell's husband."

"Ooh," they all chorused, "didn't she just have a baby?"

"This app is so addicting," another of Madison's friends said. "I sent it to everyone in my fraternity, and, like, three guys found out their girlfriends were cheating. It's madness."

Noelle came back to the table and set out the fried cheese curds Tristan had ordered.

The noise roused Max from the little hole he had dug in the snow under my chair.

He jumped up on his hind legs and pawed at the table, sending the drinks sloshing, and made whining noises in the direction of the fried cheese curds.

Madison picked one up.

"Have you ever tried one of these, city slicker?" she joked, slowly bringing it to my mouth.

It wasn't lost on me that Noelle was watching, lips pursed.

I took the cheese curd from Madison before she could stick it in my mouth.

I felt a little strange. When I had first gone to college, I had been a little—okay, a lot—out of control. My sister had just disappeared, my parents weren't involved at all, and my brothers were busy. I had felt adrift, alone, and looking for any and every distraction.

But now, I suddenly wanted something different. I didn't want to be out at bars, even small-town ones, at all hours of the night. I wanted what my brothers had—a family.

You're not going to have much of anything if Noelle fucks you over.

In her sexy Mrs. Claus outfit, Noelle scowled as she collected several of the empty glasses.

"Could you bring us another round?" I asked her, hoping I was coming off as friendly and not someone whose business you might ruin.

"These or something else?" she asked. "We have an Elf on the Shelf cocktail made with local moonshine that will have you passed out naked in the snow in front of your crush's house."

"Do you speak from experience?" I joked. "Or are you just hoping I'll end up in front of your house?"

"Be careful," Madison giggled. "Noelle's the Ghost of Christmas Past. She'd drag you into her house, chop you up, then bake you in one of her mom's disgusting casseroles."

All of Madison's friends roared with laughter.

"I remember when your mom made that Christmas casserole for the sixth-grade holiday party," Madison continued with a mean laugh. "It was the most disgusting thing I have ever seen."

"A holiday Christmas casserole sounds festive," I said, looking at Noelle in concern. She seemed stoic and unmoved.

"It was *so* nasty," one of the other girls at the table exclaimed. "It had canned peas, canned corn beef, cranberries, and tater tots."

"So everyone wants a round of 'Grandma Got Run Over by a Reindeer' Because She Was Talking Shit cocktails?" Noelle asked shrilly.

I winced.

Madison was unfazed. "Actually, I think I'll take the 'I hate Christmas because my life is pathetic' cocktail."

"Why don't we just have a round of grinch cocktails?" I offered.

"Why?" Noelle snapped. Was it my imagination or did she sound a little hurt?

"Because I'm not being your happy little Christmas-loving waitress?"

"I was the one who defended you from those creeps earlier. Why are you jumping down my throat?" I demanded. "Not everyone is out to get you. It is the happiest time of the year; you could try to enjoy it. Maybe have a little attitude adjustment."

"And you need a reality check. Christmas is a cold, miserable season filled with people who fake being happy while they secretly resent the obligations of the holiday." She was breathing hard, her breasts pushed up high, almost heaving out of the low-cut bodice.

"Don't mind her," Madison drawled. "She's just a sour grinch. Ooh, speaking of grinch, Ms. Dottie has a whole Grinch scene set up in her yard. You and I should make plans to go look at the lights one evening. I can show you all the best ones. I'll make hot chocolate."

"Oh, I uh..."

Tristan kicked me under the table.

Noelle slammed a rag on the table to wipe up the drinks Max had spilled.

Was she... jealous? Surely Noelle couldn't want to go out with me.

She's probably mad that you're thinking about dating the girl who she got in a fight with.

To be fair, it was probably too much drama to bring into my life but...

"He'll go," Tristan said emphatically. "Right, Oliver?"

I looked up at Noelle. She wouldn't meet my eyes.

"Yeah."

CHAPTER 21

I was so furious at Oliver!

It was exactly like what had happened at Harvard.

I had spent the night with him and didn't see him the next morning. Then, when I saw him in class, he acted like he had no recollection and was flirting with a girl in front of me. A girl from a good family.

Unlike me.

I sure had tried to leave my small-town roots behind. I had straightened my hair, skipped breakfast, and worn my best Ivy League prep outfit.

But I wasn't like the girl with her Birkin bag and expensive shoes sitting on his desk in class, running her fingers through his hair.

And now here we were in my small town, which wasn't supposed to be my safe space but was at least supposed to be safe from *him*.

Oliver had clearly flirted with me then was all over Madison like I had meant nothing to him.

"You're not planning on anything drastic, are you?" Elsa asked in alarm as we careened down the dark country road.

"You mean like burning his house down and stealing his dog?" I asked shrilly.

"He and Madison deserve each other," Elsa said in a soothing tone. "You always complained about how stuck-up she was in school."

"With her horse competitions and all her hair accessories." I glowered.

"At least we made bank tonight," Elsa reminded me. "And your Moi Cheaters app is taking off. There are tons of posts. We should get together and make a few changes to the code."

"Are there any about Oliver cheating? Gosh, I would love to bring him down."

"What happened to being a modest dreamer and ruining his holiday?"

I took a deep breath and let it out. It hovered in the old pickup cab. The heat hadn't worked in that thing since the early 2000s.

"Bet Oliver has a nice fancy truck with all the bells and whistles, even though he is incapable of changing so much as a light bulb."

"Karma gets everyone eventually," Elsa said sagely.

"Only if you help it along."

I seemed to be failing at that too.

Was that my destiny? To be a complete loser, just like Madison said I was?

"Maybe I could ruin his date with Madison. I mean, seriously, they were going to drive around town in his big fancy car listening to Christmas carols and looking at Christmas lights. Lame."

"Christmas lights are so much fun, though," Elsa gushed. "I love seeing how creative everyone is. You know Ms. Dottie has a—"

"Yes, she has practically a whole nativity scene worthy of *How the Grinch Stole Christmas* all over her house. Trust me. I heard all about it. It really helped Madison seal the deal when she practically strong-armed Oliver into going on a date with her. You should have seen her rubbing all up against him. She totally has her sights set on being Mrs. Frost next Christmas."

"I'm sure he's only going out with her to sleep with her."

"Oh my god, they're going to sleep together." I felt sick. "I know she's good in bed—better than me—because she lost her virginity sophomore year with one of the Svensson brothers. Maybe that was why Oliver pretended like he didn't know me. Maybe I was terrible in bed."

"You'd never had sex before, so of course you were bad. That's perfectly normal," Elsa said in her therapist's voice. "You probably squirted all over his leg and made weird noises."

"You're right. I probably did," I groaned.

"I told you that you should have been reading romance novels instead of CEO autobiographies. Then you'd know how to make a man orgasm so hard he passes out."

"But I thought men liked sex. I would have slept with him again and gotten more practice."

"Have some self-respect, Noelle."

"I will never get over Oliver. I will be obsessing about him on my deathbed."

"You know," Elsa said thoughtfully, "now that I think about it, maybe he has a virgin fetish. Since he doesn't remember you, you can just lie to him and say you've never done this before. I bet he'll want to show you the ropes, so to speak. You could probably get a free meal out of it," she added as I parked the car next to my dad's truck.

The cold winter air cleared my head when I opened the car door. The engine fumes had a tendency to exhaust back into the cab of the truck.

"According to my business management books," I said, "the most logical explanation is the most likely. Oliver's just a selfish, self-absorbed, egotistical billionaire who doesn't care about anyone's feelings but his own." I pushed open the front door, having to shove my shoulder against it because the hinges were frozen.

"You were working at the strip club?" my mother screeched when we walked into the cramped living room.

My brother had the Facebook page for Ida's pop-up bar on his laptop screen.

"Someone has to pay for everyone's bad decisions," I said, punching my brother in the arm. "Traitor."

"She made me." He winced.

"Dear God, where have I gone wrong?" My mother wrung her hands.

"Seriously, Mom?" I said irritated. "I'm not stripping. I have some standards. Also, I've been hitting the casserole and baked goods a little too hard to be North Pole ready, as it were."

My mom ran her finger over the laptop's trackpad. "That man has his hands all over you."

I peered at the screen then scowled. "Good news sure travels fast in this town." I hated how I looked like a horny cat gazing up at Oliver as he stuffed the bills in my pocket.

"That's not the man that Deborah was saying might have gotten you pregnant?" my mother asked in a horrified whisper.

"She hasn't had sex in a year, Aunt Sarah," Elsa assured my mom.

"You're having sex?" My mother clutched her chest.

Dad slapped his hands over his ears. "La la la, I don't want to know."

"I'm twenty-two. You had a kid in middle school by the time you were my age."

"I wanted better for you." My mother closed her eyes.

"Why don't any of you love me?" Azalea wailed.

We all ignored her.

"Why can't our daughter get a real job?" my mother said to James.

"I just have to present my capstone project," I said, trying not to lose it. My mother loved to make everything about her. "Then I'll be back on track."

I hoped.

Unless Oliver was there to knock me out of orbit again.

Not going to happen. I wasn't even a person to him.

I refused to acknowledge how much it hurt.

"Here," I told my mom, handing her the wad of bills in my pocket. "Why don't you get the dishwasher fixed?"

"How come you're always giving her money?" Azalea demanded.

"Here, Azalea," my mother said with a sigh, handing her two twenties. "Maybe you and Dove could do something fun?"

"I'm grounding her." Azalea scowled and took the cash.

"For what?" I demanded.

Azalea shrugged. "I'm her mother. I can ground her whenever I want. Besides, I need her to babysit."

"Guess Azalea hasn't discovered the app," Elsa said to me in a low voice when we were upstairs in the cold, cramped attic bedroom. "If she had, we would have heard about it."

I checked the Facebook group I had set up for my app's beta testers to see what people's thoughts were. I was expecting a slew of complaints from the seniors about how they couldn't upload photos or didn't like the color or a multi-page essay detailing all the grammatical errors.

Instead, the Facebook group was flooded with positive comments.

"Dang. Guess cheating's a big problem in the senior citizen community," Elsa said, looking over my shoulder.

"Oh crap," I said, skimming the comments, "they've been sending it to their friends. So that's how Madison and her little rich-kid crew have it."

Elsa giggled, opening the app on my phone. "All I want for Christmas is to catch a cheater? Gold!"

Her eyes widened as she scrolled and scrolled and scrolled through the app. "There are tons of posts on here. What is your new user acquisition rate?"

I checked the app dashboard. "Off the freaking charts. I need to kill it. It's getting out of hand."

"No way." Elsa pushed me aside and opened her laptop. We both perched on the rickety chair at my childhood desk, which was wedged in between the two sets of bunk beds.

"We should tweak some of the colors. I'm going to make you a nice graphic."

“Forget the graphic,” I said, checking the server stats. “I need more cloud storage. I don’t have money for server space.”

“Go get your credit card. You need this. Success is self-care.”

“Guess it’s another sleepless night.”

The smart thing to do would be to can the app. It wasn’t as if I ever would make money from it.

But then I would have to lie awake in the dark and the cold, trying not to think about Oliver’s hands and tongue all over and inside me.

Or even worse, dream about him making me come again and again and again then tossing me aside.

CHAPTER 22

Oliver

"Look who climbed back in the reindeer saddle."

"I don't think people ride reindeer," I told Tristan as we walked through the Christmas market the next morning. Tristan had insisted on buying another of those deer sausages.

"Sure they do. Like in that movie *Frozen*? My little sisters love it." He was cheerful.

I wasn't.

I wasn't sure Noelle wouldn't flay me and stick me on the grill if she saw me. She had been really upset at the pop-up bar the night before. Or maybe I was reading into it. Sometimes I thought my sister was upset with me, but really, she just had other stuff going on.

You're being paranoid and crazy.

Just stay friendly and polite with Noelle and it would be fine, right?

I stood in line at the Naughty Claus.

"Damn, no sausages today," Tristan complained.

"Get me a coffee, will you? Whatever the special is today."

"I'm not your secretary."

"Thanks, man!" Tristan called as he hopped out of line.

Noelle was standing behind the counter. While her coworker was bubbly and full of Christmas cheer, Noelle seemed to have a black cloud around her.

It didn't make her any less attractive in her flouncy skirt and red and green corset that curved down to flare at the waist, framing her cleavage.

Noelle looked up, and her brown eyes caught mine.

I gave her an easy smile.

I thought I saw her face soften. Then the scowl was back as Madison slipped her arm in mine.

"Mind if I cut?" She was wearing a pantsuit, and her hair was back in a bun.

"Going to work?" I asked with a pained smile.

I could practically feel the daggers from Noelle's eyes piercing my neck.

"Hi, Max. Who's a good boy?" Madison cooed at the corgi.

The dog ignored her. He seemed a little more interested in Noelle, who was slamming cups of coffee on the counter. Or maybe he was just hoping she would take pity on him and give him a snack. The corgi was not amused by the diet I had put him on.

Madison seemed like she was expecting something from me.

I wasn't sure if I really wanted to go on a date with her, but then maybe Tristan was right and I should get back out there.

It's not like you have to marry her, I reminded myself.

We were a few people away from the counter.

Now or never.

At least it would get Tristan off my back.

"Do you want—" I began.

Madison perked up.

"Maybe we could go grab a drink or dinner?"

"Dinner sounds amazing," Madison exclaimed. She reached up and kissed me on the cheek.

"If you're not going to order, then go to the back of the line," Noelle said sharply. She knocked back a shot of espresso. I noticed she still had the black eye, though her nose wasn't swollen anymore.

"Could I get the special and a black coffee?" I asked rapidly. "And what do you want, Madison?"

"Well..." She gazed up at the menu. "I want a..."

"Back of the line," Noelle barked, pointing.

"I want an eggnog latte."

"Too late," Noelle said stubbornly.

"Noelle, please be reasonable," I said.

"Your little girlfriend should have had her order ready." Noelle wouldn't budge. "Considering how high and mighty you were when you stole my dog, I'd think you and I were on the same page."

"You could have already had our order taken by the time you sat here and argued with us," I said, jaw tense.

"Whatever," Madison said. "Svensson PharmaTech has a break room. I'll just get coffee there. Because I have a real job." She blew me a kiss. "I'll see you for dinner tonight."

I half thought about going back to my office. But I did want a coffee. And besides, I didn't want Noelle to think she had run me off.

I had tried being nice, and I had tried being professional. I was done. I wasn't letting her push me around. She was just doing it because I was letting her get away with it.

"I know what you're doing," I said to Noelle, leaning over the counter. "It's okay to be jealous, but now that you ran her off, why don't you give me my coffee, and I'll just be on my way."

She leaned forward so our noses were almost touching. "Back. Of. The. Line."

I seethed as I stood in line.

Noelle was literally ruining my Christmas, my favorite time of the year. She was being vindictive and dour. It was time to face that she was going to try to tank my factory project as soon as word got out. I needed to head her off, neutralize her.

Twenty minutes later, when I was back in front of the counter, Noelle asked, "Welcome to the Naughty Claus. What's your order?"

"The special and a black coffee. Same as last time," I said, shoulders feeling tense.

"We're out of the special." She crossed her arms. The bell on the end of her hat jingled softly in the wind.

"Then I'll just have the coffee."

"No coffee left. We have hot chocolate."

"I literally see coffee in the pot."

She turned then looked back at me. "It's empty."

"So you just had me waste my time and stand in line just to fuck with me?" I demanded.

"Aww, I'm sorry. I didn't realize you were under the impression that the world existed to cater solely to you so that you could live in a bubble of your own ignorance and ineptitude."

"Hiiii." Noelle's coworker shoved Noelle aside. "Did you say you wanted the coffee and a holiday special?"

"I'm having a moment here, Elsa," Noelle hissed at her.

Elsa slid the drinks across the counter to me and took my card. "Merry Christmas!"

It wouldn't be if I didn't do something about Noelle.

CHAPTER 23

Noelle

"The betrayal. From my own best-friend-slash-cousin."

"We cannot afford to get fired," Elsa reminded me. "Your mom's going to have a nervous breakdown, and I think something fishy is going on with the Christmas tree business. You might be paying off a couple of mortgage payments or some credit card debt this holiday season."

"I'll gladly sleep outside in a shed if it means Oliver has to be miserable too."

"You have a problem."

"Yooo-hoo!" Ida power walked up to the coffee stand.

"Hey, no cutting," someone shouted at her.

"I'm here on business," Ida shot back, "because some of us aren't mooching off of our elderly in-laws even though we're in our sixties."

The old man in line grumbled.

"What's up, Ida?" I asked as I assembled one of the holiday special drinks. "Do you have any more shifts at the bar coming up?"

Ida shook her fist in the direction of the police station near the town hall building. "We live in an authoritarian hellscape. The anti-Christmas Gestapo shut me down. You can't make an honest living in this town anymore."

"To be fair, you didn't have any sort of documentation from the health department," Elsa reminded her, "or a business license, or fire marshal approval."

"Unnecessary red tape," Ida scoffed. She leaned over the counter and said conspiratorially, "I've rebranded. Transitioned to fine dining. Holiday tapas. Only people I trust are in the know—clients and staff. I already got that Frost brother and a couple of Svenssons to make a reservation for tonight."

Crap, was Oliver taking Madison there?

Wait.

An evil smile spread across my face.

This was my shot to get back at him and ruin his Christmas romance.

"You're not going to rat me out, are you?" Ida asked, glaring at me.

"This conversation never happened." I zipped my lips.

"Good. Be in front of the nativity scene at eight. Fight the power!"

"I'm just not sure how spying on him is going to help you get your revenge?" Elsa said in concern as we handed off the stand to the next shift of elves.

"Billionaires like him always have some sort of pep talk, strategy session, or ritual before their date," I said confidently. "It's like that movie *American Psycho*. This way I can get in his head and see what he's planning then put him off-balance during the date."

"What if your quirky antics during the date just bring him and Madison closer together and they bond over how weird you are?"

I paused. "Then I'll sneak back over to his house, wear a ghost costume, and scare the living shit out of him while he's balls deep in Madison."

"And I'll save some tip money to bail you out of jail for breaking and entering." Elsa sighed.

"I'm not going inside the house. I'll just plaster my face to the window."

That was going to be a little more difficult than I originally thought, I decided when I was standing in front of Oliver's house.

The historic Victorian was not the ancient squat woodland cottage where I had grown up, in which you could easily reach up and touch the ceilings and the windows were squat and tiny because glass in the 1850s was expensive.

This house was a Victorian mansion. It loomed up against the night sky, illuminated by the tasteful lights strung up to make it look like a gingerbread house. It had twelve-foot-tall ceilings and huge glass windows.

Oliver's bedroom was on the second floor somewhere.

I hiked up my stockings then jumped up to a branch of a tree that grew close to the house. The only reason I had the barest minimum of upper body strength was because I had been hauling Christmas trees with my dad.

Trying to climb up the big evergreen tree was slow going. I used to climb trees when I was a girl, one of the few pros of growing up as the daughter of a Christmas tree farmer. However, I wasn't even sure if it would lead me to the master bedroom. I might just end up in front of a dark guest bedroom. But I was rewarded when I heard Max barking.

I pulled myself up onto the next branch, hands covered in sap, arms screaming in pain.

Then I was right there, staring into Oliver's master bedroom.

Max, deeply amused that I had appeared in the window of his new owner's bedroom, was hopping around in front of the window, making happy yapping noises.

"Shh, shh," I hissed at the dog, trying to silently communicate to him that he needed to stop drawing attention to me.

The corgi kept barking.

"Max," I heard Oliver say.

I cursed the fact that I wore my glitzy Mrs. Claus costume. I tried to bury myself in the snowy pine needles as much as possible, praying Oliver wouldn't see me as he walked into the master bedroom, slowly removing his jacket. His height and broad shoulders filled the space.

"Is there a possum out there?" Oliver asked, bending down and beckoning to the dog.

Max raced to him, tongue hanging out, then raced in front of the window, barking his head off.

"I guess I should be glad you're getting some exercise."

The wind blew. I bit my lip to keep from shrieking when a cold wet clump of snow slid down the back of my neck.

"What do you think Madison would like to see me in?" Oliver said jokingly to Max, who, now winded from all his physical exertion, had flopped down on the plush rug in front of the fireplace because, fuck me, Oliver had a freaking fireplace in his bedroom. It was bedecked with Christmas garlands and little holiday knickknacks.

I bet it's a real wood-burning fireplace too.

If I had a better angle, I would be able to see if there was a stack of wood ready for a cozy fire.

"Can't go wrong with a white shirt and black sports coat," Oliver said to the dog.

He undid his cuff links then unbuttoned the top three buttons of the faintly patterned blue dress shirt he was wearing. I started to drool a little bit as I saw the flash of muscled chest.

Then he went into the bathroom.

Dang.

Probably for the best. None of what was transpiring here could possibly be considered healthy behavior.

But it was like after I'd had that hit of him a year ago, I couldn't help but crave his touch. Like I would never feel whole until I was in his arms again.

Oliver came back into the bedroom, carefully carrying a shallow dish. He set it down on the floor by Max's snout.

The corgi rolled over and plunged his snout into the bowl, lapping the water noisily.

Oliver smiled.

I swooned. He had a gorgeous smile. And hot rich guys who loved dogs were totally my type.

Oliver quickly unbuttoned the rest of his shirt, and I gripped the tree, leaning forward as he shrugged off the shirt, shook it out, then headed to what I assumed was the closet.

He reappeared still in his undershirt, undoing his belt.

My nether regions lurched. Even though it was freezing cold out, I felt hot and flushed as I tracked the motions of his hands.

His belt slithered off, and he laid it on the bed.

I was hyperventilating. He reached for the buttons on his pants, first one button then the other.

The year-old memory of him doing that in my dorm room was crystal clear.

I could practically hear the rasp of his zipper.

He grabbed the belt and headed out of my field of view.

No! I needed this. I'd had a hard Christmas, and it wasn't anywhere close to being over. I deserved this.

I held onto the tree, leaning over the branch, needing to see him. My heart beat furiously. I could peek into his closet. He had his undershirt off, and I had a glimpse of the muscular back.

I remembered how he had shivered when I ran my nails down the ridges of his muscles.

His pants were coming down now. He was turning...

I craned my head, needing all of him.

Crack!

I shrieked as the branch I was holding onto snapped, sending me—and half a tree's worth of snow—tumbling to the ground.

"Ouch! Dammit." I bounced off several branches.

"Ooof!" I wheezed, the wind knocked out of me as I gazed up, dazed, at the large evergreen tree, half buried in a snow drift.

The window opened. Oliver stuck his head out, looking for the noise.

"Guess that must have been a big possum," he said to the dog as he shut the window.

I think this might be a new low for me.

CHAPTER 24

Oliver

I did not trust Max alone in the house, especially since he was acting extra crazy that evening.

Fortunately, Madison didn't seem upset when I showed up for our date with Max in tow.

"Hi, handsome," she cooed.

"Hey," I said, unsure if I should hug her or shake her hand.

"Not you, the dog," she joked.

I smiled at her. Maybe Madison wouldn't be so bad to date after all. She seemed fun and down-to-earth, I decided, as Ida, acting as the hostess, led us to a table. The pop-up restaurant was half-hidden by the nativity scene.

It contained life-sized figures and piles of golden hay in the temporary wood structure. Our table was situated next to one of the three wise men, who was being eyed by a fiberglass sheep.

"I just love Harrogate at Christmastime," Madison gushed. "I just don't understand people who hate Christmas. It's the best season."

The evening was picture-perfect. Even though it was chilly, there were several of the tall heat lamps out.

At least Madison was more pleasant company than Noelle.

"I'll get you all started with some waters. Do you know what you want to drink? Maybe the Ebenezer Scrooge?"

Seriously? Would I never have a break from Noelle?

"Can we get a different waitress?" I asked, looking up to meet her eyes.

"Sure," Noelle said with sticky sweet politeness, "you're free to go to any of the other restaurants around town, but good luck trying to get a reservation. We have lots of tourists in town for the Christmas season. No takers? You just want to stay here? Thought so."

"Can I have a whiskey?" I said darkly.

"I'll have the same," Madison said.

Noelle had left to get our drinks.

"We can go somewhere else," I offered to Madison.

"No way am I letting her drive us off. She is the worst," Madison said. "Never had a boyfriend. Peaked in high school. Now she's bitter and angry and taking it out on those of us who made better life choices."

She flipped through the menu, which had been printed on card stock. The cover showed a snowman in a three-piece suit sipping a martini.

"Honestly, this is why I don't have any female friends. They all want to go start drama and be mean then wonder why they can't get or keep a boyfriend when they're out there stepping all over some poor guy's balls."

I inwardly winced. That sounded like she was describing my sister. Maybe Madison and I wouldn't be that compatible.

Noelle came by and slid the drinks onto the table. "Are you ready to order?"

"Yes, can we get—"

"That menu's just for show. We only have one dish available, and it's the venison with the rosemary cherry sauce, grilled carrots, and fennel with garlic cheese mashed potatoes. Take it or leave it. Dessert is the gingerbread and white chocolate mousse trifle, as featured on *The Great Christmas Bake Off* yesterday. My mom made it, and it's actually pretty good. I hope you don't order it so I can eat the leftovers."

"I guess we'll take two," I said.

Noelle flounced off, swishing her hips. The overall effect was ruined, however, when Max, who had positioned himself right behind her, yelped when she stumbled over him.

"Keep trying your luck," she scolded the dog, but then she leaned down to give him a pat.

After Noelle left, Madison said, "She has no self-control." She clinked her glass to mine. "Noelle was a mess in high school and a mess today, just like her parents."

"What's wrong with the parents?" I asked, wondering if something horrible had happened.

Madison scoffed and took another sip of her drink. "The usual small-town horror story. Preggo freshman year. They get married to make a go of it, and poverty and more unmanageable children follow. People like her family bring this whole town down."

"It is statistically difficult for relationships formed because of a teen pregnancy to stick long-term. Sounds like the marriage started off with a handicap."

Madison rolled her eyes and finished off her whiskey, "They're still married. They live in a hovel. Noelle's mom sells food she makes in her kitchen. My mom is going to call the health department on her one of these days and shut her business down. I hope they'll just get out of town then."

"Does she make sausages?" I asked before I could stop myself.

Madison made a disgusted noise. "You didn't eat one of those, did you?"

"I thought it was pretty good." I argued. As someone who grew up raised by an older sister because his parents forgot he existed, I was well aware that my situation might be described as trashy. As such, I suddenly had a lot more empathy for Noelle.

"All I'm saying is, if we want to attract more people from good families like yours, Harrogate needs to keep the country chic and lose the white-trash element."

"What's a good family?" I asked with a frown, swirling my own drink.

"Parents who are actually successful and live in a nice house. People who have some basic level of education. No one got pregnant before they could legally apply for a learner's permit. You know, those types of old-fashioned family values."

That did describe my life on the surface, but I knew from experience that materialistic outward approaches weren't the whole picture and did not necessarily a happy family make.

"I'm sure there are examples," I said carefully, "of loving, happy families that don't have the best economic circumstances."

"If you're trying to imply that I come from an unhappy wealthy family, let me tell you I don't," Madison said defensively. "My family is very close. We go on family vacations together, and if you hold my family up to Noelle's, there is no comparison."

"Some people aren't as fortunate as you are," I said sharply, ready to just cut the date short. Unfortunately, we had already ordered, and I was starving. It wasn't like I was a cook or anything, and I didn't have any food at home.

"Oh, I get it." Madison gave me a smug smile. "You're a contrarian. You're going to argue with me just because. Well"—she leaned over the table—"while I do love a man who knows his own mind, we might just have to agree to disagree on some things."

I knew my attention should be on my date, but I was suddenly very aware of Noelle sliding steaming plates of food in front of happy diners at a nearby table.

Madison narrowed her eyes at me.

"Do you want another drink?" I asked, trying not to make it seem like I had been staring at Noelle.

Madison snapped her fingers at Noelle, who slowly approached.

Max ran between her and me, barking excitedly.

"Max, no," I told him.

The dog didn't listen to me.

Madison trailed off when she saw I wasn't paying attention to her and was instead watching Noelle stuff Max silly with treats.

"Seriously, Noelle?" I demanded.

"These are vegan dog treats." She stuck her tongue out at me. "It's just cauliflower and egg white. Lighten up."

"Oliver's dog is supposed to be on a diet. It's not shocking that you overfed that poor animal," Madison dug at Noelle.

"It wasn't me. It was my sister, and some of that is still puppy fat," Noelle countered.

"I'm not here to listen to your worthless opinions," Madison said, cutting her off. "So why don't you just run along and fetch us more drinks?"

CHAPTER 25

How could he want to be with someone like her?" I fumed, stomping into the tiny kitchen. I washed my hands and stirred the cherry sauce that simmered on the gas stove.

"Sociopathic birds of a feather," Elsa said as she seared venison on the griddle. "I bet she ends up making his life miserable. He's going to be forty and married to her and wishing he had stayed single."

"You seriously think they're going to get married?" I felt heartbroken.

"They were having some sort of intense conversation," Elsa said with a grimace, "and usually when people give their meet-cute story, it goes something along the lines of 'we had a date and talked for eight hours then fell in love.'"

"So not 'we drunkenly hooked up, and then the guy pretends the girl doesn't even exist'?" I asked desperately.

"You're supposed to hate him, remember?"

I blinked back tears.

"I guess I have to acknowledge that an emotionally unstable part of me was hoping it would be a horrible misunderstanding and I was going to have my Cinderella moment when he told me he'd been looking for me forever."

I picked up a large spoon in the potatoes and slapped some on a plate then scooped up the venison.

That was it. My deep dark secret. I hadn't dropped out because of the humiliation—well, that was part of it. But if I hadn't fallen in love with Oliver and started building a future with him in my head, I wouldn't have been so devastated and heartbroken when he'd shattered my world by pretending he didn't even know who I was.

I swallowed the lump in my throat. No way was I going to face Madison and Oliver with puffy eyes. I scooped the piping hot plates onto a tray, put on my big-girl pants, and stepped back outside into the cold.

"Noelle," a middle-aged woman from a nearby table drawled, waving to me. "Hiii. I keep meaning to catch up with you, but you're always working. She's always working, isn't she, Deborah? I saw your mom at Costco. She looked a little tired. Is everything okay?"

As if I was going to give these busybodies fodder for the small-town gossip mill. They might have all gone to school with my mom, but I wasn't sure they were what anyone would call friends.

"I know she has her hands full."

"Four grandchildren, Carrie," Deborah said. "Such a blessing." Her face said that it was anything but.

"Have you worked out what your next step will be?" Carrie asked me.

Ugh, no.

"Just trying to make it through Christmas," I said with a pained smile, "then regroup."

"You can't take too much time off; you don't want to lose any momentum," Carrie said with a tight smile. "You don't want to end up like your poor sister. So out of control. We always thought you were the one with a good head on her shoulders. Can't believe what happened to you." She sighed.

"I was wondering if you could come to Stacey's school. You know, talk about how to avoid flunking out of college," Deborah said.

"I'll have to check my schedule." I gave her a tense smile.

"Before you go," Deborah called, "can you be a dear and bring me another of these?" She shook her nearly empty cocktail glass.

As much as I didn't like my mom's friends, who had clearly never left high-school-girl drama behind, maybe this was the kick in the pants I needed to finally get my degree.

Harvard had let me come in over the summer to do makeup tests to bring my grades up from failing to at least a C. For someone who used to pride herself on being an A student, that was devastation.

You should be thankful they even gave you that option.

Even if I had had to lay it on thick with the angle of having grown up the child of impoverished teen parents in a dying Rust Belt town.

For my senior-level business class however, the professor told me that since I had missed so much class, I needed to launch a product and start a business, and then he would change my grade to a C instead of an F. Otherwise, I would have to enroll for another semester and retake his class. That was not an option because I no longer had a scholarship and could not under any circumstances afford tuition and housing, especially for just one class.

Just schedule the meeting.

I needed to do it before the end of this year. I had the small business app and all the data.

I was so lost in my thoughts that I didn't see the dog leash stretched across the narrow walk path until I was already pitching headlong into Oliver's table.

"Fuck!" I cursed, firmly grasping the tray because of course food was more important than my physical well-being.

Fortunately, the table and my face broke my fall.

"That's how you know you're a good waitress," I said with a pained laugh. "You don't spill the food. Or, uh..."

Madison opened her mouth then screeched as the dark purple cherry sauce and slabs of venison dripped down her pristine white ski jacket.

"Yikes," I said, "you might want to go home and get changed. I think... yeah, it's definitely going to stain."

"This is a very expensive coat. You did that on purpose. You're just like your mother," Madison raged.

"Now, Madison," Oliver began.

She jerked away from him. "Don't you dare."

"Stop gaslighting her. Noelle did that on purpose," Carrie slurred from the table across the way. "She's trying to get rid of you. He was staring at her boobs all night. I took a picture, and I was going to put it on the Moi Cheaters app, but I'm trying to be a mentor to young women, and I just decided I had to tell you face-to-face. Isn't that right, Deborah?"

Deborah let out an earsplitting scream. "Fire!"

People jumped up from their tables.

A fire was cheerily burning the hay piled in the nativity scene. I picked up a nearby vat of liquid and dumped it onto the flames.

"Wait!" Elsa screamed as the dark amber liquid left the large bowl. "That's the holiday grog!"

The last part of her plea was drowned out by the roar of the inferno as it consumed the roof of the manger.

The three wise men's faces were melting, the plastic dripping on the sheep. Someone had used real wool to make the coats. They went up like one of those Victorian Christmas trees when a candle tipped over and suddenly burned your whole house to the ground.

"You are so going to hell for this," Madison screeched at me.

The angel that was hung up at the top of the nativity scene exploded, raining flaming fiberglass everywhere.

"So are you." Madison turned on Oliver. "They're right. You were so staring at her tits."

"I was not," Oliver choked out.

"Are we seriously going to have this conversation right now?" I hollered. "The nativity scene is on fire. Priorities, people." I ran toward the kitchen and bar on wheels, promptly tripped over Max, and careened into one of the gas heat lamps. It toppled over and wiped out three tables. The tablecloths went up in flames.

The corgi yelped, indignant.

"You," I raged at Oliver, "need to do something about this animal."

"Are you seriously yelling at me about an animal when you just set half the town on fire?" he shouted over the fire's roar. He grabbed me and shook me. "Stop screaming at me and tell me where the fire extinguisher is."

"We don't have one." I waved my arms.

"What do you mean you don't have a fire extinguisher?"

"None of this is legal or permitted."

"Hey!" Ida demanded. "Snitches get stitches."

In the distance, sirens blared.

"Everybody run," I yelled at the top of my lungs. "The cops are coming."

Most people ignored me in favor of filming the chaos.

"We better go." Madison tugged on Oliver's hand.

He looked at her, incredulous. "We can't just leave. The fire department will have questions."

She made a disgusted noise. "I thought billionaires were supposed to be ruthless. What kind of man are you?"

"Apparently one with enough sense to know he doesn't want a leech like you in his life," I snapped at her.

She shoved me. "Deborah was right. You are trying to steal him from me."

Oliver jumped between the two of us to prevent another fight. He was promptly clocked in the ribs for his trouble.

"Stuff like this does not happen in Manhattan." He groaned, clutching his ribs.

I put up my fists. I was angry enough that I felt like I had a pretty good shot to redeem myself—until a blast of water sent me tumbling backward.

"Sorry, Noelle," Cliff, one of the local firefighters, called to me.

The arc of water from the hose sprayed over me as I sputtered and wheezed in a puddle on the floor.

The fire department quickly extinguished the nativity-scene inferno. All that was left were the smoldering ruins of Christmas.

"At least this matches my mood," I croaked, trying to psych myself into picking myself up out of the mud, slush, and ash. I needed a shower but knew that all the hot water at home was probably gone. And really, if you couldn't have a shower after burning down a local Christmas landmark, then what was even the point?

Elsa appeared in my vision. "Oh, thank God. We thought we'd lost you."

"Oliver was worried?" I perked up.

Elsa grimaced. "No. I meant it more in like the metaphysical sense of me, myself, and the spirit of Oprah were concerned about you." Elsa grabbed my arm and hauled me to my feet.

The police were impounding the food truck while Ida complained loudly to the fire marshal.

"Yes, but this is your second warning."

"And you get three warnings," Ida was arguing.

"No, you really shouldn't get any warnings, Ms. Ida." The fire marshal sounded exasperated. "I should have just taken you to jail after the first illegal restaurant. Someone could have been killed."

"People need to toughen up." The elderly woman put her hands on her hips. "Back in my day, you could sell pasta out of your house. You didn't have to go through all this government nonsense."

"Ms. Ida, we're shutting down this establishment under the authority of the mayor. If you open another," the fire marshal warned, "you might go to jail."

"No respect!"

"What are we going to do with all the extra food?" Elsa asked. "And drinks?"

The firefighters perked up.

Ida smiled craftily.

"I think these fine servants of the community need some sustenance."

"No," the fire marshal warned.

"Aw, Captain," Cliff said as one of the police officers unlocked the door of the food truck. "It's not good to waste food. And we have to stick around to monitor the situation anyway."

"Seriously?" Oliver complained as I topped off drinks. Several of the restaurant patrons had returned to finish their meals.

I was not happy to see Madison.

"Half the fire department is drunk and probably most of the police force," Oliver said.

"Lighten up," I told him. Though I had been drenched, the heat still radiated from the smoldering pile of the nativity scene, and I was feeling pretty toasty. The air was, dare I say, festive. Max wandered around begging treats from the firefighters who perched in all their heavy gear on the rickety metal chairs, chowing down on all the leftover food.

"I watered down their drinks. Not to mention the mashed potatoes are loaded with cheese."

"Still," Oliver said, clearing a heavy grog tureen from a table before I could lift it, "you can't seriously think any of this is normal behavior."

"It's a small town. Most people find it charming. You're just upset because you're not getting laid tonight," I told him, taking the two steps up into the food truck.

Oliver followed me. "Why are you so obsessed with what I'm doing and who I'm with?" he demanded, setting the tureen in the small sink.

I was suddenly very aware of the tightness of the space between the sink and the griddle on the other side of the narrow aisle.

Oliver was huge; his head almost brushed the ceiling of the truck.

I craned my neck and looked into his ice-blue eyes.

"Just hate to see you waste your life with someone like her."

He paused, then turned on the water in the small sink and narrowed his eyes.

"What?" I demanded.

"Nothing. Just wondering if Madison was right about you after all."

CHAPTER 26

Oliver

"Dude, how did you ruin it with Madison?"

"Good news travels fast." I did not have the patience to deal with Tristan.

I had been up all night with Max, who had consumed his weight in mashed potatoes and was in pain but unremorseful.

And I kept spinning over my conversation with Noelle in my head.

Why did I care so much? Noelle was unhinged. The whole evening had been an insane fever dream.

"I follow Madison on Instagram. She posted a post-hookup picture, and imagine my surprise when it wasn't you. No worries," he continued, handing me a ticket embossed with silver foil and crimson lettering. "You'll find someone at the holiday alumni party."

"I'm not going." I handed him the ticket back.

"Okay, don't find a girlfriend. They're going to be all over me anyway," he said. "But it's a good networking opportunity. We're going to need to go through a massive hiring effort soon."

"Fine, but stop trying to set me up with women. I think last night was a sign," I told Tristan, "that I'm not supposed to be dating. I need to concentrate on my family. I have this dog, which is still untrained. Not to mention our company."

"Nothing more inspirational than a king practicing self-care. Oh, shit," Tristan said, ducking behind me.

One of his older brothers had zeroed in on him.

"I might have maybe borrowed Beck's watch without asking," he whispered. "I didn't think he would find out but... got to go." He took off running.

I sipped my coffee as I walked through the Christmas market. I had not stopped at the Naughty Claus. Instead, I had waited in the extremely long line at one of the local coffee shops on Main Street.

I needed to regroup and figure out what to do about Noelle.

She was clearly unhinged in some way and seemed to always be involved in drama. That made her dangerous and unpredictable.

It was too bad I had blown it with Madison. She seemed to have all the dirt on Noelle. Sure, someone who was less of a businessman and naiver than I was would write off Noelle as a simple small-town girl until everything blew up in his face.

Not me.

I dealt in systems and probabilities of systems. And Noelle was the type of person who disrupted systems.

As if to confirm my hypothesis, there was Noelle, wandering through the crowd with a canister of Snowman Surprise.

"Five dollars!" she said.

"Is there booze in that?" one woman, trailed by five screaming children, asked her.

"There can be." Noelle waggled her eyebrows.

The woman held out a large thermos, and Noelle filled it then added a generous portion of bourbon.

"Bless you."

I itched to go talk to her.

Don't court disaster.

Instead, I headed to where they were getting ready to film another episode of *The Great Christmas Bake Off*.

I was so glad I hadn't let my brother rope me into participating. This Christmas season was difficult enough without trying to bake every week.

Besides, Max, who I had dressed in a Christmas-themed sweater, was the real star.

"Can I take a picture of Harrogate's two most handsome men?" a woman with a camera and a press pass begged.

I let her snap a few photos.

The atmosphere was festive and a perfect small-town Christmas scene. A man in a Santa costume was selling raffle tickets for charity.

I bought two.

"Merry Christmas," he said. "Drawing is at noon. We have an extra special prize today."

If only Noelle weren't here, this would be a perfect December morning.

"Did you dress Max in a Christmas outfit?" Noelle said from under my arm. "Appalling."

"It keeps him from getting anxious," I said, glaring down at her, forgetting all my earlier promises to myself that I would stay the hell away from Noelle. "And it has the added bonus of attracting a lot of women."

"Hey, hot stuff!" a group of young female tourists catcalled me.

Noelle yelled at them, "He's not worth your time."

"Depends on how long his dick is," one of them shot back at her.

"Don't look so smug," Noelle snapped at me. "Men are disgusting."

"That drink you're serving is disgusting."

"This is a very popular drink. Have you even tasted it?"

"I don't want to drink anything called elf vomit," I retorted. "Besides, knowing you, you're just going to spill it all over me or yourself."

"You wish I would," she replied hotly. "You're totally dreaming of a wet-T-shirt Christmas. Didn't get enough of a look last night?"

"It was dark," I said before I could stop myself. "And I barely saw anything."

"So now you want to get a look?" she asked, doing a little shimmy.

Did I?

Maybe sleeping with her is the way to get her on your team.

Or maybe it would just be inviting more craziness into my already turbulent life.

CHAPTER 27

For a second, I thought Oliver was going to kiss me, or at least invite me back to his office for a quickie.

The loudspeaker screeched.

The spell was broken.

You're delusional, I told myself, breaking away from him and hurrying away.

I normally didn't spend money on the raffle, but after last night, I felt like I deserved my own bottle of whiskey. Not to mention it was an extra-large bottle shaped like a corgi. That was a sign it was meant to be.

After the conversation with Oliver, I definitely deserved it.

Had we been flirting? I wondered as Dave, the chairman of the raffle committee, shook the large glass bowl filled with raffle tickets.

Surely not.

But it had felt very similar to the last time we had flirted, right before Oliver had asked if my roommates were gone because he was sure I got pretty loud when I came.

I shivered, not from the cold but from thinking about his hands all over me.

"And the winner is," Dave announced, "489. Is the holder of ticket 489 here? You have one minute to claim your prize."

I checked my ticket. "Crap, I need that whiskey."

"Hey, that's your number," a guy said behind me.

I turned to see who had stolen my whiskey.

"*You*."

Oliver smirked at me as he headed up to the stage, Max in tow. He was met with "aws" and "so cutes" from the townspeople gathered in the square in front of the gazebo.

Max wagged his tail and then sat on Oliver's polished dress shoes.

"How dare he?" I fumed. His very existence was an affront.

Elsa patted me on the shoulder sympathetically.

"I know it's not fair, but remember that even if you did win it, your sister would probably drink the whole bottle."

"You ready to go sell some Christmas trees, Dad?" I asked my father later that evening.

He rocked back on his heels.

"Don't you have the Harvard alumni holiday party?"

"I'm not exactly an alumnus," I said bitterly.

"You're practically an alumnus," Elsa said, "and your app is totally amazing. I bet it's way better than anyone else's project."

“I didn’t even buy a ticket.”

“We pitched in and bought you one! Surprise!” Elsa and my parents jumped up and down.

“Happy early Christmas present, honey.” My parents hugged me.

“Worst Christmas present ever.”

Elsa snapped our picture and grinned at me. “This is a good networking opportunity for you. You could shop your app around,” she cajoled.

“You don’t want to go, Candy Cane?” My dad was crestfallen.

Ugh. Stop being such a grinch.

“Of course I want to go,” I said, trying to muster up the last drop of enthusiasm from a very dry well.

“You’ve been working so hard, and I thought this might help you get in with some of the other Harvard people around town.” My dad lightly punched me on the arm.

“It will be a fun event,” my mother coaxed. “It’s ugly Christmas sweater themed. You used to love ugly Christmas sweater contests. Here.” She pulled out a garment that looked like someone who had only read the Wikipedia entry for *How the Grinch Stole Christmas* had decided to get drunk and knit a sweater.

“Thanks, Mom,” I said, trying to sound happy.

My mom beamed. “I knew you’d like it! You can wear it with the Ann Taylor loft skirt I found at the thrift store for you.”

“Maybe someone in there will ask you to join their startup,” my dad said in excitement as he parked the pickup truck in front of the boutique hotel where the alumni event was being hosted.

My poor father had no idea how any of this worked. I couldn't blame him. I, too, had been naïve when I had first attended Harvard. I, too, had thought that because I was now in the hallowed halls of the college, the universe would unroll a red carpet for me.

Not.

"I can swing by and pick you up after we finish selling Christmas trees," my dad said, reaching over and giving me a hug.

"I probably won't stay that long," I told him. "I can come over and help you all out."

"No," my dad argued, "you're going to be there all night. You'll see. They're all going to want to be your friend."

"Sure, Dad."

I walked in. The too-tight sweater had started to give up the ghost in the car when a thread of yarn had snagged on a spring sticking out of the seat cushion and begun to unravel.

At least there will be booze, I told myself.

I had worn my one good bra, the one that never let me down and kept my boobs from sagging. Unfortunately, just like the rest of my life, it, too, had decided that this Christmas was the one on which it would check out.

The underwire stabbed me in the ribs every time I took a step.

I tried to adjust the bra under the sweater.

There better be food here.

I handed the girl at the door my ticket.

"Oh," she said in excitement. "I'm so glad you wore an ugly sweater. I thought I was going to be the only one." She giggled.

Oh no.

I walked into the historic art deco ballroom, where Harvard alums were milling about. Literally no one was wearing a sweater. They all wore some mix of business formal, like they had all just come from work, which, I guessed, they all probably had.

Should have brought a backup shirt. Stupid, stupid, stupid.

"Here's what we're going to do," I decided. "We're going to stay twenty minutes. By that time, Dad should be super busy with the Christmas tree stall, and I can hide in the nativity scene and surf Instagram on my phone."

Wait, crap, the nativity scene was gone. Maybe I could just hide in the hotel bathroom like I was back in middle school.

I loaded up a plate with snacks and was trying to decide between red and white wine when a guy said practically in my ear, "What year?"

I bit back a curse as I tried not to drop my snacks everywhere.

"Excuse me?" I asked desperately.

A man with thinning hair stood in front of me. His glasses slid down as he twitched his nose. "What, um, year did you graduate?" He pushed up his glasses.

"This one," I lied.

It isn't a lie as long as I present my capstone project.

"Two years ago for me."

We stood there in silence for a moment.

"I'm Sydney," he said. "It was traditionally a boy's name."

"Like Sidney Poitier."

More awkward silence. I inched toward the wine.

"Where are you working?" he asked. "Some place cool?"

"Just doing a startup thing," I lied.

Creating an app to publicly shame my sister and another app to keep my parents from running their home businesses into the ground was hardly making me the next Mark Zuckerberg.

"That's excellent," he said, following me as I took another step toward the wine.

"I've been trying to dabble into seed fund investing myself. My grandma gave me a little bit of money to get started. The startup I funded didn't do very well." His shoulders sagged.

"If at first you don't succeed," I said, finally making contact with a bottle of wine.

"I could probably secure a loan," he said hopefully, "and invest in your startup."

Seriously? No wonder this guy went broke.

Did I want to drink wine alone in a bathroom stall, or did I want to set someone straight on their terrible business practices? Guess which one I chose.

"You don't know anything about my company," I argued. "You can't just invest without doing the research."

"The other investors I follow on YouTube really stress that you have to go with your gut and invest in people, not products," he said stubbornly.

"You're getting investment advice from YouTube. Dear Lord. Look," I told him impatiently, "you can't just invest because you think you'll be friends with a person. Honestly, you can't even invest because the other person has some sort of proven track record. Friendly personalities can be faked, and people can also lie about past successes. Anyone that's really been successful will not come to *you* to invest in their company."

"You don't know anything," Sydney sputtered.

"How much funding have you received, huh?" I demanded.

"You're such a—"

"Grinch? You're just mad because she's right," a deep voice said behind me. Oliver poured himself a glass of wine.

Sydney's eyes bugged out of his head.

"Oh my god," he babbled, "Oliver Frost. It's an honor to meet you. I've been following your hedge fund. I'm very impressed with your accomplishments. You should think about starting a YouTube channel. There are lots of us out there who would benefit from your sage wisdom."

I almost puked all over my snacks.

"I'll just excuse myself, since it sounds like you two boys are about to have a very enlightening conversation."

"Actually," Oliver said, cutting off Sydney before he could launch into a long, boring discussion about finance YouTube, "I wanted to introduce Noelle to some friends of mine." He grabbed my arm, steering me away from the wine and the exit.

"If you're going to kidnap me, you better get me a drink," I said, shaking him off.

Oliver handed me his glass then grabbed the duck slider from my plate and took a bite.

"A thief and a kidnapper."

"I didn't realize you went to Harvard." His eyes narrowed.

My heart started pounding. Was this it? My big moment, when Oliver finally remembered who I was and—sure, maybe it was too much to ask that he recover from his little amnesia episode and declare me the love of his life, but at least pity sex might be on the table?

"Um, yeah."

His tongue darted out and licked his lower lip.

I was totally not remembering how it felt to have his tongue do that on my clit.

"When did you graduate?"

I stammered, "This year. When did you graduate?"

"Strange," Oliver said, tilting his head.

"You don't remember?" I asked desperately, hating my voice's pleading edge. "I think we were in a couple of business lectures together."

He shook his head. "Not at all. Though there were a hundred people in some of those lecture classes."

He doesn't remember.

If I didn't need the alcohol, I could have thrown it into his stupid face.

I felt so dumb. I never should have come to this stupid party. Oliver wasn't going to remember someone like me. I was just a nameless, faceless girl he'd hooked up with one night who was invisible to him when he wasn't actively fucking her.

"Look who showed up after all," Tristan called out, sauntering over to Oliver. Several giggling young women hung off Tristan's arms like those little parasite-eating fish on sharks.

"And you found a friend. Hey," Tristan said, lowering his voice, "can you hit me up when you have more of those deer-meat sausages?"

"Sure," I whispered, "if the cops don't shut us down first."

Tristan laughed and slapped Oliver on the back. "Professor Hoffman is here. He does some consulting work with the Department of Defense. See ya in the Christmas market," Tristan called to me.

Oliver turned back.

Hope sprang eternal.

"Oh, Noelle?"

Had he remembered?

His eyes flicked down to my tits then back up to my face. "Nice sweater."

CHAPTER 28

Oliver

It wasn't a lie—Noelle did look good in that sweater. I wondered why she was wearing it. It sure grabbed attention. Not that it was as low cut as her other shirts, which made her tits practically spill out. This sweater had a high neck but just hugged her curves in an enticing way, making her look like a Christmas present waiting for me to unwrap it.

It was weird that I didn't remember her. We had graduated at the same time.

I was very aware of her through the event. Noelle mainly prowled around the drink table but occasionally chatted with other alums.

It wasn't lost on me that I wasn't the only man who had noticed her.

"Dr. Hoffman," I said to the director of the business school. "Didn't know you lived in Harrogate."

"I got married again," he admitted, "and she wanted to buy a second home out here. Our first date was at the Harrogate Christmas market, and she fell in love."

She, of course, was a former student of his turned teaching assistant turned lover.

Dr. Hoffman was old enough to be my grandfather.

"Hi, Cathy," I said to her. "Congratulations. I didn't realize you two had gotten married. That's... brave."

She clung onto the much older professor's arm and beamed up at him.

"I know you're not supposed to date students," he said to me defensively. "So we waited until after she had graduated."

"I was going to get a master's," Cathy gushed to me, "but then I decided to be a stay-at-home wife."

"I'm traditional, I admit." Dr. Hoffman kissed her hand.

"I think you and I have a lot in common, Oliver." He rested a hand on my shoulder.

I tried to keep my expression neutral.

"You're going to want a traditional wife, what with being a billionaire and all," he continued. "You need someone to keep up the home."

This guy sounds like my father, who is a grade-A dick.

"I'd rather have someone who hustled and wasn't going to be a mooch," I replied. "I didn't get rich running a charity, after all."

"No," Dr. Hoffman said, "I suppose not."

After the professor had moved on to other partygoers, Tristan said into my ear, "It's awkward, because his first wife is here too."

He inclined his chin toward an older woman in an animated conversation with Noelle, who was nodding along sympathetically.

They both glared in our general direction.

If looks could kill...

The woman was looking at her ex, but Noelle's anger was clearly meant for me.

It seemed personal.

I wondered if she had found out about the factory I was building.

Must have.

There was no other explanation.

CHAPTER 29

"Screw Oliver," I slurred as I walked along the snowy residential street, bottle of wine in hand.

Everyone else at the alumni holiday party had been using it as a way to network.

Not me.

I had drunk my way through the wine table while offering free therapy to several women whose husbands had left them for students, interns, or, in one case, the woman's own niece.

"Men are such pigs."

I had seen how Oliver chummed it up with Professor Hoffman.

Reminder to self—crank out a paper.

After I finished talking to his wife, Dr. Hoffman had cornered me to remind me I was supposed to come meet with him prior to my final capstone presentation.

"I'll be back in Harrogate in a week or so," he'd said. "Email me to set up a meeting."

He had given me a patronizing look. "I know you've had some difficulties compared to other, more prepared students. I want to see you succeed."

The exchange had left a sour taste in my mouth. Though I had loved the historic buildings, the dark academia vibes, and, of course, the library at Harvard, I hated that I would never fit in with the people from good families, with their money, effortless luxurious style, and casual exchanges about the exotic places they had gone. I had longed to be part of that world.

Did I really care all that much, since I hadn't gone home to start the paper?

I didn't want my parents to ask me why I hadn't stayed at the party longer.

"Gee, I don't know. Maybe watching the man who ruined my life get treated like the prince of England wasn't all that conducive to maintaining a stable mental state?"

I took another swig of wine as I stumbled down the sidewalk.

I didn't really have a clear goal in mind. I just didn't want to go home. If I was in any way the type of person who still got giddy on Christmas, I *might*—emphasis on the *might*—think that the Christmas lights decorating the rows of Victorian houses were beautiful.

However, I was in full-on grinch mode.

"Won't someone think of the poor raccoons who have to deal with this injustice?" I declared to one particularly nauseating house that was lit up like a nuclear bomb with lights on every single window, eve, and column.

"Wait a minute," I slurred, recognizing a metal reindeer in the yard. "What're you looking at? I don't know where your friend is."

I emptied the last of the bottle of red wine into my mouth as I stood there and regarded Oliver's house.

"A man like that," I told the reindeer, "doesn't deserve this."

I stumbled through the snow toward one of the windows decorated by a wreath with big red bows.

I tripped over one of the reindeer and face-planted into the snow.

"Ow," I groaned, grabbing at my boobs. My stupid bra had almost impaled me.

"Dear Santa," I told the sky. "I want a, oh, never mind. It's useless." I rolled over on my back, fished under my sweater, and unhooked the torture device. I breathed a sigh of relief when I was free from the underwire.

"Santa is not going to bring you a new bra *or* revenge for Christmas," I told myself. Now that I was lying down and the world wasn't spinning quite so much, my head was much clearer.

"A real businesswoman takes charge of her life," I declared, pushing myself up on all fours then staggering upright.

I headed for my old friend: the pine tree.

"Why is that man so hot?" I groaned as I swung up onto a branch. "That horrible mother-freaking, *ow*!" I cursed as I stabbed myself with a particularly sharp pine needle.

How did he literally not remember me, even though he was balls deep in my—er... Well, let's just say I lost all of my virginity that night.

I huddled on one of the branches near Oliver's master bedroom window, which was also decorated with a Christmas wreath. Max was stretched out on Oliver's bed, flat on his back, snoring loudly.

The dog's black nose twitched, and his tongue lolled. He flipped over and started barking at me.

"Ungrateful wretch. Whoops!" I called as I almost slipped off the branch. "Not today, Father Christmas." I reached out to the window. Of course, it was locked.

"Open it up, Max," I slurred to the dog. "Oliver doesn't deserve those wreaths. My grandmother made those wreaths. I don't even have a wreath."

The window stayed shut.

Max ran back and forth in front of it.

I peered up; the tree extended to the roofline.

"And hurry down the chimney tonight!" I sang off-key as I swung up to the next branch.

As a child of lower-income teen parents who lived in the middle of the forest, I hadn't had much else to do in my childhood except climb trees. I could climb trees drunk and in my sleep. Come to think of it, that was what I was doing.

"I'm on top of the world!" I crowed when I reached the top of the peaked roof.

I slid like a squirrel straddling the roof peak, scooting along the ridgeline to the massive brick fireplace. I pried the round ceramic top off and stuck my head inside.

The Victorians liked their fireplaces.

While my parents' wood-burning fire was more of a stovepipe, this house had been built to hold a massive fire.

I swung my feet over and shimmied into the chimney. Below me, Max must have figured out what was up because he was barking, the noise echoing up the chimney shaft.

"Dang, I can't believe I fit," I marveled. The cold air whipped my face, and I had a moment of clarity.

"Maybe this was a bridge too far," I said and tried to hoist myself back up.

The chimney rim was slick with ice. My hand slipped. Then I fell down into the sooty black tube.

I stopped abruptly, my teeth knocking together.

"Help," I squeaked.

I was stuck in the chimney, my arms wedged up above my head. Every time I let out a breath I slid farther down. My skirt was wedged under my boobs, and my sweater was wrapped around my head and neck.

"Help!" I rasped, kicking my legs. "Max, get help."

The dog's frantic barking changed to excited yips.

A pair of strong arms wrapped around my soot-covered thighs.

In any other scenario, I would have been really put out that Oliver was finally touching me only after I had flaked on working out the past year and developed a layer of winter flab. But I just wanted to be free. It was difficult to breathe.

"Save me," I forced myself to whisper.

"Shit," Oliver said, giving a solid tug on my legs.

I wedged down farther.

"I think you're stuck in there." His hands disappeared.

"Don't leave me," I begged.

His hand was back, his thumb stroking me reassuringly on my ankle.

"Don't worry. I'm going to call the fire department. We'll probably have to dismantle the chimney. I'm sure my neighbors will complain to me about it." I heard the eye roll in his voice. Then his phone emitted beeps.

I kicked my feet. "Don't you dare, Oliver Frost. Don't you dare call the fire department. My mother will find out. I'll be the talk of the town for years. Decades. It will be on my tombstone."

"I can't leave you here," he said, voice echoing up the shaft.

"Oh, yes you can. I insist. I'll be dead and done rotting in about three weeks. Then we can all just pretend this never happened."

"Are you insane?"

Oh God. I had a horrible thought.

He can probably see straight up my crotch.

Was I wearing my nice underwear? Did I even own any sufficiently nice underwear?

"Please," I begged. "My life is shit. Please just try pulling me out one more time?"

"I'm afraid to make you more stuck. Embarrassment won't kill you."

"It literally will," I shrieked with my remaining breath.

Oliver muttered something that sounded like "God save me from this woman."

"Fine," he grumbled, moving the logs and the metal grate out of the way. "I'm giving this one shot. Then we're going to host the fire department for the second time in as many days."

After a rustling of fabric, his large hands slid up my bare legs.

"Sorry for manhandling you like this."

His bare arms circled my waist, and I squawked as he wrapped them around my bare torso, connecting my body with his.

I could feel his bare chest against my thighs.

His head was somewhere in crotch vicinity, and he squeezed me tight.

Maybe I could just tell him to eat me out and then die happy.

Oliver gave a sharp hard tug. My sweater slipped up.

He adjusted his grasp and pulled, grunting hard.

"I think I'm moving," I called.

He gave one more strong tug. My sweater ripped, and then I was free, tumbling down in a heap of ash and yarn on top of him.

He was covered in black soot. It was all over his pale skin, turning his hair a dark gray and making his eyes a startlingly bright blue.

"See," I said, spreading my arms. "I knew you could do it. And you wanted to call the fire department."

He didn't say a word. He was staring at me, or more specifically my boobs.

I looked down.

"Elf balls."

Oliver quickly turned around, his bare, soot-covered back to me.

"So not only did you try to sneak down my chimney, but you weren't even wearing a shirt?" he demanded.

I hastily pulled down my ripped skirt. I was not wearing my good underwear. FML.

"No," I countered, "I wasn't wearing a bra. I definitely had a shirt on. It's the middle of winter. You think I'm just going to walk around making nipple Popsicles?"

He let out a slight growl.

"You were wearing a bra earlier in the evening. Where is it?"

"In your front yard," I said primly.

"Do you have a therapist we can call?"

"Nope. I get by with unqualified self-help gurus on TikTok and inspirational quotes on Instagram."

"Did one of them advocate stalking me?"

The rest of my sweater dropped out of the chimney. I clutched it to my chest.

"I'm not stalking you," I said, pulling what was left of it on. I coughed and sneezed as a cloud of soot enveloped me. "I was just here to steal your wreaths."

"*I bought them from you.* Just make some more."

"It's a little more complicated than that."

"Your eighty-something-year-old grandmother seemed to be making them out of scraps lying around, so I can't imagine it would be that much of a hardship." He glanced at me over his shoulder then, seeing I was covered, turned around.

Damn, his chest is fine.

I crossed my arms. I was not built to go without a bra.

"Hey," I challenged, "Gran isn't a day older than sixty-seven."

"Really?" He was shocked. "I said eighty to be nice. She looks like she's a hundred."

"That's what a lifetime of drinking will do to you. Speaking of," I said with another cough, "could I have a drink?"

Oliver's lips parted slightly.

I wanted to throw him in a bubble bath and soap him down, wash all the soot from his skin, then kiss it.

Don't get in a knife fight with the universe. You've already pushed your luck today. Need I remind you that you almost died earlier?

Yeah, but it would be amazing if you could get laid. Maybe this is the re-meet-cute moment.

Oliver narrowed those blue eyes at me.

"I'm not giving you a drink; you're lucky I don't call the police. Now I have to clean up the mess you made in my living room."

"Oh." I looked around at the black dust covering everything. I tapped two fingers together awkwardly. "I can stay and help you clean. I've been told I look cute in a maid's outfit."

Oliver pointed at the front door.

"Get out of my house."

CHAPTER 30

Oliver

I couldn't stop thinking about her in the chimney, the curves of Noelle's body underneath my hands, the way her breasts hung, full and round, the thin coat of the black soot barely hiding the pink of her nipples.

She's crazy.

Bet she would be good in bed, though. Her riding on my cock.

Get that out of your head. She's unhinged.

Maybe I shouldn't have been so quick to kick her out.

It wasn't like I had actually cleaned up the living room. I had paid an expediting fee to have specialized cleaners come remove all the vintage furniture, pillows, and rugs then carefully clean the walls, trim, and floors.

I wasn't sure why, after Noelle cost me a high-five-figure cleaning bill, I was going over to the Naughty Claus the next morning for coffee, but it absolutely did not have anything to do with my desire to stare at Noelle's tits again.

It was later in the morning. Max, who was starting to get the hang of walking on a leash, trotted smartly next to me as opposed to running ahead, choking himself on the leash, flopping over, running under my feet, or otherwise not acting like a normal dog.

Because he had been covered in soot, we'd just come from the groomer, and his fur was extra fluffy under the little Santa vest the dog shop owner had begged me to buy.

Noelle didn't even notice me when I approached. She was busy mediating an argument between her niece and a woman I assumed was her sister.

"I can't believe that, after I had to wake up in the middle of the night to change your little brother's diaper and clean him up, that you're going to sit here and ask for an expensive Christmas present. You only just started Christmas break, and you're already being a whiny, entitled brat."

"Azalea," Noelle said.

"I'm dealing with a lot right now," her sister snapped at her. "Some bitch in this town put me all over that Moi Cheaters app, and my boyfriend broke up with me to go back to his wife."

"Surprise, surprise," Noelle said.

"Of course you can't show a little empathy for your own sister." Azalea banged her fingers on her chest. "There goes my income stream for this month. Guess none of us are getting any kind of Christmas."

She stomped off.

Dove seemed resigned.

Noelle took a deep breath. "Here," she said to her niece, "just give me your Christmas list. Aunt Noelle will take care of it."

"There's only one thing on it," Dove pleaded. "It's what everyone is asking for. All the girls in school are going to have it, and I'm going to be the only one left out. Trust Aunt Noelle and the magic of capitalism. Speaking of." She pursed her lips and met my eyes.

"Tell your friend we don't have sausages today," Noelle said.

"That's fine. I'm sure he'd like the holiday special drink."

Noelle turned to making the green and red swirled concoction.

"So you don't have a big list for Santa?" I asked Dove, to try to break the tension.

"Santa's not real," she said automatically. "It's just an excuse for rich people to give their rich, obnoxious children lots of presents they don't deserve."

"Harsh but accurate," Noelle said, sliding the large steaming cup across the counter to me.

Dove leaned down and petted Max.

"And can I have a black coffee too?" I asked.

"Oh my god, do you only drink black coffee?"

"Why are you letting your aunt be so mean to me?" I teased Dove.

She smiled up at me. "Don't mind her. She just hates Christmas. Also, she's not boy crazy like my mom, so you can't use your looks to win her over."

I grinned. "Good to know. And," I said, lowering my voice conspiratorially, "can you tell me what will win her over?"

"Hm," Dove said, tapping her chin and looking seriously at Noelle.

Noelle gave an exaggerated huff and put her hands on her hips. "I cannot be bought."

"Can I go watch *The Great Christmas Bake Off* with Stacy and Oakley?" Dove begged, clasping her hands together and jumping up and down.

"Sure," Noelle told her.

"What are your friends' favorite snacks and drinks?" I asked her.

Dove wrinkled her nose. "They're all on diets, so they like the skinny almond lattes."

"That doesn't sound like a merry Christmas."

"I know! How could you not want a snowman sugar cookie?"

"Why don't you put three of the health-food lattes on my tab and some snowman cookies," I told Noelle. I smiled at Dove. "You and your friends have to start winter break off right."

"Thank you!" She beamed at me.

My heart warmed. I loved seeing kids happy at Christmas. It made the season all the more magical.

Noelle slid the drinks and cookies across the counter. Then Dove scampered off.

"Ugh," Noelle said, slumping over the counter and burying her head in her hands. "What a shit show."

She pulled a bottle of bourbon out from under the counter.

"Geez, it's like ten in the morning."

"I've been up since four, so it's more like happy hour for me."

"No, I think even with that math, it would still be unacceptably early to be doing shots at work."

Noelle stuck her tongue out at me and poured a splash of bourbon into a Santa mug.

"I feel like I need to buy you a Grinch mug."

"Har, har." Her face reddened. "I guess you were up all night cleaning. I can seriously come by after my shift and—"

"No need," I assured her. "I have people cleaning."

"Right, people." She wrinkled her nose.

"You're awfully judgmental for someone who was breaking and entering and causing all sorts of property damage," I said sharply. "Not to mention, you left your bra in my front yard. My elderly neighbor was not amused."

Noelle hastily pulled out her phone and scrolled. "Fudgsicles. It's all over the Harrogate Facebook group."

I took the phone from her and read the latest post out loud. "'Whose undergarments are these? They seem to belong to a well-endowed woman. They were found on Oliver's lawn. He's such a nice boy. I hate to think that someone untoward is attempting to lead him astray.'"

I snickered. "The elderly sure are national treasures."

Noelle snatched the phone back. "Mrs. Horvat is like a beagle. She'll never rest until she finds who did it. Ugh, I can't believe it. Can I come pick it up after my shift? I'll trade you a Santa cupcake."

"I don't have it," I informed her. "Mrs. Horvat took it hostage for evidence. I think she's planning on bringing it up at the town hall meeting."

"Why does this keep happening to me?" Noelle wailed.

"I don't know, but you seem to be the common denominator in all your terrible life choices."

I picked up the black coffee and took a sip.

"I owe you for ruining your living room," she said as I grabbed Tristan's coffee, which I really should have poured down a storm drain because it was going to rot out his teeth. "Just tell me how much."

"Instead," I countered, "why don't you let me have first dibs on the next batch of venison sausage. I highly doubt you'll be able to fund the cleanup, especially since you have to make all your niece's Christmas dreams come true."

Noelle grimaced. "If she only wants one thing, I think I should be able to manage."

"What's her one special gift?" I asked, curious.

"Some sort of deluxe Hello Kitty-themed makeup gift set."

"Cute," I said as Noelle typed in the product name on her phone.

"Holy crap, no, not cute," she said. "How is this thing twelve hundred fifty dollars? It's just a mirror, accessories, and a few makeup kits."

I leaned over the counter to look at her phone. I was close enough to breathe in her scent. She smelled like spiced apples. I wondered if it was her shampoo. She had missed a little bit of soot behind her ear.

"It's a smart mirror," I murmured.

Noelle played the video on the purchase page. There were several happy-looking little girls doing their makeup, marveling at their reflections, and watching YouTube videos on the smart mirror shaped like Hello Kitty. The other accessories were artfully arranged around them.

"Ugh, I don't know if I'm going to be able to afford that."

"You may not even be able to get one," I said pointing at the little icon that said Sold Out.

"Crap. Maybe I can get her some Hello Kitty merch from the dollar store—oh my god." She threw up her hands. "I sound like my mother."

Noelle didn't seem as antagonized as she did in our previous interactions. Soot all over my living room aside, maybe finding Noelle and her huge fucking tits in my chimney was worth the money I spent having it cleaned after all.

Now she owed me.

Maybe the town hall would go smoothly after all.

CHAPTER 31

Beep Beeeeep Beep Beep Beeeeep!

I sat up groggily in bed. I had been in the middle of a very spicy dream in which Oliver and I were in a big tub full of hot chocolate, and he kept licking marshmallows off my tits.

"Is there a fire?" Elsa said sleepily.

On the bottom bunk below me, Gran was snoring like a freight train.

"I don't smell smoke," I said, pulling the covers back over my head.

There were heavy footsteps on the narrow staircase that led up to the attic.

"There's a carbon monoxide leak," my dad said, frantically throwing open the door. "That's the carbon monoxide alarm. Wake up."

I ignored him.

"Oh my God," Dad cried, shaking me and turning on the lights. "Oh my God, you've already succumbed. I feel faint. This whole room is filled with it. Mom? Mom, are you dead?"

Clearly, I wasn't getting any sleep.

"She's snoring at a decibel level that really deserves to have an OSHA complaint filed about it," I said loudly. "Obviously, she's alive."

Gran snorted awake and sat up, feeling around. "Where are my teeth?"

"We have to go outside now," Dad insisted, picking up Dove out of her bed.

My niece complained as my dad ran downstairs.

"We all have to get out of the house before we die," he shouted.

"I don't think it's sustainable to operate on this little sleep," Elsa mumbled as we pattered downstairs and pulled on boots and coats while my dad freaked out on the phone with the fire department.

I stuffed the cat down my coat and joined the rest of the family in the yard in the dark and the cold.

My mother had handed my nephew off to Dove while she held Azalea's little girl. My brother, his daughter asleep on his lap, had set up his laptop on a nearby rickety table my dad had found on the side of the road ten years ago. He was always about to fix it, so he told us not to throw it away.

"How long is it going to take the fire department to show up?" my mom asked my dad.

"They said they were on their way. Good thing I installed all those carbon monoxide detectors, huh?"

A horn blared, and a car swerved down the driveway, narrowly missing one of the metal reindeer I had stolen from Oliver.

"What in the world, Azalea?" my mother said shrilly as my sister jumped out dressed in a club outfit, almost breaking the heels on her platform stilettos.

She slammed the door and stomped over to us, her impractical shoes sinking in the snow.

"You," she fumed at me. "This was you."

"This isn't about the bra, is it?" I asked carefully.

"What bra?" my mother demanded.

My sister tried to slap me in the face. I skidded away from her, and she almost fell over.

"Girls," my mother yelled at us, "stop fighting this instant."

"She started it," Azalea screamed. "She made that app and put me all over it. I got thrown out of the club because the bartender thought I was there to cheat with her boyfriend."

"Well, were you?" Gran asked pointedly.

"They just had a baby, and she hadn't been taking care of his needs," Azalea argued.

"Speaking of not taking care of the needs of family members," Dove mumbled as my baby nephew started crying for his mom.

"I swear you're not getting a single thing for Christmas," Azalea snapped, snatching up her crying son.

She pulled out her phone, paused her ranting, and filmed herself making sexy faces at the camera then kissing his cheeks. Instagram content done, she handed the baby back to Dove.

"You," she yelled at me as she posted the video, no doubt with a caption full of typos, "are jealous. You're sad, and you're bitter, and you're lonely. You—"

Fire engines drowned out the rest of the rant.

"I hope they sent over hot firefighters." Gran rubbed her hands together.

Azalea perked up. "You think they're going to be hot?"

"A man with a steady government job and a pension is hot," my mom said firmly.

My dad looked crushed. "We're selling a lot of Christmas trees this year, thanks to Noelle."

"Oh, not you sweetie." My mom leaned up to kiss him. "I love my big Christmas lumberjack so much. But Azalea really needs to find a man who can take care of her."

"And all her kids," Gran added.

Azalea pushed up her boobs under her skintight blue sweater dress. She waved to the firefighters.

"Hi, boys, thank you so much for coming all the way out here to save us."

"Yes, ma'am," one of the firefighters said to her, jumping out of the truck. He was not young and attractive. He was more the been-around-the-block-and-seen-some-shit-and-you-can-take-or-leave-my-mustache type.

"Hubba hubba." Gran elbowed me in the side.

The fire captain stomped up to the house as the rest of the firefighters jumped out of the truck.

Azalea preened. "Do you boys want some Christmas cookies?"

"They better run," Elsa said under her breath, "or they're going to have a single mom and her three kids and her suitcases full of drama moved into their apartment by Christmas Eve."

"At least she would be out of the house."

"Hey," a younger firefighter said, peering at Azalea.

"Hiii." She twirled her hair around her finger.

"Aren't you that girl from the Moi Cheaters app? My girlfriend checks it daily just to make sure she doesn't find me on there."

"I think you created a monster," Elsa whispered in my ear.

I grimaced.

"Turns out," the firefighter continued, "she was the one cheating all along."

"I could, ah, help you rebound from her." Azalea wasn't giving up.

"Oh, er... uh..." He hastily stepped back. "I'm actually trying to just date women my own age."

"Your own age?" Azalea shrieked.

The firemen looked like they wanted to go run and hide behind their truck.

The captain came out of the house and pulled his gas mask off his face.

"The house is safe."

"Did you find the leak?" my dad asked anxiously.

"The sensors didn't pick up anything, sir. The battery just needed changing in your smoke detector. That's why it was beeping. Cliff, you got any double A's?"

"Yes, Captain."

"You didn't check the battery?" my mother screeched at my dad as the fire department packed up.

"There was an emergency, Sarah," my dad begged as my mother swept back into the small house. "Why don't I rub your feet while you try to fall back asleep?"

My mother aggressively filled up the coffee maker. "No point in it now. Besides, I need to finish that big order of pastries for the town hall."

"You can't go to the town hall, Mom," my brother complained. "I need you to watch the baby."

"I thought Krystal's mother was going to come take her."

"She's going to Atlantic City."

"So she has money for that but not her own grandchild."

Gran settled on the couch, turned on *The Great Christmas Bake Off,* then promptly fell asleep.

"Noelle, could you do the town hall refreshments?" my mom pleaded.

"Sure thing. I'll wear something extra sexy."

"I don't want to know." Mom poured herself some of the piping hot coffee.

I poured a cup for myself then headed to the bathroom to wash my face and do my makeup. Between the cold and my chaotic family, I was wide awake.

"Get out of my way. I need the bathroom. I have a splitting headache," Azalea announced.

I rolled my eyes, grabbed my laptop, and sat down next to Gran. I opened the dashboard for the finance app.

"Don't forget, Dad," I reminded him, "I need to see the rest of your financial information."

"I'll do it in a little bit. Need to go check the other smoke alarms," Dad said gruffly.

"I need it to finish my capstone project," I told my dad. That was true, but I also had a suspicion that things at the Christmas tree farm were dire.

I opened my Word document, needing to finish the paper that I had to submit with the app I had created.

It was a common misconception that a professional paper had to be boring. Wrong. A paper should be entertaining, gripping.

When I had written my application essay for Harvard, I knew talking about what a roller coaster high school was wouldn't cut it. People wanted drama.

I had really played up the teen-mom angle in my college essay. A pregnant fourteen-year-old got people's attention, especially when you laid on the hardship extra thick. My essay was practically Dickensian.

Of course, I hadn't let my family read it. I had given them a fake one. They just wouldn't understand that in business, sometimes you had to be cutthroat to make the sale. As evidenced by the fact that my father had barely been breaking even with the Christmas tree stand where he had free watered-down hot chocolate and low-priced trees. You had to spice it up in business.

Then I opened my old essay so that I could recycle part of it for my paper. I had to pull out all the stops. Not graduating was unacceptable.

I'd already been seen at the alumni holiday party. Couldn't you be arrested or at least blacklisted for pretending to be a college grad?

Panic took root in my chest. I typed furiously in the Word document.

I bet no one ever made Oliver feel small and worthless. Gosh, it was gross how they were all sucking up to him at the holiday party. Especially Professor Hoffman.

The hurt threatened to drown me.

Oliver got everything, got to just ruin everyone's lives.

He didn't call the police, I reminded myself.

He did rescue me and didn't post about it on the Facebook group. Maybe he wasn't completely terrible.

What if there was some sort of reasonable explanation for his behavior a year ago? Maybe he had been drugged? Maybe I had run into his identical twin?

I couldn't go down that road. After the shock of his rejection of me, I couldn't concentrate or do my work. When I should have been studying, I had spent hours and hours every day obsessing online about what I had done wrong and how I could get him back, bargaining with the universe, until finally it was midterm time, and I was failing.

No, we were not going to start that spiral again.

Oliver was an asshole, selfish, self-centered, and not anyone I would ever date, let alone sleep with. Well, sleep with again.

You cannot let Oliver ruin your last shot of earning a Harvard degree, I told myself as I finished typing up the email to Professor Hoffman to schedule a meeting.

Even if he does look good without a shirt.

CHAPTER 32

Oliver

"Is she going to be a problem?" Tristan nudged my arm and jerked his head to Noelle.

Noelle scowled across the room when she saw me. Gone was the grateful and ever so mildly flirtatious girl from yesterday.

"Does she know? Did someone on the planning commission or the mayor's office give her a heads-up about our factory development?"

"Do you have a plan?" Tristan hissed.

"Of course," I said, straightening my tie. It was too bad I didn't have photos of her stuck in the chimney. If all else failed, I could have used those as a nuclear option.

You just want to see the curve of her thighs up to her hip and the hint of her slit through the tear in her panties.

Focus, I scolded myself, but it was like I was drawn to her.

Noelle's eyes widened slightly when I walked over to the refreshment table. It was laden with the snacks and drinks my company had paid for in hopes of making the townspeople more receptive to my announcement that I was looking to put a factory outside of town.

Noelle scowled. "I should have known this was for your company."

"Who else?"

"One of the Svensson brothers. They're constantly trying to get one over on the town and buy up all the land in Harrogate."

"But they're creating jobs," I argued with her.

"They're ruining the character of the town."

"They've rehabbed a number of old buildings," I countered. "Really, you could say that they're helping to save this town."

"You're just so full of yourself," she said in annoyance. "What are you building in town, huh? Is that why I've been seeing you everywhere? You're just trying to butter us all up before you screw us over."

"That's quite the visual."

Her face turned red.

Two older women jostled me trying to reach the table.

"Out of the way, buddy. I need to get a good seat. Mrs. Horvat has a bone to pick with all the sex people have been having in front of her house."

"She's just jealous that her husband would rather eat a hamburger than take his Viagra and isn't man enough to go down on her," the other woman added.

Nothing like listening to the play-by-play of the perils of elderly sex.

Probably should just end it all before it gets to that point, I decided as I took my seat by the Svensson brothers.

"I call this meeting to order," Mayor Meghan Loring announced, banging her gavel on the lectern.

"First matter of business, we are not discussing the death that occurred recently at the Christmas market during this meeting. There will be a special town hall on the matter tomorrow."

"Thank God," Tristan muttered to me. "I feel bad for the lady, but honestly, no one liked her, and that meeting is going to be eight hours long."

"Old business," the mayor continued. "*The Great Christmas Bake Off* is still filming, and that means that the moratorium on parking within three blocks of the town square is still in effect. Do not park on the grass."

"But I own a stall at the Christmas market," one woman called out.

"You can unload, but you cannot leave your car parked there for the duration of the evening," Meghan said.

"That's baloney. I say we have a referendum."

"No new business. Please keep in mind that we have an agenda to follow, and if we have time, we will have an open forum at the end, God help me. And yes, as you can see, the nativity scene is on the agenda," she said to a crowd of angry people holding signs at the back of the large room.

"I have an item for open forums," an elderly lady stood up and announced loudly. She was my neighbor, Mrs. Horvat.

I shrank in my seat.

I chanced a glance at Noelle, who was still handing out refreshments to stragglers. Her skin was blanched, with only two spots of color high on her cheeks.

"There is a problem in this town with people who are unable or unwilling to have sex indoors," my neighbor said loudly.

"Mrs. Horvat," Meg warned.

But my neighbor steamrolled on. "I found this in Oliver Frost's front yard."

"Holy shit."

Tristan's brothers snickered, except for Greg and Hunter, who gave me furious looks.

"Now," Mrs. Horvat continued, "I don't know if he and the large-bosomed young woman to whom this brassiere belongs actually had sex in his front yard or not, because I can't get that dratted Ring camera to work on my TV."

What in the world?

"However," she said loudly, cutting off Meghan, "I live in a nice neighborhood and do not appreciate that I saw it in Mr. Frost's front yard."

Behind me, Noelle knocked back a shot of something strong.

I wished I had a glass of bourbon right about now.

"I took this brassiere to an amateur detective in town..."

A what?

"...and she was able to find a clue!" Mrs. Horvat held the bra aloft. "On the bra strap was embroidered a name. Noelle. Did it mean the brassiere was a Christmas garment?"

"Mrs. Horvat," Meghan pleaded, "this is not an open forum."

"That assumption proved to be incorrect. In fact, the word was the name of the brassiere's owner." She pointed at Noelle, who was topping off her drink. "That woman has been seen at Mr. Frost's house on a number of occasions."

A number? I wondered.

"The evidence points to one person. The mystery has been solved. Arrest this woman for public indecency."

"Public indecency?" Noelle exploded. "The only reason you were in Oliver's yard in the first place was because you were going to dig up the pansies in his garden. You need to be arrested for trespassing."

"I would never." Mrs. Horvat held a hand to her throat.

"Yes you would! You stole all the tomatoes from the houses on Ashby Street to make that jam that you sell for an obscene amount of money."

"Wait, so I was buying back my own tomatoes?" a woman complained.

"We're not talking about tomatoes, Bettina," Mrs. Horvat thundered. "We are here to discuss the fact that Noelle is sullying the reputation of the handsome bachelor billionaire Mr. Frost." She wiped away a tear. "He's like the son I never had."

What the fuck, Greg mouthed to me.

"The son you never had is a sleaze ball," Noelle shouted. "He's here buying you all drinks and Christmas cookies and being helpful around town because he's planning on building some huge development. It's probably a giant mall, and he's going to bulldoze half the town!"

After a horrible moment of silence, all hell broke loose. People were fainting. Several townspeople yelled threats at me.

"Fuck." I jumped up and headed to the front of the room.

"Mr. Frost," Meghan demanded. "Sit down. We are not at your agenda item yet."

"Please, Mayor, one minute," I begged, needing to get this situation under control. "Everyone listen."

The townspeople ignored me in favor of yelling out their preferred doomsday predictions.

"A new factory and subsequent offices would bring lots of new jobs into the area—"

"We don't want a strip mall," Noelle yelled out over the din of the crowd.

"I'm not building a strip mall," I exploded.

"Then what are you building?" one resident demanded.

"It's a high-tech factory building. We're in the early stages, still gathering information—"

The mayor banged her gavel on the lectern.

"Since Mr. Frost went early, we will move on to the next order of business. The rebuilding of the manger and nativity scene."

"But I have a whole presentation," I protested.

"You wanted to skip your turn. I need to control this until it turns into a replay of the Halloween riot. Order," Meghan yelled.

Noelle stuck her tongue out at me then grabbed up the empty food and drink containers and headed out the door.

I zeroed in on her and followed.

CHAPTER 33

I whistled the tune to "Santa Baby" as I walked through the Christmas market back to my car.

Was I one of those people who abused their Christmas market loading privileges? Yes. Yes I was.

Fortunately for me, my brother occasionally worked under the table at the tow company, and they knew not to take the truck.

"Dammit," I swore as I realized what I was whistling. I switched over to a funeral march.

It had felt good to finally watch Oliver Frost get taken down a peg. And if it ruined his business? All the better.

Harrogate did need factory jobs, though, I thought.

I felt guilty.

That was what had really screwed my family over—when the last of the big factories had closed and laid off my father.

Some people in town needed high-paying working-class jobs that only required a high school diploma.

Oliver's a billionaire. Of course he's going to come out on top and build the factory. Stop wasting your energy on him, I told myself as I unlocked the coffee stand to stack the empty containers.

The wind blew freezing cold through the propped-open doorway.

I shivered.

Even though the tiny cabin I shared with my family wasn't what anyone would call luxury digs, I would still rather be there than here in the dark and the cold.

The wind blew harder, sending snow flurries inside the stall.

"Why do you hate me?"

I screamed and grasped around for a knife, a rolling pin, or another makeshift weapon.

"Why are you trying to ruin my life?"

"Oliver, what are you doing here?" I gasped, heart pounding when I realized it was him.

He advanced on me, his blue eyes almost glowing in the low light.

My hand finally made contact with the blender. I swung it at him.

He grabbed my wrist. The blender crashed to the table, and he pinned my hand to the wall behind me.

"Get your hands off me," I demanded, though the sex-starved part of me was gleeful we had only a couple of inches between us.

Oliver closed the distance, his hard body pressed against mine.

"Not until you tell me why you're doing this."

"Doing what?"

If I was half the woman I liked to think I was, I would have grabbed him by the tie and let him know how I really felt. But instead, I settled for ineffectively wiggling against him.

"You're fucking with me. Deliberately," he said, jerking me against the wall with every word.

I was practically panting now, my breath hovering in a cloud between us.

"I don't even know you," I lied, even though I knew every inch of his body. "Why would I want to?"

His eyes flicked from mine to my mouth, back up, then down again.

St. Nick have mercy on me.

"Funny," he said, his deep voice sending shivers all over, "because this feels personal."

"Just the Christmas holidays making you a little crazy." I licked my lips. His eyes followed the motion.

"Must be, because otherwise, why would I do this?"

He leaned in and kissed me.

It was not a chaste under-the-mistletoe kiss. This was spiked eggnog in front of a Yule log that was about to burn your house down. This was "I'm going to ride that Christmas tree all the way to the North Pole."

He still had one of my arms pinned above me.

His other large hand he cupped around my head, tangling in my hair. He tilted my head so he could take my mouth, kissing me hard, like he wanted to repeat the best night of my life right here in the Naughty Claus.

His hand moved to my chin, and he gripped me hard as he tilted my head back.

"You gonna tell me now?"

"Say wha—?"

Fuck, I'd do pretty much anything right now for his cock, up to and including singing a Christmas carol.

"Come in me first," I gasped, arching against him.

"Jesus, what am I doing?" Oliver released me and stepped away. "You're crazy. I'm not going to sleep with you."

"All talk and no action," I said with a lot more confidence than I felt. I craved his body, and it was taking all of my willpower not to beg him to fuck my brains out.

Oliver suddenly grabbed the ribbons on the front of my costume, pulling me back to him.

"Do you ever wear anything normal?" he murmured then kissed me again.

It was a promise of many fun things underneath my tree.

I moaned, wrapping my arms around his neck. It felt so right to be in his arms. I wanted to marry him and spend the rest of my life with him.

Alarm bells started ringing.

I pushed him off.

"I have to go," I stammered, grabbing my bag and brushing past him out into the mostly empty Christmas market.

"I can walk you to your car."

"No need," I yelled over my shoulder. I hurried around the stall.

Oliver's heavier footsteps crunched in the snow behind me.

"You're not supposed to park here," he reminded me when he saw the rusty old pickup truck.

"This is how you know you're a real local," I said, then slammed the door shut and cranked up the engine.

I was so glad it started. If it hadn't, that would be bad. All of the willpower I'd reserved had been used up. Oliver might have offered to give me a lift or wait with me for a tow truck, and then we would have had sex in the café or at his house or—

I rubbed my hand over my face and turned on the radio. Vintage Christmas tunes warbled out. My fingers were freezing on the steering wheel, since I'd forgotten to put on my mittens.

I was in shock.

It had happened.

Oliver was back.

With me.

He only was kissing you because he was trying to manipulate you.

Or maybe it was because he thought I was cute.

It didn't feel like a kiss you would use to try to convince a girl to do something for you.

I knew what his real kisses felt like and this—well, these, multiple, plural—long, steamy, spicy Christmas kisses had been exactly that. No, better.

This didn't end well the first time, and it's not going to end well now.

I had been a good girl my whole life. My parents had always been very strict about no sex before marriage. Not that my siblings had internalized that message. But I had not wanted to ruin my life, like my sister or my mother.

Until I had met Oliver. Now I literally could not think about anything else.

I had paid for it, yet now I was about to compromise myself again.

Maybe I just hadn't been aggressive enough, part of me tried to reason. Maybe it had been a miscommunication last January.

Don't get ahead of yourself.

He kissed me in a shed in the middle of an empty Christmas market. It wasn't like he declared his undying love for me in front of the town hall.

I wrenched the steering wheel, and the car slid in next to the broken-down truck that my dad had been working on fixing for the last five years. It was supposed to be a graduation present for my sister. Except, of course, she had never graduated high school, and my dad had never gotten the car to work.

The Great Christmas Bake Off was blaring from the TV when I walked into the living room.

If you ignored my mom and Gran yelling at each other and the random elderly gentleman in an elf costume standing in the corner, you could even call the scene cozy.

"I'm allowed to have guests over," Gran was arguing.

"James," my mom yelled at my dad.

"Why don't you have some hot chocolate?" my dad offered, coming into the living room with a tray of mugs.

"Seriously, James?" My mother's eye was twitching.

"It's Christmas." My father looked crestfallen. "What's wrong with a little hot chocolate on Christmas?"

"He's been here all day," my mother said, pointing at the elderly elf who looked like it was twenty-three minutes past his bedtime and he just wanted his recliner.

"He's not allowed to drive after dark, so he has to spend the night," Gran said stubbornly.

"He looks like he's not supposed to be driving at all," my brother added.

"Just because the city took away his license doesn't mean he's not *able* to drive," Gran insisted. "Just don't drive with him at night."

"Why can't we all have a nice family viewing of *The Great Christmas Bake Off*?" my dad said jovially, handing out hot chocolates. "We sold out of Christmas trees again. Let's all get in the Christmas spirit."

My mother's face was red.

"Brought you some extra alcohol," I whispered to her. "Saved it from those lushes at the town hall."

"Bless you," my mother said, opening the thermos.

On the TV, the hosts were announcing which contestant was going to get booted.

"There's a casserole in the oven," my mom told me.

Elsa followed me as I was standing in front of the stove, dishing up the broccoli casserole.

"You look a little bit shocked," she said.

"I almost had sex with Oliver," I said in a high-pitched whisper.

"You what?"

"Shhh!" I hissed at Elsa as she jumped up and down, her hands clapped over her mouth.

"How far did you get? Did you see his Santa's little helper?"

"Don't call it that, and no, we just made out."

"Oh." Elsa's hands dropped.

I made a come-on gesture. "That's a big deal."

"Yeah, totally," Elsa assured me.

"But you made it sound like you were one cookie away from a merry Christmas."

"We could have been," I insisted.

"I know how strong you make your holiday punch," Elsa argued. "Maybe he was drunk. He was drunk the last time, right?"

"I'm not crazy. I'm not making this up," I said stubbornly. "There was something there."

Elsa sighed. "I just think that you might be going back down the same dark path that led to ruin and flunking out of Harvard last semester. You finally were back to your old self—better, even, because you were an ass-kicking boss. You can't let Oliver get in your head again. Even if that means keeping him out from under your skirt."

"I can't stop thinking about him," I admitted, pacing around the small kitchen.

"You know what you need to do." Elsa placed her hands on my shoulders.

"No."

"Yes."

"No way!"

"Just rub one out; you'll get a little post-squirt clarity."

"Gross."

"It's perfectly natural to masturbate. Ida's selling gift cards to her sex positivity workshop in January. I'm going to buy you one."

"I'd rather have a new rolling pin. And English toffee. Besides," I said rapidly, "I literally have no privacy in this house."

"You're an almost-Harvard grad. I think you could figure something out. Turn on a little porn. I'll send you some good romance novels."

"I'm a prude! I've only had sex once in my entire life, and it was when I was twenty-two! I don't even watch sex scenes in movies, let alone something like porn."

"All I hear are excuses that are leading you down the path to never getting over Oliver." Elsa wagged her finger.

"I don't need to do that to get over him," I grumbled, knowing she was right.

I wasn't dumb. I could see myself rolling down that same hill.

"I don't care about Oliver. I'm going to stay away from him. I swear on Frosty the Snowman's watery grave."

CHAPTER 34

Oliver

I couldn't stop thinking about Noelle, about kissing her. It was like I got a hit of something that awakened an addiction in me. Which was bad because I was dealing with the Svenssons.

They were not happy about the town hall meeting.

I shifted my weight on my feet as I stood in front of Greg and Hunter in the conference room of Svensson Investment's Harrogate branch.

"Did neither of you have a plan going into yesterday's town hall meeting?" Greg asked slowly, fixing his flat gray gaze on me.

My sister sat next to him, arms crossed.

"I don't know why she has it out for me," I argued.

"Could it be," Greg said, opening up a leather portfolio, taking out a set of papers, and sliding them across the table to me, "that one of the parcels you are looking to potentially purchase is owned by Noelle Wynter's family?"

I swore.

"Did neither of you do research on the parcels?" my sister demanded.

"I was about to mention that same point," Greg said, turning and smiling at her. "See, Belle, we make a good team."

"No we don't. You're just deadweight. You said that you were going to be taking the lead on this project. It's obvious to me that you didn't do a shred of due diligence. Is this honestly how you're running a business? Do your investors know?"

Greg scowled and turned his ire back on me. "Have either of you been doing any research or have you just been wasting your time at the Christmas market?"

"Of course I did research on who owned the parcels," Tristan insisted. "The Christmas tree farm is de facto owned by the Harrogate Community Bank at this point. There's, like, five mortgages out on it."

"It's not a good look," Belle told us. "This girl, Noelle Wynter, is clearly not stupid. She knows how to play the crowd to her favor. You need to start looking for alternate locations in counties more accepting of this type of factory."

"The rest of the towns close to Manhattan are either wealthy enclaves where people want to play Marie Antoinette in the countryside and would faint at even a rumor of a factory, or they're so run down that I'd have to bus in employees an hour each way every day and wouldn't be able to find anyone to work there," I argued.

"Then I guess you'll have to find some way of winning Noelle to your side if you have to have the Christmas tree farm land."

I thought I had a pretty good idea how.

CHAPTER 35

I felt twitchy.

Oliver hadn't been by the Naughty Claus café all day.

"It's best that he stays away," Elsa reminded me. "You need to detox. You can't let him ruin your life again."

"But it feels like he already has," I said miserably. "What is wrong with me? Why am I lusting after some guy who slept with me then tossed me aside? Now he's trying to ruin my town."

"I thought you didn't like this place."

"Of course Harrogate is obnoxious. It's a small town," I explained, "but it's still my small town. Office buildings are one thing, but he's building some sort of factory complex? Where? If he puts it in town, it's going to ruin the aesthetic, and if he puts it outside of town, who knows how much of the forest is going to be clear cut. He can't just come to my hometown and start a multibillion-dollar business right under my nose."

"Exactly," Elsa said, "which is why you can't sleep with him. He can't go to a Christmas party potluck, not bring any food, not remember the host's name, and not even wear a festive garment and then take a to-go plate without even helping clean up."

I felt a little anxious as I looked out over the Christmas market. We were halfway through December, and the townspeople and tourists were busy with their Christmas shopping.

When I was a little girl, I detested Christmas shopping.

No, it wasn't the same songs played on repeat or the crush of the crowds, or the fact that every single shop sprayed the most toxic concoction of patented Christmas scent into the air. No, it was knowing that my family could never have afforded the gifts that the other girls in school received.

Even while the Thanksgiving turkey carcass was still warm, the girls I had gone to school with would talk about all the gifts they were going to buy for their friends. One group of mean girls always liked to tell everyone loudly that if you couldn't afford to buy your friends a nice gift, then you weren't really friends.

I had been so excited one year when one of the girls gave me an American Girl doll, Samantha, all dressed up in her Victorian Christmas finery.

I had thought we were great friends. Until I got back to school, and she told everyone that she had given me an amazing gift and I had given her a handmade ornament.

I still cringed ten years later, thinking about how they had all laughed at me.

Like I said, Christmas villain origin story. Bah humbug.

"Noelle!" Gran called over the crowd, waving at me. She pushed her way to the front of the line.

"Hey, no cutting!"

"We're friends and family," Gran retorted to the guy. He was waiting on his order of seven hot chocolates for his brood of unruly children, who were presided over by a mother more interested in her phone than the kids licking the stall, throwing snow at one another, and generally being menaces.

"I'm out of brandy," I told Gran, "so if you want hot chocolate, you'll have to spike it yourself."

"See, Mom?" my dad said, rushing up to the counter. "Noelle's busy. We should go."

"She's not too busy to help out her family," Gran insisted.

"The best I can do you is a discount on drip coffee."

"We're not here for coffee," Gran said. "We need you and your tits at the Christmas tree stall pronto."

My dad looked like he was about to cry.

Gran patted his arm. "You tried your best, James, but nothing sells like sex. Isn't that what they taught you at that fancy business school, Noelle?"

"You said you were selling out," I reminded my dad. "That my marketing was working."

"He keeps giving away free trees." Gran was exasperated.

"It's Christmas." My dad wrung his hands. "I can't look a little boy or girl in the eye and tell them they can't have a Christmas tree because it's too expensive. Besides, you doubled the prices," he argued with me as I slowly shook my head. "So it's like I'm selling out."

"Oh, Dad."

He started crying. "You're my little girl, and I'm a terrible father." The bells on his Christmas sweater jingled off-key as his shoulders heaved. "I keep ruining your Christmas."

I fished under the counter for the emergency vodka and poured him a shot. "Drink that. You're not ruining Christmas." I stepped around the counter and gave him a hug.

"Don't worry, Uncle James," Elsa assured him. "We'll be over as soon as our shift ends."

"This is just business." Gran patted him on the back. "Fran's place has literal reindeer. We need to break out the big guns."

I checked my hair in the small compact mirror. I had been wearing a gingerbread girl costume at the Naughty Claus, and stuffing my bra with tissues had raised my cleavage alert level from yellow to Santa Claus red.

"Maybe we need to start coming here every night if your dad isn't selling out," Elsa said to me as we walked through the rows of trees.

"I should have been checking up after him," I fretted.

"You've had a lot going on."

"But not anymore," I swore. "I'm totally over he who shall not be named."

"Selfie." Elsa held out her phone. "We need to drum up interest."

"No need," Gran said, power walking back into the Christmas tree lot. "I just put up signs all over the Christmas market advertising hot girls and cool Christmas trees. They'll be flooding in here."

The trickle of customers from earlier in the evening turned into a surge. Trees were flying off the racks.

My dad kept busy with the tree-bagging machine, an off-brand used model that I'd helped him buy on eBay.

Whenever someone bought a tree, Elsa would ring a bell and do a little dance, and the noise and applause would attract even more customers. Gran was manning the cash register and loudly catcalling all the men that walked through the arbor of Christmas garlands we'd put up.

I started to relax as the money flowed. I'd been working since I was ten, trying to help out my family. Sure, this wasn't my own high-paying career, but it was nice to help out my parents.

"Check that one out." Gran nudged me and pointed at a customer.

"Gran, you can't just point at people. Oh shit."

"I know, right? Hubba hubba!"

I crouched down behind the sales counter as Oliver Frost walked into the Christmas tree lot.

"Oh my gosh, he can't be here."

Gran leaned down. "You know hot stuff over there? Word on the street is he's a billionaire. He bought a nice house on Oak Street. Hey, wait a minute." Gran slapped me on the shoulder. "You're the one who was having sex on his front lawn."

"You were doing what, Noelle?" my dad yelled, leaning over the countertop.

"Keep it down," I hissed. "Aren't you supposed to be bagging trees?"

"I need some twine."

"It's fine, James. You get so worked up over the smallest things." Gran rolled her eyes dramatically. "Noelle is sleeping around with a rich guy. Not like that trash Azalea scrapes up. Now here's the plan." Gran rubbed her hands together. "Get preggers and—"

"No!" my dad said loudly.

I shushed him.

He lowered his voice. "Not until you get a college degree. Or finish it, rather."

"I'm working on it," I hissed, covering my head with my arms.

"Noelle, we have customers."

I stood up slowly, praying that Oliver had left.

Unfortunately, there would be no miracle on 34th Street tonight.

His deep blue eyes met mine, and he gave me a slow, lazy smile when he saw me.

Ugh. I just wanted to melt into a puddle in front of him and beg him to take me back, which was the source of my problems because he apparently never realized we were an item.

"Merry Christmas! Looking for a Christmas tree?" my dad cheerfully asked Oliver.

"No," I said, grabbing Oliver by the arm and turning him back toward the exit. "He already bought a ton of trees from us. He clearly wandered in like a lost badger and needs to go back to the dirt hole he crawled out of."

"He's a grown man," my dad insisted. "He can buy more Christmas trees."

"My last one was actually covered in soot," Oliver explained in that intoxicatingly deep voice that wanted me to rip off my Christmas outfit and burn it on a pyre of my desire for him.

"We have a lovely—oh, hey, is that Max?" my dad said happily as the corgi barked and wagged his tail at him.

"I hope you're behaving yourself," my dad said to the dog, playfully cupping his face.

I crossed my arms.

Fraternization with the enemy. Really, Dad?

"Once he got a little training, he leveled up to my standards," Oliver said imperiously.

He made a hand signal, and Max stopped barking and posed handsomely in his plaid Christmas vest at Oliver's feet.

"And still with the lame outfits."

"Christmas isn't lame, Noelle," Oliver said to me. "This is the happiest time of the year. How can you dislike Christmas? The lights, the music, the smiling children—it's a chance to reconnect, to appreciate all the wonderful things that have happened during the year."

"How can you like it?" I argued. "It's nothing but people pretending to like each other, racking up credit card debt, and drinking too much."

"I like you," my dad assured Oliver. "Anyone who has ten Christmas trees in their house is a friend of mine."

"You want another tree, then?" I said loudly before my dad could offer Oliver some of the peppermint hot chocolate my mom had made or, God forbid, invite him over for dinner.

"There's a very healthy Douglas fir we just cut down earlier," my dad suggested. "I'll show you."

"Looks like there's a line at the tree-bagging station, James," Oliver said, then gave me a wicked smile. "I'm sure Noelle can assist me."

I hurried away from him, down the row of slightly spicy-smelling streets. The scent of sap in the air mingled with the snow, the smoke from nearby fires, and the peppermint hot chocolate, making the place smell like a perfect Christmas.

"Here's the tree," I said, pointing. "And I'm marking up the price, so I hope you brought your credit card."

He stepped up to me.

My heart started fluttering.

I do not like him. I do not think he is attractive. I have had way too much caffeine today and am about to have a heart attack.

Oliver's arm circled my waist.

"For someone who claims to hate Christmas," he breathed, "you do have quite the Christmas clothing collection."

His fingers grazed lightly up the lacy pinafore over my gingerbread girl costume.

My nipples hardened as Oliver's fingers trailed along the lace edging that framed my cleavage.

I panted in anticipation, drowning in those blue eyes.

"You sure you don't have a little Christmas spirit?" he murmured, his breath slightly cool on my mouth.

"Never," I rasped.

Push him off. Leave. Tell him you never want to see him again.

Except that I did. The irrational crazy part of me wanted to see him every day for the rest of my life.

Oliver leaned in to close the distance between us. The kiss was heavier than last time, and I melted against the familiar strength of his body.

He angled me toward him, running his hands over my curves as he kissed me hard, his tongue tangling with mine. His large hands cupped my tits, and I inwardly cursed the thick fabric I wore. I needed to feel his hands on me.

They moved, tracing the curve of my waist to my ass, grabbing me and grinding my hips against his.

My legs spread slightly. I needed to feel him, *there*.

Just as it seemed like his hands might be moving to the South Pole, there was a huge bang, and several people screamed.

"Oh my god," I gasped. "Dad?"

CHAPTER 36

Oliver

Noelle raced past me to the tree-bagging machine.

Thin, dark wisps of smoke wafted out of the barrel, and her father seemed flustered as he fanned it with several pine branches.

"Call the fire department," he said frantically.

The burning plastic sent an acrid smell into the cold air.

"I have to bag all these trees," James fretted as I fished in my bag for my tool kit. "What am I going to do?"

"Can't you fix it, Dad?" Noelle said.

Max hopped around, barking at the commotion.

"I don't know what's wrong with it." He patted his jacket. "Where are my tools? Just one moment, please, everyone," her father announced. "We appreciate your patience. There is hot chocolate and cookies."

"I have a holiday party I'm supposed to get to," one of the men in line complained.

"Oh no," Noelle's father said, flustered. "Oh, where is my screwdriver?"

"You don't have to watch the wheels fall off our janky Christmas tree farm," Noelle grumbled at me.

I set the tool kit on a nearby table. "And let all these good people go home Christmas-tree-less? Absolutely not. That isn't in the spirit of the holidays. Here." I picked up Max and handed him to her. "Hold my corgi."

"You can't fix this thing," she argued as I took off my jacket. "It's a hunk of junk; it leaks oil."

"Yes, I see that," I said, undoing my cuff links and handing them to her. Since she was trying to juggle the corgi, I slipped the gold cuff links into the small pocket on the front of her uniform, satisfied when she squeaked.

I quickly unbuttoned my dress shirt and slipped it off.

"Oh my god." Noelle hid her face in Max's fur.

"Yeah, baby!" her grandmother crowed. "Suck it, Fran! We have the hottest guy in town."

"You're seriously able to fix that?" Noelle asked breathlessly, hovering around me.

"Not only that, but I'm going to make sure your customers don't go anywhere." I winked.

I gently moved her father out of the way so I could look at the machine before he ignited a fire with all his fanning.

"I think it's probably the hydraulic fluid," James said rapidly, "or maybe the compressor."

"This machine doesn't have a compressor," I said, sliding on my back under the tree-bagging machine.

It wasn't the basic ones I knew from childhood Christmas tree picking. This was a higher-end model with multiple settings.

I popped off the side of the electrical box under the machine.

"Do you think there's a clog in the machine? Maybe it's the brakes." James paced around the tree bagger.

"I'm sorry, Oliver." Noelle's head appeared under the machine. "As you can see, my dad is not great in a crisis."

"I can hand you screwdrivers," James offered.

"Got it already," I said, reaching up and carefully unscrewing the little microprocessor.

It smelled like burning plastic. One of the wires had been fried.

I crawled back out from under the machine, went back to my tool kit, and plugged in my mini soldering iron.

While it heated up, I took a picture of the part number with my phone.

"Is that a computer?" James marveled. "But this is just a basic machine."

"Nowadays, every piece of machinery has a computer onboard."

"Is it salvageable?" Noelle asked me.

"We'll see," I said. "I'll order you a new part, but this should see you through the weekend."

I unwound some wire to replace the broken one and crawled back underneath the machine. After quickly rewiring the processor, I plugged my phone into the USB on the underside. Luckily, the machine ran on a similar piece of software to what I used to power the fabrication robots I normally worked with.

I played with a few settings until I got rid of the error message. Then I replaced the cover and scooted back out.

Noelle handed me a paper towel; I wiped my hands.

"Give it a try," I said to James.

He turned on the machine, and it cranked up.

"It's a Christmas miracle, everyone!" he exclaimed.

Noelle rubbed the palm of her hand over her face.

"Nothing about this is a miracle. This is literally Oliver's job, to play around with computers."

"There's a little more to it than that," I told her.

"I have a truck," her dad began.

"Dad, no!" Noelle shouted.

He barreled on. "It's my pride and joy. It was where Noelle and her siblings were conceived."

Noelle had her hand over her face.

"I can take a look at it, sure."

Her dad spontaneously hugged me. "You are a brilliant man. Just brilliant. Your dad must be so stinkin' proud of you."

As if. I didn't think my father even remembered I existed.

"You can have a free Christmas tree." James patted me on the arm.

"No, Dad." Noelle sounded incensed. "This is a business."

I smiled at her.

I wanted to lean down and kiss her, finish what I'd started earlier, but her dad had probably seen enough excitement for one evening.

"No need. I do what I can to bring the holidays to everyone."

Her father beamed at me.

"Don't worry," I whispered to Noelle. "You can make it up to me later."

CHAPTER 37

Noelle

"You should have seen it," my dad crowed when we walked back into the cramped living room later that evening. "Oliver Frost saved Christmas!"

Dove was sitting on the couch, staring numbly at the TV while the three little children were crying and grabbing onto her.

I went over, picked up the closest one—my nephew—and patted him on the back.

"We sold out. I just don't even understand where all this money came from," Dad said, showing my mom the thrifted Christmas cookie jar we used for tips.

"I was charging for photos," Gran said matter-of-factly. "Even though there's all that porn on the internet, people still will pay for the real thing."

"You girls didn't take your clothes off, did you?" My mother closed her eyes.

"No, but Noelle's boyfriend did," Gran announced.

"He's not my boyfriend," I shrieked.

The kids stopped crying then immediately started up again.

My mother tied a green and red ribbon around the box of cookies she had just assembled and set it in a crate with others for the next morning's delivery.

My dad declared, "He fixed the tree-bagging machine right up."

"There was a huge fiery explosion," Gran said, already exaggerating the incident. "It scorched his shirt, then he ripped the rest of it to reveal rippling muscles. And then he fixed the machine right in the nick of time."

"And saved Christmas," my dad repeated.

"Will I have to hear about this for the rest of the holiday season?" I complained.

"Probably. You really missed a show, Aunt Sarah," Elsa said with a giggle.

"Christmas would have been ruined," my dad said reverently, staring down at the cash-stuffed cookie jar.

"You better take Oliver something nice," my mother said.

"I think he already got his reward lined up," Elsa said under her breath.

I elbowed her. "Oliver's rich. He doesn't need anything."

"Now, Noelle," my mom warned, "that's not how we do things in this family. We thank people for their efforts."

On the couch, Dove snorted.

"I'm going to put together an extra-special goodie basket for him," my mom added. "You can drop it off tomorrow with the other deliveries."

"As if I'm just going to roll up in front of his house in the morning," I scoffed as I assembled a huge coffee order for an office.

"What are you going to do with the cookies?" Elsa asked me. "Your mom's bound to run into him sometime."

"She's got a ton of orders," I countered. "She's super busy."

"She loves the Christmas market," Elsa reminded me as we stacked the cups in the to-go trays. "That's not a plan. Oliver's probably at work now. Just go drop it off now on his doorstep."

"Fine," I huffed and took off my apron.

Fresh snow had fallen last night, and my feet crunched on the ground as I hoofed it through the Christmas market and turned onto Oliver's street.

"Are you here for another conjugal visit?" Mrs. Horvat called out from her window as I approached Oliver's house. From his front window, Max was barking furiously when he noticed I dared to stand on his property.

Even a dog lives a better life than I do.

I turned around slowly.

"Merry Christmas, Mrs. Horvat," I said through gritted teeth.

"And that outfit," she said, sounding scandalized.

"I work at the Naughty Claus," I said, sidling up to Oliver's front door. "I have to represent."

"My word." The elderly woman slammed the window shut.

I scurried up to the porch and rang the doorbell. I'd count to ten then leave the cookies and be on my way.

Ten... nine...

The door unlocked...*Santa's balls.*

CHAPTER 38

Oliver

"Yes, thank you so much for your time," I said, hoping the engineers from Taiwan didn't hear Max going crazy in the background.

Because of the time difference, I had been up all night on conference calls with various entities in Taiwan.

I yawned.

I was going to take Max for a walk then work out and try not to think about Noelle—how it had felt when she had rubbed up against me, the noises she had made, her soft curves under my hands.

For all that she claimed she hated me as much as she hated Christmas, it was clear she desired me. It wasn't lost on me how she had practically drooled when I had removed my shirt.

Sure, this was the perfect way to keep her too distracted to whip the townspeople up into a mob over my new factory, but more than that, I wanted her.

I wanted to feel her under me and on top of me. I wanted to watch her as she came.

"Max," I scolded, heading into the living room, where the dog was still barking.

Someone was on the porch. I made out a red and green silhouette through the artisan glass.

The doorbell rang.

"Max, go to the kitchen," I ordered the dog.

I didn't want him to chase another Amazon delivery person. The last thing I needed was a slip-and-fall lawsuit.

I wrenched the door open.

Noelle was standing there with a huge white box tied with red and green ribbon. Her mouth made a little O.

A slow smile spread across my face. "Is Santa's elf doing a little recon?"

She clamped her mouth shut and thrust the box at me.

"This is a thank-you present for fixing the tree-bagging machine. Enjoy. Got to go."

I hooked two fingers into the loop of ribbons that hung from the ridiculous costume she was wearing.

It could only be described as German Christmas Barbie with a tightly laced corset that flared into a flouncy short skirt.

"A thank-you present, huh?" I tugged her toward me. "I think I'd rather see your tits."

"Ah, um..."

She didn't protest as I led her inside and softly shut the door.

I kissed her, hard, letting her know exactly why I had brought her into my house.

I pushed her down onto a nearby sofa.

In a frilly skirt fit for the holidays, her bare legs parted, like she was ready for my cock.

Not that I was going to give it to her just yet.

I stole another kiss from her, my hand traveling down her curves.

"What are we doing?" she whispered.

"Just trying to get you into the Christmas spirit is all."

"I'm thinking that we have a gross disagreement on what the Christmas spirit is, but I'm willing to hear your argument."

She gasped as I continued my ascent up her thigh.

"I wonder, are you the kind of dirty girl that wouldn't wear panties?"

"This is a work outfit," she squeaked.

Her panties had some frills, matching her outfit. I ran my finger against her panties, making a firm touch on her pussy, causing her to gasp. I laid my touch on harder, feeling her heat, her warmth. I kept the pressure on, letting her shake with anticipation of what I might do next.

My touch slithered around her panties and past them. After going to her clit, feeling it shudder against my finger, I started my steady massage, flustering her.

Noelle had intoxicated me with her presence for so damn long, and I yearned for more of her.

I was going to take my time, unwrap her carefully like an expensive Christmas present.

Her gasp of pleasure echoed through the room. She was a bit mixed up on how to reply to my very sensual massage, and I pushed it further, sliding fingers into her opening.

Feeling how tight, hot, and absolutely wet and ready for me she was.

I wanted nothing more than to tear off that festive dress of hers, bend her over something, and fuck her raw.

I unlaced the top of her gown, smirking when she moaned. The dress accentuated her tits, and they spilled out as I unlaced the corset. I kissed her hard, tugging out her huge tits.

"One day, I'm going to spill my hot come on these," I whispered against her mouth.

My free hand ran down her chest, around those huge tits, enjoying her curvaceous body. Her nipples were already rock hard for me, poking out, as if I needed any more confirmation of how much she wanted me.

I circled my fingers around them, teasing them and making her giggle with my touch, before I brought my kiss down to her chest. I showered my kisses down her breasts until my lips met her hard nipples, and I suckled on them, letting her gasp out from the additional stimulation that I gave her.

I threw myself wholly into her pleasure. Sucking on her tits, fingering her slit, enraptured with her. She carded her fingers through my hair but was soon consumed by the pleasures I gave her. The storm of delight inside her, her shaking and twitching from my hands and mouth, her gasping.

I steadily increased my pace until my fingers were like pistons, and I tried to suck her tits, nipping occasionally.

She cursed as I felt her body tremble under my fingers.

I kissed her as she rode my hand over the edge.

I was hard, but I was going to eat her out before I fucked her. I wanted to feel her come again before she came on my cock.

Noelle made an *eep* noise when my phone rang.

I pulled it out to silence it then frowned when I saw the call was from Tristan.

"What?" I said more harshly than I intended.

But Tristan didn't seem to notice.

"Dude, you need to come into the office now. We have a problem."

CHAPTER 39

Noelle

"Where is the emergency alcohol?" I asked, running into the Naughty Claus café stall.

"It's the Santa read-along today," Elsa reminded me, "so all the alcohol sold out faster than you can say 'deck the halls.'"

"I'm doomed."

"Did you run into Mrs. Horvat?"

"Worse. Oliver."

"Oh no." Elsa's face became a mask of horror. "You didn't. Noelle? Tell me." She grabbed me by the shoulders.

"I couldn't help myself. He opened the door, and his house was perfect, and he smelled so freaking good, and *his hands*! They're like Christmas magic on a stick."

"Oh my gosh."

"I'm turning into my sister," I wailed.

Across the square were several wine moms whispering and pointing. Also in attendance were a smaller number of gold-star moms who seemed totally enraptured by a slightly confused Santa trying to read "'Twas the Night Before Christmas" and periodically giving dirty looks to the wine moms, who were making scandalous comments about the ripped elf accompanying Santa.

My sister was on the periphery, flirting with one of the few dads who had come to the read-along.

She had dumped her kids with my mom. While I was glad my mom had a chance to get out of the house and enjoy the Christmas market, it was too bad she had to take care of my nieces and nephews and couldn't enjoy time to herself.

See? This is what sleeping with Oliver has cost you. You ruined your mom's golden Christmas years.

"You're not as bad as Azalea. You're not about to be on baby daddy number four. But," Elsa added, "you have to build a very tall wall between you and Oliver's penis."

"It really needs to be a big wall." I giggled.

Elsa hit me on the back with an Elf on the Shelf.

"Repeat after me. Oliver's dick is not—"

"That thick," I interjected and snorted with laughter.

The Elf on the Shelf gave me a disappointed look.

I cleared my throat. "I am taking this very seriously."

"You cannot let him ruin your life again. He does not inspire good decision-making in you," Elsa scolded.

I held up my hand. "I'm totally on the revenge train. I've had an orgasm. Clear mind. Non-horny pussy, can't lose." I smiled craftily. "Speaking of revenge, what if I found some incriminating evidence on him? I could blackmail him or something?"

"How are you going to do that?" Elsa asked, incredulous.

"Guys like him tend to spill their secrets during pillow talk..."

"So you want to have sex with him," Elsa said flatly. "Again."

"I have a problem." I buried my face in my hands.

"This is terrible. We need to detox you," Elsa said firmly. She pulled out a box from her bag and opened it. The box was filled with essential oils, candles, and bunches of dried herbs. She took out several little bottles and started dousing me with the strong-smelling oils they contained.

I sneezed as some peppermint oil dribbled on my forehead.

"This is gross," I complained, wiping the oil off with a napkin.

"Your face is caked with three days' worth of makeup, and I don't think you've washed your hair since Thanksgiving. Honestly, this is an improvement." Elsa lit several bunches of herbs on fire and wafted the smoke around me.

My eyes watered.

"Hold this candle and chant after me. 'Begone Oliver, oh ghost of hookups past. I release you.'"

I mumbled the chant after her.

"Does this detox come with food?" I asked. "Or alcohol?"

"Do you feel cleansed?" she asked.

"Not really."

"I'm assuming he wasn't enough of a gentleman to offer you a shower, so that's not unexpected."

"It's not like we went all the way."

"So there's still hope."

My friend wafted the last of the herbs at me.

“You’re lucky. If you and I actually had our lives together enough to afford our own place, I would totally make you steam your vag.”

“No vag steaming necessary,” I swore. “I’m totally over him. I’m focused on family and making money.”

And wondering when I would be able to be with him again.

CHAPTER 40

Oliver

"What's the problem?" I asked, trying not to sound as irritated as I felt. If I played my cards right, my company would make me into one of the wealthiest men in the world. Whatever business issue had arisen was much more important than hooking up with Noelle.

But I had been so close to tasting her.

Focus.

I rubbed my jaw and tried to concentrate on the document that was on the screen at the front of the conference room.

"The preferred property is the Christmas tree farm, right?" Tristan said.

I wondered where this was going.

"Noelle's father and other relatives have taken out five mortgages on it."

"Who even let that slide?"

"Small-town bank, man." Tristan shook his head. "The mortgages were taken out over a period of fifty years. If we want to buy it, it'll incur not just all these mortgage fees we have to pay but also the cost of the property."

"So what's the problem? This is easy. We can just buy it from the bank."

"The loan taken out was some sort of under-the-table deal where if the mortgage isn't paid off in full by the owner—that means if we pay it off instead of Noelle's family—then the mayor gets to rezone it or add any new restrictions they want."

"So this property is not happening," I said flatly. "Fine, then. We'll do the expo site."

"We received the soil tests," Tristan said, "and the thing is soaked in lead, oil, and other nasty stuff. It's going to take at least two years to clean it up and treat the soil and groundwater before it's ready to build on."

"Dammit. And the one by the river?"

"Your sister read through the report and nixed it. Said she worried about potential flooding or soil instability because of drought."

"So unless I want to push everything back two years, I need to somehow convince the whole town to approve the factory on the Christmas tree property. After the town hall meeting the other night, that seems pretty much impossible. Especially once Noelle figures out that it was me who bought her beloved family Christmas tree farm. She will haunt me for the rest of my days." I ran a hand through my hair.

"I guess we'll have to recalibrate. We'll work on a new financial pro forma for using the exhibition site." I scowled as I did the mental math. "It won't be fully up and running for four, maybe five years, depending on the supply chain.

How can one small-town girl in an atrocious Christmas outfit be so much trouble?"

I stood up and opened a window, letting the cold winter air inside. This factory was supposed to catapult me into the financial and technological stratosphere. I was going to be the kingmaker when it came to microprocessors in America. Now?

All my dreams were dashed.

Because of Noelle.

Why is she trying to ruin my life?

I scowled. "We'll have to tell your brother and my sister. They won't be happy about the setback. We just have to figure out a way to spin it, I guess. Any ideas?"

Tristan shifted his weight on his feet.

I recognized the motion. It was the same movement he and his brothers would make when an older brother was about to come down hard on them for hatching a batch of baby chickens they found on Craigslist in said brother's bed.

"So, I have an idea..."

"I'm not going out Christmas barhopping with you."

"I mean, you are," Tristan said. "But no, I have an answer to our land problems."

I raised an eyebrow.

"You could marry Noelle and transfer the money to her to pay off the debt on the property," Tristan suggested. "Then it doesn't technically leave the family."

I froze for a moment. "Marry Noelle? That's insane. I'm not doing that."

"You saw her at the meeting," Tristan reminded me. "Even if we buy the expo site today, which, need I remind you, has to go before the town hall, she could make a huge stink. It could take years to even get approval to purchase that site."

"And if I do something as crazy as marry Noelle, who, *need I remind you*, hates me—"

"She doesn't hate you that much," Tristan interjected. "You saved her Christmas tree machine."

"Eventually, she's going to find out that I only married her for the land, and then she's going to divorce me and take all my shit."

"Prenup, my dude."

"If I do this, especially during Christmas, it'll be the worst bad karma dump ever."

"Her family is terrible at finances," Tristan argued. "Either way, they're losing this land. If you swoop in and save them, you'll always be the favored son. If she divorces you, you'll have her parents on your side. After all, we don't need all the land. Her dad can still run his Christmas tree farm. You'll build them a fancy new house. You'd be the Christmas miracle."

I rubbed my jaw.

Financially, it made sense. And it wasn't as if Noelle hated me completely. She had certainly loved what I'd done to her earlier.

"This is a crazy, terrible idea."

But what if it worked?

After running the numbers for purchasing the expo site, just marrying Noelle and slamming a factory onto the Christmas tree farm was looking more and more appealing by the minute.

"You don't actually have to decide right now," I told myself as I walked through the Christmas market.

I'd stayed to work late, make a few calls with people in Japan, and distract myself from Noelle.

I'd been with women before, though not lately. I'd had so much work stuff and personal stuff going on. Now that I'd had Noelle moaning and shuddering on my hand, she was all I wanted.

"You're just thinking that marrying her to steal her land is a good idea because you haven't been laid in almost a year."

That was a perfectly reasonable explanation for why I was even considering Tristan's crazy, immoral plan.

Those Svensson brothers were a terrible influence.

My sister had always warned me to be careful around them, that they had no sense of limits. They would do anything and everything to make money.

The lights were still on at her family's Christmas tree stall when I approached.

Noelle was sitting at a table, humming along to the Christmas carols that filtered through the snowy night air as she wove pine boughs into a dark green wreath.

She casually reached up to pull at the laces holding her huge breasts in the sexy gingerbread girl costume. She uncrossed her legs then recrossed them.

My eyes were drawn to the milky skin of the thighs that I knew from experience were warm and soft under her skirt.

"We're out of trees," Noelle called when I stood under the elaborate pine bough arbor that marked the entry to the Christmas-tree stall.

She looked up from where she was carefully tying a big red bow on the garland.

"For someone who hates Christmas, you sure know how to make a wreath," I remarked.

She scowled.

"They're made out of leftover Christmas tree branches, and we sell them at a steep markup. What's not to love?" She put her fist on her hip, the gesture making her chest stick out even more. "I thought you were supposed to be a big bad businessman," she shot at me.

I let my gaze slowly drift down from her mouth to her chest then back up, glad to see the red flush creep up her neck as she noticed where my gaze lingered.

"How many times do I have to let you insult me before you let me put my tongue in your pussy?"

CHAPTER 41

I swallowed.

Guess that cleansing didn't work at all. Because all I wanted to do was to strip off my panties and let Oliver fuck me on the big pile of pine boughs on the table.

"I'm, um..." My voice cracked. "I'm supposed to be working."

"Working on what?" he asked, taking a step toward me.

His deep voice was entrapment. His blue eyes were dark, like those of a winter fairy prince that liked to kidnap pretty young women and steal them back to his kingdom to be his princess for all eternity.

"All your Christmas trees are gone. I bet you ran out of that alcoholic hot chocolate hours ago."

It was true. My dad had taken Gran home along with a load of kitschy Christmas stuff I'd made him remove from the Christmas tree lot. I was going for a certain retro

Christmas aesthetic, and the Christmas Cabbage Patch Kid he'd found at the thrift store was not it.

Oliver's hands rested on my hips. Like I was his puppet, I spread my legs on the stool, and he stepped in between them, the barest brush of thigh between my legs.

I whimpered softly.

He hooked two fingers in the lace of the bodice and pulled me toward him. Then he was on me, kissing me hard, making me remember why I'd lost my mind for him.

His hands gripped my hips, digging into my ass, then moved up my tightly laced costume. I wanted to feel him all over me.

He cupped my tits through the costume, and I arched up against him.

When he unlaced the front of the bodice, the pressure finally released, and my tits spilled out.

Oliver pushed the top down so he could dip his head and suck on one breast. I gasped as the cold air hit my nipple, making it pebble hard. He left my tits and kissed my neck then under my jaw.

"I could fuck you right here," he murmured into my ear.

"But," he added, stepping back as I hastily tried to gather my clothes together, "it's too bad you're working."

"I'm not really working," I croaked, having about as much success resisting his siren call as I did a plate of freshly baked Christmas cookies.

He smirked. "I'll leave you to your not working, then."

This man had an obnoxious amount of self-control.

I needed to muster up the same.

I forced myself to sit there on the stool and watch him saunter off.

Who cares if he's leaving. Again.

I cared.

I wanted him.

And I wanted him to want me. I wanted to be special, to know that I was worthy, to know that a wealthy Harvard guy thought I was good enough to be his girlfriend, to be the love of his life.

"We had a connection, goddammit," I muttered as I grabbed my bag, turned off the lights to the stall, and locked the front gate.

Oliver was waiting around the corner. He had a smug smile.

"I knew you couldn't resist me."

See? He's a dick.

"I'm just going home," I claimed. "The Christmas market is pretty empty, and some of us have real jobs to work in the morning."

"I thought you were waiting for your father?"

"I, uh—" *Dammit.*

The loudspeakers started playing "Baby, It's Cold Outside."

Not helping.

"Let me give you a ride," he crooned.

"A ride on what?" I said, then caught myself.

Oliver stepped up to me and pressed another hot kiss to my mouth.

"Not my sleigh, if that's what you're asking."

"That really doesn't make any sense," I babbled as we walked through the Christmas market.

Sure, it was late, and hardly anyone was out, so it wasn't like he was showing me off or anything, but baby steps. Maybe this was the beginning of a long, beautiful marriage.

"If you think about it, the girl should be the sleigh, and the guy should be the North Pole or something," I said.

Oliver was amused. "I meant in a cheesy Christmas sense," he said, resting his hand on my ass, "but good to know where your priorities lie."

Crap.

Maybe Elsa was right, and I needed to go on a serious spiritual cleanse.

We're not sleeping with him, just bumming a ride home.

Oliver clicked a button on his key ring. A large SUV in an alleyway beeped.

"You're not supposed to park here." I stuck my tongue out at him.

"It's funny," he said, opening the back door of the car for me. "They let you get away with a lot when you're attractive and rich."

I climbed into the car.

"You look good enough to eat." His handsome face was in shadow as he crawled in after me. He leaned in, running a gentle touch down my cheek and to my chin. He guided my lips to his and hit me with another sudden, powerful kiss.

His embrace went lower down my curves.

Oliver then slid down before me, hands all over my thighs. He reached under my short skirt and grabbed hold of my panties.

I gasped as he pulled them down my legs. Then he spread my legs and went down deep between them.

He kissed me right on the clit, his hands roaming up my legs, that strong touch of his feeling so perfect against me. He licked me down from my clit to my slit and all around me.

I couldn't help but shudder as I sank into the pleasure. Every little sensation down there sent shivers up me—from the more obvious touching and sucking of my pussy, to even feeling his cheeks rub against my thighs, his hands holding me in place and rubbing me as they joined together into something truly magnificent.

I ran my hands through his platinum hair and let the fire build up inside me. It was cold outside, but I was hot and aching.

The intensity of it all built inside me quickly. He looked up at me as he devoured my pussy, giving me everything I wanted. I was panting and throwing myself back hard into the plush leather seats. I was crying out for him already, my words growing more incoherent. This man knew just how to turn me into a blubbering mess.

One more lick, one more finger thrust, one more whatever else he did to work his magic, and I was lost. I tried to stifle my cries as I came.

"Damn, that was just as good as I remembered," I groaned, sprawled out in the back seat of the luxury SUV.

"From this morning?" he asked, brow slightly wrinkled.

"Er, right, yeah." I hastily tidied up my clothes. "I'm not riding your North Pole in the car," I said flatly, climbing over him and into the passenger's seat.

A girl had to have some standards, even if they were fifty feet below ground. Besides, it was freezing cold.

I shivered in the front seat as the sweat rapidly cooled down my body.

Oliver didn't seem to notice the cold at all when he climbed into the driver's seat.

He's driving you home after you hooked up! my inner wannabe popular girl cheered.

Well, half a hookup.

But still, he was driving me home like we were a couple™ with all the emojis.

Wait, did I really want Oliver driving me home? He was going to see the house and my dad's hoarder junk yard that surrounded it.

It's all covered in snow right now, I reminded myself, so maybe Oliver wouldn't notice?

Or maybe he would and then remember why he didn't want to sleep with, let alone date, girls like me.

Oliver drove down the snowy road, Christmas carols drifting softly out of the car stereo.

If I was in any way a Christmas lover, which I totally was not, this would be the perfect holiday Hallmark movie moment.

As if my life was ever a Hallmark movie.

"You can just drop me off here," I said as Oliver approached the road that led the mile down to my parents' cabin.

"Isn't it a far walk? I don't see your house," he asked, turning briefly in the dark to look at me.

"Nope, just a quick hop," I said as he turned on the road. "I need to pick up the mail anyway."

He kept driving. "Your house is pretty far down, isn't it?"

"No, of course not," I lied, starting to sweat.

I didn't want to lose the one shot I had at a second-chance romance, or at least a second-chance hookup.

Oliver frowned in the dark while I silently freaked out as the first mound of snow-covered junk appeared in the headlights.

Somehow, seeing my family's properties through a potential boyfriend's eyes gave me a newfound horror of just how depressing they were. Here was the old VW bus that my father had bought on a whim because he was planning for us to all go on road trips as a family before we kids got too old. A month later, Azalea was pregnant. There was the two-story tall rocket engine my dad had bought me for my birthday one year. He got it for a steal and claimed it was the real engine from a NASA rocket. Turned out it wasn't, and now it was rusting among the Christmas trees.

"You have those reindeer too," Oliver remarked when he pulled up in front of the house.

"Yeah, they're pretty much everywhere in Harrogate," I said, tugging at my collar.

"It's a cute house."

I cringed at the sagging roof accentuated by the slightly lopsided string of lights. It was nothing like Oliver's professionally decorated home.

"It looks so cozy and Christmassy. Also, it smells like cookies out here."

"I think that's just me."

He turned off the car.

"Why don't you come home with me instead? I'm sure your parents won't miss you for a night."

I hesitated. Everything with Oliver was moving too fast. "I don't know. I had fun, but I'm exhausted and really looking forward to going to bed."

I reached for the door. Oliver stilled my hand.

"Is that what you really want?"

"I wouldn't have said it if I didn't want it."

"I guess you need further convincing."

"Convincing? What do you mean?"

He hugged me all too suddenly, his hands sliding down my body, his movements gentle. Through the top of my gingerbread costume's skirt, he slid his fingers into my panties, and his touch went back to my aching and yearning clit. He had made me come not long ago, and the memory of that wonderful feeling still ached within me.

Kissing me, he pressed on, and I couldn't help but giggle at his forwardness. His fingers slid into my pussy, which was still wet for him, and I guessed from how intense that feeling was that I'd always be wet for him.

"You know you love this, dirty girl."

I was like putty in his hands, feeling him rub me, the fire inside me spreading so easily as he commanded it. Oliver pressed me against the car, keeping me warm through the cold and shielding us from any onlookers who might happen to pass by.

Knowing where we were, though, did add an element of intensity that I couldn't deny. How his desire for me was so damn strong that there was no such thing as risk for him.

As he fucked me with his fingers, he laid a kiss on me, letting me purr for him. My legs were already trembling, my body still way too sensitive from what his lips started earlier.

I nibbled my lip, but it was all too hopeless. Oliver, though, was right there with me. Laying a kiss right on my lips, sucking up my moans of pleasure, silencing me from screaming about the end of the world and how good it felt.

He held me close as he brought his fingers back up to me and licked them. Then he leaned in and kissed me.

"Don't you want my cock in that wet pussy?" he whispered, his deep voice making me soaking wet for him.

I was about to tell Oliver that I had actually just decided to abandon all of my former moderately high standards and have sex with him in the car when I felt eyes on me.

Outside in the snow, on the rickety porch, my mother and grandmother were standing in their Christmas-themed robes, staring into the car window.

"Oh my god," I screeched and wrenched the door open. "Thanks for the ride, Oliver. I'll see you at the never-ending hell of the Christmas market."

The last thing I needed was for Oliver to deal with my family.

"I cannot believe it," my mother said as Oliver waved to me and pulled away. "How could you do this to me?" She started sobbing.

"Pull it together, Sarah," Gran interjected. "Noelle's a grown woman. You had kids in middle school when you were her age."

"I wanted her to make better choices. I'm a terrible mother. You don't want to end up like your sister."

"The man is drive-a-BMW rich," Gran said, patting her on the shoulder. "Even if Noelle gets preggo, she'll have a steady paycheck."

My mother wailed louder. "Please don't get pregnant," she begged me. "That will be the worst Christmas ever."

"No worries there," I assured her. "When I have sex with him, he's wearing a condom."

"Atta girl!" Gran hooted.

"I feel weak."

"Get this woman a drink."

I poured my mom a glass of wine. "I am not and never will be pregnant with Oliver's baby." Not that a part of me didn't want it. "He was just giving me a ride."

My mom perked up. "Did he like the baked goods?"

"I didn't ask."

"You sat in the car with him in the long ride over here in the cold," my mother argued, "and didn't ask him how he liked the pastries? I put some savory ones into the box with the sweets. It was a spinach pastry. I made the dough myself, you know. Dorothy uses the pastry dough you buy at Whole Foods, but I make it myself out on the porch so it stays cold."

"Yes, I know. I've had to freeze my bits off outside helping you make the spinach turnovers." I stomped up the steps.

"Did you even give them to him, or did you eat them yourself?"

"Geez, Mom, have a little faith in your daughter."

CHAPTER 42

Oliver

Noelle's mother's pastries had been amazing, and she'd written me a beautiful note. Something about the careful handwriting in the loopy cursive on Christmas stationery was so endearing.

I contemplated Noelle as I ate another spinach pastry. It was divine.

My own parents would have sneered at Noelle and her family and especially their house. They would have said they were low-class, made terrible decisions, and were not worthy of our family's attention. However, that humble cottage nestled amongst the trees had more Christmas spirit than my parents' overly decorated yet still sterile house.

I hadn't seen them in years, and I didn't intend to. It wasn't like I really had a relationship with them. My sister had basically raised me.

Noelle was lucky her parents adored her.

I smiled, thinking about her mom waiting for her to come home. Then I frowned. Would I really be able to pretend to love Noelle so that I could steal her family's land?

I wasn't sure.

What I did know was that I needed to see her again.

Noelle wasn't at the Naughty Claus when I walked over there through the Christmas market later that evening. Nor was she at the Christmas tree stall.

Instead, she was near the charred ruins of the nativity scene, selling alcoholic beverages where two elderly men wearing Santa costumes brawled while the crowd cheered.

"Is this a sanctioned Christmas-market activity?" I asked, wrapping an arm around Noelle's waist.

"Hell no."

She turned around.

I smiled at her. She was wearing her sexy elf costume with the frilly green skirt.

"And you better not snitch," she warned.

I leaned in and kissed her. "Come have a drink with me."

"I have to sell the rest of these." She wrinkled her nose.

I kissed it. "Do you take credit cards?" I asked.

"We're totally high-tech here in Harrogate," she bragged.

"Good," I said, taking out my wallet. "I want to buy your whole inventory."

"For what?" she asked, automatically pulling out her phone with the square card reader attached.

I took it from her and swiped my card then called out, "Free drinks!"

The crowd crushed around us, clamoring for the free alcohol.

"Courtesy of Mithril Tech," I told them as Noelle handed out drinks to anyone who wanted one.

"And a merry Christmas to you, sir." One of the elderly men watching the fight saluted me.

Noelle scowled.

"It's called marketing." I smirked. "See? I am a big bad businessman." I tugged her hand. "Come on. I want to take you out."

"Funny," she said. "Because I'd like to get fucked instead."

CHAPTER 43

I barely even registered the impeccable Christmas decorations as Oliver tugged me into his house.

He picked me up and carried me upstairs to the luxurious master bedroom, which was legit probably bigger than my family's tiny cabin. He set me on the bed, kissing me hard, then turned and took off his jacket. I admired the lines of his body.

He started a fire then returned to me.

"You're all my Christmas fantasies in one pretty package."

"Christmas is a wholesome holiday, Mr. Frost."

He ran his hand down my cheek and caressed my chin, looking at me with such anticipation. The fireplace crackled, its warmth feeling so good that I could definitely stand to wear something with less faux-fur lining.

Oliver then guided my face toward his, the first kiss of many that I was sure I would receive that night. Intense as always, leaning into something messier and more passionate with him, our tongues twisting. We leaned into one another as we desperately wanted so much more.

His hand flowed down my back, using my bare midriff to let me feel the power of his touch on the small of my back, the other going down my side. His fingers slithered into my skirt and across my panties, as he had done many times before already. But it was a feeling I'd never grow tired of.

I gasped as the first shock of his digits against my clit shot through me. He knew exactly what I liked and how exactly to do it for me. We fell back onto his massive bed. I clawed at him as he continued to finger me.

All the while, he watched with intent. He loved nothing more than to see me struggle to keep my composure as he pumped his fingers in and out of me, me fighting to stifle my moans as they grew louder. It wasn't like I had to worry about anyone hearing me in his place, but it was more of a point of pride, as if I were trying to win some game we were playing.

I could only take so much of his touch before I was putty in his hands. I cried out as I came. The thudding pleasure that my clit sent through my body in wave after powerful wave made me tip my head back.

"I think it's time I unwrap my present," he said.

"What about me? Do I get to unwrap my present?"

"Only if you're a good girl and tell me how much you love Christmas."

"Never," I stated as he pulled my skirt down my legs, exposing my panties.

Greedy and craving him, I ripped his shirt, sending buttons bouncing over the bed, and gazed on his smooth, muscular chest. It was just as good as I'd remembered and all for me.

Next came my top. It was always hard to wear a decent bra with some of these outfits, and with how tight it was, I got a bit of visceral pleasure just from no longer having to deal with the discomfort of wearing it. When Oliver looked at me hungrily, as if my tits were freshly baked cookies he wanted in his mouth? That was just a bonus.

His pants came off, then came my panties. He wasted little time, taking hold of them and pulling them right off me, leaving me only in my stockings, held up by red and green garters.

As soon as my pussy was exposed to him, he parted my legs and slid his head between them. I gasped as he licked my thigh coming in before he latched on to my clit.

I groaned from the sudden pleasure, and he followed it with more. Lick after lick, he devoured me, looking at me, watching me come undone. My head fell back, and I shot my hands down and grabbed hold of his head. Not to stop him but to make sure he didn't go anywhere.

He had done this before, yes, and now I wanted more. Oh so much more. He laid on the pressure, lick after lick, his tongue thrusting deep inside me and driving me a bit wild. He paid all of me proper attention, building the sensations up all along with one another, making that fire within me a well-managed yet oh so delightful chaos. Tongue lash after suck, fingers deeper, a constant massage. He played me like a master musician played his instrument, and I sang a song that was absolutely beautiful.

To him, anyway, and right now, that was all that mattered.

To me? All I cared for was that I was absolutely loving the intensity of everything I was feeling. That blissful energy shooting through me, making me cry out again and again, riding the waves of pleasure.

Soon I was lying naked and panting on his bed, covered in sweat and staring up at the ceiling. Everything I'd experienced so far should have been more than enough to leave me oh so very satisfied. But I was a bad girl and wanted more.

"I hope you brought me to your bed to do something more intense than just eating me out," I rasped.

"Don't worry, I fully intend to fuck you until you scream."

Pushing myself up on my elbows, I looked at him as he shoved his boxer briefs down his legs, his cock thick and throbbing, jutting out from his perfect marble body.

Better than I remembered.

"Fuck me," I said, looking at the daunting thing in front of me. "Give me what I want."

Before I realize just how much of an incredibly bad idea this is.

"You're getting coal for Christmas if you don't watch that mouth." Oliver smirked and went to his nightstand, slid open a drawer, and brought out a condom package. He opened it and slid it down his cock.

Protection secured, he climbed onto the bed beside me, his heavy presence radiating over me. He ran his hand over my cheek then rested it against my neck.

I arched up against him. Craving him.

"Fuck me," I begged.

Destroy me.

"I knew you'd be naughty this Christmas," he whispered and kissed me hard.

His cock slid down and over my pussy, playing in the hot wet slit. I moaned as he parted my pussy lips and slid into me, the pressure immense. I shuddered as he slowly inched into me, bit by bit, while I cursed and begged him for his cock. I felt so overwhelmed when he was finally inside me, the sensations vibrating through me as we were now together as one. Finally. Again.

I ran my hands down his back, toward his ass, feeling all of him, enjoying all of him. His manliness was so much, everything I could ever want.

He pulled out then slammed into me again. The reverberations of pleasures echoed through my being with each and every thrust. He took me again and again. I couldn't help but cry out as the bliss washed over me with every movement, every bit of friction between us building on our pleasure.

I met his movements with my own, bucking into him, making every stroke all the more intense. I pulled his hips into me, as if I could force him to fuck me harder. He obliged, angling my hips so his cock hit my clit as he fucked me hard. Soon my cries of pleasure echoed more loudly through the bedroom.

It was a sensual overload. Every penetration sent vibrations through me, making me cry out again and again. I nibbled on my lip and scratched at him, my hips making needy circles against him.

Oliver hooked my leg as he slammed into me again and again, using his leverage to give me anything and everything. The way he fucked me was perfect, as if he had found the fabled G-spot with ease, but still I fought, knowing the longer I held on, the more intense my payoff would be.

I never want this to end.

Because I wasn't sure if I'd ever be able to have him again.

Then I was arching up against him. Sheer bliss pounded through me, leaving me moaning for him as I crested. Oliver followed, spilling into the condom.

I lay sprawled on the bed as he wrapped his strong arms around me, burying his face in my hair.

The sex had been mind-blowing and amazing and somehow even better than the last time.

Men are like wine, right? I thought, my brain racing as Oliver snuggled me against him.

The déjà vu was disorienting. This was exactly what had happened last time. We'd had amazing sex. Then cuddles, then more sex. He'd said he adored me. I had started planning our future together. Then came disaster. Humiliation. Failing.

It's going to happen again. It's happening again.

I needed to run.

"Don't go," Oliver murmured when I made a move toward the edge of the bed. "I want to come on your tits next."

CHAPTER 44

Noelle

My breath caught as he pulled me back toward him. His cock was still throbbing.

"You're still hard?"

Damn.

"Remember? Cold-hearted businessman. Work hard. Play hard. Plus, your tits are fucking amazing."

He stroked his hand over my breasts, the nipples sensitive and hard.

"That looks uncomfortable. You might want to take care of that," I teased.

He narrowed his eyes. I smirked.

His fingers trailed down to my still-glistening slit.

"Too intimidated to do it yourself?" he asked. "Not surprising."

I scowled, took hold of his cock, and stroked him, smirking when I felt him shudder and pulse in my hands.

"You wanna come on my tits?" I teased, giving him the sexiest look I could manage.

My body rubbed against his, his hardness against my abdomen. I shimmied down his muscular form. He hissed when I rubbed my tits on his cock. I took his length and squeezed him between my breasts.

He moaned as I pumped his flesh against my own. I leaned in and licked the head of his cock, lapping at him. Oliver reached down, caressing me, encouraging me.

Up and down I went, bouncing on his length, teasing his cock with my lips. He reached down, squeezing my tits with his huge hands, holding me in place so he could fuck my tits. It was extremely hot, him taking his pleasure from me.

Or maybe I was just a naughty elf.

My pussy ached. With my free hand, I reached between us and began to massage it in rhythm with his thrusts.

I was close, and so was he. I could feel the subtle shifts, the subtle quivering of his cock, how he wouldn't be able to hold back much longer.

"I'm going to—" I gasped as I shuddered on my hand.

His cock pulsed and exploded all over my tits and chin, marking me.

Oliver tugged me back up to him, tracing his initials in the come as he gave me a crooked smile.

"You're mine now."

My heart leapt.

I wanted more than anything for that to be true.

I woke up alone in bed with a snort.

"God, I need to stop eating so late at night," I mumbled. "That was a crazy dream."

Crazy good. I kept my eyes shut, not ready to face the day and fight for the small bathroom with the cracked pink tile that had had its heyday in the early fifties. I just wanted to stay asleep in the dream in which Oliver had said he wanted me and that I was his and had done amazing things to my body so much better than the last time I'd been with him.

I opened my eyes and stared up at the intricately plastered detailing on a ceiling that was a far cry from the wood paneled ceiling in my parent's house.

"Holy crap," I whispered. "It was real."

And he didn't even throw me out after the hookup.

In fact, he had asked me to stay.

"What if this means he really did like me all along?" I whispered to myself.

Maybe I wasn't crazy, and Oliver was the man I was supposed to spend the rest of my life with.

"This is definitely the house I'm supposed to spend the rest of my life in," I decided.

I didn't even feel my inner Krampus clawing to get out as I stepped out into the hallway, which was decked out for Christmas.

"Oliver?" I called out just to make sure I wouldn't be caught snooping.

I checked the time on a large antique grandfather clock. He should be at work right now.

Shoot, so should I, but the Naughty Claus could wait.

If there was a repeat of the last time I'd slept with Oliver, also known as the one and only time Noelle had sex, I would never be as close to being Mrs. Frost as I was right now.

I draped a Christmas-themed quilt around my head and shoulders and wandered through the house like a hobbit.

The holiday decorations that had made the downstairs look like a postcard carried through all the upstairs rooms of the historic Victorian home. I marveled at the impossibilities I saw, like the fact that every one of the bedrooms had both a fireplace with a mantel draped in garland and its own bathroom.

Speaking of bathrooms, I was going to take the world's most luxurious bath in Oliver's tub.

I tossed the quilt onto his bed and went into the bathroom to turn on the water. It was like walking onto a movie set. Expensive hand-painted wallpaper, imported Italian marble tile, mahogany vanities, and a large claw-foot tub.

"As if a man needs a tub like that," I said as it filled with a rush of steaming hot water.

The bathroom held more Christmas garland and other holiday touches. I lit one of the candles, and the familiar scents of Christmas filled the room.

In the steam from the bath, the pine boughs gave out a slightly sharp scent.

"I could totally get on board with Christmas if this was how I got to spend my December," I said, sprinkling Christmas-scented bath oils in the tub.

Then I slipped in the water, practically submerging myself into the hot tub.

"Merry Christmas to me," I sang, leaning back, my whole body relaxing for the first time in over a year.

Outside of the window, which was of course decorated with a wreath and a big red bow, snow was softly falling. Yet I was warm and safe inside this beautiful bathroom.

"It's beginning to look a lot like a working hot water heater!" I sang at the top of my lungs, "Every—"

"There you are."

I shrieked then submerged myself in the tub.

Wait, crap. I didn't put any bubbles in here. Above me through the water Oliver's shadowy form appeared.

I surfaced, the water running over my face as I stared up at his bare chest, the jogging shorts he wore riding low around his waist.

"And here I was," he said, sliding off the running shorts, "thinking I was going to come back here and make you all hot and wet. But you already beat me to it."

I drooled as I took in his body, the broad shoulders, his muscular torso, those washboard abs, and yeah, that thick, hard cock.

"There's room for two."

"I'm not sure if there's room for me and your tits."

I hissed as he stroked his hands over my wet flesh.

He withdrew his hand and rummaged something out of a nearby cabinet.

Then he stepped in the tub. His hands ran down my body, igniting my flesh again. I was still hungry and yearning for him.

He rolled me over in the water. I braced my hands on the rim of the tub, my back arched.

He slid his hands down my wet body, lightly cupping my tits, then running his hands over my hips and sliding down to my ass. His deft tongue slithered up between my legs, and he began to lap at my pussy.

I grabbed at the edge of the tub as he licked me, spreading my legs for him. The heat within me was spreading quickly as he lapped at my pussy, which was wet in more than one way. I didn't think I'd ever tire of his tongue. His large hands gripped my ass, spreading me, opening me up for his tongue and lips.

With every lick, I gasped. He fingers slid into my opening, making me moan as he finger fucked me. The pleasure was searing through me, and my legs trembled as I rocked back against him.

My cries echoed on the tile as I came, shuddering.

I heard a condom packet rip as I panted.

He carefully repositioned himself in the tub, hands on my hips, and thrust into me in one smooth motion.

I groaned as his thick cock filled me. Even though I'd just come, I wanted him to make me scream again, not caring how aching and sore I already was.

He wrapped his hands around my hips then went to my breasts, cupping them, playfully tweaking them as he took me. He drew back then slammed into me again, working up to a furious pace. My breasts splashed in the water from the power of his thrusts. I held onto the edge of the tub as he fucked me.

Not long had passed before I was once again seizing up with absolute bliss. Everything became so tight only for me to be hit with that wonderful release.

But he wasn't done.

I moaned deep and low in my throat as he continued to pound into me. His fingers dug into my ass as he buried himself in me. One of his large hands tangled in my hair, pulling my head back. My torso arched, and I felt a little lightheaded.

I was cresting over the edge again. This time, he was there with me.

I came, calling his name as he shuddered in me.

He turned my head and kissed me messily. Then he set me back down into the warm water with gentleness, before stealing one more kiss from me.

“I thought you were at work,” I said, leaning against his chest.

He tugged a wet lock of my hair off my cheek. “I had to take Max out. He needs a lot of exercise.”

“Seriously?” I closed my eyes and rested my head against his broad chest. “All Max did at my house was lounge around and beg for food.”

“He’s a corgi,” Oliver murmured against the side of my head. “He’s a working dog. He was bred to chase sheep around the Welsh countryside all day. I take him on a three-mile run twice a day. It’s really helped calm him down.”

“Oh,” I said, feeling bad. “I didn’t know that. On Instagram, I only saw them sleeping.”

The excuse sounded ignorant and lame to my ears. Max wasn’t my dog, but I had lived in the house. I could have taken him for runs.

I felt the burning rush of shame, just like when I had first moved into my freshman dorm and my roommate was appalled that I had brought those little microwave packets of macaroni and cheese. My mom had found them at Costco and stacked manufacturer’s coupons to be able to afford them. My roommate had told me that it was plastic food and would ruin my skin. I had heard her laughing about it later with her friends.

Maybe Oliver had been right. Maybe this was why he wouldn’t ever date someone like me, because I was trashy and neglected a puppy.

“You want to go grab an early lunch?” Oliver offered, kissing me and running his hands over my breasts.

“I actually have to go to work.”

Going out with Oliver in public like an actual couple was what I had dreamt of since that fateful night. Yet now that he so casually offered, all I wanted was to go home and freak out with some Christmas cookies and wine.

"I'm sure the Naughty Claus can spare you for a few hours more," he said, pulling me back to him and kissing me again.

As if I would put on the same stained sexy gingerbread girl uniform and walk into a nice restaurant with him and my tangled wet hair and torn tights. The easiest way to avoid humiliation was to pretend you didn't care.

"I know it would shock you," I told him, trying not to let the anxiety creep into my voice, "but I'm kind of one of the most important people at the Christmas market."

CHAPTER 45

Oliver

What did she mean she was the most important person at the Christmas market?

I frowned as I stood in the town square near the gazebo, where people stood in line to get in to see Santa Claus.

Had it been a threat? A warning? Did Noelle know what I was up to?

What do you mean "up to"? You haven't said one way or another if you're going to go ahead with Tristan's crazy plan and ask her to marry you.

Even so, what if she was on to me?

I did a hasty mental review to try to remember if I had left anything incriminating out in my study.

I needed to stop being so cavalier. I had gotten caught up in the holiday romance with Noelle. Not to mention those too-tight costumes that pushed her tits up and the necklines that scooped down to almost reveal her nipples every time she breathed.

See that? Where all you can think about is sex? That's a problem, a weakness my enemies could exploit.

I was running a business now, and if my company ever actually found a piece of land, I would be manufacturing high-tech processors needed for America's military equipment. Spies would crawl down the chimney trying to get one over on me.

Maybe Noelle was one of them.

She is not working for the Russians, I told myself firmly.

But she might be working for her own interests, or for one of the many small-town factions.

Tristan had said his brothers had had multiple issues with the feral cat committee, for example.

For my brothers, I picked out a box of Christmas firecrackers that were supposed to be shot out of a miniature cannon. Jonathan, I knew, would love them. The rest of them would act like they didn't, but they would totally use them.

The shopkeeper at the stall wrapped the gifts for me while I went to look at the dog toys at another stall.

"Do you have anything that will stand up to a husky?" I asked the shopkeeper.

She hefted up an oversized rawhide candy cane. "How about this?"

"Perfect."

I wandered through the stalls. Even the shops on Main Street were decorated for Christmas and doing brisk business, especially the jewelry shop.

Can't hurt to have a backup plan.

"Interested in a proposal in front of the Christmas tree?" the shopkeeper asked me, noticing I didn't have a ring on my left hand.

"I just wanted to see what you had," I said carefully.

The man took in my suit and guided me to what I assumed were the most expensive engagement ring options.

"This is a very fine five-carat diamond," he said, showing me a ring.

"It seems a little plain."

A different ring caught my eye. It was a large diamond surrounded by smaller ones so that it resembled a snowflake. The band was silver and studded with smaller diamonds.

"I'll take that one." I pointed.

"An excellent choice."

I tried not to feel guilty as I paid for the ring.

You don't have to use it, I reminded myself.

The ring rested in my breast pocket as I headed back out into the Christmas market.

The holiday atmosphere helped calm me.

Christmas was always a big affair at our house when I was a child. My mother had always insisted that the presents be wrapped perfectly. Gift-giving was a skill that showed you were observant of the people around you. It was about the appearance of being a good friend, brother, or spouse more than actually being any of those.

Still, I had been the youngest, and who wasn't excited by Christmas as a kid? As long as my siblings and I behaved exactly as my mom wanted, she was in a better mood that day than she was all year long.

"There he is," Jonathan said loudly, sauntering down the path that wound through the stalls. My brother Jack was trailing him. Jack's large husky practically bounced along beside him.

Jonathan had his cat in a baby carrier.

"Jack's really gotten into the Christmas spirit," Jonathan informed me. "Every time I turn around, he's stopping to sniff the Christmas potpourri."

"No, I'm just trying to stay as far away from you as possible so that people don't think we know each other."

Jonathan threw an arm around Jack's neck. "Cindy Lou Who is having separation anxiety lately."

I petted the cat's head. She hissed at me.

"Someone's not having a Merry Christmas."

My brothers and I grabbed drinks from a nearby stall and found a table. The air was cold. The snow had stopped falling, and a frigid breeze was blowing the gray snowy clouds across the sky.

I took off my sports coat. The people in the market all bundled up against the wind looked at us like we were insane.

My siblings and I had a high tolerance for the cold, and, of course, so did Jack's husky. The cat was wrapped in a parka, and the corgi wore his own Christmas-themed vest.

After Jonathan took a sip of his drink, he said, "Word on the street is that you're trying to get married?"

"What the—keep it down," I hissed at my brother.

"Holy fuck, it's true."

"No," I hissed, leaning over the table. "It's not. I mean it might be. It was Tristan's idea."

"He's been bragging to his brothers that he's going to be the next Greg," Jonathan said.

"I have to say," Jack said reproachfully, "that is a pretty underhanded thing to do."

"Does Belle know?" I asked them.

"Not yet, but she will."

"So you're seriously considering going through with it?" Jack shook his head.

"Not seriously considering. Obviously," I scoffed.

"Good."

"But..."

"Shit, man." Jack scowled. "You can't let the Svenssons get in your head."

"Funny. Belle said something similar."

I knew it was wrong. But maybe I could just be with Noelle and see where that led. Just because I was sleeping with her didn't mean I had to commit to marriage.

There had to be some other way to get around the deed restriction on the property—a sympathetic judge or a clause or caveat in the documentation might be all I needed to make the property mine.

Then I wouldn't have to marry Noelle or feel bad about being in a relationship with her.

CHAPTER 46

As I headed back home later that evening, I tried to keep the horrible thoughts from bubbling up. The Christmas market had been busy with people out shopping. It had been easy to go on autopilot and pretend it was all just a dream.

Who wanted to forget about amazing, mind-blowing sex with a hot guy? Me, that was who.

I kept waiting for the anvil to drop out of the sky on me, to have to relive the same humiliating moment I had that dark afternoon at Harvard.

Oliver had left my dorm room sometime in the night after the mind-blowing sex.

I had spent the day on a cloud of cotton candy, deliriously happy that I had found a boyfriend, sure that we were going to have the perfect life and the perfect marriage. I had started planning my wedding and daydreaming about how my parents would cry and how jealous my sister would be, how I would finally have it all, finally be able to save my family. I would ride off into the sunset with my degree and my Prince Charming.

Except… Oliver hadn't texted me that day.

Like at all.

I had told myself it was because he had lost my number. I was sure I would see him in class and it would be like one of those old romantic comedies my mom and I would watch on Saturday afternoons.

Oliver was going to whisk me off my feet and tell me he loved me and couldn't stop thinking about me and was so glad he'd found me.

I wasn't going to be like my sister, clingy and crazy and getting pregnant by guys just so they would stay with her.

No, not me! I was perfectly sane.

To show just how okay I was, I had grabbed my books and hiked through the winter snow and cold to class the next afternoon, worrying that maybe Oliver had been abducted by aliens or hit by a car. Maybe he was in the hospital, needing me.

My business classes had been filled with several elite Harvard students, the ones whose parents gave them credit cards and sent them on summer trips. The girls all liked to gather around the boys, who looked like they had just walked out of a Polo Ralph Lauren ad, and flirt and revel in how perfect and beautiful their lives were.

I usually avoided them at all costs, sat in the corner, and never raised my hand to answer a question.

Not that day.

I had been drawn to Oliver, his platinum white hair, his intense blue eyes.

But when I'd greeted him, he wasn't happy or ecstatic or full of love. He'd just said, "Excuse me. Do I know you?"

The girls in their expensive preppy clothes like they had walked out of a dark academia inspo video on YouTube, shrieked with laughter.

"Maybe you slept with her and didn't remember," one of them had cackled.

My face had burned. I had wanted to shrink and disappear inside the secondhand sweatshirt and jeans I had been wearing. My tennis shoes were soaked from the snow. I couldn't afford the warm leather boots the other girls wore over their stockings.

I longed to hear Oliver claim me, say that he was sorry, that he had been drunk and of course he remembered. I wanted him to kiss me in front of the class, to show those girls that I, too, was someone who mattered.

But he had just scoffed as they ribbed him. "Of course I wouldn't just sleep with someone like her. Who do you think I am? Honestly, I'm offended." He had been so cold, so aloof.

The entire class had laughed. Even the teacher had snickered.

I had turned and run away, skipping class for the first time ever in my life. But I hadn't cared about grades. I had crawled into bed and didn't leave for a week. It didn't help that someone had anonymously invited me to join a Facebook group about the incident. I lay in bed, just crying and scrolling through the comments people had written about the sad, pathetic girl in class, wishing it was all a joke and he would come make a grand apology gesture, that he would find out about the group and come to my defense.

"How could I have been so stupid?" I yelled at myself as I drove down the driveway to the dilapidated cottage. "You were supposed to be the smart one."

The humiliation sat like a lump in my chest. My lips felt numb in the cold.

"Elsa was right," I told myself as I parked the car.

I shouldn't have gotten back with Oliver.

But at least this time he had remembered me.

But was that really enough? Was that what I wanted?

I needed it to be real. Was I ever really going to have what I wanted? Even if I could figure out exactly what that was?

Maybe I needed to live in the moment, stop taking life so seriously. This could be a fun holiday romance. Just as long as I kept emotions out of it.

At the very least, aside from mind-blowing sex, being with Oliver for the Christmas season would keep me out of the shitstorm brewing in my parents' house.

"You let her spend entirely too much time on that phone," my mother was chastising Azalea when I walked in.

"She's on winter break," my sister huffed at my mom, gaze fixed on her own phone. "And she's my daughter, not yours."

"I've practically raised her," my mother reminded Azalea. "And I want Dove to be successful in life."

"Still trying to prove that you don't raise crappy kids?" Azalea sneered at my mother. "Well, guess what? You do. We're all failures. Maybe the guidance counselor was right and you and Dad should have put me up for adoption."

"You don't mean that." My mother started crying, which set the three small children playing on the floor wailing.

"Admit it," Azalea yelled at my mom. "I'm a failure. I suck as a mother. My children are bratty and useless. You think I'm a bad mom, and you regret me."

"I don't," my mom insisted. "I just wish you'd make better choices."

"It's not like I had a great role model, is it?" Azalea grabbed her coat.

"Ah, the prodigal daughter returns," she jeered when she saw me.

"Where were you?" my mother snapped.

"I told you," I said, taking off my coat, "I was staying at a friend's house."

"I bet she was with a boy," Dove said in singsong.

"Seriously?" I said to my niece more harshly than I intended because she gave me an angry look.

"Dove, could you please get the children?" my mother said, exasperated as one of the toddlers pawed at my niece's ankle.

"Why do I always have to take care of them?" Dove asked.

"Who do you think took care of you?" my mother exploded at her. "Why can't anyone show a little gratitude once in a while for everything I've sacrificed?"

"Dove, can you please?" I begged her. "You and I can go out for snacks and hot chocolate at the Christmas market later."

"This is supposed to be my break," she argued.

"Yeah, well, life sucks."

"Is that why you're sneaking around?" she grumbled. "Bet you end up pregnant like my mom."

"You shouldn't be dating," my mother scolded, following me as I headed to the bathroom.

"I'm twenty-three," I reminded her. "I can spend the night with a guy if I want to."

"Think about your future," my mother begged. "You need to be a good role model for Dove and the other children."

"Look," I told her, "I can't do this with you right now. I need to shower and change and meet with Professor Hoffman so I can earn my degree and finally start my life." I slammed the door.

Would this miraculous new life have Oliver in it?

Would it be so bad if it did?

CHAPTER 47

Oliver

After shaking our hands, the banker said, "It took my assistant a while to dig up the original mortgage documents."

Tristan and I sat down on the large leather chairs on the other side of the desk. The Harrogate Community Bank was in an old building from the 1890s.

"Tristan mentioned to me," I said as I flipped through the copies of the original documentation, "that if the land title was exchanged, not inherited, it went before the town council to vote on any zoning or other use restrictions. We're hoping to try to find a way around that."

"Understood," the banker said. "I did have a read through the documents, and that clause is very clear. In the 1950s, when the Wynter estate was sold off, several of the other surrounding wealthy landowners feared that the property could be developed into less desirable housing types. There is a certain upscale charm where those large Gilded-Age estates are located that the landowners didn't want ruined."

"What happens if Noelle's father is unable to pay the mortgages and the bank puts the property in foreclosure? When does the trigger happen, exactly?"

"What are you thinking?" Tristan asked me.

"If the bank technically owns the property because Noelle's family loses it for not paying, which it sounds like they're getting close to, there's not as much political buildup. We can spin it like it's just a formality. The bank can tell the zoning and land use commissioners that they'd like the land zoned for industrial estate because that gives them the maximum flexibility to sell the land. That zoning code will allow for an operational farm with one lodging and a certain type of factory, but the commissioners will probably overlook that."

The banker seemed a little nervous at the conversation.

"I'm not sure that we can help you all with that."

I fixed my gaze on him.

"Really? Because we were planning on opening a very large account at this bank in anticipation of our new business's large capital expenditures."

I knew that would get the banker's attention. This bank offered bonuses for new accounts. This guy was looking at a very merry Christmas if he helped us.

"Like I said, we wouldn't be building low-quality housing. The factories of today are high-tech and robotic, and we're manufacturing very small products. It won't destroy the quality of the countryside to build our factory on the Christmas tree farm, so you can sleep easy at night."

Tristan handed him the preliminary site plan the architect had produced.

The banker relaxed as he studied it. "I think we can help make this deal happen."

"James Wynter has missed several payments and only made a partial payment last month. If he doesn't make another payment in the next two weeks, we'll put him in foreclosure. He's already had a number of notices go out. We'll call you when we're closer to the turnover."

"See?" I told Tristan as we stepped outside onto the sidewalk, which had been freshly cleared of snow. "And you thought I'd have to get married like this was one of those trashy historical fiction books."

"I still think you should buy a ring just in case," Tristan told me, slipping on his sunglasses. "Can't hurt to have a plan B."

"I already have a ring," I said as we walked down the street. People were strolling along, carrying their Christmas parcels. "Maybe I'll even propose to her for real one day."

"Actually," Tristan said, pulling down his sunglasses and pointing, "you might be too late."

CHAPTER 48

I tugged at the hem of my burgundy turtleneck sweater dress.

It had a couple of moth holes in it when I bought it from the thrift store. My mom had tried to fix them, but if you looked closely you could see that the thread she used did not match the exact shade of the dress.

I adjusted the skinny leather belt at the waist of the pleated wool skirt, which was a little—okay, a lot—too tight on me. I could barely breathe, and I longed to undo the pearl buttons.

These were the nicest Ivy League prep clothes I owned. Now that I was standing in the foyer of the packed restaurant, I wondered if I shouldn't have worn business casual instead. Maybe I looked too cutesy, too much like a little girl trying to pretend like she came from a good family. I should have worn a no-nonsense black skirt and starched white blouse to show that I was serious about business and finishing my degree.

I chewed on my lip.

What if Professor Hoffman didn't even show up?

That would be bad. I needed him to give a preliminary approval of my project so I could go before the capstone project committee, who would grill me on it. He was doing me a solid and giving me eight hours of credit for an independent study so I could graduate. I just had to make it through these last few weeks.

And then?

Then I would try to find a low-level entry job at one of the offices in town. Though most of the firms hired in the early summer right after college graduation, maybe there would be a position open somewhere.

The door to the restaurant opened, and Professor Hoffman strode in.

He had been the hot young professor back in his day but had now crested into late middle age. He still acted like he was the twenty-something wiz-kid PhD candidate.

When he saw me, his eyes clearly swept from the top of my hair, carefully pinned in the approximation of a popular New England hair style, and down my curves and back up again.

"Glad to see your depression seems to be wearing off," he said finally. "I'd give you a hug and kiss on the cheek, but Harvard doesn't let us touch students."

Gross. Yuck.

"I didn't have depression," I said hastily. "Just some family stuff came up."

"Ah, yes, family stuff." He shook his head as we waited for the hostess to lead us to a table. "My girlfriend just told me she's pregnant, and now she's trying to act like she has a disability. As if I don't have three other children. I know how pregnancy goes. I've decided I'll give her a week to throw a tantrum, then I'm putting my foot down."

The hostess grabbed two menus, and we followed her to a table.

I ordered the French onion soup and a water.

Professor Hoffman ordered tomato soup.

"My girlfriend keeps trying to cook," he complained. "She's terrible at it."

"I'm sorry to hear that," I said, feeling awkward.

"I hope you know how to cook," he told me. "Otherwise you're going to make your future husband very disappointed."

"I'm probably pretty far away from that," I replied, twisting the straw wrapper between my fingers. "I'm going to take some time in the workforce first."

He snorted. "Really? Doing what? You have a generic business degree. You're qualified to be a secretary."

"I have a computer science minor," I said, trying not to seem annoyed. "That was the whole point of doing this capstone project—so I could get my computer science credits and business in one go."

"Firms won't hire women as software engineers off the street. You should have majored in it."

"A business major seems to have worked out well for you."

"It's because I have a PhD in economics," he bragged. "Stanford."

"Not to get off track," I said, tapping my nails on the table, "but we were going to talk about my progress on the capstone project?"

"Right."

"I emailed my paper over to you."

"Honestly, I didn't have a chance to read it. Just give me the elevator pitch."

Figures.

"Millions of people start small businesses in the US every year, and at least half fail during the first five years. Based on several papers I read, which are documented in my report, many businesses fail because of improper management of cash flow, poorly managed marketing efforts, and failure to set realistic benchmarks. Many people end up worse than they started after the business fails." I took a deep breath. "For my capstone project, I developed an app to help small business owners manage their companies and keep them on track."

"Sounds like every other app out there," Professor Hoffman said as the waitress brought our food. "I must say this is not something I would invest in."

"Fortunately, I'm not asking you to invest." I forced a laugh. "I just want you to sign off on my credit."

He took a bite of his soup. "So let's see this app."

"A big issue with small businesses is that people get easily overwhelmed." I pulled up the app on my tablet and handed it over.

"All the other small business apps out there—and again, a review of them is in my research report—are difficult to use, require high levels of executive function, and assume a knowledge base that someone who's, say, operating a bakery out of her home just may not have the mental bandwidth to deal with. My app is designed to be accessible for people of all education levels and abilities and to be aesthetically pleasing so that you want to use it."

As Professor Hoffman flipped through the app, which was loaded with my mom's bakery information, his eyes widened in surprise. He was probably expecting one of those banking apps with the generic circle graph and bad font. Mine was fun to use and had little stickers, inspirational quotes, and a nice font. It was designed to automatically customize based on your business type so that someone who wasn't super technologically literate or who didn't have a lot of time on their hands could easily set it up.

"It generates invoices, payroll, and ninety-day, one-year, and five-year business plans based on past data. It makes projections and links to card readers and bank accounts. It could be monetized, if it were a real business, to make credit card or loan offers or adversity course options."

"Interesting," the professor said as he continued to play with the app.

I was secretly pleased. I had studied game design to make the app fun and a little addictive to use.

I had to. My mother was scatterbrained, and if I didn't make it something she would automatically reach for and which sucked her into monitoring her finances, she would just forget about it.

Whenever Mom would hit her account, the app showed off a happy dancing cat in an apron shooting off fireworks. She would thrust her phone in my face, delighted she was earning money for her baked goods.

He looked up at me with a frown. "You're just a girl. How did you even know how to make something like this? Are you sure you coded this yourself? You can't have help with a capstone project, you know. That's cheating."

He handed the tablet back to me. "Did your parents do this for you?"

"No," I said slowly, "my parents didn't help me at all. They're high school dropouts."

"Oh," he said. "Right. You're the one with the teen mom."

He reached over and grabbed my hands. "That must have been very difficult for you growing up."

Uh, what the hell?

He stroked his fingers over my knuckles. "All those men coming in and out of your house. I bet your mom was jealous when her boyfriends thought you were more attractive than her. You've probably been having sex since, what? Age thirteen? All those daddy issues."

I yanked my hand away.

"My parents are still married to each other," I hissed at him, furious. "And my siblings and I all have the same father."

Apparently having multiple degrees from multiple fancy colleges didn't give you a lick of home training.

"Now don't be like that," Professor Hoffman scoffed. "It's a fair assumption. You can't deny the stereotype exists for a reason. Especially if you wear such a short skirt. Now eat your soup and stop scowling. It's Christmas."

This motherfucker.

A man rested his hand on my shoulder before I could pick up my French onion soup, throw it all over Dr. Hoffman, and thus ruin my chances of ever earning my degree.

I whirled around in my seat to accost whoever had the balls to touch me.

Oliver leaned down slowly and kissed me.

"Good afternoon, Dr. Hoffman," Oliver said, voice chilly. "I had no idea you knew Noelle."

"Mr. Frost." The professor looked between us in confusion.

The waitress came over. "Do you need another chair for your party?"

"No need," Oliver said with a sharp smile. "Professor Hoffman was just leaving. He'll have his soup to go, please."

CHAPTER 49

Oliver

After the waitress packed Professor Hoffman up and pointed him to the exit, I took his chair.

"So, birds of an arrogant and entitled feather flock together, huh," she said bitterly. "Guess you two are super buddy-buddy."

"Professor Hoffman is a creep," I said simply. "He was sleeping with his teaching assistant, and he left his second wife as soon as she graduated. Now they're off spending all his money so he can relive his youth for the second time."

Noelle snorted. "Not sure how much youth he's going to be reliving with a new baby on the way."

"You're kidding me," I said in shock. "She's pregnant?"

"Apparently," Noelle said with a slight smirk. "And making his life hell."

I sat back in my chair. "Good."

The waitress came over.

"Can I get you anything?" she asked me.

"Could I have the pepper crusted lamb with roasted potatoes and an old-fashioned?"

"You want the St. Nick old-fashioned?" she asked.

"Sure."

Noelle shook her head.

"And Noelle wants your Christmas cocktail and the Santa's special to eat."

"I already have French onion soup."

"I told you I wanted to take you out on a real date."

I had been so fucking pissed when I had seen her and Dr. Hoffman. At first it was jealousy when I thought they were having a romantic lunch, then it turned into rage when I saw her jerk her hand away.

"What were you doing with him, anyways? I hope you don't end up on the Moi Cheaters app," I joked. "That thing is really taking off."

Noelle grimaced. "My sister sure isn't happy that she was featured."

"I'm sure it will blow over once the novelty wears off."

The waitress came by with the drinks.

The old-fashioned was only mildly holiday-themed and came garnished with Christmas spices.

Noelle had been given a bloated-looking Santa mug overflowing with red and green foam.

"Merry Christmas," I said, a smile playing around my lips as I clinked my glass against the oversized mug.

"What is even in this?" she asked.

I picked up the specials menu, which was on a little Christmas placard on the table.

"Eggnog, almond spritzer, ice cream, Christmas spice whipped cream, enough rum to kill an Elf on the Shelf, and the patented happy Santa spice blend on top with Christmas graham cracker crumbles."

"I thought you liked Christmas," she countered, stirring the drink with the red and white striped straw. "People who claim they like Christmas can't make dark jokes about the Elf on the Shelf."

"It's literally on the placard," I said as she took a long slurp of the drink through the straw. The straw was oversized so that the ice cream didn't clog it, and I couldn't keep my eyes off the way her lips pursed over the straw and her cheeks hollowed slightly as she sucked.

I wonder if she sucks cock like that.

I really wanted to find out.

I swallowed.

"It's not the worst thing I've ever had in my mouth," she said, her tongue darting out and licking up the small dab of green whipped cream on the side of her mouth.

I shifted in my seat.

"But if you dipped your cock in chocolate, I'd probably get more enjoyment out of it than this drink."

I almost choked on my drink.

"Did you like eating my pastries?" she asked innocently.

I gave her a long look. "The cream filling was a nice touch."

She ran her booted foot up my leg. I grabbed her knee, laughing.

"Seriously, tell your mom thanks for the pastries. She should open a shop."

"She wanted to," Noelle said, ducking her head. "That was her dream—to have an adorable little bakery on Main Street that would serve seasonal pastries, and then she would branch out into running a quaint bed and breakfast in the woods. I think she was hoping my sister or I might work there with her but..."

She sighed heavily.

"Does your sister not like to bake?"

"My sister doesn't like to do anything." She scowled. "Azalea working with my mom would be a Christmas miracle on par with when the Germans and the English stopped fighting World War One and had a soccer game that one Christmas Day. Now, instead of expanding her business, my mom is having to take care of my brother's and sister's kids."

The waitress brought our meals over.

Mine looked normal with only a small tuft of Christmas-inspired garnish.

Noelle's plate looked like the elves and reindeer had gotten drunk and made an art project in Santa's workshop.

"Is this supposed to be Santa Claus?" she asked in a low voice.

"It looks horrific." I reached my fork out and poked at the round scoop of white something that I supposed were meant to be his cheeks.

"I think it's mashed potatoes, though using two olives for his soulless eyes was a bit much."

"You have to switch with me," she said.

"No way." I cut off a bite of my own lamb. You need to be filled by the Christmas spirit. There are only so many Christmases a person has on earth. You have to make the most of them. Hang out at the Christmas market. Spend time with family. Go to holiday parties."

"Christmas is only fun if you have money."

"Looks like someone didn't learn the cardinal lesson from *How the Grinch Stole Christmas*. Presents and material goods don't make the holiday special." I wagged my fork at her.

"Easy for you to say, Mr. Billionaire," she snapped. "I bet you grew up rich too. Did your parents have decorators come to the house the day after Thanksgiving? Did your school throw tasteful holiday parties? Did you get nice presents you could show off to all your other rich private-school friends?"

I frowned. "Yes, but that wasn't what made Christmas fun."

"Guess what, Mr. Holly Jolly Christmas. In the real world, the rest of us have to work to make Christmas magical for spoiled children like you. I have to get up at four every morning to open up the Naughty Claus and make those fun Christmas-themed drinks. I have to freeze my tits off delivering Christmas pastries all over town so they can be a cheerful holiday gift for friends, clients, and loved ones. I have to stick a coffee IV in my arm every evening and dance in a thin polyester outfit to sell enough Christmas trees so that our electricity doesn't get shut off. Christmas isn't fun. It's stressful, and tensions are high because you have one shot to save up enough money for the next year. Oh, and did I mention it's snowing the entire time this is going on? Christmas sucks. I hate it."

She stabbed at the radish that made up Santa's nose.

"Guess I'm not good holidate material," she said, pushing her chair back.

I stood up and grabbed her hand.

"Look, I know I probably came off as privileged and tone deaf. But you should have at least one afternoon where you get to be immersed in Christmas. And you're with the right person to do it." I leaned in and kissed her. "Come to the Christmas market with me."

"Ugh."

I kissed her again. "Come on. It will be fun and romantic."

"Fine. But I won't like it."

I grinned. "I think you will."

CHAPTER 50

Noelle

Walking arm in arm with Oliver was everything I had dreamed about for a year.

Well, everything except that we weren't on a promenade in Paris in the spring but instead in my small hometown, wandering through the snow-covered Christmas market.

I had been so freaked out when Oliver had shown up, worried that Professor Hoffman would spill the beans that I was not in fact a Harvard alumnus. I was sure Oliver would yell at me in the middle of the busy restaurant accusing me of lying to him.

It was kind of sexy that he just saw me and stepped in to save me. Not that I couldn't handle Dr. Hoffman. I did work in food service, after all, and had dealt with far worse customers.

Still, it was nice to be taken care of.

The wind blew, lifting my skirt and blowing out any of the body heat I'd managed to accumulate. I was trying to look cute when I met with the professor, so I hadn't worn the oversized men's winter coat I had found at the thrift store a couple years ago. I had thought I would go straight to the Naughty Claus to work, and I'd left it there to change into when I was done with my meeting.

Now I was walking around the Christmas market like a tourist or someone with money to burn on Christmas presents.

"Are you cold?" Oliver murmured in my ear.

"Nope." No way was I promenading around the Christmas market in that ratty coat while he walked beside me like a model in his bespoke suit. All it would do would highlight just how much Oliver and I did not belong together.

"Really? Because I can see your nipples through your sweater."

"Crap." I looked down.

Oliver released me.

Was there a non-trashy way to tell a guy maybe you should just skip the romantic holiday date so that you could go have loud sex in his multimillion-dollar home?

Oliver shrugged off his wool overcoat then draped it around my shoulders.

"Here," he said.

"Aren't you going to be cold?" My eyes bugged out as he stood there in just his suit jacket.

"No. It's not that cold out."

I drew the soft wool coat around me. It was a deep charcoal and very warm. It also smelled like Oliver. I let his scent wrap around me.

All the rum from the Christmas cocktail was starting to hit me. It was a blustery winter day. The rich smells from the food stalls filtered through the market, mingling with the scents of Christmas trees and snow.

Oliver squeezed my hand as we walked.

"See?" he said. "It's beautiful. Where I grew up in Connecticut, it was a suburb that liked to pretend it was a small town. They had a Christmas market, but it was never this lively."

"You mean no one was illegally selling roasted chestnuts from the back of a llama?" I pointed at one of the many elderly characters who populated the Christmas market.

"No, it was all the same generic mass-market-produced kitsch with a steep markup." He nudged me over to a stall where a grandfather and his grandson were selling handmade toys.

"You can't find stuff like this everywhere."

"Merry Christmas," the young man said cheerfully. I recognized him from high school.

"Oh, hey, Noelle," he said. "I ran into your mom earlier when she was dropping off pastries. She said you had made her a business app? And a website? We're getting a lot of requests for sales because wooden toys are the hot item right now. I downloaded it from the app store and wanted to see if it could set up a specific type of report."

"Email me, and we can set up a time to talk," I promised him. "If it can't produce what you need, I can just amend the code."

"Awesome! I need something to help manage the business. Gramps uses pen and paper, and that is not cutting it."

The grandfather nodded at us as he sat in front of a little metal stove, carving a wooden boat.

Oliver picked out several of the wooden toys that were marked as for babies and toddlers.

"My brother's wife is about to have a baby," he told me. "I fully plan on spoiling the little girl."

"Be careful with that," I said as he swiped his credit card. "My nieces are the most spoiled, ill-behaved little girls in town. Love them but probably should have given them some discipline for Christmas."

He handed Oliver the bag.

"You make apps?" Oliver asked me as we strolled on.

I grimaced. "It's just something I did on the side for my parents." The type of girl Oliver wanted was not a college dropout. Of that I was sure.

You're about to graduate, I reminded myself. Soon. I hoped. Just had to make it through Christmas.

Across the square was the Naughty Claus. There was a line, and my boss was there, yelling at Elsa.

I felt suddenly guilty.

Elsa made eye contact with me, waggled her eyebrows, then made a grinding motion with her hips.

I rolled my eyes.

"I think she's telling you she'll be your wing woman and cover for you while I fuck you 'til you come. After our wholesome afternoon in the Christmas market, of course," Oliver whispered in my ear.

My face felt flush.

"I hope Elsa survives that long."

"If you really have issues with your boss, I'll flirt with her for you."

"Gosh, no." I shoved him lightly, making him laugh.

"She'll probably think you're serious and surprise you in your house when you come home one night."

With a laugh, he leaned in and kissed me.

"You mean stuck half-naked in my chimney?" He smiled against my mouth.

"I think you're the one who has to get stuck in my chimney," I whispered.

"There are worse ways to go."

We kept walking arm in arm.

"There sure are a lot of stalls here," I marveled.

When I was a kid, the Christmas market stalls lined the town square, and that was about it. Oliver and I were walking all over town, it seemed.

"This is the biggest Christmas market in New York State," he said.

"Seriously?"

"People visit from all over the region. It's really ramped up in the last few years, though."

"Wow," I said, feeling suddenly proud of my humble little town. It did look magical as we walked through the stalls. Café lights crisscrossed over the streets between the stalls. Each streetlamp had a wreath attached to it. The stalls were all decorated with lights and garland. Children laughed as they raced through the Christmas market.

"Raffle ticket. Get your raffle ticket," Dave said. "Support the Harrogate Arts Foundation."

"I'll take two," Oliver said.

"Are you giving away anything good?" I asked Dave.

"We're giving away artwork by a local artist."

"No more whiskey?"

"There were complaints it wasn't family friendly."

"Geez."

Dave took Oliver's ten-dollar bill.

After Dave left, I told Oliver, "I think that guy is secretly taking bribes to pick certain ticket numbers."

"Conspiracy theories at the Christmas market. Next you're going to tell me Santa is in league with the wooden toy makers on a price-fixing scheme."

I stuck my tongue out at him.

"Just for that, when I make moonshine this fall, I'm not giving you any."

"You make moonshine?" he said in shock.

"Uh yeah. I live in the woods. We make moonshine, jam, and canned vegetables. Before my sister got pregnant, she was the jam queen. Won prizes and everything. People have gotten in knife fights over her apple butter."

"She stopped making jam?"

"She'll still make it. Fall is the time of the year when she and my mom mostly get along, because they make jam together." I smiled at the memory.

"We have tons of blackberry brambles near the back of the property by the creek, and of course all the apple, pear, and cherry trees. Fall is when we all pitch in and harvest all the fruit, or as much of it as we can. It's the best. Everything feels hopeful. Then Christmas rolls around, and it gets cold and dark and snowy, and everyone is stuck inside."

"Does your sister have a stall here?" Oliver asked as we strolled down another street lined with stalls.

"No, it all gets sold off pretty much immediately. There's a waiting list."

We stopped at a stall with cat toys. Oliver selected a Santa on his sleigh that you could attach to one of those cat wand things.

"Do you have any Halloween-themed cat toys?" he asked the stall owner.

The woman rummaged in a box under the stall. "We have a pumpkin."

"I'll take it. My brother's girlfriend is also not a lover of Christmas."

"Sounds like she and I would get along," I said dryly. "I assume she's the one with long black hair and the witch's cauldron?"

Oliver paused a moment, frowning.

Crap. He didn't know I had been creeping around his house, spying on him and his siblings, a couple of weeks ago.

"I've seen her around town," I said weakly. "Small town. You know all the local characters."

"Right," he said.

We headed back toward the town square. A jazz band was playing Christmas music by the small ice-skating rink.

"Do you ice skate?"

"I did some with a youth group. It's easy here to just make an ice rink in your backyard. I was in love with American Girl, and there's one book where they flood the woods and make little ice-skating paths with candles. My father used to make one when my siblings and I were kids, and I would skate on it and pretend I was a princess."

"We have to go ice skating, then," Oliver said, wrapping his arm around my waist and leading me over to the skate rental.

"Surely you don't want to wear used skates," I said, desperate not to ice skate. It had been years since I'd put on skates. I was totally going to wipe out and humiliate myself in front of Oliver.

"I don't mind," he said. "A thirty-minute rental is nothing. This is supposed to be your Christmas afternoon extraordinaire. You can't skip ice skating."

"What size shoe?" the rental guy asked in a bored tone.

I mumbled a number.

"What's that?" he said loudly.

Ugh. When I'd been in high school, I'd always been teased for how large my feet were. Other girls had small, dainty feet made for ballet and flip-flops and summers by the pool.

I had extremely large feet made for trekking across the US on the Oregon Trail.

"Nine and a half," I whispered, hoping Oliver didn't hear.

"Nine and a half," the guy said loudly. "Nine and a half. I'm not sure if we have a women's nine and a half."

I wanted to melt into a puddle like Frosty the Snowman on a balmy summer afternoon and drip into a storm drain.

"Here you go," he said, plunking two ginormous skates down on the counter. "Nine and a half."

So much for a good, romantic date.

My face felt hot as I sat on a nearby bench while Oliver and I laced up our skates.

"I guess you probably played hockey when you were a kid," I said, desperate to keep him from thinking about my large feet.

"I wasn't great at it. My older brother Owen was better. But it wasn't like I was ever planning on being a pro hockey player. It was just fun to play with friends. I never got that worked up about winning or losing."

"Sounds like an emotionally healthy attitude to have," I said as we stepped onto the ice. "I hate losing."

"You must be fun to play Monopoly with," he teased as we slowly joined the crowd of skaters drifting over the ice.

"Monopoly is for amateurs. You need to play poker with my gran. Talk about a sore loser. She threw a chair once when she lost a hand."

Oliver laughed as we skated hand in hand, just a normal couple out enjoying the Christmas market. There was something nice and wholesome about skating out in the winter air, the lights from the large Christmas tree in the center of the ice glinting off the smooth surface.

Everyone was bundled up—except for Oliver, of course. With the historic town as a quaint backdrop, the scene was as perfect as a postcard.

"Are you having a nice holidate?" Oliver asked me.

"Yeah," I said, my mouth in a wide smile that surprised even me. "I am."

In one fluid motion, he switched on one skate blade to face me and kissed me long and slow as he skated backward.

"Show-off," I grumbled.

He grinned at me. "You thought it was sexy."

I rolled my eyes. "I mean, it's figure skating."

"It's a sport that takes strength and stamina, according to my sister, at least." He let go of my hand, skated into the middle of the rink, then did a jump and spun around in the air three times.

The whole crowd applauded, and he took a bow.

I was too shocked to be annoyed by it. "Did you do figure skating during the hockey off-season?" I asked in amazement when he skated back to me.

"Ha!" he said. "No, I had an older sister who was forced to babysit me. She treated me like her wind-up doll and made me do figure skating with her." He grinned at me. "It's better than dancing. I almost broke my foot when she made me dance the nutcracker to her Clara."

I clapped a hand over my mouth as I laughed. "Okay, now I have to see you do ballet."

"Absolutely not. Besides, it wasn't like I knew what I was doing. There was a lot of flailing and falling and my sister yelling and chasing after me with a ruler."

"She sounds like someone I need to be friends with."

"I think men turn out better when they have older sisters. Older sisters don't let anything slide."

"It's nice that you're close."

He squeezed my hand.

"I'm sure your sister will come around eventually. I think it's hard to be the oldest sibling," he said thoughtfully as we skated around the tree. "Your parents don't really know what they're doing. They're scared and out of their depths. They don't want to screw up the kid, but everyone is telling them anything they do is wrong. Then they have more kids, and shit really hits the fan. Maybe they rely too heavily on the older sibling, want them to grow up too fast because raising kids is difficult, and it's easier to lean on someone else even if it's your oldest child."

"That's not right," I argued. "Did your parents check out and your sister raise you? I have zero sympathy for people like that. She didn't get to have any sort of life."

"It's not right, obviously. Everyone gets screwed over," he agreed. "But I'm just saying I can see how it happens. You make a bad choice after a bad choice because of anxiety or you're insecure, and suddenly your whole personality is the sum of your bad choices, and none of your kids want to talk to you."

"Sounds like you're speaking from experience. Are you planning a big Christmas miracle to make up with your parents?"

Oliver shook his head. "My brothers have tried that with varying degrees of failure. At one point, I thought about it, but my sister has some personal stuff going on, and I don't want to stress her out anymore. So I'm staying away."

He squeezed my hand. "I don't really know your parents, but from what I've seen, they seem nice. They clearly love and adore you. You're lucky. What's that face?" he asked.

I was scrunching my nose. "You're not exactly who I thought you were, so I'm having to readjust my original assumptions, and it's a painful and unpleasant process."

"It's that time, folks," the loudspeaker blared, "for the afternoon Christmas raffle drawing. Make sure you have your tickets at the ready. Ticket C382. Does anyone have ticket C382?"

"I won! Yes! Whoo!" I jumped on the ice and immediately lost my balance.

Oliver caught me, spinning me around and kissing me as we spun slowly on the ice under the twinkling lights.

It was hands down the most romantic moment of my entire life. To be fair, it was the only romantic moment, but I would take what I could get.

We turned in our ice skates, and I headed to claim my prize. "I hope it's one of those metal penguin sculptures we saw earlier," I gushed to Oliver as we walked through the seating area in front of the stage where the committee members were announcing the raffle.

"Oh my word," I said as we approached the stage and my prize.

Instead of an adorable Christmas-themed sculpture, it was... something else.

"How," I said slowly, "is this family friendly?"

"It's an abstract reindeer," Dave said with a scowl.

"It looks like a penis," I said flatly, "with some sort of growth."

He narrowed his eyes at me. "It needs to be out of here in the next hour. I am not taking home any unclaimed prizes. I know where you work, Noelle Wynter, and don't think for a moment I won't dump this sculpture in front of your coffee stand."

"I can't take a giant penis home," I said, shaking my head. "My mom's been on the edge this Christmas season, and she's going to lose it if I show up with this."

"Get it out of the Christmas market." Dave pointed toward Main Street.

I sighed. "Freaking figures that the one time in my entire life I win a raffle, it's this monstrosity."

Oliver was walking around the sculpture with his arms crossed, studying it like it was a Michelangelo statue.

"Got anyone you hate who needs this in their front yard?" I asked.

"I think it's kind of interesting. You can sort of see the reindeer."

My mouth fell open. "We cannot be friends if you think this is artistic."

He laughed at me. "I'm just messing with you. It's actually pretty disturbing."

He tilted the sculpture over on its side. I flitted around him as he easily lifted it over one shoulder.

"I'll get the back," I said, "and carry the packages."

Oliver was so tall I had to raise my hands above my head to hold up the ball-sack end of the sculpture.

Oliver moved easily through the crowd, and I trotted after him.

"Guess I have my brother's Christmas present," he called to me.

"Or you could just leave it on your parents' front lawn the night before Christmas. Then, when they wake up, they'll see this disaster staring back at them."

He roared with laughter. "You are in a whole other class of petty, Noelle," he said, glancing at me over his shoulder, blue eyes dancing.

"You have no idea."

"Are you sure you don't mind keeping it?" I asked him as we approached his house.

"It might keep Mrs. Horvat from coming into my yard."

"You have to put it in your backyard. You're going to give several of these old people heart attacks. The ones who don't keel over are going to complain about it the entire time at the town hall. Mayor Loring will be upset, and you don't want the mayor annoyed with you." I released the ball sack, which I guessed was supposed to be a set of hooves, but someone failed horribly. Then I ran around Oliver and opened the side gate to the backyard. We set the sculpture by a small gardening shed.

We were laughing as Oliver let us into the kitchen. Max barked at me then ran out into the fenced yard.

I set down the bags of presents Oliver had brought.

"You want a drink?" he offered.

I unbuttoned his coat. "Actually, I was thinking of something a little more filling."

He chased me up the stairs to the master bedroom.

There, he pulled off his shirt while I discarded my skirt.

"Fuck me," I commanded, jumping on him all too suddenly, my weight crashing into him and sending him down onto the bed.

After a brief kiss, I shimmied up to him, holding him down with my weight.

"Didn't know you had an aggressive streak in you."

"I do. When I need to," I replied.

One hand slipped under my panties and stroked my wet pussy.

I gasped, arching my back against his touch.

I pulled off my sweater and unhooked my bra. He sucked on my tits as he stroked me.

He pushed my lacy panties down and tossed them aside. Then, in one smooth motion, he pulled me up to his head.

I squeaked and held onto the headboard.

My pussy in his face, he got right to work. His tongue lashed against my folds, kissing my clit and dipping his tongue in my opening. Lick after lick, all I could do was enjoy the ride.

My head fell back as I gasped for him, moaning and rolling my hips against his mouth. He held me steady as he tongue fucked me. I felt the pleasure tighten then explode as I came.

"Ready for another ride?" he asked as I panted.

"Are you?" I would not be beaten.

I reached down to his slacks, unzipping him and finding his rock-hard cock. I didn't have any doubts about how hard he'd be. He'd probably been erect ever since I jumped on him.

I shuffled down his body, and with his cock poking out of his slacks, I rolled my still-slick pussy across his cock, teasing him with my pussy lips.

"Fuck," he cursed and pulled off his pants while I fished in his nightstand for a condom.

I grabbed hold of his cock and rolled the condom right down his throbbing length, all the while looking at him with the anticipation of someone oh so very hungry for him.

With everything ready, I guided him right into my pussy, yearning for that thick, throbbing cock inside me. Goddamn, he felt so good. Hands on his chest, I started to ride him, bouncing up and down on his cock, letting that steady thumping pleasure spread through me and enjoying it to the fullest.

Oliver's hands crept up my side, to my breasts. He cupped and played with them, pinching the nipples as I continued to ride him. Bucking up and down, I cried out in bliss as delight hit me again and again.

My legs were starting to tremble. Oliver was there for me, holding me steady. His hands went to my hips and helped me keep the rhythm strong and fast, since he wanted this every bit as much as I did.

He dug his fingers into my ass and adjusted the angle so he was jackhammering up into me. My tits thumped his chest with every thrust, my hips rolling against his. I needed to feel every thick, hard inch of him.

His thrusts became more erratic. He was close and so was I. He rolled me backward so his cock hit my clit one more time. Then I was a goner. The erupting pleasure shook through me, leaving me screaming his name. I moaned as he thrust into me a few more times. Then he came hard in me.

He gathered me to his chest.

I lay on his chest, tracing patterns on the ridges of his muscles. One of his large hands rested on my ass.

It felt comfortable and right to be with him.

Except for one nagging noise.

"Is that your phone?" I asked him.

"I think it's yours."

It stopped ringing then started up again.

I sighed heavily. "Hold on."

I fished my phone out of my skirt pocket.

"This... this has to be a wrong number," I said in shock and disbelief as I read the text messages on my phone.

Mom: *Where are you???*

Mom: *You need to come home RIGHT NOW.*

Mom: *Dove is pregnant.*

CHAPTER 51

Oliver

"What happened?" I said in concern as Noelle sank down on the floor.

"I think I'm going to throw up," she groaned.

I picked her up and sat her on the bed then ran to the bathroom and grabbed her a cup of water.

She was sitting on my bed like a rag doll.

I lifted the glass to her mouth. She swallowed then coughed.

"My niece," she said.

I grabbed her hand and squeezed it tight.

"My niece. She's pregnant."

"Holy shit," I said after a moment.

"She's only eleven. She just turned eleven." Noelle started bawling.

I cradled her to my chest. "Come take a shower, and I'll drive you home."

Noelle sat with her teeth chattering in the front seat of my car.

I had been planning on a relaxing evening with her, one that involved maybe watching a Christmas movie, probably ordering food, and making her come. It felt so right to be with her, to hold her in my arms, laugh with her. We worked well together and complemented each other.

I had always wanted a true life partner, not just a girlfriend. It felt like I had more of a connection with Noelle than with any of the girls I'd dated while in college.

Now I would support her while her family was going through a crisis.

"How did this happen?" Noelle kept repeating. "Where did we go wrong? Did it happen at school? A friend's house? She never talked to me about a boy. Why wouldn't she even tell me? Oh my gosh, I was snappish with her lately. This is my fault. I should have been a better aunt."

I rolled down the window so that she could get some fresh air on her face.

"I'm sure you'll get some answers when you're at home," I told her.

"I cannot believe you got wrapped into my family drama."

I took her hand.

"I'm here for you," I promised. "I'm not going anywhere."

Except that you're going to buy her land... or did you forget about that?

Fuck off, I told my conscience.

I would think of something.

I wasn't going to lose Noelle or my business.

"My family is cursed," Noelle said forcefully. "The whole family. It's not just my parents getting pregnant when they were fourteen. It's all our extended family too. Elsa's brothers live in a trailer, and they're all crazy. Gran keeps bringing home weirdos. My sister got pregnant when she was fourteen. My brother got his girlfriend pregnant when he was a junior, and I—"

She clamped her mouth shut. "Never mind. I need to figure out how to help Dove."

"I know some good lawyers," I said delicately.

"Lawyers?" she forced out and looked at me with wide eyes.

"You know, in case you need to deal with the police..."

Noelle burst into tears.

She was sobbing and hysterical when I pulled up in front of the house.

I turned off the car, got out, and walked around to help her out of the passenger's side. I handed her my handkerchief when she stepped out, and she sobbed into it as I helped her up the stairs.

Inside, her whole family was in hysterics.

"You're so kind to bring Noelle back," her mother said through her tears, running to me and hugging me.

I patted her on the back.

"I'm here for you all. Whatever you need," I promised her.

"Do you want some casserole?" she asked me. "Or cookies? Noelle, get him some coffee."

"Are you kidding me, Mom?" Noelle shrieked. "Dove is pregnant, and you want me to make Oliver coffee?"

"This is Azalea's fault," a young man I assumed was Noelle's brother said.

"Fuck you, Jimmy," Azalea raged at him.

"He's not wrong," Noelle's grandmother hollered. "You're a terrible mother. Your eleven-year-old is pregnant. She learned to make bad choices from you."

"And I learned it from her." Azalea pointed at Susan.

"Don't talk about your mother like that," their father raged.

"Why are you pregnant?" Noelle screamed at her niece.

I winced.

"I'm sure it's not her fault," I said kindly.

Noelle grabbed Dove by the shoulders and shook her. "Who is it? Tell me!"

"I… I don't know," she said.

"See? She doesn't even know the father."

"Gran, shut up," Noelle raged. She was so furious.

Dove looked frightened.

"Tell her," Azalea yelled at her daughter.

I didn't know a lot about parenting—okay, probably nothing at all—but I suspected that this was probably not the best way to handle the situation.

"I can give you a few recommendations for therapists," I offered, trying to keep my tone even. "Maybe she can talk with one."

"You will talk to us now," Noelle said forcefully.

"Stop lying. You know who did this." Both sisters turned on Dove. Azalea was screaming at her. Their mother was sobbing into her apron.

Noelle shook Dove again while the girl sobbed hysterically.

"Stop it right now," I roared.

They all immediately went quiet.

"That's not how you treat a child. She's been through a lot."

"I—" Noelle seemed to come back to herself.

Azalea sucked in a breath to continue screaming at her daughter.

Noelle grabbed her arm. "I'm sorry, Dove," she said. "Oliver is right. We're not being very nice to you. We're all just scared, and we want to help you, but we will get through this together."

Dove wiped her eyes.

"Yeah," Gran said, petting her on the hair. "It will be okay. If the father is from a rich family, then we can all go to Hawaii."

"Gran," Noelle hissed at her.

Dove wrapped her arms around herself. She didn't look at me. Her lower lip trembled.

Then she blurted out, "I do know who the father is." She pointed at me. "It's *him*."

CHAPTER 52

Noelle

"*What the fuck?*" I screamed at Oliver. I ran across the room and shoved him.

"You horrible, horrible monster. How could you? My poor niece. My poor Dove. How could you? I never should have trusted you."

He looked shocked.

Dove was crying again. She was hysterical and upset.

"I swear to God," Oliver said in a low tone, "I did not even touch her. She's just a little girl."

"Liar! You're a fucking liar!" Noelle said. "Like I'm going to believe you over my own niece. You're so full of shit. You're just like all the rest of those sociopaths at Harvard. I wish I'd never met you."

My dad was clutching his chest. He staggered over to the couch.

"I'm having a heart attack," he wheezed. "I'm having a heart attack. I need to go to the hospital."

"Now you've killed my father," I screamed at Oliver as the tears ran down my face. "Get out. Get out of my house. Fuck, get out of my town. I better not see you again or I'm castrating you!"

Oliver looked sad and hurt. He took in a breath like he was going to say something then let it out. He slowly turned and opened the door. Before he stepped out into the snow, he turned to me and said, "I swear, Noelle. I didn't do it."

I wiped away my tears and hurried over to my dad.

"Come on. I'll drive you to the hospital," I said to my dad, who was sweating and groaning on the couch.

Gran took one look at him. "He's not having a heart attack. He ate half of your mom's casserole earlier, and now he has an upset stomach. Get him some seltzer water and turpentine."

"Old-timey medicine isn't fucking around, huh, Gran," my brother joked.

"How far along is she?" I asked Azalea.

She shrugged. "Mom found the pregnancy test." She handed me a pregnancy test in a Ziploc bag.

"So no one has taken her to the doctor yet?" I asked, incredulous. "Am I the only adult in this family?"

"No, you're the only adult that brought a predator around my grandchild," my mother yelled.

"Maybe if Azalea kept better track of her children, Dove wouldn't be pregnant," my brother called.

"I don't want to go to the doctor," Dove said in a small voice.

"You have to," I told her. "I'll make you an appointment."

"You're not her mom," my sister shot at me.

"This is a crisis," I said slowly, trying to resist the urge to slap my sister. "Step the fuck up and be a mom."

"I'm tired of her. She's been a problem since day one. She ruined my life," Azalea spat at Dove. "I was going to be a beauty queen and have my own jam line, and she ruined it."

"Fine," I said in a dark voice. "You don't want to deal with her? Sign her over to me. Mom's right. I brought Oliver into our lives. This is my fault, not yours, Dove. I'll handle things."

"He may have just targeted her through you," my brother said.

We all looked at him.

He shrugged. "Gran watches a lot of true crime while I game. They're kind of our things. When I went out to the Christmas market to make deliveries for Mom, Oliver was always hanging around your stall."

"We're cursed," my mother moaned.

"That asshole, that fucking asshole." This was literally my worst nightmare. "I'm going to ruin him."

"Let's just cut out the middleman and have us a good ol'-fashioned Christmas bonfire!" Gran pumped a fist.

"First," I said, pulling my niece to me, "we're going to take care of Dove. I'll make an appointment for first thing tomorrow. It's going to be all right." I petted her hair. She was tense in my arms.

Once I made sure she was okay, I would destroy Oliver.

CHAPTER 53

Oliver

My sister was furious. Her cold stare burned. In a voice as soft as cracking ice, she said, "A twelve-year-old girl accused you of *what*?"

"Actually, she was eleven."

"You f—"

"I swear to God," I interrupted, raising my hands, "I didn't do it."

"That's what they all say," Greg said coldly. "You see, Belle?" He turned to my sister. "This is why I have lots of brothers. If one of them goes missing due to his own poor choices, it's not such a great loss."

"I can't fucking believe you." Belle shook her head at me.

"Obviously I didn't do it," I begged her. "Do you really think I would be capable of something like that?"

"Who the fuck knows?" she railed. "You think you know someone, then they stab you in the back and cut out your heart."

"I hardly think a business tiff is as serious as what this little girl is accusing your brother of," Greg said, voice steely. "I don't jump to conclusions. We'll have to gather more information."

"You want to get cops involved?" Belle lowered her voice. "This could ruin his company and ours."

"No. Of course not," Greg said slowly. "We're going to find out exactly what happened. If she's telling the truth, I'm going to call Crawford. He's going to kill your brother and dump his body in the Pacific Ocean. We'll tell everyone he died in a tragic yacht accident."

"You don't mean that," my sister said, her eyes wide.

Greg's eyes were cold. "I assure you I don't make empty promises."

It was a tense ride over to Noelle's house later that evening. I felt like I was going to my execution.

Greg's brother, Crawford, who had been doing God knows what in the military, was sitting in the back of the SUV with Tristan and me. I was wedged in the middle.

Greg had rounded up several of his lawyer brothers, and they and Belle had sat around discussing a game plan before the drive. The lawyers had not seemed pleased to spend their Christmas season dealing with a man an eleven-year-old girl had accused of getting her pregnant.

I felt sick. I knew I didn't do it. I couldn't really blame Noelle for siding with her niece against me. I was about to be an uncle, and shit, I'd do the same.

But my own sister didn't seem like she believed me. And that fucking hurt.

She was sitting up front with Greg, who was driving.

The clear skies from earlier had turned dark and stormy. The snow blew as the cars drove down the country roads, headlights reflecting on the flurries.

We pulled up in the turnaround in front of the small cottage. Through the narrow windows, I could see Noelle and her family pacing around the living room, yelling.

Crawford opened Belle's door then dragged me out of the car.

Belle and Greg had their corporate masks on as they walked up the wobbly steps. Greg reached out and knocked on the door.

Noelle opened it. She seemed confused to see my sister and Greg standing there. Then she saw me.

"I thought I told you to get off of my property."

"Ms. Wynter," Belle said, enunciating the words, "it has come to our attention that you have an eleven-year-old girl in your family that may be carrying my brother's child."

It sounded so horrifying.

"May we come inside? I'd like for us to talk."

"Is this the part where you threaten us with lawyers?" Noelle snapped at her as we all stepped inside.

Her family stared at our group. Everyone was wearing suits, even my sister, who wore a neat skirt suit and expensive leather heels. We looked like movie villains coming to harass the poor wholesome country family.

"Noelle," I begged, "please believe me, I didn't do anything. I would never hurt you or your family."

"Actually, I think you would," she spat. "So no, I don't believe you."

"So that all of us are working from the same evidence," Belle continued, "we would like to have Dove be taken to a gynecologist for a pregnancy test and DNA test, depending on how far along she is. Once we see that her story checks out and my brother is in fact the father, we will, of course, offer a generous payout. We understand that will not make up for your family's pain and suffering, but as mentioned, it will be generous."

"And he goes to jail," Noelle demanded.

"Of course, at that point, once things are confirmed, we can involve the cops," Belle said. "We'd ask that we not involve them yet so no one is jumping to conclusions."

"Too freaking bad," Noelle shot at me. "I'm bringing your whole house of cards down. We're going to the cops tomorrow. We're blasting this on every single news station in America. I'm bringing your family down. And I'm going to laugh when they haul you off to jail."

"What? Jail?" Crawford drawled. "Greg, you said I'd get to shoot him."

My stomach sank.

The Svensson brothers had grown up in a dangerous cult in the middle of the desert. I was a hundred percent sure that Greg Svensson wouldn't hesitate to have me eliminated, especially since Noelle was gearing up to go scorched-earth.

Dove started crying.

"I'm going to end you," Noelle raged. "You're going to pay for what you've done."

"Stop," Dove begged.

"You're going to be ruined," Noelle yelled, "and dead."

"Please," Dove cried hysterically, "please just stop."

"This isn't your fault," Sarah said soothingly.

"Yes it is." The little girl hiccupped. "I—" Her mouth moved. "I lied." She started crying again.

What the fuck?

Dove picked up the pregnancy test. "I bought it online. I didn't mean for this to happen. I just..." She wiped her face. "I'm sorry. I used my Christmas gift card. See?" She tapped on her phone. "I have a receipt. I'm sorry, Oliver. I'm so sorry."

A horrified Noelle slowly took the phone and stared at it. "It... it's a receipt," she said, averting her eyes from me.

"Shit."

Dove ran past us out into the night.

Noelle gave me a helpless look then ran after her.

CHAPTER 54

Noelle

"What the fuck?" I cried as I ran through the dark. "What the actual fuck?"

My head was spinning.

I felt sick.

If I'd eaten anything that day, I would have puked it up.

"Dove!" I cried into the night. "Dove!"

I wandered through the Christmas trees, the falling snow muffling all the sound. In the moonlight, I found Dove's small footprints.

I followed them deeper into the grove of Christmas trees to find her sitting on the stump of a recently fallen Christmas tree, crying. She had her arms tight around her knees. I sank down into the snow next to her, where I wrapped my arms around her and rocked her.

"What were you thinking?" I said softly. "Dove, what in the world?"

She sobbed in my arms. "Nobody likes me. None of the girls at school want to be my friend. My mom hates me. Grandma doesn't like me. I always have to take care of the kids, and they aren't even mine. I don't have my own room. I don't have anything nice. You're never here. You're the only one who likes me. I just wanted to be special. I wanted people to pay attention to me."

"Well, you got your wish."

"But I guess you hate me now." She sobbed.

I rubbed her back. "I don't hate you. I just don't understand. Why did you say it was Oliver?"

"He was so nice to me."

"Then why did you try to ruin his life?" I cried.

"I don't know," Dove blubbered. "I didn't think he would be really angry with me because he was nice to me."

This was so fucked up.

"I didn't mean to ruin his life. I don't want Oliver to be killed," she pleaded.

"I don't think they were actually going to kill him," I said, closing my eyes. "It is Christmas, after all."

"Christmas sucks," my niece said vehemently.

"Yeah."

"Am I going to go to jail?" she asked after a moment. "For lying?"

"I don't know." I sighed heavily. I was exhausted. "They'll probably sue us. Not that we really have anything to take unless they want some old cars and acres and acres of Christmas trees."

"I'm sorry," Dove said again. "Please don't hate me."

"I don't hate you," I promised her. "You're my niece. I'll always be here for you. But if you're having trouble, please come talk to me. We can work it out. Blowing up someone's life because you want some more drama in yours is not the way to do it. You could have destroyed Oliver."

"I'm sorry. I guess he's not going to want to be your boyfriend anymore," she said sadly.

"Probably not."

We sat in the falling snow in silence until Dove stopped crying.

"Come on," I said, standing up and offering her a hand. "Let's go inside."

"Do you think Oliver is still there?"

"I hope so. You have to apologize."

"I don't want to see him." She started crying again.

"Time to take responsibility for your choices."

When we walked inside, my parents were crying and pleading, grabbing onto Belle's arm.

"We can't afford that. We don't have any money. Please don't sue us."

"Fine, then we're going to take your land and the house," Belle said. "You can keep your businesses."

God, these fucking billionaires.

But could I blame them? When I had thought Oliver had hurt Dove, I was ready to go scorched-earth. I had come after Belle's little brother. Of course she would pull out all the stops.

"I'm sorry," Dove yelled. She turned to Oliver, desperate. "I'm sorry. I didn't mean to say it was you. You were there and I panicked. Please don't punish my family because of me."

"Please have mercy," my mother begged. "We are so very deeply sorry. I will bake for you every day. You can have any Christmas tree you want."

"And jam," Azalea said. "Everyone likes my jam. Shit, you want a baby?" She picked up my nephew. "You can have a baby."

"You all wanted to play hardball," Belle said, voice icy. "You came after my little brother with no evidence. These are the consequences. I get what's due to me. I have lawyers here, and they can draft up documents right now. We can do this the easy way or the hard way."

When my mother saw Dove, she grabbed her and shoved her in front of Belle.

"We will ground her; she will not have a Christmas."

"I already never go anywhere and take care of children and clean and live in a freezing cold attic and never get anything nice for Christmas, so I guess my punishment is just to continue to live the rest of my life." Dove set her jaw. "I think I'd rather go to jail." She held out her hands. "Arrest me."

"This is not a joke, young lady." Azalea hauled back and slapped her daughter across the face.

"Azalea, don't hit people," I scolded.

Azalea slapped me.

I yelped in indignation. My mother hit us both over the head with a pillow.

"This is your fault too," Azalea said to me. "You put ideas in her head."

"No, it's your fault," Gran hollered at her. "Now we're ruined. We'll be homeless. Where is your mother supposed to bake? How will we sell Christmas trees or make jam? Your daughter is bringing ruin to us all!"

I felt like I was going to pass out. They were going to take our land, our home.

"Ruined!" Gran cried, wringing her hands as Belle and the men in suits stood uncomfortably in the crowded living room, watching my family fall to pieces.

But really, if ever there was a call for hysterics, now seemed like a pretty good time.

"I will not be moved," Belle stated. "Start packing your things. Choose the easy way so you don't rack up lawyer bills you won't be able to afford."

The front door creaked open.

"Uh... hiiii..." Elsa sidled into the living room.

Everyone turned and stared at her.

"So good news, we sold out of all the Christmas trees. Bad news, since no one answered their phone or showed up to the Christmas tree stall, I had to beg Ida to help bag the trees so I could man the cash register. She's surprisingly strong for a very old woman. But she asked for a penis cake in exchange, and she wants it filled with custard so it, quote, oozes when you cut it." Her eyes darted around in confusion.

"Is this one of those prank shows? Are we getting a home makeover and a trip to Disney? Wait, you're not here about that missing inflatable elf, are you?" she demanded. "I have no idea what happened to that."

"Crap. Elsa. I completely forgot." I grabbed my phone from my bag. There were a thousand text messages and missed calls from her.

"Oh, Elsa, you're so sweet to handle the Christmas tree stall while we're dealing with this." My mother clasped her hands to her chest.

The lawyers all watched her walk past them.

She kept her eye on them as she slowly crab-shuffled through the room then tripped over the coffee table. "Damn it."

One of the suited men snorted. Another elbowed him in the ribs.

Belle crossed her arms. "She a family member?"

"Cousin," Elsa chirped, "and best friend."

"Fine. We're suing you too."

"You can't sue me," Elsa squawked. "I declare bankruptcy!"

One handsome, gray-eyed lawyer's mouth turned up in an almost imperceptible smile.

Elsa giggled and winked at him.

I couldn't help myself. I looked at Oliver.

But his eyes were kind.

"No," Oliver said. "Dove is just a kid. She made a mistake. We're not suing anyone. On one condition."

"Anything," my mother assured him.

"Get Dove into some therapy."

"You don't get to make that decision, Oliver," Belle said coldly.

"Yes, I do," Oliver countered. "I'm the accused. Noelle's family didn't go public with the accusations, so there are no damages against my company or Svensson Investment."

"You're lucky," Belle told us, "that my brother's such a pushover."

"It's Christmas, Belle," Oliver said, tone mild. "Have a heart."

"I don't; it's just a block of ice."

I watched them leave.

If this were the end of some horribly misguided Hallmark film, I would run after him and declare my undying love.

But this was real life, and I was sure Oliver did not want the person who had just been trying to ruin his life to run after him and beg him to pretend everything was okay.

It was not okay.

"You're grounded and on punishment for the rest of your life," my sister told Dove. "Go upstairs and stay out of my sight."

My niece trudged up to the attic.

We all slumped on the couch.

"There's casserole in the oven, Elsa," my mother said, her hand draped over her closed eyes.

"Thanks, Aunt Sarah, I'm starving," Elsa replied.

"If you're in there, can you make me a drink? This has been a godawful holiday season, and it's not even Christmas yet."

CHAPTER 55

Oliver

"I can't believe none of you trusted me," I yelled at my friends and family.

"You honestly thought *I* was going to give you any benefit of the doubt?" Greg asked, incredulous.

"No," I shot back, "because you're an asshole. But you're my friend, Tristan, and you, Belle, are my own fucking sister."

Belle's mouth turned down. I hated that I was yelling at her. But seriously?

"I'm sorry, Oliver. This was a crisis. We had to handle it assuming the worst-case scenario," Belle explained.

"I could have just had you shot," Greg added.

"You know what?" I snapped at Belle. "You and Greg deserve each other. Both of you are coldhearted and like to throw people under the bus."

"That's not fair, Oliver."

"Life's not fair," I snapped at her.

"Oh, please," Belle said. "As soon as we found out that little girl wasn't telling the truth, I immediately pivoted to make sure that you came out on top."

"By stealing their land? Their home? Their livelihood?" I argued.

"You mean the land that you need to build your factory?" My sister raised an eyebrow.

"There's a deed restriction," Tristan said softly then cringed when Belle swiveled her furious gaze on him.

"As if you couldn't work around that once you had the land in your possession and the Wynter family under your thumb."

"I have to agree with Belle." Greg nodded. "We're both very disappointed in how you just let this deal fall through."

"It's not a deal. These are real people. Clearly, they have a lot going on. We can't just profit from other people's misery."

Greg tilted his head. "I mean we can."

"You certainly did," Belle spat at him.

"Remember how it felt to get kicked while you were down?" I said to her. "And you want to do that to someone else, especially during Christmas?"

Her mouth turned down. "Noelle was going to ruin you and drag you through the mud. My own little brother."

"She didn't," I reminded her. "I appreciate you being there for me. You're an awesome big sister, but I can handle it from here out."

"He can't," Greg said simply.

"I'll have his phone and email tapped," Crawford said.

His brother saluted him.

"Thanks," Belle said to Crawford.

"Oliver is correct, though," Greg said, smiling at her. "This is Christmas, the season of forgiveness."

My sister was unmoved. "I despise you."

My house was quiet when I returned. Max was asleep in front of the unlit fireplace. Belle had offered to come over, but I just needed the quiet and to clear my head.

"Up, up," I said to the corgi, nudging him.

He woke with a snort.

"Some guard dog you are." I picked him up and hugged him.

Max shook himself when I set him back down. I slipped his leash on and pulled off my shirt.

The cold air felt bracing against my skin as Max and I ran through the neighborhood.

Were Belle and Greg right? Should I have gone scorched-earth? Was it weak not to?

Maybe. But that wasn't the kind of man I wanted to be, the kind of man my father was.

Noelle's family didn't have a lot. They had their land, but even that they were about to lose, according to the bank. The truth had come out after only a few hours. I still had my dog and my family and my nice house. In the end, there wasn't really any harm done, though I was still a little shaken up.

If Belle had insisted it go to court, I wasn't sure if the judge would give me any real amount of money. Certainly not the land.

So to get it, we'd have to threaten and strong-arm the Wynters into signing documents.

It felt shitty to do that.

It was why I was cashing out of the hedge fund business. I'd rather invent new technology and help people than try to profit from people's misery.

Lots of high-and-mighty talk from someone who, a couple of days ago, was going to marry this girl to steal her land.

Belle's method would at least be more honest.

Because at the end of the day, I did need that land, and I would have to do something underhanded to acquire it.

Guess I was just as bad as Greg and my dad after all.

Letting Dove and Noelle off the hook was just my attempt to pretend I was a good man when I really wasn't.

CHAPTER 56

Noelle

"Mom, I don't think it's a good idea to show up at his house after we almost ruined his life."

"It wasn't me," my mom insisted as I drove the truck into town. "Dove accused him, and then you went scorched-earth. Threatening to go to the news media. Honestly, Noelle, you must have given the poor man a fright. Your father certainly hasn't recovered from the ordeal."

"Yes," I said, turning down Oliver's street, "and I think that maybe the best thing to do is to just give everyone some space. Send a nice apology note and some cookies."

"Cookies aren't going to cut it." My mom sniffed.

She had a large hamper in her lap. She'd been baking all night since Oliver and his sister had left our cramped living room.

Not only did the hamper contain Christmas cookies, but there was also an entire fruit cake that literally oozed rum—along with three casseroles, a mountain of spinach turnovers, and two rings of freshly baked cranberry bread. In the back of the truck was a ginormous Christmas wreath Gran had put together, festooned with holly berries, dried fruit, and spices.

The hamper also contained my mother's homemade cranberry cordial, which she had been saving for an emergency.

I felt sick as I parked the car in front of Oliver's house. He had barely looked at me last night. I felt like such a bitch. I shouldn't have jumped to conclusions.

"He's probably at work," I whispered to my mother as we walked up the sidewalk to his front porch. "We should just leave the basket and run."

"So Mrs. Horvat can steal it?" she replied. "Absolutely not."

She reached out and rang the doorbell while I juggled the Christmas wreath and the oversized hamper. Max barked on the other side of the door.

Please don't answer. Please don't answer.

"If he's not here, we're going to his office," my mom declared.

Footsteps approached the door.

Please let it be a maid who can take this so we can just leave.

St. Nick was not smiling down on me this winter morning.

A key turned, and the deadbolt unlocked with a dull metallic noise. Then I was standing face-to-face with Oliver.

I looked at my toes. I was wearing my scuffed-up leather ankle boots that semi-went with the Mrs. Claus outfit I was wearing. I pulled at the hole in my ripped tights.

"Can I help you?" Oliver asked in a clipped tone.

"We came to apologize," my mother said forcefully. "What happened yesterday wasn't right, and we greatly appreciate your mercy." Her voice cracked. "It's all my fault. I clearly raise terrible children."

"Noelle's not so bad," Oliver said in his deep voice. "Why don't you come inside?"

"We don't mean to trouble you."

"You can't stand out on the porch. My neighbors will have a fit," he said, a slight bit of humor in his tone.

We stepped inside the warm foyer. My mother twisted her knitted wool cap in her hands. I looked around at the decorations; Max, who was hopping up and down at my feet; and the fancy rug that probably cost a semester's worth of tuition.

"We brought you casseroles," my mother began. "Noelle, show him."

"I don't think he wants the whole spiel, Mom."

"There's a note that goes with it too," my mother said, soldiering on.

Oliver took the basket from me.

I hid my face with the wreath.

"Are those spinach puffs?"

My mother beamed. "Freshly made just for you."

"Apology accepted, then." He smiled.

"You're such a darling," my mother told him. "And you're coming for dinner tomorrow."

I grimaced. "He does not want to come back to the place of his trauma and eat dinner, Mom. We dropped off the gift basket. Can we please go? Oliver is busy."

"I was hoping to talk with you," Oliver said to me.

"I need to go take the deliveries to Ida."

"I can take them," my mom insisted.

"I won't be able to get back home," I protested from behind the wreath.

"I'll drive you," Oliver offered.

"Don't insult him by being ungrateful." My mother rapped me on the head with her hat and walked away. "Merry Christmas, Oliver. See you tomorrow for dinner. Bring an appetite!"

The door shut behind her.

"Do you want me to take that?" Oliver asked, gently lifting the wreath from my hands.

I looked up into his face and immediately started crying. "I'm so sorry. I don't know what happened. I was acting horribly."

Oliver wrapped me in his arms, squeezing me tightly against his chest.

"You had a shock."

"Why are you being so nice about this?" I stepped back and looked up into his face. "You should have sued us, ruined us. Isn't that what billionaires do?"

He tipped my chin up with two fingers.

"Dove is a child and in a difficult and chaotic situation. Just because I'm wealthy doesn't mean I'm a psychopath."

He hesitated for a moment then said, "Are you sure your niece is okay? Sometimes... kids who have been sexually assaulted can accuse people not responsible as a cry for help."

I made a disgusted noise.

"She said she did it because she wanted to be special and felt like none of us liked her or were paying enough attention to her." I looked away from him and crossed my arms.

"She's right," I continued. "My sister's a terrible mother; I'm not the greatest aunt. Dove probably spends way too much time taking care of the toddlers. I can't imagine life without Dove, but..." I blinked back tears. "Azalea was originally thinking about putting her up for adoption. Maybe if she had, Dove would have been in a better household, with her own room. She could have had wealthy parents who were able to dote on her and aunts that weren't such disasters, who could do cool things like take her to Paris instead of making her hawk spiked hot chocolate at the Christmas market. You saw how trashy and dysfunctional we all are."

"Noelle." Oliver petted my hair. "It seems like there's a lot going on at your house. But clearly your family loves each other. Look at how you all rallied around your niece when you thought someone had come after her. You can't buy that kind of love and loyalty. Trust me. I grew up in a well-off household, and there wasn't anywhere near the love that your family had."

"Thank you for being compassionate and understanding. It's not what Dove or I deserve. You're a good man, Oliver Frost," I told him seriously.

He gave me a twisted smile. "I'm not really."

"You are," I insisted. "You're the best man I've ever met. Besides my father, of course."

"Naturally."

I scuffed the toe of my boot into the carpet then stopped myself. I didn't need to dig a hole into a rug worth tens of thousands of dollars.

"I guess I need to get back to the Naughty Claus. Elsa's had to cover for me a lot the last couple of days. You don't have to drive me," I said hastily when he opened his mouth. "It's not a long walk."

"I'll drive you," he insisted.

God, why was Oliver so wonderful, and how had I ever thought he was awful? He was amazing, and I didn't deserve him.

He had been right last winter. He would never date a girl like me because he was wholesome and kind, and I was a complete grinch.

"Let me just unpack the food so it doesn't spoil," he said, heading to his kitchen, "and then I can give your mom the hamper back."

"Speaking of," I said as I ran after him, "you do not have to come to dinner tomorrow. It's going to be a shit show. My mother likes to think she can host dinner parties, but we do not have the space, and my family drinks too much."

"An excellent meal and entertainment?" Oliver said, turning and smirking at me from the doorway to the kitchen. "Sounds like my kind of dinner party."

I helped him unpack the hamper on the kitchen island. I put the cordial in one of his cupboards and found a glass storage jar with a lid for the pastries, another jar for the cookies, and a glass cake stand for the cranberry breads.

"Also, you don't have to eat these casseroles. My mom loves a casserole, but I'm sure these are not your usual high-quality fare."

"What's not to love about a casserole? It feels like home," he told me. "My mother hated them. Said only bad mothers fed them to their children. Ironic, considering she never cooked so much as a piece of toast for us."

He set one of the still-warm vintage CorningWare dishes onto the counter.

"Oh no, she didn't give you the fish casserole. I swear to God. I told her not to put that one in the hamper."

Oliver pulled out a spoon and took a bite. His eyes lit up. "This is amazing." He took another bite.

"It's got frozen peas," I said flatly.

"The fish tasted very fresh."

"Well, yeah, because we catch it from the stream on the back of the property. Mom made my brother go out in the cold last night and catch some."

"And the sauce?"

"I made that from scratch. Canned soup is expensive, and I'm not paying for something I can make myself and have it taste better." I squirmed. "It's not fancy. It's not what's served in nice restaurants."

"It's better. This is the type of food your grandmother makes." He took another bite. "So, you know how to cook all of this?"

I swept an arm over the food. "You can't make all this food if you're just one person. Mom and I were up all night."

He walked around the counter and wrapped me in his arms.

"Thank you."

"You literally don't have to thank me for anything. I should be offering to suck your dick after you didn't bring the hammer down on us. Gran was actually going to show up and do it, but my mom banned her from coming near your house. You're welcome."

Oliver's mouth twitched with a smile. He leaned in and brushed my lips with his.

"I don't know if I want you on your knees in front of me giving me a blow job." He nipped my bottom lip then kissed me harder. "I think I'd rather eat out your pussy while you do it. If you're offering."

"Good to know you can't stop thinking about how I was sitting on your face."

"I told you I love Christmas; I just want to come down your chimney."

CHAPTER 57

Oliver

As soon as I set Noelle on the bed, I pulled off my shirt while she grabbed the metal of my belt and pulled at it. I kicked off my slacks and shoes then undid the ribbons of her sexy Christmas costume, unwrapping her like a present.

I kissed her, kneading her breasts, running my thumb over her nipples. Before I could go down on her, her hands were at the bulges under my boxer-briefs. She then snatched them down, letting my cock pop out in front of her and filling her eyes with desire.

She wrapped her hand around my cock and pulled me forward, her touch sending shocks down the length. She jerked me up and down a bit, pumping it in her fist, before bringing it toward her lips. Once again, she coyly kissed my cock and teased it with a bit of tongue. She then rolled a lick all the way down my length, teasing my balls with a few tongue lashes and getting them roaring for what she could possibly be up to next.

Back up the length, her hands still wrapped softly around my hard cock as she ran her pink tongue on it. Then she opened wide for me and inched down my cock, bit by bit, wholly consuming me.

Deep inside her mouth, her tongue continued its seductive dance all over my length. I groaned, my hand drifting down, caressing her hair, her face, wordlessly encouraging her to keep going.

And she went hard. Deep. She challenged herself with my length, and I was most definitely there for it. Up and down, she eagerly took me, nearly choking in her effort to please me.

It was so damn sexy. And yet? I wanted more than her mouth. I wanted all of her.

I pulled her head back. Her mouth made a little O when she popped off my cock.

"Am I that bad?"

"Hardly. Lie back."

She nodded along, obeying my command. Confused but intrigued, she lay back on the bedspread. I climbed up on the bed beside her but not in the way she expected.

I hovered over her, my cock brushing her still-wet mouth while I brought my face to her panties. I mouthed her through the soaking wet fabric then promptly yanked it down her legs. I went right for her as soon as I could. I sucked on her clit, teasing her pussy.

She grabbed hold of my still-hard cock, jerking me, and took me deep into her mouth again, holding me tight, jerking me sensually. I cursed then returned to her clit, feeling her moans vibrate through me every time I licked her.

She was close. When I twirled my tongue around her clit, she was mine. Her entire body trembled beneath me, against me. Even in our unusual position, I held her close and savored her experience. My cock still throbbed with anticipation.

"Just give me a moment, then I'll take care of you," she said, breathless.

I sat up a moment, taking in her beautiful naked form on my bed, the swell of her breasts against her chest.

"What I really want is your pussy tight around my cock," I said.

She squealed as I flipped her over on the bed. I fished out a condom and rolled it on.

I rubbed two fingers in her soaking wet pussy. She moaned and bucked her hips back against me.

I helped her up to all fours, digging my fingers in her ass. I wanted her. Needed her. I positioned myself then buried my cock in her hot, tight pussy, savoring her sudden moan. Hands on her hips, I bucked into her, starting to fuck her good and hard, my balls slapping against her ass. Her tits swung on the bed as I took her, her loud cries echoing around the room.

I took her harder and faster, wanting nothing more than to reduce her to a quivering orgasmic mess.

Hands tightly on her hips, I felt her thighs tremble as she came, her entire body clenching my cock. She called out my name as she came. I continued to fuck her, her pleading gasps spurring me on until I came inside her.

"Shit." She collapsed in a heap on the bed. "You're so good at that. Why are you so good at everything?"

She rolled on her side, and I trailed my fingers over her huge breasts, fondling her nipples with my fingers. Every so often, my hand would dip down and caress the V where the slit of her pussy started.

I was going to have her again later but not right now.

I pulled out the remote and turned on the TV.

"You know what the best part of Christmas is?" I pulled her to half lie on my chest.

"I'm not watching a Christmas movie." She trailed her candy-cane-striped nails down my bare chest.

"Get in the holiday spirit, Noelle," I said as Jim Carrey, covered in green makeup, paraded around on the screen as the Grinch.

Her hand crept lower. She tugged on my cock.

"Really? The best part of Christmas is movies?"

I hissed as she ran her thumbnail over the slit.

I flipped her over and kissed her hard against the pillow, and I grabbed a condom out of the nightstand.

"I'm not letting you fuck me while the fucking Whos are dancing around on TV," she said against my mouth.

"Of course you are." On screen, the Whos cheered.

Her legs opened for me and curled around me as I slid into her, her low moan vibrating through my jaw. I wrapped my arms around her and decided to mix it up. Rather than taking her madly, I wanted to savor it. Every little movement between us I enjoyed to the fullest, smiling as I felt her pussy shudder around me.

My kisses rained down her body, and I let my hand explore her, memorizing every curve. I dipped my head and sucked on her breast, running my tongue over her pebble-hard nipple. She was everything I ever wanted in a woman.

She arched up against me, sensual, every time I slid into her, drawing out the pleasure, slow and deep.

I ran my hand down lower between us, toward her dripping wet slit. I began to caress her clit with every thrust, and she let out a deep-throated moan.

We were both close. I grabbed her hips, angling her to give her deep, hard thrusts. Then she was coming around me. After two more quick thrusts, I came with her.

I planted one last kiss on her lips before collapsing next to her, still holding her tight in my arms. I nuzzled her neck as she panted. A part of me felt like I was falling for her.

She's going to hate you when she figures out you took her land.

Or not. Belle was right. I could use the fact that I was a gentleman about her niece's accusations to keep Noelle from pitching a fit.

But I would lose this—I would lose her soft, warm body pressed against mine, the little noises she made, the way she rolled her eyes and bit her bottom lip to keep from laughing when I teased her about not liking Christmas.

My company was worth the sacrifice, though, wasn't it?

CHAPTER 58

Oliver

"Mom, this is insane."

"Oliver is our guest of honor, Noelle," my mom reprimanded me as my brother and I carried the couch into the cramped bedroom she shared with my father.

The small cottage did not have a dining room. It had a small galley kitchen, a living room and two bedrooms and a bathroom downstairs, and the small attic bedroom upstairs.

Normally, we all ate dinner at the large table outside, except in the coldest months, when we sat on the couches and chairs in the living room. However, my mom insisted that we have a proper dining experience for Oliver, and that meant clearing the living room.

"My god, it's filthy in here." My mother handed Azalea a broom and a mop. "Where did this hole in the floor come from?"

"Probably Azalea's dog," my brother remarked. "Don't all the worst things come from her?"

"Your daughter is drawing all over the wall," Azalea screamed at him.

"You know," I interrupted, "I tried to talk Oliver out of coming for dinner."

"Noelle, how could you?" my mother scolded.

"He insisted on coming because he thinks we're quaint and loving. But we have to step it up. He's going to take one look at this disaster and run away screaming."

"I already have my outfit picked out and topics of conversation ready," Gran promised. *The Great Christmas Bake Off* was blaring on the small TV in the corner of the room. "Your butter's burning," she yelled at the TV.

The front door opened, and my dad came in, dragging a freshly cut Christmas tree.

"Dad, we already have a tree."

"I was looking at Pinterest," he said enthusiastically, "and some dining rooms have two trees. You know, for symmetry."

I pointed at the cased opening that led to the kitchen. It had a jagged piece of trim missing and was covered by a ratty stained curtain. "This," I said, "is not the type of space that can handle two Christmas trees. Besides, it will clash with the hole in the floor, the fireplace that's belching smoke, and the smoke stains on the ceiling."

"That's why your mom told you to paint the ceiling earlier this year," Jimmy reminded Dad.

"You know how to use a paintbrush," I told my brother.

"It's too late to paint now," he protested.

"We'll cover it up with some Christmas decorations," my dad declared. "Sarah, where are all those Christmas streamers?"

"You're getting sap in my hair," my sister yelled at my dad when he shoved past her with the tree.

"James," my mother said, poking her head out of the kitchen, "what in God's name? You take that back outside."

"I just cut it down," he protested. "Dove, why don't you help me decorate the tree. Can you help Gran find the rest of the Christmas decorations we need to make this a nice dinner for Oliver?"

"I can't come to the dinner," she cried from the stairs. "I'm staying in the attic."

"You can't just cause all this commotion then not even attend the apology dinner," Azalea hissed at her, grabbing her by the back of her shirt and hauling her downstairs.

"Nothing we do is going to make this in any way a nice dinner." Dove crossed her arms.

"Bathroom's free," Elsa called, parading out in an eighties holiday dress.

"Go get dressed," my mother coaxed Dove. "Your outfit is laid out on my bed."

"What in the world are you wearing?" I asked Elsa. She corralled one of the toddlers, who were wandering around yelling nonsensically and pointing at the TV, to keep her from roaming out the front door.

"We all need to wear matching outfits," my mom said as I picked up a footstool and carried it into her bedroom.

"I modified our old outfits from our family Christmas photo a few years ago." She followed me into the bedroom and waved a hand over the dresses she had painstakingly sewn.

That Christmas photo was taken back when I was in high school and dieting heavily so that I could blend in with the other svelte Harvard girls.

"I guess it's a small blessing that you and Oliver are done, since his dick is going to shrivel up and die when he sees you in this dress," Elsa whispered to me as she helped me drag the coffee table outside. Because of course the first thing someone coming up onto our front porch wanted to be greeted with was a random coffee table. That definitely said classy.

My cousin tugged at her black velvet dress with the oversized puffed green taffeta sleeves and big bows.

"He sort of slept with me last night."

"He still wants to sleep with you after..." She waved in my family's general direction. "All that?"

"I don't know why?" I whispered.

"Maybe you made a bigger impression last year than you thought."

"He still doesn't remember me, though."

"At this point, does it matter? You're having a holiday hookup, and he's not suing you. Shoot, if you play your cards right, he might even give you a loaded-up gift card for Christmas."

"What if I don't just want a gift card?" I said in a small voice.

"Are you expecting an engagement ring?" Elsa laughed at her own joke. "Wait." She grabbed my shoulders. "You're not serious, are you?"

"No, of course not," I promised her. "I don't love him."

"Or even like him," Elsa added.

I squirmed. "I mean, I kind of like him."

"Girl..."

"He's a good man," I protested.

"Is he?" Elsa made a face. "For the past year, all we've talked about is how terrible Oliver is, how Oliver humiliated you, how Oliver ruined your life. Now you got a few good orgasms in, and suddenly, he's Mr. Perfect Boyfriend?"

I twisted my bracelet.

"It's just—he didn't sue us after what Dove did," I said lamely. How could I express how he made me feel like the best version of myself, that he looked at me like I was important and cared about me? How I felt safe and, for once in my life, relaxed, in his arms?

"So give him a blow job. If you're really feeling grateful, let him in the back door a couple of times and send him on his way. Don't suddenly hand your heart over to him."

"What if I was wrong? What if it was all a misunderstanding? What if I wasn't crazy to think that there was some deeper connection between us, that he did really care for me?"

"Or maybe," Elsa countered, "like last time, he's just using you for sex, and he's going to throw you away and stomp your heart into pieces. You don't have time to fall in love with him. You have to graduate. Remember?"

"I'm super close. I have my paper done, and my presentation for the capstone committee is ready to go," I swore. "I'm totally graduating. No one, not even Oliver, is going to prevent that."

I thought about Elsa's warning as I showered with the lukewarm water.

The bathroom was a far cry from Oliver's.

I let my mind wander to what it would be like if he and I were actually a couple, if we were actually married. Every day would be like Christmas. I would have a happy ever after. He liked my parents. Maybe he would build them a new house.

So you just want him for what he can provide for you, not for him as a person.

Great. You're just as bad as Azalea.

I blow-dried my hair in the upstairs attic bedroom, tipping my head upside down and trying to dry my thick tangled curls. Oliver would be here soon. I shouldn't have even bothered to wash my hair. It was never going to dry.

Then I stuffed myself into the dress.

Fortunately, the velvet was stretchy, and I just barely managed to zip it up. Through the small attic window, the snow was falling. I hoped it put a fresh blanket over the junk that was piled haphazardly in the front yard.

Oliver's car was coming down the drive. Crap.

"He's here," I yelled to my family as I pounded down the narrow attic stairs. The smoke alarm was blaring.

"Stall him," my mother cried, rushing out of the kitchen. "This place is a pigsty!"

The table had been brought in from outside, a Christmas tree propped against it. Gran was deep in the whiskey and slurring at *The Great Christmas Bake Off* on the TV while my brother was on a stool, trying to paint the smoke stains on the ceiling.

"This dinner is going to be a disaster."

CHAPTER 59

Noelle

Noelle seemed slightly out of breath when she ran outside, tripping on something buried underneath the snow.

Before she could crash-land into a snow drift, I caught her and kissed her.

"Merry Christmas." I swung her up onto her feet. "For a self-proclaimed grinch, you look very festive." With my finger, I tapped the bell on the big bow tied around her head, making it jingle merrily.

She scrunched up her nose. I kissed the tip of it.

"My mother has been running on coffee and Christmas carols for the past two days. I don't dare cross her. I just decided to accept my fate of eighties purgatory."

I traced her tits, the velvet stretching over them enticingly, their round swell outlined against the thin velvet. I thumbed her nipples through the fabric.

"I would absolutely fuck you in that dress."

She shivered under my touch.

Actually, I wanted to fuck her right now in that dress, but I forced myself to have some self-control.

"Shall we go in?"

Noelle made a face. "My mom is still trying to finish dinner. I'm supposed to be out here, distracting you. She'll kill me if I let you inside to see the current state of the living room."

"Distraction, huh?"

"Don't get any ideas." She stuck her tongue out at me. After she skipped and turned around to face me, she laced her fingers in mine.

"This isn't some fancy Regency period estate with adorable little cottages dotted around the woods where we can have a quickie. I'm not doing it in the woodshed. There are spiders, and the old depot on the rail line to the east is infested with bats. This used to be a big logging property," she explained, "so they had a spur line. It's mostly overgrown now."

She slipped and slid through the snow toward the grove of trees that came right up to the cottage.

"Do you need me to help shovel the drive off?"

"It's supposed to be my brother's job. We had a snow blower, but it broke, and my dad has been trying to fix it but..." She rolled her eyes and gestured to several snow-covered objects in the yard. "When we get a little more snow, my mom will make me help her turn all the random pieces of junk into snowmen."

There were a few snow flurries in the air, but the wind was still when we walked among the trees.

"You're beautiful," I said honestly.

She laughed self-consciously. "Not in this dress."

I pulled her to me, kissed her hard, and caressed her curves under the thin velvet.

"Yes," I said, voice dropping an octave, "in this dress."

The temptation of seeing her in this dress had been too much, and I didn't think I had it in me to wait until I got home. I wrapped my arms around her, stealing a kiss. I ran my hand down her body, shifting the fabric away from her tit, letting it fall free into the chilly air.

She gasped in the cold, her nipple hard and round.

With her breast exposed, I couldn't help but tease that nipple in my fingers and bring it to my mouth. I suckled it and heard her gasp.

I kissed her hard then pulled a condom out of my wallet.

Her eyes bugged out.

"You can't be serious. Out here?"

"No one can see us. Besides, your mom said you were supposed to distract me."

She licked her lips as I undid my slacks, bringing out my already hard length through my boxer briefs.

I kissed her hard again, our tongues tangling. "Tell me how much you want my cock," I murmured against her mouth. I pushed my hand up under her skirt to feel the wet heat between her legs.

She bit her lip then whispered, "I want you."

I turned her around in one quick motion, rolled the stretchy black fabric up over her hips, and pushed her panties to the side to expose her pussy. I gripped her wrists, pulling her arms back, and thrust into her, making her groan with pleasure. She arched and strained against me as I started to fuck her, jackhammering into her hot, wet pussy.

Noelle ground against my cock, half bent over, as I held onto her. She whimpered and moaned, her ass jiggling so seductively as I took her. I rammed her hard, fast. Needing to make her come.

Her breath came out in high-pitched gasps, then she was shuddering and moaning as she came. Her pussy tightened around my cock and I came hard.

Noelle stumbled a little when I righted her. She half collapsed against my chest. Her lips were flush and plump from the exertion. I leaned in and kissed her heavily. She melted into me.

"Do you need my coat?" I offered.

"I need another shower. Gosh." She fanned herself and flapped the dress. "I'm so sweaty."

"I like you hot and sweaty," I said, pulling her to me for another hard kiss.

"We can skip the dinner," she whispered to me. "Go back to your place. I can give you my best Christmas stripper elf impression."

"How does that differ from a normal stripper?"

"The pole is candy striped."

I draped my arm around her shoulder, tucking her next to me as we walked through the woods. The property was perfect for building my factory.

Sure, in the distance was an old-growth forest I didn't want to touch, but in this area, where Noelle's house was located, were only the dilapidated cottage and these Christmas trees. This was the area I would clear-cut so that we didn't take down any of the high-value hardwoods. I would leave a small patch that her father could cut down to sell at the Christmas tree stand, just as I'd leave any fruit trees.

I felt slightly guilty that right after having sex with her, I was secretly plotting to take her land.

She's going to lose it either way, I tried to tell myself. At least now she and her family could still run their businesses.

Or I could... not buy her land. I could just pay it off for her and use the expo site. Sure, it would put us a few years behind, but we could use that time to hire people, do training, and design the facility. Then I could have my business and Noelle.

It was doubtful the Svenssons or my sister would approve of that plan.

Just enjoy today. You'll figure something out.

I had to.

Because I didn't want to lose Noelle.

CHAPTER 60

I poked my head in the front door.

"Is everyone decent?" I asked.

I felt terrible.

Actually, no, I felt great. Who knew sex outside could be so invigorating? But I felt bad that I'd had to tramp Oliver around the Christmas tree farm.

If my family had a real house, I could have entertained him in the drawing room while the dining room was being prepared for dinner.

I could have made him a fancy drink and offered to take his cloak. We would have sat in front of a fire that didn't belch smoke.

"It's just an old nest or something that fell off a tree down the chimney," my dad assured me before I could complain. "It will clear itself out soon. We have a window open."

Dove was standing by the open window, fanning an apron at the fireplace.

I inwardly cringed. I wish I didn't like Oliver so much. Then it might be easier to swallow that this would not be a fancy dinner like he was used to.

The table was set with mismatched Christmas-themed plates my mother had collected over the years either from thrift stores or because my siblings or I had given them to her. A tureen of clam chowder sat steaming in the center of the table, surrounded by thick slices of brown bread on a platter with a pattern of laughing elves. It smelled amazing, and after all my physical exertion, all I wanted to do was make myself a bowl and curl up on the couch in my pajamas.

But I needed to keep it together for this family dinner that no one needed or asked for.

"We're ready," my mother sang.

"Wait, Noelle," she cried as I was opening the door to let Oliver in. "We have to give him the grand welcome. Oliver, dear," she called, "Noelle's going to come inside, and then you can knock on the door."

My eye twitched. "Mom, this is insane."

"Just go with it," my dad begged. He, too, was wearing a velvet outfit. It was a onesie, decorated with a green belt made from the same taffeta.

If it wouldn't leave us all homeless, I would have prayed to St. Nick that the fireplace finally gave up the ghost and sent this whole dinner party up in flames.

I shut the door behind me and slunk over to stand in the line of my family. The room was too small to contain the table, the Christmas trees, and all the random decorations. We were crammed in a line behind the narrow space between the table and the wall.

With all of us in matching outfits, even the cat, we were giving off some definite Christmas-cult vibes.

Oliver knocked hesitantly on the door.

We waited a beat.

When the door didn't open, I asked finally, "Is someone going to let him in?"

"Shoot. Noelle, he's your boyfriend. Go let him in." Gran nudged me.

Oliver peeked through the window.

I tried to wave, but he didn't see me.

Because my family was blocking my exit, I crouched down on my hands and knees and crawled under the table, banging my head on the underside.

"Ow." I stood up, rubbing my head, only to see Oliver giving me a confused look through the window. My face turned hot.

When I was in college, starting to finally wonder if now was my time to find the financially secure, well-educated husband of my dreams, what held me back from fully pursuing my goal was that eventually, he would have to meet my family.

I had known it would be awkward, that there would be cultural differences, and that my family would embarrass me. The reality far exceeded even my worst nightmare.

"Welcome to our home, Oliver," my family chorused when I opened the door, *again*, to welcome him inside.

He leaned in to kiss me.

It was too late to stop him.

"You're... you..." My dad's mouth opened and closed.

"Get with the program, James," Gran exploded. "Why do you think he didn't have Dove shipped off to the gulag? Behold the power of the pussy!"

I wanted to die.

Dove cringed. My sister elbowed her.

Dove crept over to Oliver and handed him a sealed envelope. "I just want to apologize," she said in a small voice. She handed him a little gift bag, then she shuffled behind me as Oliver pulled back the tissue paper.

He held up a small, hand-painted Christmas ornament.

"We made them in class," Dove said.

"You're giving him a Christmas ornament?" Azalea shrieked at her. "I told you to give him something nice."

"I love Christmas ornaments," Oliver assured her. "I'm going to put this on my Christmas tree." He held out a large bottle of very expensive whiskey in my parents' general direction. My family was still shoved awkwardly behind the table.

I took the bottle and stashed it under one of the Christmas trees. "You seriously didn't have to."

"To welcome you into our home, Oliver," my dad began, "we'd like to offer a song."

"No," I said firmly, "we would not."

My family warbled through "O Tannenbaum" with lots of heart but not a lot of technique.

"Can we please eat before the food gets cold?" I yelled over the singing.

I couldn't even look at Oliver. We were only five minutes into the dinner party, and it was already a shit show.

"The man is starving," Gran said to my mother. "Let's do the singing later."

Oliver was shoved into a chair at the place of honor at the head of the table.

My family all stared at him with wide, toothy grins on their faces, even the kids.

What in the...

"Would you do the honors?" my father asked Oliver.

I snorted.

My mother pinched my arm.

We were not a family that said grace. We all just dug in and stuffed our faces as soon as the food arrived like heathens. But now my parents were trying to pretend like we were civilized.

"As we gather around the table during this busy time of year," Oliver began, bowing his head, "we'd like to give thanks for the things that matter. Family, friends, and good food."

"Amen." Gran crossed herself, even though my family had been run out of Europe a few centuries ago for being drunkards and heretics and couldn't even spell *Catholic*. "Short and sweet, God bless him. Someone give this man a drink."

"I will." I was closest to the kitchen. Also, I would combust with the pressure of trying to force my family to be normal by sheer force of will.

"Do you want red or white?" Gran asked Oliver.

I thought we weren't doing wine. My father had rolled in a keg of hard apple cider earlier that afternoon.

"Red is fine," Oliver said.

"Noelle," Gran called loudly, even though she was like five feet away from me in the dining room-slash-living room. "The red food coloring is with the baking supplies."

I sucked in a breath. "I'm not putting red food coloring into his apple cider," I shrieked at Gran as I poured the cider.

I had worked in food service all through high school. I could put a tray of drinks together like no one's business.

Soon, I came out of the kitchen laden with trays of the mugs of apple cider.

"I want red," Gran complained as I set down the tankards.

"Yeah, me too," my brother said. "It makes me feel like I'm drinking the blood of my enemies."

My mother gave him a death glare, and my brother shut his mouth and accepted his mug of hard cider.

My mother had won the tankards in a Christmas raffle when I was in elementary school, and they were her prized possessions. They were handmade out of pewter with individualized scenes from various Christmas stories on each mug.

"Make sure Oliver has the *Christmas Carol* mug," my mother said.

I slid it across the table to him. I had the Grinch mug. The Dr. Seuss character smiled evilly at me as I took a swig of the alcoholic drink. I needed it.

"I hope you like clam chowder."

"If it's anywhere near as good as your fish casserole, Mrs. Wynter, I'm sure I'll love it."

My mother beamed at Oliver as she dished him up a heaping bowl of clam chowder and sprinkled some chives, cheddar cheese, and bacon bits on top.

She set the bowl carefully in front of him and balanced a slice of bread on the side. Then she dished him up a bowl of salad.

Crap. We didn't have any bread plates, butter knives, or salad forks. Shoot, there was only one set of forks and spoons. We didn't even have soup spoons.

I was hot and itchy under the velvet dress. Before going to Harvard, I had spent days at the library, reading old etiquette books and rehearsing with Elsa so I didn't embarrass myself. Not that I had even been invited to a fancy dinner my entire time at Harvard, but it never hurt to be prepared.

Oliver ate his soup just like the manners books dictated.

He elegantly brought the soup up to his mouth as opposed to hunching over his bowl and shoveling his soup in his mouth, alternating with bread and spoon in each hand like my father, or picking up the entire bowl and pouring it in his mouth like my brother.

I tried to eat my soup like Oliver did and only succeeded in spilling half of it in my lap.

"This is the best clam chowder I've ever eaten," Oliver complimented my mother.

"Noelle did the hard part," my mother trilled, "cleaning and shucking all those clams. You have to have them fresh. I cannot stand canned clams, and they're so expensive."

"Fuck!" The cat sank her claws into my leg, trying to get a lick of the cream and the clam that was in my lap, and I jumped up and banged my knee on the table.

"Noelle, behave yourself." Now my mother turned her death glare in my direction.

"This is the first time Noelle has brought a man over for dinner," Gran said as she mopped up the last of her soup with a thick piece of brown bread. "This is the first time she's brought anyone over for dinner, come to think of it."

"Noelle didn't have any friends in school." My sister smirked. "She wasn't popular."

"Maybe you could ask Oliver for a job, Azalea," my father suggested mildly.

"Or if he has any single brothers," Gran added.

"Like they're going to want Dove for a stepdaughter," my brother joked.

I cringed.

Dove looked upset. "I said I was sorry."

"She shouldn't be eating any dinner; she should have bread and water," Azalea snapped.

"This bread is actually homemade," my mother interjected. "Brown bread is a New England staple."

"He's from Connecticut," I said to my mom.

"I knew a guy from Connecticut," my dad said. He was on his second mug of ale, which did not help the fact that my dad was like me and easily flustered in high-stakes situations. "He went to jail for smuggling a baby moose onto an airplane."

My spoon clattered in my empty bowl as I struggled not to laugh.

My mother's eyes were twitching.

I knew that her lifelong dream was to be one of those perfect Instagram moms who lived in an impeccably decorated house, served restaurant-quality food, and had children that made all her friends envious. This was her moment, and she would rain hell down on anyone who ruined her dinner party.

"Sorry, Sarah," my father mumbled into his ale.

"On to the next course," my mother chirped.

"Another course?" Oliver seemed a little surprised.

"We're not as trashy as our first impressions might have led you to believe," Gran cackled, whacking him on the back.

My mother came back out of the kitchen, carrying an enormous turkey pot pie covered in a flakey golden crust. My mouth watered, even though I'd just eaten a bowl of chowder.

The turkey pot pie was decorated with a hand-cut Christmas scene made from the extra pie dough. Dove followed her, carrying a platter of fried potato croquettes. Elsa snapped pictures, and we all oohed and aahed.

"This is beautiful, Mrs. Wynter," Oliver told her.

"Please call me Sarah. James's mom is Mrs. Wynter."

"Fat lot of good that ever got me," Gran said, adding rum to her apple cider.

"Noelle was telling me you were thinking about opening your own restaurant and lodge," Oliver said to my mom.

"I was thinking more of a bistro," my mom preened as she sat down. "But then I had all these children."

"And a useless husband," Gran added and hiccupped into her cup.

My dad cringed. Gran patted him on the arm.

Oliver looked a little alarmed.

"My son is handsome and sweet but doesn't offer a lot in the financial department, I'm afraid. Just like his father, that rat-faced bastard. Did you know I saw him all over the Moi Cheaters app, out with Mrs. Russo? Her husband's half-dead. She keeps him propped up alive in her guest room. She's collecting his pension payments."

"Have some chicken pot pie," I said, scooping up a generous helping onto Oliver's plate.

"Turkey," my mom corrected.

"Mom," I hissed. "We're trying to make a good impression."

"I can't just lie," she said through gritted teeth while Oliver watched the whole exchange. "What if he has an allergy? Did you ask him if he has any allergies?"

"I don't have any food allergies, Mrs. Wynter, I mean, Sarah."

She beamed and dished him up more of the turkey pot pie.

This pot pie was one of my favorite meals. It had a thick, flakey pastry crust and was filled with a rich creamy sauce, dotted with chunks of carrots, potatoes, bright green peas, and caramelized onions.

"The turkey is a heritage bird," my mother said as Oliver took a generous bite of the dish, still with that same elegant motion. "Bought a few big ones on sale after Thanksgiving. Noelle made the sauce. No need to buy that in the store. She's really good at making creamy white sauces."

Azalea and my father started snickering.

"Grow up," my mother snapped at them.

I speared one of the croquettes.

"What do you do for work, Oliver?" my mother asked politely. "Besides cleaning up our family's messes."

He seemed to freeze for a moment then dabbed his mouth with his napkin. At least it was a cloth napkin, embroidered with a poinsettia.

"I have a hedge fund," he said smoothly. "And I'm looking to build a microprocessor factory."

"Too bad you didn't stick with the hedge fund. It sounds more glamorous than being out here in the country."

"Noelle was trying to go work for a hedge fund after she graduated and she was acting all high-and-mighty," Azalea said, "like she was too good for this town and was going to live it up in Manhattan."

I threw a croquette at her. I didn't need my sister to spill the beans to Oliver that I was a college dropout. He would get up and walk out of here.

"Stop throwing your food." My mother's voice was dangerous.

"Where are you putting the factory?" my dad asked, dishing up more of the turkey pot pie.

"We're not sure yet," Oliver said, his deep voice sophisticated and reassuring.

"You should put it in Dorothy's yard," Azalea said with a smirk.

"I wish." Mom stabbed at her own pot pie. My mother and I followed Dorothy and her perfect home and life on Instagram. She would never have been caught dead throwing a dinner party like this one.

"I'm afraid we'll need a bit more land than that," Oliver said, chuckling.

"There's the old county expo site," my mother suggested, "or the next town over where the Bauer factory is. James used to work there until they closed."

"They tore up the rail line and sold it off," my father said. "Oliver probably wants a rail line."

"I don't think Oliver wants to talk business," Gran insisted. "Get the man another drink."

She tipped more rum into her apple cider.

"None for me, thanks," Oliver said when she held up the bottle.

I shuffled around a Christmas tree to get him more cider. My dad made it strong, and I was feeling pretty warm and a little bit woozy.

My family was starting to relax around Oliver. Well, everyone except for my mom, who was still in hostess mode and not amused that the rest of the family was using their thumbs to scoop the last of their turkey pot pie onto their forks.

My brother was laughing as Oliver regaled them with the tale of the latest town hall meeting.

"Did you ever get your bra back from Mrs. Horvat?" Azalea asked.

"She probably turned it over to the police department," my dad said, shaking his head.

"The police are involved?" My mother sounded appalled.

"It's the authoritarian government in this town." Gran slammed her tankard on the table.

"Just because they wrote you a ticket for riding a lawnmower drunk through the Christmas market that one year doesn't make them authoritarian," my mother told Gran.

"Why would I live in a small town if I couldn't ride a lawnmower to the store?"

"You stole that lawnmower, Mom," my dad said to her, still snickering.

"You think Dot's husband was ever going to use that thing again? His prostate's the size of a cantaloupe, and he can't walk five feet without having to pee."

Elsa offered my mother the rum bottle under the table, and she took a swig.

"Why was your undergarment even in Oliver's yard in the first place?" my mother demanded.

Oliver looked at me expectantly.

I was not going to admit to my mother that I'd been breaking and entering down his chimney. She would throw me out, which would not work for me because she had made apple pie, and I was not missing out on that.

"Just a Christmas miracle. Who wants dessert?"

The apple pie, which my mother had baked in the big cast-iron skillet that had been in her family since the late 1800s, was decorated like a Christmas wreath.

"Where's the cheddar cheese?" my brother complained when my mom set her masterpiece on the table.

"We're trying to have a fancy dinner," she said.

"Cheddar, cheddar!"

Even I started chanting.

Oliver looked extremely confused.

"Oh, sweet winter child," I said as I went and retrieved the cheese. "This is the greatest food combination in the history of New York." I plunked the block of extra-sharp cheddar on the table.

My mom served Oliver a huge slice of apple pie.

I picked up the cheese cleaver, a Christmas present my dad had made for my mom out of an old plow blade.

Oliver jumped at the noise.

I slapped a hunk of cheese on his plate. "My dad likes his melted on the pie, but I like mine cold on the side."

"I have never heard of this."

"It's the only way to eat apple pie," my brother assured him. "And you have to melt it because that's the traditional way."

"That makes the crust soggy," I argued. "Mom and I know what's up. You don't ruin an apple pie crust like that."

Oliver was still politely inspecting his hunk of cheddar.

Maybe we should have skipped the cheese.

My family waited with bated breath as Oliver bit into the apple pie then the wedge of cheese.

"This is surprisingly good," he said after chewing (with his mouth closed. Take note, Jimmy).

I breathed a sigh of relief, and the evening progressed.

Oliver didn't seem disgusted or annoyed by my family's antics. He wasn't even just humoring my father's drunken ramble about proper forest management. He was asking engaging questions.

He literally is the perfect boyfriend.

I felt starry-eyed as I looked at him. Maybe this would be the perfect Christmas after all.

"Game time," Gran hollered, topping up everyone's glasses.

"Oliver doesn't want to play a board game," I protested, and I lowered my voice. "Where are we even going to play it?"

"In the living room," Gran slurred.

"It's currently packed up in the bedroom."

"We can just play at the table," Dove suggested.

"Or we could just call it a night."

My family wasn't the greatest at board games. For one, it took half an hour to finish arguing over the rules, especially since people either didn't want to read them or started making up their own.

Out came a plate of jam-filled butter sandwich cookies. The tops of the cookies had a Christmas tree cut out of them so that you could see the homemade jam underneath.

My father set the tattered old box on the table. "Oliver, have you ever played Santa's Workshop?"

"Can't say that I have."

"Why don't we play something normal?" I said desperately. "Like Clue or Life?"

"That's not the Christmas spirit," my dad argued.

"Santa's Workshop is like Settlers of Catan except with Christmas presents, and the elves mine coal and sex toys for all the little boys and girls." Gran hiccupped.

My mom shot her a dirty look.

"Let's get lit!" Gran hollered, pouring everyone a generous glass of her homemade moonshine.

I was not drunk enough to manage this board game.

"You're laying them out wrong," my brother complained to my sister. "You're supposed to do it randomly."

I took another sip of my whiskey then decided, *Actually, I think I'm going to slow down.*

Gran was pounding the moonshine back.

My brother picked up the die to roll it.

"He's cheating," Azalea complained to my mother.

"No I'm not."

Mom was pinching the bridge of her nose. She drained her glass.

I switched our glasses, since it looked like she needed the whiskey more than I did.

My younger nieces started crying.

My siblings were squabbling, ignoring their respective children.

"You can't put all the coal mines in one spot," my brother complained.

"This is how the cards came out randomly." Azalea bared her teeth.

"Are there directions for this game?" Oliver asked.

"Yes," my dad said loudly, "but we lost them. However, I remember them perfectly."

"He doesn't. Can't we just look online?" I asked, experiencing serious déjà vu of family Christmas game nights of Christmases past.

"I think we all need another round," Gran said, hauling herself up from the table and staggering to the makeshift liquor cabinet that was hung on the wall, another of my father's woodworking projects.

My father was a woodworker with more heart than skills, and as soon as Gran opened the narrow cupboard, the door fell off.

"I told you to fix that, James," my mother practically shrieked.

"No one panic," Gran said loudly as she tried to jamb the door back on the cupboard.

"Gran," I said, hurrying over, "let me..."

The cat, who had been sitting in the Christmas tree, surveying the dinner, chose to leap to the cabinet.

We gasped. The cabinet shuddered but held.

I breathed a sigh of relief.

"My son sure does know how to make 'em right." Gran slapped the side of the cabinet for emphasis.

The cabinet gave up the ghost and pitched forward.

"Man down," Gran cried as I lunged, trying to catch all the falling bottles.

"Oof." I lay on the floor, whiskey soaking into my hair.

"We only lost one," Gran said cheerfully, peering down on me. "Fortunately, you were blessed with those big honkers."

I was feeling a little woozy, and my boobs hurt from catching the falling bottles.

I stood up, nausea rolling over me, then I doubled over and puked behind the Christmas tree.

My mother stood up and slammed her hands on the table.

"*You all ruined my lovely dinner. I hope you're happy.*"

CHAPTER 61

Oliver

Noelle was half draped on me as we stood on the front porch.

"You think that was bad?" She hiccupped. Her grandmother had declared that more cider was all the cure Noelle needed and given her a refilled tankard and an ice pack for her ribs.

Sarah had huffed and yelled at her family while packing me an elaborate basket of leftovers.

The sconce was out on the front porch of the small cottage. The only light came from the stars, a brilliant strip across the night sky, glimmering through the trees.

"It's beautiful out here," I said to her.

"You're beautiful," she slurred and gave me a warm smile.

I couldn't help but lean in and kiss her softly on the mouth.

"I have to tell you a secret," she said in a stage whisper.

"Oh yeah?"

"I'm in love with you." She took a swig of her tankard. "I think I always have been, ever since I first saw you. But you can't tell anyone else. Elsa would kill me and then make me go through a whole green-juice-and-sage-smoke cleanse."

"Elsa doesn't like me?" I whispered back, still a little shocked Noelle had said she was in love with me.

"She agrees that you're incredibly hot, but she thinks you're bad news, like the fruitcake your crazy neighbor brings over the day after Christmas that's been marinating in her root cellar since last Halloween."

Noelle giggled at the horror on my face.

"They leave those things out all year?"

"That's the British way to do it," she said with a fake Cockney accent. "Don't you follow the royal Instagram? The Queen and Prince William were on there, making fruitcakes for next year."

"That's horrifying."

She wrapped an arm around my neck. "Your face. You're so appalled. See? Christmas is the worst. People leave fruitcakes rotting in the basement then give them to innocent bystanders. When we get married, I will never, ever allow us to give a fruitcake as a gift." She smiled up at me drunkenly.

My heart caught in my throat.

Noelle wanted to marry me.

I allowed myself to imagine what it would be like—the warm though admittedly somewhat dysfunctional family, the Christmas-market traditions, a quaint cottage in the woods.

"Oh no," I teased her. "If the Queen's doing it, we have to give out fruitcakes."

"Never!"

"I'm sure you can make the tastiest fruitcake. You'll be the sexiest fruitcake baker this side of the Hudson River," I told her, picking her up and kissing her.

"No, *you* will, because I'm not touching them."

I swung her around in the falling snow, making her laugh.

"You're spilling my drink," she shrieked.

Under the stars and the snow flurries, surrounded by Christmas trees, we were in the perfect Christmas moment.

"I love you," I heard her whisper.

I wanted to say it back.

I should. If Noelle were in love with me, that would fix a lot of my problems. Especially because I was falling in love with her too.

But should you really view falling in love as a problem-solving measure?

Probably not.

Noelle was nursing a hangover when I showed up at the Naughty Claus the next morning.

"I brought you a Christmas biscuit," I said. "It has fried chicken on it."

"What makes it Christmas?" She wrinkled her nose.

I kissed it. "It's dressed with hot sauce—green and red." I handed her a raffle ticket. "The hot sauce is also being given away at the raffle today. It's not whiskey, but I figured you had enough."

"Ugh, I was hoping you would have drunk enough to have blacked out all the embarrassment."

Slowly, she unwrapped the chicken biscuit, not looking at me, and asked, "Did I completely humiliate myself last night?"

"Aside from destroying your mom's living room, puking up ten-thousand-dollar whiskey, and declaring your undying love for me? No, you were the perfect picture of a lady."

"Fuck my life." She *thunk*ed her head down on the stall's counter. "I can't believe you even want to be seen with me. I'm a complete mess."

"I'd take you back to my place so I could show you just how much I like a girl making a mess all over my cock," I whispered in her ear, satisfied when she shivered. "Unfortunately, you'll have to sit there thinking about me because I have a meeting."

"Dick!" she called affectionately.

One woman in line clapped her hands over the ears of a teenage boy who was playing a game on his phone.

"This is a Christmas market," she yelled at Noelle.

"Do you see the sign, lady?" Noelle shot back in her New England accent. "The Naughty Claus. *Naughty*."

I laughed as I headed back to Main Street. Tristan was waiting for me in front of the bank.

The banker had called us in for a meeting and said it was an emergency but didn't say much else on the phone. He had the blinds drawn when we walked inside his office.

"I'm not supposed to be telling you this." He lowered his voice. "But I heard the secretaries talking by the spiced wine stand last night. Rod, he's like the GOAT at this place. The president of the bank loves him."

Tristan was nodding, trying to get the banker to spit it out.

"He's got all these Silicon Valley investors. He did his MBA at Stanford." The banker took a deep breath. "He has investors interested in the Christmas tree farm and ready to purchase. The Wynters didn't make the last payment, and the deadline is today."

"You have to put a bid in for us," I said.

"The head honchos love this guy. I mean, I get it. He has amazing hair, and he's, like, six feet tall. What's not to love?"

"I need that property."

The banker made a helpless gesture.

"We have to let the family have a chance at paying off their debt. Honestly, that's the preferred option. No one at the bank wants to deal with the city, since we would officially be the transfer of title. It's a big liability for us. Lots of paperwork. The city could be difficult to work with, not to mention the feral-bunny coalition."

"Excuse me. Harrogate has a feral-rabbit coalition?" I asked.

"Bunny," the banker corrected. "They're the archrivals of the feral-rabbit coalition. Apparently, Harrogate has a huge problem with people dumping their pet rabbits out here. My wife is very involved. We already have five in our house. Her mom is knitting them sweaters."

"God help me," Tristan muttered.

"The land?" I prompted.

"Right, so if the family shows that they can pay something, anything, then we can pause the clock. If not, then it goes down the ol' hierarchy," he said, making stair-climbing motions. "You guys are third on the list."

"Fuck."

After a moment, Tristan said, "Do fiancés count as family?"

The banker seemed thoughtful

"Why not? If there's a ring exchanged and a public promise of marriage, then there are some common laws that could apply. Why, is someone in the family engaged?"

"Not yet," Tristan said, "but Oliver's about to be. He's proposing to Noelle today."

The fuck?

"Congratulations!" The banker beamed. "If you can make the proposal before lunch, then I can slip this in with the president of the bank and have him sign off on not foreclosing on the property for another month."

"Done," Tristan said.

"What the hell," I snarled when we were back out on the street. "I'm not proposing to Noelle."

"What's your solution, then?" he demanded as we hurried back to the office.

"I don't know, but it's not that."

"I thought you said you liked her."

"I don't even know her."

"My mom married my dad after talking to him for like an hour at a polygamist meet and greet in someone's backyard," Tristan argued.

"Your mom is crazy and abandoned you and your brothers, and your dad is in federal prison," I said flatly. "It's hardly the type of life I want to lead."

"Dude." Tristan clapped a hand on my shoulder. "This isn't something we can be wishy-washy on. We have to be decisive."

"I can't steal her land."

"Why, because you love her?"

"Maybe."

"Okay, then marry her. Because guess what? Noelle's family is losing that land one way or another. Either it's going to a foreign investor who'll kick them all off, or it's going to you. If it makes you feel better, after you propose to her and sort out the property, you can tell her the truth. Then tell her if she wants any of the land, then she has to play ball. You two marry. The land transfers to you as a family member, you split off part of it or we can organize an access easement, and then you divorce. Everyone wins."

"Maybe I should just tell her now."

"Fine by me," Tristan said snidely. "Is she a reasonable businesswoman?"

"I think so," I said slowly.

"You want to bet fifteen billion dollars on it? Because that's how much money we lose if we have to go with the expo site as opposed to this one. But you know, your choice." Tristan threw up his hands.

"I have to walk Max," I said, not answering.

I grabbed the dog's leash. He'd been asleep under my desk, and he shook himself when we stepped back out into the cold December air to return to my house.

I couldn't propose to Noelle. It was wrong, on so many levels.

But could I have a rational conversation with her, right now, immediately, and have her agree before lunch?

Noelle was stubborn. Emotional. She worked at a coffee stand. It wasn't like she was some high-powered businesswoman at a big consulting firm or hedge fund who breathed, ate, and slept money.

Worse, then it would seem like I only wanted to be with her because of the land, when that was furthest from the truth.

I was falling for her.

I didn't want to lose her.

What if I did propose, and we just stayed married? I could play off buying the land as something I did just because I cared and then slip in my plan about building the factory there. I bet I could get her family on my side, especially if I spun it that I was saving the land from an evil investor.

"You're really reaching to make yourself the good guy," I told myself as I approached my house.

I opened the front door and headed to my study, leaving Max on the porch.

The ring was where I'd left it in the drawer, a single perfect, gleaming snowflake.

No one has to know.

You love her.

Maybe this was the start of my great Christmas romance.

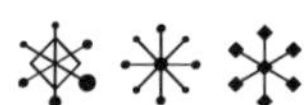

Dave was standing on the stage with the raffle bowl. He raised an eyebrow as I approached him.

I took a deep breath.

"Could you help me make a Christmas miracle happen?"

CHAPTER 62

Noelle

"You don't want to see if you win any of this hot sauce?" Elsa asked.

I had only just now been able to eat my fried chicken biscuit. The line at the stall had been long. Tensions were high; Christmas was less than a week away. Many people—mostly men but also a fair number of women—had not even begun their Christmas shopping, and they needed caffeine and sugar to do it.

Elsa took another bite of the chicken biscuit before I could grab it back from her.

"Oliver and I won a giant metal reindeer dildo the other day," I said with a scowl. "I think I've pushed my Christmas raffle luck about as far as it can go."

"This sauce is amazing, though," Elsa said, her eyes watering.

I took another bite. My nose tingled; the biscuit was spicy.

"Also, are you and Oliver, like, a thing now?"

I grimaced. "I confessed my undying love for him, and he didn't run away."

Elsa's eyes bugged out. "So you're, like, really into him."

"Don't hate me."

"Your funeral."

"Maybe we could just see where it goes?" I begged.

"No judgment here. To be fair, he's better than anyone your sister has brought home or not brought home, since no one's even sure who the father of the latest kid is."

"I keep imagining a life with him," I admitted, the words spilling out. "He wants to make Christmas traditions with me. He has a ready-made life I can just slip into and have the perfect happily ever after. The cute, well-trained dog, an amazing house, a yard, a loving husband."

"Yeah, but you're building that life on a foundation of lies," Elsa reminded me. "At the very least, you should come clean about how you two really met and that you haven't graduated."

"Absolutely not," I said. "If I'm seriously going to have the happily ever after I deserve after all the shit I've had to put up with, I can't just tell him the truth. I can't tell him that, actually, he and I hooked up last year but he didn't remember me and instead humiliated me in front of his friends, thus causing me to go crazy, drop out of college, and spend the next year obsessing about him and then stalking him when he turned back up in my hometown. He thinks I'm a wholesome small-town girl who wears fun outfits and bakes. I can't let him know I'm crazy."

"Spoken like someone who is totally mentally stable," Elsa said, raising her eyebrows.

"I have to seize my moment," I said, pacing around the stall. "Oliver seems to think our family is quaint, wholesome, the salt of the earth. I just have to keep him amused for the next six months. Then we'll be official. I'll get a real job but still keep enough of my small-town-girl charm to hold his attention."

That earned me another snort from Elsa. "Then you'll get married and have babies and really have it made."

"No," I said defensively, "I will be a good wife and a slightly above-average mother. We will be a normal family."

"Your eye is twitching. Are you sure you're in love with him, or was it the expensive whiskey and all that apple pie and cheddar cheese talking?"

"I am," I said with false confidence. "I was since the first time I laid eyes on him."

But what if I wasn't? Maybe I was just as bad as my sister.

Maybe I just needed a therapist.

Who has money for therapists in this economy?

The gong sounded at the stage set up in the center of the town square.

"Raffle time," Elsa sang.

"I have to do my capstone presentation later today. I'm going to ride home with my parents," I told her as she skipped next to me on our trudge through the snow to the stage.

Dave was on the stage with the large glass bowl.

I crossed my arms. "Why can't they have any decent prizes? Like a suitcase full of cash."

"We have a special prize today," Dave said, the microphone screeching as he tapped it. "A very special prize. And stop leaving raffle donations at my house, people. Take them to the thrift store."

He pulled out a ticket. "Number E622," he said in a monotone. "E622, come claim your prize."

No one moved.

I yawned.

That sauce had actually been good. I might need to go get another fried chicken biscuit.

"Number E622," Dave called louder. "Can someone in the audience please check her ticket? My blood sugar is low. I need to go eat lunch."

Someone in the audience coughed.

"Where's your ticket?" Elsa hissed at me.

I huffed and patted my pocket.

"She won," Elsa yelled out, grabbing it from me and holding it in the air.

There was polite applause as Elsa dragged me through the crowd.

Oliver was waiting at the stage. He had a weird expression on his face. Tristan was standing next to him and gave me a wan smile.

"Another day, another Christmas raffle," I joked. "I hope it's not a dildo."

"We do not give out dildos, Noelle," Dave said loudly into the microphone.

I cringed. I saw my family out in the audience. *The Great Christmas Bake Off* had just finished filming the second-to-last episode, and the town had turned out to watch.

My parents waved to me.

"Your special prize," Dave announced as Oliver climbed up onto the stage, "is a very beautiful diamond ring!"

The wind rushed in my ears as Oliver pulled out a blue box from the breast pocket of his coat.

Elsa squealed and clapped her hands while the townspeople watching let out gasps as they realized what was happening.

Cellphone cameras flashed, the light reflecting off the dazzling diamond ring that resembled a snowflake nestled in the box that Oliver held out to me as he slowly dropped to one knee.

I was getting proposed to? Me? I clapped my hands over my mouth. I stared down at Oliver in complete shock as he held the ring out to me, a hopeful, slightly wary smile on his face.

This was what I had wanted, right? Or at least I had last night when I had drunkenly confessed my undying love for Oliver.

Clearly, he was a romantic at heart. Someone who loved Christmas that much also probably believed in true love.

Could I really trust him? He never remembered that we were together.

He was super drunk. You can't judge.

Maybe his soul remembered and was yearning for me this past year.

This was why I could never get ahead in life—I overthought things, and then, when something good happened to me, I found every reason to reject it.

You're scared of change.

Seize the moment.

This was every girl's dream—being proposed to by a wealthy, handsome, tall, kind, amazing man.

You literally will never do better than this.

But...

"Say yes!" several townspeople shouted.

I looked out over the crowd. Women were crying. My parents were clutching each other, huge smiles on their faces.

Of course people who got pregnant and married before they were fifteen thought it was a perfectly good idea for their daughter to marry some guy she only met a few weeks ago.

You've known him for a year.

"Noelle," Oliver said in that familiar deep voice that I wanted to wrap around me like a blanket warmed by a fire. "You said last night that you loved me the moment you first saw me."

In hindsight, that love was starting to feel a little bit like unrequited lust built up over ten years. Also lots of stress and more than a little alcohol.

"I feel the same way," he said. "I love your sense of humor, your love for this town, and how much you value your family. Would you please do me the honor of making this the most wonderful time of the year and becoming my wife?"

"I..." I pressed my hands to my chest.

"Say yes! Say yes!" the crowd was chanting.

"I..." *You have to say yes. There will be a riot.*

"Yes. I say yes." I stuck out my hand.

Oliver slid the ring on it. It glinted dully in the overcast sun.

My fiancé wrapped me in his arms, kissing me like he loved me.

My heart thudded.

This was what I always wanted.

So why didn't it feel good?

CHAPTER 63

Oliver

"I'm sorry. You're engaged?" Matt demanded. "Does Owen know about this?"

"He does now," Jonathan said, waving his phone at me.

Owen: *What the fuck?*
Owen: *Jack, did you know about this?*
Jack: *Fuck no.*
Owen: *I'm coming to Harrogate right now.*
Owen: *I can't fucking believe this.*
Owen: *Have you lost your goddamn mind?*

No, but I couldn't necessarily explain my grand master plan to my siblings.

We were in my house along with Noelle, her family, and several people from the town who wanted to celebrate the holiday engagement.

I took out my own phone.

Oliver: *I'm going to Manhattan today to meet with Tristan's brother, so I'll stop by your office after.*

Oliver: *I'll explain everything then.*

Belle: *If what I think is going on is going on, then this is a problem.*

Oliver: *I bet Greg thinks it's a great idea.*

Belle: *You little shit.*

Tristan hurried up to me. "Got confirmation from the bank they're holding the property for us to make the payments. We have to go to Manhattan and get my brother Greg to sign off. Now."

I stuffed my phone in my pocket as one of the town's elderly residents yelled to me, "You're ignoring your beautiful fiancée."

Fiancée.

I felt a little nauseated.

This wasn't how I had envisioned getting engaged.

Noelle seemed blissfully happy as various family, friends, and neighbors congratulated her and made her show off the ring.

I went over to her and wrapped my arms around her.

"Mistletoe," I said, pointing.

She gave me a shy smile as I leaned in and kissed her.

Tristan hovered a few steps away from me, antsy.

"Business calls?" Noelle said with a laugh.

I felt doubly bad.

"I actually have to go to Manhattan," I said, hoping I sounded sorry that I was leaving her, though I desperately needed to get away, to clear my head.

What had I done?

"You can't just leave your fiancée," her father joked.

"He's busy, Dad," Noelle said tersely. "He can go."

Shoot, she was angry.

"I promise I'll make it up to you later," I told her.

"Sure," she said, but her voice sounded strained.

What had I done?

"As much as I love my beautiful soon-to-be bride," I said, hoping the words didn't sound as crazy coming out of my mouth as they felt, "I do have a business to run."

"It takes money to be this extra," Noelle teased.

I felt horribly guilty.

Noelle really did love me.

Scratch the original plan.

She could never know that this proposal was fake. I need to stay married to Noelle for the rest of my life and take this lie to the grave.

CHAPTER 64

Am I seriously getting married?

I twisted the huge diamond ring around my finger.

I was standing in Oliver's living room. My parents were chattering on, excited, as the townspeople marveled at Oliver's Christmas décor.

I watched through the window as he climbed into a waiting black SUV.

People seemed a little confused that he was leaving right after a big public proposal, but his leaving worked very much in my favor. I was supposed to be in Boston that evening for my capstone presentation. I needed him to vamoose so I could make it to the presentation in time.

Go, go, go.

The car drove off.

I could not have Oliver know that I had never graduated. I needed to get to Boston now.

"Gran," I whispered, "can you please get everyone out of here?"

"I'm opening a keg in the town square," Gran hollered.

Keeping an eye on the clock, I rushed to stash perishable food in the fridge and let Max out one more time.

"We need to go," I urged my parents, hurrying them to the car.

"My daughter, engaged!" my mother said happily as I raced the car down the winding country roads.

I should be ecstatic. I was about to graduate. I had a handsome fiancé. But I just felt stressed.

You'll feel better once you have the signatures on your graduation paperwork.

It wasn't like I was getting married tomorrow. We could have a very long engagement. It would probably be a mature, responsible adult decision to talk to Oliver about how exactly we were going to handle our relationship.

A relationship. Me!

After only sleeping with one guy in my entire life, I was now about to marry him. I had probably spent more hours of my life watching *Gilmore Girls* reruns than I had in total with Oliver.

My parents were whispering to each other as I screeched to a halt in front of the cottage. I needed to change and get to the train station. Driving would be way faster, but who knew if the truck would make it? Dashing out of the car, I rushed into the house and up to the attic, where I threw on the preppy Ivy League outfit I'd prepared.

"USB, printouts, tablet with the app. Check. Check. Check."

My parents were still whisper-arguing when I clattered down the attic stairs.

"Just ask her," my mother hissed at my father.

"What?" I shifted my purse strap on my shoulder.

"Nothing, sweetie," my dad said. "We're just so proud of you." He started bawling.

"Lord help me." My mother threw up her hands. "James."

"We're going to lose the farm," my dad admitted.

"Lose the—what farm?"

"The Christmas tree farm."

"Our land?" I was shocked. "How? We own it. We've owned it for over a century."

"There are a number of mortgages that were taken out," my father admitted. Then he added defensively, "Not all of them by me."

"Why didn't you tell me?" I demanded, my head spinning. "Why are you telling me now?"

"I told your mom I didn't want to say anything because this evening was your big presentation."

"Today's the deadline, Noelle," my mom said desperately. "We hoped that you would land a big fancy job when you graduated earlier this year and could help pay off the debt."

"Then you had some troubles," my dad interjected.

I felt sick. Fuck. Oliver did that.

No he didn't. That was you. You need to start taking some responsibility for your life. You got obsessed with a boy. Now your family's land is on the chopping block because you don't have a high-paying career like you were supposed to. This is on you. Fix it.

My tongue darted out and licked my lips.

"Dad, you should have told me earlier. I could have taken out a loan."

"It's not your problem."

"Yes it is," I screamed. "This is my problem."

"But now you have a fiancé," my mother begged. "Can't you ask Oliver to help us with the payments? We can pay him back."

"God help me." I paced around. "We need to go to the bank. I have a few thousand in my account. I can't believe you didn't tell me."

"I'm your dad. I'm supposed to take care of you." He started weeping.

"We are a family. We take care of each other," I said, trying not to start yelling again. "We can stop the bleeding, at least. Then, after I do my presentation, we'll figure this out."

My mom nodded.

"We cannot," I warned them, "ask Oliver for money. Ever. That's going to look... It's going to look like I'm just a gold digger, like I told him I loved him because I wanted his money."

The ring sparkled on my finger as we headed back into town.

My dad was crestfallen in the passenger's seat next to me.

No wonder my dad had refused to show me the full picture of the Christmas tree farm's finances. Why had they lied to me? I could have done something earlier.

"Do you have an appointment?" the lady at the bank's front desk asked when we walked in.

"I need to talk to Randy," I said.

"Let me check his schedule."

"We were in kindergarten together," I told her. "He paid me a lollipop to lift my shirt up. Then he cried. I think he owes me one."

She frowned. "That doesn't sound like him. He has a boyfriend."

"Like I said, there were a lot of tears."

Randy looked exactly the same as he had in high school, same stick-out ears, same red hair, same glasses slipping down the end of his nose.

"Merry Christmas!" he said excitedly when he saw me. "Congratulations on your engagement. I saw it on the Facebook group."

"Cool, cool. Look, I need you to let me make a payment toward a loan someone in my family took out against our land and then schedule me a meeting to discuss some way of paying off the mortgages."

"Let me pull up that account," Randy said, rustling papers on his desk then going to his computer.

I drummed my fingers on the desk and checked the clock. I had missed my train.

Guess we're driving. Hope the car can make it. Maybe I can hitchhike.

"Here it is. It says you all owe one million four hundred thousand thirty-two dollars and twenty-seven cents."

"What's the minimum payment?"

"You need to pay four thousand two hundred thirty."

"Can you transfer everything in my bank account?" I said, rummaging in my purse. "And here's the remainder." I dumped a fistful of cash and coins onto his desk. "That should more than cover the minimum. Then we have another thirty days to reset the clock, right?"

His nose twitched nervously.

"Randy," I warned.

"The system says that there's been a hold placed on the account."

"We're too late," my mother wailed. "We're going to be homeless!"

Santa's balls. "Fine, I'm going to buy out the full amount of the mortgage. Can you make that work, Randy?"

"I only just started here this summer. Let me ask around. All the higher-ups are in a meeting, but I'll text you, okay?"

"Sure. But when you talk to them, tell them I'm coming back here to pay off the debt in full."

"You're driving to Boston now?" my dad asked. "Do you want us to come for moral support? We can stand outside."

"The car won't make it," I said tersely as I searched on my phone for venture capital firms in Manhattan. "And I missed the train."

My dad's shoulders fell. "But you have to graduate."

"I'm not graduating. I'm going to Manhattan. We need money," I told them. "We are not losing that land, not on my watch. Give me a ride to the train station, please."

The short ride over felt like a funeral procession. All my hopes and dreams of being a Harvard grad?

Gone.

Poof.

Not to mention my relationship with Oliver. He wouldn't want to marry a liar.

There was no question I would sacrifice my college degree for my family. I didn't even feel bad about it. But I was sad about losing Oliver.

"You don't have to do this," my mom told me as I parked the car in front of the train station. "We can work something else out."

"How are you even going to get that much money?" I argued. "I think I can find some sucker in Manhattan to invest in my finance app. Shoot, I have a pitch deck all ready to go," I said, holding up my tablet.

"But your degree. You would have been the first person in the family to graduate college." My mother started sobbing.

"I'm sure I can work something out with my professors," I lied to her. I had been shocked they had even made the original capstone deal possible. There was no way I would graduate.

"I know you'll make a Christmas miracle happen," my dad said optimistically. "Even if you don't, I'm so proud of you!"

CHAPTER 65

Noelle

Manhattan was busy. The vibe was faster paced and more stressful than Harrogate.

I had been hoping to find a women-led investment firm. I had thought I might have better luck securing funding there, but Svensson Investment had just bought up the two main ones. I had emailed a few people while riding into the city on the train but received no response.

Therefore, we were going to do this the hard way.

I shuffled my feet on the sidewalk as I stood in front of the huge glass tower while people in suits streamed around me and a guy in a Santa costume loudly clanged a bell near the street corner.

"I'm here to see someone in Svensson Investment who does consumer app funding," I said to the receptionist.

"Do you have an appointment?" she asked in that syrupy customer-service voice that let me know she wanted me to fuck right off.

"Nope, this is a cold pitch."

She rolled her eyes. "Uh-huh."

"I have an app to help small businesses be successful, and the investors in Svensson Investment will want to see it." I handed her the booklet.

"I think we had someone else pitch that idea earlier this week," the receptionist said, handing the booklet back to me without looking at it.

"It's a two-for-one deal," I said desperately, "with my other app called Moi Cheaters that a lot of people are catching their significant others on."

"Oh my god!" the other receptionist exclaimed, eyes bugging out. "You designed Moi Cheaters? I'm, like, so addicted. I saw my sister's fiancé on there. Someone uploaded his photo with another girl who was not my sister. He claimed she was his cousin, but she was not, *and* she thought he was single. They are not getting married this Christmas."

I winced. "My condolences."

"Good riddance. We're having a big fancy party instead." She tapped a few numbers into her phone and held it up to her ear.

"Hey, Marnie. I'm sending the creator of Moi Cheaters up. Do you have any investors free? Amazing!"

She set the phone on the cradle. "One request. Can you let people make private groups so you can discuss potential cheaters without tipping them off? Please and thank you!"

I went up to the investor's offices in a daze. I hadn't really considered monetizing Moi Cheaters. Other than monitoring server-space usage, I had relegated it to the back burner.

Belle Frost was waiting for me in the elevator lobby when I stepped off.

I sucked in a breath.

"It's you."

"Crap."

"No hard feelings." She shook my hand and looked down at my ring. "You could have just had Oliver text me that you wanted to talk."

"That seemed sleazy." I followed her to her glass-enclosed office and sat down heavily across the desk from her.

She snorted. "Men do that shit all the time. Just call up one of their buddies for special treatment."

Then she held out her hand. "Let's see it."

"This is just my personal finance app," I said, handing it over. "Designed for small businesses. I don't have anything for Moi Cheaters. It was designed on a bit of a whim, and then it took off."

"It's a flash-in-the-pan app," she agreed, "and we can ride that wave until it crests then sell it for an obscene amount of money to one of those idiot executives at a tech firm. But this app is actually interesting. It has the potential to interface with some other finance products we're currently investing in. Since you already have both these apps off the ground and have a solid user base, we're going to go ahead and offer you Series A funding. Moi Cheaters will be fifty million, and the finance app will be thirty."

My eyes bugged out, and I legit almost peed myself.

"*Really*?"

Belle typed a few things on her computer. Then the printer spat out several documents. "Sign here. This is just the statement that you're not going to go look elsewhere and that we are promising to invest. We'll have actual lawyers draw up the contracts."

"Okay, but why?"

"It's the holidays, and it's hard to get anyone to do anything. This will have to tide us over until we can get the lawyers to actually do their jobs. I can't stand Christmas."

"I hate it, too, but I mean, why are you investing in me? My family tried to ruin your little brother."

"Why not?" Belle asked. "You know how many idiots come through here with some crackpot app idea? At least you, one, coded it and, two, actually have it out in the world. How much money did you spend marketing Moi Cheaters?"

"I paid my gran in elf beer to get her friends to download it. So, like, ten bucks?"

She seemed shocked. "That app is everywhere, and we want in on it."

After signing the promissory contract, I folded my copy and stuck it in my purse.

"'Tis the season of making money." Belle shook my hand. "We'll be in touch."

Eighty million dollars. *Total.* I needed to hire people. I needed to find office space. Holy shit, I was running a real business.

I called my parents as soon as I was out on the sidewalk.

"Did you get any money?" my father asked as soon as he answered his phone.

"James," my mother barked, "honestly, stop putting so much pressure on her. Look at what happend to Dove. We need to be better parents. It's okay if you didn't," my mom said to me in a louder voice. "We know you tried your best."

"I got it!" I was grinning.

"You did?" My dad sounded unsure.

I took a picture of the contract and texted it to them. My parents started screaming over the phone, and I pulled it away from my ear.

"We're saved! You did it, Noelle! You saved the farm. It's a Christmas miracle."

Tears pricked the corners of my eyes.

"It's not a Christmas miracle, Dad," I said, though I was too deliriously relieved to be annoyed.

"Merry Christmas! Merry Christmas!" he shouted.

"I have to go. Got to catch the train."

I wiped away the tears that flowed down my face.

I wasn't sure if I was sad or happy. I was saving my family's land, but I was going to lose Oliver. Not only that, but I would forever be a loser college dropout.

On the bright side, I had money and my own company.

I fished in my purse for a tissue to blow my nose and wipe away the tears.

The door of the tower opened, and I moved out of the way for people to pass me.

"Crying out in the middle of the sidewalk? That's almost a Manhattan Christmas cliché."

"Oliver?" I hastily wiped away my tears. "What are you doing here?"

"I told you I was going to be in Manhattan for a meeting," he reminded me.

He handed me a handkerchief. "But what are you doing here?"

"Uh, surprise?" I said helplessly.

He frowned. "Did you think I was here cheating on you?" he demanded.

"Gosh no," I said, waving my arms helplessly. Of course that was what a guy would think if his fiancé showed up randomly outside of his business meeting crying.

"I, um..."

You cannot marry him. You cannot sink that low. Better to do the breaking up rather than the one who gets dumped.

I twisted the ring off my finger and held it out to him.

"Why?" he asked, shocked. He stepped back from me. "Noelle, we can work this out. I can explain."

"I have to tell you something," I said desperately. "I never graduated from Harvard."

"You were at the alumni holiday party." He frowned.

"I somehow ended up on the list," I explained, starting to cry again, "but I didn't graduate, and"—I blinked back tears—"I was going to do a capstone project for credit, but then stuff came up and..." If I got into my family's situation, I would sound like a gold digger. Any rich person who had a bunch of people in debt sucking up to them would automatically assume that they were after his money. I didn't want Oliver to think my family was that trashy.

"...and I missed the train. I can't get to Harvard."

"Oh, is that all?" Oliver let out a relieved laugh. "Noelle, seriously, don't worry. It took my brother seven years to earn his undergrad degree. He dropped out, spent time in Ireland, switched majors, reenrolled."

"You don't care?" My mouth fell open.

He smirked. "I care that you're a bad girl for crashing the alumni party."

"Why are you so goddamn wonderful?" I was getting choked up.

Oliver wrapped me in his arms and kissed me. Then he laced his fingers with my left hand and used his other hand to slide the ring back on.

"I love you. I don't care if you graduated college or not, especially since it sounds like it was my fault." He turned me around to face him. "I proposed to you and threw a wrench in your schedule."

"Um, yeah, that's exactly what happened."

"We're going to fix that, then," he said simply as a black SUV pulled up.

"We can't drive to Harvard now," I argued. "Traffic's too bad."

"No, but we can take my helicopter."

CHAPTER 66

Noelle ran her fingers through her slightly windswept hair as we hurried from the helicopter in the direction of the main Harvard campus.

The university was on winter break. There were only a couple of students in the Harvard Yard, giving campus tours to their parents and grandparents. The sun was setting, and the deep cold was settling in.

"Don't be nervous." I tucked my arm around her waist. "They aren't going to just fail you. I'm sure your presentation is fine. It's not a good look for Harvard to have too many people flunk out, especially if they're first-generation college students."

When I'd seen her there outside of Svensson Investment crying, I'd thought the worst, that she'd figured out I was trying to put a factory on her parents' property.

But this? I could be the supportive fiancé and fix this problem.

Several professors, including Professor Hoffman, were waiting in a large conference room in the business school.

After we all introduced ourselves, I explained, "I'm just here for moral support." I took a seat on one of the chairs against the wall.

One large table faced the projection screen. Noelle loaded her presentation and handed out the packets she'd prepared. I didn't know what I was expecting. Maybe something light and fluffy that barely scratched the surface of business theory. But when Noelle started her presentation, it was clear that she knew what she was doing. I was impressed with the quality of the data and the complexity of the app she'd developed.

Dr. Hoffman crossed his arms to interrupt her.

"I understand that you've had a difficult semester and had to drop out, and of course I think this is more than enough for a passing grade. But I do want to challenge you for the future to go above and beyond a placeholder app. Maybe find a nice young man who can code this app for you and find a larger user group." Professor Hoffman's tone was condescending. "Just because Steve Jobs used images for the iPhone unveiling with the intent to code it later doesn't mean that you should too. As people who dabble in investing, we like to see actual apps with actual users."

"This is an actual app," Noelle corrected him, still maintaining a professional tone. "You can go on the app store right now and download it for iPhone and Android."

"Oh," he said, surprised.

I pulled out my own phone and downloaded the app.

"I like all your stickers," one woman said. "My daughter has been acting like she wants to start homeschooling so that she can be a beauty influencer on TikTok. I think this app will firmly disabuse her of that notion."

"As you can see in this graph," Noelle continued, "the users that have started tracking their small businesses with this app have seen exponential profit growth in just a few short months. It certainly has been a come-to-Jesus moment for several users."

"It just seems a little derivative," Dr. Hoffman said sourly. "Not to mention there are numerous regulations around financial products."

"Oh, Dr. Hoffman," another professor said, exasperated, "this is just a college project."

"Actually," Noelle interjected, "we just received thirty million in funding from Svensson Investment, and they plan, further down the line, on integrating this app with some of their other financial investment products. While the issue of regulations is certainly on our radar, it's not considered too big of a hurdle for our investors at this moment. But thank you for your concern."

She did what?

I started to panic. Had she seen me in there signing off to get the money transfer to purchase the property and start exploratory site work?

"Guess you've earned an A plus on this project," the professor with the daughter said with a laugh. "I look forward to seeing your career progress. Sounds like you're going to be quite the popular alumnus around these parts once the investor gravy train really gets going."

I hung back as Noelle shook hands with the professors and accepted congratulations.

Dr. Hoffman and one of the professors from the computer science course both signed her paperwork.

"Just email the dean of students and CC us both," the computer science professor said. "Merry Christmas. Have a wonderful holiday."

"You are amazing," I said simply when we were alone in the conference room. "You didn't tell me that you received funding. Now I don't have to feel too guilty that you almost missed your presentation."

She squirmed. "I just completely forgot. I was so surprised to see you there," she replied in a rush. "You want to grab a drink?"

I was still feeling antsy as we headed down the empty halls of the historic classroom building. I had no idea how to pose the subject of putting my factory on her land without essentially strong-arming her into it.

Noelle clearly wasn't stupid. I wouldn't be able to just sweet-talk her into it. I needed to ask her soon. Greg was under the impression that we could begin moving toward the construction of the new factory right after the holidays.

Maybe an appeal to her ego?

"We're quite the power couple," I said to her.

She grinned up at me. "I'm so glad it's over, but now I have to somehow run two whole companies."

"Two?"

"Got fifty million for the Moi Cheaters app," she admitted.

"Damn. You really are the woman for me." I smiled down at her. "I couldn't imagine anyone else I'd want to take over the world with."

"Gosh."

"But before you walk out of here as an official Harvard alumnus," I said, "there's one more important fact I need you to tell me, and be honest."

She chewed on her lip, seeming nervous. "What's that?"

"Did you ever do it in a classroom?"

"What?" she squawked. "No way. Someone could walk in and see you."

"Guess I'll have to pop your classroom-sex cherry." I tried a nearby door.

"This isn't a classroom," Noelle said in a rushed whisper as we walked into the oversized lecture hall. The lights were off, but there was enough to see from the light that streamed in through the windows.

I winked. "It's more fun if you're afraid of getting caught."

I came up behind her. She seemed nervous about something, and I knew just how to loosen her up about things. My hands went down her sides, enjoying her curves and holding her tight. She was not dressed in some ludicrous Christmas-themed costume this time. Instead, she looked nice and respectable. A sweater and a preppy skirt, not too out of line with the other students who wandered Harvard's halls.

I massaged her hips, making my intentions known. My hands slid up her sweater and went to those soft, huge breasts of hers. I held her tight, squeezing her against me, hearing her pant. Her nipples went erect so damn easily from my touch, her so hungry and yearning for everything I could do to her.

One hand continued to massage her there, and the other went low. It slithered into her skirt toward her panties and found her sex, so hot and ready for me already. She shuddered wonderfully against me as I held her close, my digits' infiltration going deeper into her still. Flesh to flesh, she dripped for me, ached for me. For all her protests, her body wanted me, and it wanted me bad, her low purr putting an exclamation point on that.

And I wanted her too. My cock throbbed with need for her. I had her not too long ago, but my desire for her was unquenchable.

As I held her close to me, I whispered into her ear. "Noelle..."

She turned in my arms, even if it broke my sensual massage, wanting to look me right in the eye. "What do you want?"

"You. Now." I lifted her up and planted her ass right on the edge of the nearby desk.

I must have pushed her literal button in the right way, because she was now fully on board with this. Grabbing at my crotch, clawing at my belt, pulling my cock out from its prison, as it yearned for her so badly.

A brief kiss we shared, as I pulled a condom out of my pants pocket.

I wanted her, right here, right now.

Condom on, I grabbed hold of her with one hand while I pushed her panties to the side with the other. Then I thrust right into her, stifling her cries with my mouth. Her pussy squeezed my cock when I entered.

Mindful we might be caught, I took her at a furious pace, seeing her writhe with every thrust, her entire body trembling, her breasts jiggling under her sweater. She tried to stifle her moans, not wanting the whole university to hear how hard she was getting fucked.

Every moment inside her was so fucking intense, so fucking powerful. I relished each and every moment of taking her, the intense pleasure that spread through me as I fucked her. And knowing that she was feeling much the same was a fucking rush that I couldn't get enough of.

It didn't take long. The sudden and powerful release pulsed through me, and it did the same to her. Noelle couldn't help but let out a loud moan for me, and it echoed through the empty lecture hall.

She was panting under me on the desk. I kissed her one more time before I withdrew from her.

"That strangely fulfilled a fantasy I didn't know I had," she said as she pulled at her clothes.

I immediately wanted to take them off her.

I wrapped my arms around her and ran my hands up under her shirt to cup her tits.

"I might have to bend you over that desk again," I said, slipping my hand between her legs. Her ass was soft, and as I squeezed it, I leaned down and kissed her, my tongue tangling with hers.

I was hard again. I discarded the condom and rolled on another as I pulled her skirt off and let it pool on the floor.

Then I spun her around and folded her over that desk. She gasped but made it clear she didn't protest. Her panties pushed to the side again, I slammed myself into her, and she immediately moaned in pleasure from my thick cock shoved all the way in her. The first fucking had only left her more sensitive and more ready for me. God, she just got better and better.

Hands on her hips, I went at her hard. The sound of flesh against flesh echoed through the room, covered only by the sounds of Noelle's cries. Her ass rolled back against me as I took her fast and hard.

Fuck, I was in love with her.

I tangled my fingers in her hair, and she let out a low moan of pleasure as I adjusted the angle.

Her back arched. Leaning in as I took her, never slowing down, I brought my lips to her ear and whispered, "I love you."

She came moments later with a hoarse cry, and I followed, spilling myself in her.

She staggered a little when I let her upright.

I kissed her swollen mouth.

I'll tell her after Christmas, maybe, I decided.

Fucking her, being inside her, the way she slipped her hand in mine? I didn't want to lose that.

I just need a little more time.

I started a fire in the fireplace while Noelle made drinks.

It felt so homey and comfortable.

"You want to watch a Christmas movie?" I asked. I pulled her to me and kissed her. She tasted like bourbon and spice.

"Fuck no. I want you to come down my chimney."

CHAPTER 67

I was riding high.

I graduated.

I was going to be a millionaire.

I was saving my family's land.

Oh, and I was marrying a hot, rich, amazing man.

Life was freaking good.

And I was about to get laid again.

My skirt slid down my legs, and I stepped out of it.

"You sure you want to watch a movie instead of my show?" I asked, pulling off my sweater. I meant to do it seductively, but it was a little too small for me to begin with, and then it got caught on my hair clip.

"Ow! Dammit." I just ripped it off and followed with the bra and panties for good measure.

Slowly, I sank down to my knees on the plush carpet in front of the fire, rubbing my clit as I looked his way. Then I got on all fours, grinding my ass.

"You gonna put your cock in me?" I purred, looking over my shoulder at him.

He smirked as he undid his tie. "Of course. I just wanted to see how far you were willing to go with the performance."

I licked my lips as he pulled off his dress shirt then kicked off his pants.

My pussy was dripping wet in anticipation. I felt his bare chest against my back, and he cupped my chin in his large hand to turn my head just enough to kiss him. His hands roamed down my curves, electrifying my skin, teasing my nipples, caressing up against my ass, then stroking my pussy.

I moaned softly and gasped as he spread my legs and mouthed me from behind. I gasped in pleasure as he teased and licked me. My skin was hot, both from him and from the pleasant warmth of the fire in front of me.

He spread me wider, dipping his tongue in my opening then running it along my folds to twirl around my clit. His large hands dug in my ass, keeping me from bucking back against him. My legs trembled, and my stomach tightened as he brought me closer and closer.

Then I was coming for him, shuddering, as he milked my orgasm.

I moaned softly as he repositioned himself, whimpering as I felt his cock against my soaking wet pussy. He slid it up and down my slit, teasing my clit. My nipples were hard in anticipation of that huge cock in my pussy.

But instead, he rubbed his cock on the outside of my pussy lips. Never going in but just teasing me. He almost parted my folds, only to pull himself back.

"Fuck me, Oliver. You know how much I want you."

"Say please."

"Please fuck me, Oliver."

He chuckled, his cock still prodding my pussy but denying me everything I wanted.

"Say it like you mean it. Beg me."

If I wasn't completely addicted to his cock, I would have dumped my drink on him.

"I want you to take your huge, thick cock. I want you to thrust it into me. All the way. Until you can't go in anymore. I want you to fuck me. I want you to do it, fast and hard. I want you to do it now, Oliver. Give me it. All of it. Please."

He paused to roll a condom onto his cock. His fingers were back.

God, I hate you.

I thought you loved me.

Then he slammed his cock in me. He hit me hard, but I took every thick inch of him. My body rocked as he thrust into me. He grabbed a handful of my hair to hold onto me as he took me, making me squeal and moan as he rutted into me. It was hard and fast, and soon everything was so tight within me, leaving me ready to erupt and explode, turning my moans into screams. I could barely hold myself up anymore because I was so overwhelmed, but Oliver wrapped one strong arm around me, and the other held my hips in place as he took me over the edge.

My arms collapsed as I came. He continued to thrust into me a few times more, then he was coming.

We came down from our high, and he wrapped his arms around me, holding me close to him, kissing me gently on the neck as he embraced me next to the fire.

"I love you," he whispered in my ear.

"I love you too," I said automatically.

But maybe I shouldn't. Elsa was right. This relationship was built on a lie.

What if Oliver woke up one day and remembered me and was like, "Why didn't you tell me?"

You're paranoid. If he hasn't by now, he never will.

Ring!

I rolled over, snuggling against Oliver in his large bed, in a room I wasn't sharing with three other people.

"I think that's your phone," he murmured.

"Probably Elsa," I said, rolling over again with a yawn.

For a moment, I was hit with my usual morning wave of stress and anxiety. Then I remembered—literally all my problems were solved. I had Oliver, I had graduated, and the Christmas tree farm was saved. Best of all, I didn't have to go back to work at the Naughty Claus. Shoot, Elsa didn't either. She was going to come work with me at my brand spankin' new companies.

I did need to call Randy to schedule a meeting, though. His name flashed on the screen.

"Just let me take this."

I didn't need Oliver to know the massive bullet I'd just dodged. Now that he was finally mine, I wasn't doing anything to ruin it. He wanted an equal, not some girl who needed her husband to give her handouts.

I slipped into the hallway to take the call.

"Hey, Randy," I said, sneaking into a guest bedroom also impeccably decorated for Christmas. "Good news. I just got funding for my business. I'd like to put up a portion of it as collateral to take out a loan to pay off my family's property."

Randy laughed. "Is this a 'Gift of the Magi' situation? That Christmas story always made me cry."

"A what?" I was confused.

"You gave up something you loved to pay for your property so Oliver could build his factory, while Oliver already must have given up something he really loved so that... Wait, that doesn't make any sense. Oliver's a billionaire. He'd have no problem paying off the money owed on the land. I guess he was always going to build his factory."

It felt like someone had just thrown me naked and screaming into the Arctic Ocean.

"His factory?" I asked, barely able to get the words out.

"Yeah." Randy laughed. "That's what the hold on the account transfer was. Oliver was going to propose to you so he could count as a family member, and he wouldn't have to worry about the rezoning issue on the deed restriction. The proposal was totally romantic, by the way. You're so lucky! I wish my boyfriend would propose to me at the Christmas market."

"Oliver wanted to buy the land?" I felt sick.

"Yep! I finally got one of the partners to explain it all to me. He was not in a good mood." Randy lowered his voice. "His third wife got caught on the Moi Cheaters app, sooo apparently his first and second wife teamed up to spill the beans. Guess sometimes you have to make your own Christmas magic."

"Cancel the hold."

Randy giggled. "They barely let me use the printer here. The account manager has to sort it all out. You two lovebirds need to come down in person. Maybe talk with Oliver on how you want to handle the payment of the debts, then I'm sure the account manager can set it up."

Oliver was just coming out of the shower when I walked into the master bedroom.

"You want to grab breakfast and—"

"Breakfast?" I snarled, the delayed anger rising in me. "You want to go have breakfast, you lying sack of shit? You were going to marry me to steal my land."

The shock and guilt on his face let me know it was true. Tears pricked at my eyes. I blinked them back.

"Noelle, I can explain," he begged. "It's not what it looks like. I was trying to help you."

"No, you were trying to help yourself."

"You don't understand," he said, taking two steps toward me. "The bank wouldn't just let me buy the land. One of the higher-ups has these California investors. They wanted it. I had to be your fiancé. I'll let your family still have a few acres for Christmas trees. The California investors would just clear-cut it. I can buy your family a nice house in town where they can live."

"Right. We have to move so that you can build a goddamn factory on the land that has belonged to my family for centuries. That's our home. That was where I grew up, where my dad grew up."

My chin trembled. "How long was this your plan? Since day one? All those nice things you did for me and my family were you just trying to butter us up, weren't they? You thought we were stupid and simple and poor and you could just breeze in and march us around like your personal nutcracker collection."

"No, of course not, Noelle. I adore your family."

"My god." I threw up my hands. "I can't believe I fell for it."

"It was real," he pleaded. "It is real. Noelle, you love me, and I love you. Now that we're honest with each other," he said, taking me in his arms, "this is a good thing. I mean it. I've always wanted a woman like you as my wife. We're a power couple. A dream team. We can help each other reach our goals."

I threw him off. "You really can justify anything and do anything to make yourself look like the good guy."

"You're a businesswoman," he said, tone a little colder. "Let's talk it over rationally and see if we can come to an arrangement that benefits us both. I still do want to marry you. I love you."

I wanted to believe him—it would be the easy way out. I could still have it all—well, most of it—and he could have what he wanted.

Except...

"I loved you from the moment I first saw you," he was saying. "I don't want to lose you. I can't lose you. Don't break my heart."

Except... I knew he was lying because I *knew* the truth.

The tears ran down my face now.

"I was right about you all along." I let out a sob as I pulled off the ring and threw it at him. "You never cared about me."

I straightened my back and wiped at the tears. "I don't need you. I'm going to buy the land all by myself. Merry fucking Christmas."

CHAPTER 68

I hated Oliver.

As soon as I had my family's land paid off, I would use all the junk and old Christmas tree branches to create an effigy of him then burn it to the ground and roast marshmallows over the fire of my hatred.

"I'm sorry," Randy said nervously as he typed on his keyboard. "We can't approve you for a loan."

"This is all of the paperwork from Svensson Investment," I said desperately. "The companies are incorporated. This is more than enough to put up for collateral for a one-and-a-half-million-dollar loan. Not to mention your bank will make a hefty profit from my business."

"I know," he said helplessly, "but you don't have office space or employees."

"My company produces a very popular product," I said shrilly.

"Noelle." My dad, who was sitting in the chair next to me, patted my arm. "Randy's trying his best."

I bared my teeth.

Randy cringed. "I can give you a personal loan," he offered.

"How much?"

He cleared his throat. "Twelve hundred dollars. Thirty percent APR."

That was not good enough. I needed the whole amount to pay off the property, since the bank refused to let me pay a partial amount, thanks to the freaking backroom deal Oliver had worked out to put a hold on the account.

"If I were a man, I bet you all would approve me," I said darkly.

The laughing vintage Santa hanging on the wall mocked me.

I'm going to burn you to the ground, too, Santa. Just try to sneak into my house. TRY. ME.

"Can't your fiancé pay cash?" he asked, doing that twitching thing with his nose to keep his glasses from slipping.

"I'm not engaged anymore."

"Give Oliver another chance," my dad pleaded. "He was just trying to do the right thing."

"No," I said, trying not to lose it and go off on my dad. It wasn't his fault, after all.

Wait, yeah, actually it was.

I took a deep breath. "We are not going to talk about this right now. Randy, you and I have known each other a long time. Isn't there anything you can do?"

"Actually," he said, brightening, "since you're not engaged anymore, I have to talk to my boss. I think that means the hold is expired."

"Great. Fantastic."

"See?" My dad grabbed my wrist. "It's a Christmas miracle. Everything works out okay."

But when Randy came back into the office, he was wringing his hands, followed by his manager.

"Since you're no longer engaged," the manager, a balding man with a messy tie, explained, "we are going to lift the hold on the account."

"I am ready to start paying the outstanding balance."

Randy looked like he wanted to crawl in a hole and hide.

"The payment was due several days ago. At this point, the bank has assumed ownership of the property," the manager explained.

"So this Christmas, the bank has decided to steal a Christmas tree farm?" I yelled.

"Ma'am, I need you to calm down," the manager said, holding out a hand.

"No, I will not be calm. I am sitting here, ready to pay off the land, and you won't let me."

"Do you have cash?"

"I need a loan using my business as collateral," I repeated through gritted teeth.

"I'm sorry," the manager said. "But it has to be all cash. If you'd just come sooner, we might have been able to work something out." He sighed. "You all need to be out of the house by Christmas Eve. We have some investors who are anxious to purchase the property. Not my choice, obviously."

"Thank you," my dad said dejectedly. "Merry Christmas."

"Merry Christmas?" I exploded at my dad in the car. "These assholes just ruined your livelihood and stole your land, our land, your grandchildren's land, and you wished them a Merry Christmas."

"It's the holiday season," my dad said in a small voice.

I stared out the window, trying to blink back tears.

"It will be okay," my dad said to me comfortingly, patting me on the back. "As long as we have each other."

"But the Christmas tree farm," I said, holding my hand in front of my mouth so I wouldn't sob.

"I'm going to be too busy helping you out to run a Christmas tree farm, and I bet you're going to buy a nice big house in town. Your mom can run her pastry business out of it. Maybe you can find one with a little carriage house and Azalea can live there?" he said hopefully.

"Sure," I choked out.

He wrapped me in a big hug.

"You'll see. It's Christmas; it's going to be okay."

My mom was standing in the living room, wine glass in hand, tears running down her face when my dad and I stepped inside.

Dove was huddled on one of the threadbare armchairs, halfheartedly working through her winter reading list.

"How the mighty has fallen," Azalea said sourly when she saw me.

Even Gran and my brother looked sad.

"Mom," I said softly, "don't cry. I'm sorry. We were so close, but... I'm sorry. I know it sucks we have to move, but I can buy us a nice house with a—"

"Is this what you think of me?" she asked in a quiet voice. Mom pointed at my laptop, which was open on the coffee table in the living room.

"What?"

"That essay you wrote. You think I'm some stupid girl, some terrible mother who neglects her kids, that you grew up with nothing, getting thrift-store Christmas presents wrapped in newspaper."

"Oh, for fuck's—why are you on my laptop? No one told you to go snooping around," I snapped when I saw my college application essay open on the screen.

"I was trying to access my business information on the app *you* made that *you* wanted me to use," she said accusingly, "and it was there. You think I'm some sort of derelict. That I never did a thing for you and you have to go to Harvard with hat in hand and beg for charity because of your horrible, stupid, simple mother."

"No, of course not." I slammed the laptop closed. I did not have the patience for this right now. I needed to pivot.

"Mom, can we please talk about this later? We have to pack up the entire house and move."

"Stop being so dismissive of me. I may not have a Harvard degree or eighty million dollars in funding or whatever you have," she said, the wine in her glass sloshing, "but I raised three children. I have grandchildren."

"Mom—"

"You're just an ungrateful little brat. I sacrificed everything for you and your siblings."

"I never asked you to," I screamed at her. "I never asked you to get pregnant your freshman year of high school. I never asked for you to neglect your education and drink too much and marry some guy with no prospects. I never asked for you to 'make a go of it' instead of giving your kids up to a rich family who would give them a car for Christmas."

"Christmas is more than presents and money. It's about love and family," she argued.

"News flash, mom. We suck. Our family sucks. We're getting evicted for Christmas. Your granddaughter accused a man of impregnating her. Your other daughter doesn't know the fathers of two of her children. Nor does she know what it's like to work a real job. Your son is a video game addict who sits on the sofa in his underwear, and your mother-in-law is a drunk."

"You're a drunk," Gran slurred at me.

"No I'm not. I'm the only person here who is keeping the family afloat, the only one who is going to make sure that we aren't homeless for Christmas."

"No," my brother shouted, "you're the one whose boyfriend is trying to steal our property."

"No one would be able to steal it if you had just listened to me," I yelled. "I've been telling Dad for months to let me look at the finances."

"Just because you went to Harvard—" Azalea said.

"Graduated," I spat at her. "I graduated from Harvard because I'm the only one who gives a shit about her future."

"Stop acting like Harvard makes you better than the rest of us," she sneered. "You think you're such hot shit."

"I don't think I am. I know I am," I said, cutting her off. "I am better than the rest of you." I felt like shit when the words left my mouth, but I was too far gone.

"Fuck you," my brother said. "Mom and Dad are better people than you will ever be. You're so snobby and stuck-up."

"Oh, go get a fucking job!" I shrieked at him. "Before you sit here and judge me. You want to know why I wrote that essay to make you all sound like delinquents? Because I needed the scholarship money. You can't get into Harvard or make it in business without playing the game. You don't understand what type of people they are, what I had to deal with there. Those guys like Oliver who go to Harvard without having to take a dime of scholarship money? They will crush you. They already crushed us. They take anything good in the world and just suck it out and leave you an insane husk of a person. God, I cannot believe I'm wasting my time with this."

Azalea scowled at me.

I turned and stomped up the attic stairs.

"So that's it? You're just going to run off?" my mother demanded.

"No," I said slowly, "I'm going to change then go to work because Christmas Eve is in two days, and someone has to sell Christmas trees because God knows neither of your other two children are going to do it."

CHAPTER 69

Oliver

In his reindeer outfit, Max trotted happily beside me as I trailed my brothers through the Christmas market. They were all in town for *The Great Christmas Bake Off*. Jack's girlfriend Chloe was one of the judges for the finale.

"Guess you wasted your time coming all the way out here," Jack joked.

Owen scowled. He detested Christmas almost as much as Noelle did.

My heart sank.

Noelle.

I couldn't quite accept that I had completely ruined my relationship with her. I didn't even know what I was going to do.

I hadn't admitted to Tristan or my sister or the Svenssons that I had not just ruined my relationship with her but cost us billions of dollars because we wouldn't be able to build the factory on her land.

You need to do something.

Going to Greg Svensson hat in hand and saying, "Please give me mercy. It's Christmas, sir," would not cut it. He made Ebenezer Scrooge look like the pope.

"I'm just glad you came to your senses." Owen clapped me on the back. "What were you thinking?"

"Just got caught up in the magic of Christmas," I said bitterly.

"This is why you can't give that much money to twenty-three-year-olds," Owen said somberly. "They're complete idiots."

"Don't you have to go be with your pregnant wife?" I snapped at him.

"Owen's not supposed to come back without bringing his weight in snacks." Jonathan threw his arm around Owen.

I seethed internally. I couldn't believe my brothers were here, just acting like this was a normal family outing, like Noelle wasn't selling Christmas trees two stalls over, while the life I had thought I would have slowly blew away like snow in a storm.

Madison, who wore an elf outfit, skipped up to us. She had a placard advertising her family's Christmas tree lot.

"Merry Christmas," she cooed to Max. "Aren't you the world's most adorable reindeer?"

She stood back up. "We're having a bonfire. I heard you and Noelle broke up." Her sad and concerned face didn't look sincere.

"I actually have to get some work done."

"Boo, don't be such a Scrooge! We're all meeting on my parents' farm after *The Great Christmas Bake Off* finishes. Come by and bring Max."

The dog wagged his tail at her.

"Also," she called over her shoulder as she sauntered away, "Christmas trees are on sale if you need one more for a little extra Christmas cheer."

"We should buy you another Christmas tree," Jonathan joked to Owen as we passed by Noelle's family's Christmas stand.

"Holly already has one in each room of the penthouse. All my clothes reek of Christmas."

I almost waved to Noelle. I just wished there was some way we could work it out. I didn't want to lose her. I wasn't an idiot, though. I knew that what I had done was beyond wrong. But I still loved her.

Maybe once the dust settled in the new year when she had bought her family's land back and her business had worked through some growing pains, I would contact her again and sincerely apologize.

The ring I'd bought her was still in my pocket. It was a cold, heavy weight. I chanced a glance over to her. She was busy ringing up someone's last-minute tree purchase.

What had I done? Why had I thought this would be a good idea? Now I didn't have the land or Noelle.

"They're going to the food stalls," Matt said to me as our other three brothers ambled off, squabbling about Jonathan's desire to purchase spiked elf juice. "I said we would grab seats."

"I think I'm just going to go home."

"You didn't seriously love this girl, did you?" Matt said in surprise.

I shrugged helplessly. "I think I did."

Matt threw his arm around my neck and squeezed me in a brief hug. "It will all work out. It's Christmas, after all."

"Fuck Christmas."

"Damn, you really are upset. I'll buy you one of those toxic-looking Christmas cinnamon buns to cheer you up," he said with a snicker.

But baked Christmas goods were not going to help me. I really needed a reset, to go back in time and keep myself from ruining Christmas and my life.

CHAPTER 70

"That fucker has some nerve," I hissed as I watched Oliver laughing with his sibling, flirting with Madison, and enjoying the Christmas market like he hadn't ruined my life.

"Screw him. He has no right." I took a swig from the bottle of whiskey I had under the table. It was the last of the bottle Oliver had brought for the dinner a few nights ago, when I had thought I was in love with him.

Why had I fallen into the same trap? Again?

"I thought you said you were taking responsibility for your choices," Elsa said to me.

"I do take responsibility for my choices," I spat. "But if he hadn't humiliated me, if he hadn't ruined my life, I would have graduated, and my dad would have told me about needing to pay off all the loans on the land earlier, and we wouldn't be kicked out, and I wouldn't have done the capstone project, and my mom wouldn't have read my college admissions essay. Every time Oliver comes into my life, it's like a bomb goes off. Then he gets to sail off into the sunset while I'm stuck picking through the rubble."

The last of the customers were trickling away. *The Great Christmas Bake Off* was filming its last live show of the season, and most people were trying to score good seats on the wooden bleachers that had been set up around the stage.

Max, the picture-perfect adorable corgi in his reindeer outfit, barked happily as Oliver trailed after his brothers.

He didn't look like a man who felt guilty for pretending to be in love with someone and proposing marriage to her just so he could steal her land and ruin her life.

I blinked back the tears.

"Oliver gets everything, doesn't he? He does whatever he wants, screws over whoever he wants, steals people's dogs and their land, then comes out smelling like pumpkin spice and everything nice. This isn't fair. The villain is supposed to get wrecked by the end of the story. Oliver didn't even get haunted by a Christmas ghost."

"I don't think that's a realistic expectation," Elsa said gingerly.

"You're right." I narrowed my eyes. "I can't just sit around and wait for justice."

"Why don't we all just calm down and eat some Christmas cookies? Your mom made extra. They're filled with anger and resentment."

"I'm not going to spend another year moping around, making voodoo dolls of Oliver, and stress eating," I said, sliding off my stool. "I can't just sit here and let him get away with ruining my life again."

"Sometimes this is just how the Christmas cookie crumbles," she said.

"He doesn't deserve to have a nice Christmas after what he did to me. He's going to be in that big fancy house with his lovely family full of siblings who aren't complete fuck-ups," I said, my voice sounding hysterical to my ears. "He's going to have a Christmas goose and lovely side dishes and unwrap presents and wake up in a bedroom with a fireplace that he doesn't have to share with half his family, and he's going to take cute pictures of my dog."

"Technically, it was your two-year-old niece's dog."

"I walked it," I said stubbornly.

"But did you..."

"This is *my* revenge spiral," I reminded her.

"Going into very supportive sidekick mode." Elsa pressed her hands together.

"Someone has to do something."

"People like him always get what's coming to them," Elsa said.

"They don't," I said, taking another swig of whiskey.

"It's just a sad reality of life," Elsa said. "After this, why don't we look on Zillow and drive around and check out the houses that you can buy."

"Since I got kicked out of my home," I grumbled.

"That you didn't even like."

"It's the principle." I scowled. Christmas carols were blaring over the loudspeaker. I had heard Mariah Carey's "All I Want for Christmas Is You" eight times already this evening. I was at my limit. It was all too much. Pressure built inside of me.

I pulled my Santa hat tight over my head and adjusted the belt on the sexy costume.

"He does not deserve to have Christmas. He doesn't deserve to have a happy new year. He doesn't deserve eggnog or cookies or a white Christmas morning. And I'm going to make sure he doesn't have it."

The Great Christmas Bake Off was in full swing when I snuck over to make sure Oliver hadn't gone back home.

There he was. I recognized his shoes as I crept under the bleachers where the seating had been set up.

The crowd gasped as one of the contestants accidentally set their soufflé on fire.

I resisted the childish urge to tie Oliver's shoelaces together. I had been drinking so much whiskey I didn't think I had the hand-eye coordination.

Suddenly, Max was there, his black corgi nose twitching. He barked when he saw me.

I froze as Oliver shushed him.

Why does he have to put this dog in a goddam Christmas outfit?

I took another swig of whiskey then gave into the impulse.

There was more screaming from the crowd. One contestant had slung a handful of icing at another.

So glad I didn't let Gran talk me into that mess, I decided as I quickly unclipped Max from his leash. I tucked the corgi under my arm, stumbled out from under the bleachers, and ducked around the back sides of several Christmas market stalls.

I huffed as I hauled Max through the Christmas market toward Oliver's street.

Max struggled in my arms when he realized where we were.

"Fine, you want to walk?" I slurred at the corgi and set him down. Then I took another swig from the bottle and stumbled after him down the street.

Oliver's house, with all its beautiful Christmas lights, glowed in the distance.

When I stumbled into his front yard, I yanked on the nearest strand of lights. Sparks flew as they came down around me in a coil.

Through the window, the huge Christmas tree gleamed. It was like a postcard.

"I hate Christmas!" I yelled at the house.

All the old hurts, of never getting a nice present, of being humiliated in school, of the fake marriage, of losing the land, being evicted—they were too much.

"I'm stealing your Christmas. Then what are you gonna do, Oliver, huh? You can just be as sad and miserable on Christmas morning as I am every fucking day of my life."

Mrs. Horvat had a whole Christmas scene set up in her front yard with Santa's reindeer and a sleigh.

"You steal my bra? I'm stealing your stupid decorations," I said around the bottle of whiskey I had firmly clamped in my teeth. I dragged the sleigh out of Mrs. Horvat's yard, cutting two lines in the freshly fallen snow as I maneuvered it across the street to Oliver's house.

I still had the key he had given me, back when I had thought that he was my one-in-a-million Christmas romance.

It took me a few tries to open the door. I threw it open, and it banged on the opposite wall. Max ran inside, the antlers on his little doggie hat bobbing.

I ripped the garland from over the doorway and dumped it into a pile on the floor.

"That's my garland that my granny made," I slurred. "You don't deserve nice things." I pulled the garland off the walls and the banister. Pine needles and bits of dried fruit were everywhere. The pine sap was sticky on my hands as I dragged it outside and threw it on the sleigh.

Then I piled the stack of Christmas dishes from the dining room table and dumped them on top of the garland. Max was following me around, confused, as I tore down all the meticulously hung Christmas decorations.

The stocking with all his siblings' names on them and even one for his new niece were thrown away onto the sleigh.

"*I'm dreaming of Christmas revenge...*" I warbled as I switched out my now-empty whiskey bottle with a new one from his liquor cabinet.

I recognized the brand. It was very expensive.

"Merry Christmas to me." I pulled the top off with my teeth.

In the fridge were platters of food that I supposed he planned to serve to his siblings after *The Great Christmas Bake Off*.

I took a huge bite out of the wheel of brie and stumbled back to the living room. There, I gathered armfuls of perfectly wrapped presents and hauled them to the sleigh.

Then I rolled up my red Santa sleeves and faced the tree—the Christmas tree my father had grown on my family's land, the land Oliver stole. I gave the tree a good shove, and it came toppling down with a crash of ornaments and glass icicles.

Dragging it through the house was difficult. The big branches knocked over furniture and swept little porcelain Christmas figurines onto the floor, where they smashed. The destruction was nothing compared to my own rage, sadness, and humiliation.

"He doesn't deserve this," I sobbed as I tried to haul the huge tree through the front door. "He doesn't get to have a nice Christmas that my family made for him, that I made for him, and then turn around and screw me over."

The tree finally popped through the door, and it and I went flying out into a heap in the yard.

"Crap," I wheezed as I lay in the snow.

Max, concerned, ran over to me and snuffled my face.

Sweating from the exertion, I hauled myself out from under the tree and hefted it onto the sleigh.

After another swig of the whiskey, I slammed Oliver's front door shut. Last thing I needed was someone seeing the open door and blowing up my grand plan.

But what was my grand plan?

The sleigh full of stolen Christmas decorations sat heavy in the snow. What was I going to do with it all? Leave it there? That seemed anticlimactic.

Another sip of whiskey made me feel pretty woozy, though the cold helped.

"Max," I said after a stroke of inspiration. "We're going to set this shit on fire. Burn his Christmas like he burned my heart."

The ropes attached to the front of the sleigh cut into my palms as I strained against them, my boots slipping in the snow.

Max grabbed another trailing rope and tugged, thinking it was a game.

"Pull with me, Max," I yelled as the fluffy dog tried to drag the sleigh back toward the house.

He ran in the opposite direction, and it was enough purchase to get some forward momentum on the sleigh. It slid along the sidewalk as I pulled it over the snow and up a small hill toward the park at the end of Oliver's street.

"How the hell did the Grinch's dog drag a sleigh all the way up a freaking mountain?" I wheezed.

With Max pulling the rope on one end and me pushing the sleigh from behind, we finally crested the hill and made it to the park.

The town was laid out below me. All the townsfolk of Harrogate were down there enjoying *The Great Christmas Bake Off* and the Christmas market. All the lights glowed cheerily, and the faint strains of Christmas music wafted over the snowy air.

"Fuck Christmas!" I yelled, raising up my arms. "And fuck you, Oliver Frost."

Like any good country girl, I always had a trusty lighter with me. I took one last swig of the expensive whiskey then dumped the rest out over the pile of stolen Christmas decorations and presents.

Then I flicked my lighter.

The dry garland went up like, well, like the nativity scene I'd burned down earlier in December.

Max and I watched the glow of the Christmas bonfire as it burned as merrily as a Yule log.

I took a deep breath, inhaling the scent of Christmas spice and pine.

"Yep," I said to Max, "this is pretty cathartic."

It was cleansing, letting all the bad feelings and bad memories burn up to the snowy sky. Tomorrow, I was going to apologize to my parents. Then I was going to find a very nice house for us all to move into. Yes, it would even have a carriage house for Azalea. Then I was going to work on my business, putting Oliver completely behind me.

The blaze had burned through the Christmas trees, and now the presents were on fire.

I was feeling like a *Game of Thrones* badass bitch as I watched my former love's Christmas burn to ash. That was until a high-pitched whining noise punctuated the soothing crackling of wood.

I screamed as a green ball of light whizzed past me and a nearby pavilion exploded.

"What the fuck was that?" I ducked.

Another firework burst out of the burning pile of presents, flying in a red arc and landing on a bench in a fiery explosion.

"Fuckity fuck, who in the fuck has fireworks wrapped under their tree? Is Oliver a lunatic?"

Another present burned, setting off more fireworks. My ears rang from the flash-bangs.

"Max, we gotta go now," I yelled to the dog, stumbling through the dark, partially blinded by the bright flashes of lights.

"Max!"

The corgi was racing around in a panic, barking at the fireworks that rocketed through the dark park.

Three fireworks shooting off red and green sparks flew up into the night sky, a beacon to let everyone in town know that drama was afoot and they might want to head on over before their neighbors got the scoop ahead of them.

"Shit, shit, shit!"

Sirens blared in the distance.

I wasn't in especially good shape, and I hadn't pushed the sleigh all that far from town. The police cars screeched to a halt in front of the park entrance before I had even taken two steps with Max.

"Stop!" a police officer bellowed.

As if.

I took off running as the cop raced after me, yelling at me to halt.

I narrowly missed being hit by a fire truck as it careened up and over the curb. Several men in helmets and Day-Glo yellow uniforms raced out with lengths of hoses.

"I need all units at the Van de Berg Park," the police officer yelled into his radio.

I dodged another cop then slid in the mud from the fire hoses.

They haven't caught me yet; it isn't over.

"There is a girl in a Santa Claus outfit carrying a corgi dressed like a reindeer," another cop said into his radio. "We are in hot pursuit."

Were we, though? I was drunk and had been stress eating Christmas cookies for the past three weeks. The cops were not in the greatest shape either.

The firemen, having easily put out the bench, pavilion, and sleigh fires, were watching as I jogged slowly around the park while the police officers lumbered after, trying to catch me.

"We need backup!" one of the officers shouted while the firemen roared with laughter and took bets.

God, this fucking town.

The townspeople, complete drama addicts, were already streaming up to the park to witness the spectacle.

"Someone make a citizen's arrest," the police officer begged, out of breath.

The fire captain smirked and squinted in the glowing light from the dying fires. Then he turned the hose toward me and signaled to one of his men.

I was blasted with a freezing cold stream of water that bowled me head over heels to land in a heap on the sidewalk in front of Oliver.

"Noelle?" he said in confusion.

The red-faced cop grabbed me and forced my hands behind my back.

"You're under arrest for... for... starting fires and breaking things and running away."

"It's called arson and evading arrest," one of the firemen yelled.

"Screw you, Cliff," the police officer shouted while the firemen doubled over, laughing.

"Noelle, what did you do?" Oliver said, looking around at the smoldering ruins of the park and his Christmas tree.

"I ruined your holiday," I spat at him. "Now we're even. Merry fucking Christmas."

CHAPTER 71

Oliver

It took forever for the police to take my statement. They wandered around my house, photographing all the damage, asking me to check and see if anything else of value had been stolen.

Noelle hadn't made it into my study, as far as I could see, but the foyer and living room were completely wrecked.

"Damn," Jonathan whistled as we walked through the house, feet crunching on the glass from the broken ornaments. "You really know how to piss off a woman."

"What did you do?" Jack asked me.

"You mean besides a fake proposal of marriage so you could steal someone's land?" Belle asked acerbically.

I cringed.

She was like the ice queen coming for some poor sod's head.

"It was Tristan's idea."

"And this is my shocked face that a Svensson brother's unethical decision comes back to bite you in the ass." She glared at me. "You better figure something out. Because you will have no kind of Christmas if you can't figure out how to fix the issue of your factory."

My brothers followed her out of the house.

I sighed and went to the bar to make myself a drink then snarled when I saw my most expensive whiskey was gone.

My elderly neighbors had all invited themselves to my ruined house to *tut-tut* about the damage and help themselves to the platters of food in my fridge.

They also were assisting Mrs. Horvat, who was sprawled out on my couch, recovering from a fainting spell after she had realized Noelle had stolen her Christmas yard art.

"I always knew something wasn't right with her."

Two elderly men pushed me aside to help themselves to my liquor collection.

I sat down heavily on the bottom step of the grand staircase, blankly staring while the townspeople streamed in and out of my destroyed house bearing casseroles and baskets of winter fruit, as if this were a funeral. Under the guise of being neighborly, they gawked and gossiped, making comments about what a tragedy this was and how Noelle was such a nice girl until she came back from Harvard disgraced last year.

"What happened?" I asked one older lady.

She balked when she recognized me and stammered. "I just came over to bring you a casserole, to help you through this time of terrible tragedy." She held out the hot dish to me.

I took it. It did not look as good as the ones Noelle and her mom made.

"What did you say about Noelle?" I repeated, suspicious.

"My daughter was friends with her sister Azalea, before she went off the rails, of course. All the Wynter girls are crazy."

"What happened at Harvard?" If Noelle was just plain crazy, then none of this was my fault and I wouldn't have to sit here with the guilt eating me for the rest of my life, wondering, *what if?*

The woman's friend muscled in. "I heard there was a boy who spurned her, and she couldn't handle the rejection. Dropped out. She was completely undone. Spent weeks crying in bed. Poor thing."

I winced.

"Do they know who?"

"No idea here," the friend said. Then she shoved a tuna casserole and bag of potato chips at me. "Now don't forget to sprinkle that with some chip crumbs before baking."

There was no way I would survive being in that house with half of Harrogate, and I didn't have the energy to try to make them leave.

Max and I trudged down the street into town.

People were still milling around up and down the road, talking about the great Christmas fire and speculating about the upcoming trial.

Noelle had been in love before? I felt terrible. A man had broken her heart twice over Christmas. No wonder she despised the holiday.

I had never wanted to hurt her.

But you did. You fake proposed to her. That's some pretty low shit.

She must have felt so humiliated and betrayed. No wonder she went crazy and tore down all my Christmas decorations—well, some of them. I had a lot.

I needed to do something to make it up to her.

I didn't want to be like her previous boyfriend, who had her hiding and crying in her bed for weeks. That wasn't who I was. That was the type of man my father was. And I was nothing like him.

The police station was crowded when I walked in.

Multiple people were in for drunk and disorderly conduct, quite a feat when Harrogate allowed you to open carry alcohol in the Christmas market and turned a certain amount of blind eye to tourists' poor behavior.

"You here for a drunk frat brother?" the lady at the front desk asked, snapping her gum.

"No, my ex-fiancée."

"Name?"

"Noelle Wynter."

The police officer looked up at me. "You got bail money?"

I handed over my credit card.

Max was making friends with a man in a dirty Grinch costume. I waited around while the guy's mom came in and yelled at him then dragged him back out the front door of the station.

Finally, the cops brought out Noelle. She reeked of smoke and pine sap.

I gave her a small smile.

"*You*," she spat.

"Just take me back in," she said to the police officer. "I'd rather be in jail than see this asshole."

The officer sighed loudly. "We're already over capacity. Check back on the bulletin board for your court date."

"My grandmother was right. This is an authoritarian hellscape!" Noelle yelled at the officer as he unlocked her handcuffs.

"Tell your grandmother she can't keep selling moonshine to tourists," the officer shot back.

"I thought this was America."

I grabbed Noelle's arm and led her outside before the officers could throw her back into the jail cell.

When we were a few steps away from the police station, she wrenched her arm away from me.

"How dare you."

"I didn't want you to stay in jail overnight," I told her. "I know it doesn't look like it, but I do care about you."

"You don't care about me. You literally fake proposed to me so you could scam me out of my family's property."

"And I fully accept responsibility for my actions," I said calmly. "And will work to make it right. I'm not a bad person, Noelle."

"Yes, you are a bad person." She was practically hopping up and down, she was so mad. "You ruined my life."

"You don't have to let my actions ruin your holiday or your life. You clearly know what you're doing. You just landed a huge round of funding for your companies."

"Stop it!" she shrieked. "Stop sounding so rational and calm just so you can make me sound crazy. Everyone here thinks I'm crazy."

"You're not crazy. I heard about what happened last year, how some bastard really sent you into a tailspin," I said soothingly.

Noelle looked at me like Frosty the Snowman and Rudolf had just materialized behind me and were doing the polka.

"But you're stronger than that. I promise I'm not mad about the Christmas decorations. I'll just buy new ones. I'll make it up to you about the proposal. You can even keep the ring. I don't want this to leave us on a bad note. We're both going to be living in Harrogate and—"

"That was you," she shrieked, jabbing her finger at me.

"Excuse me?" I tilted my head.

"You were the one who ruined my life last year. You were the one who made me depressed and heartbroken. I hate you. I've always hated you."

"I—that wasn't me; it couldn't have been. I only just met you." I held out my hands, a placating gesture.

"*Liar*." Her chin trembled. "Liar, liar, liar! We hooked up after a party one night. Multiple times. You said you loved me and wanted to marry me." Tears were streaming down her face, and she was choking on the words. "You said you had never met anyone like me before, and I made you so happy and wasn't it amazing that you had found the person you wanted to spend the rest of your life with."

"I—I don't remember any of that," I said, completely shocked. "I'm sorry."

"How could you not even remember?" The heartbreak was etched on her face.

"There was a lot going on then," I said slowly as I wracked my brain. I winced as I dredged up long-buried memories.

"I slept around a lot," I finally admitted sharply.

"So you just slept with random girls and told them you were in love with them? And people think I'm the crazy one."

"I'm sorry," I repeated, "I just—I don't remember you at all."

She fumbled with her phone and shoved it at me.

"This was from that party. I have video evidence that you were there and I was there." Her tears continued to drip down. "I watched this video over and over and over, trying to see if there was something I missed, some explanation for why you would just cast me off like that then tell all your friends that you would never date anyone like me and that I wasn't good enough for you."

Now that I saw the video, I did vaguely remember her, the party, the drinking, how stressed out I'd been about Belle, how I'd been looking for some—any—distraction.

In the video, Noelle laughed, her shy smile vaguely coming back in focus. I looked up at her.

"You look a lot different now," I said lamely.

"You mean I got fat," she said darkly and wiped a hand across her face, smearing her makeup.

"No," I said, closing my eyes.

The girl in the video was sweet and open-faced. She had carefully dyed red hair, not Noelle's frizzy brown hair. She was wearing modest clothes compared to Noelle's bright red Christmas outfit with its short skirt.

I handed her the phone back and crossed my arms.

"I thought you were going to call," she said quietly. "But you didn't. Then I saw you out with all your other rich friends from good families whose parents didn't have them when they were in high school, and you looked right through me and laughed. I can't believe I wasted the last year of my life obsessing about you." She shook her head, eyes downcast.

As she turned away, I suddenly, with excruciating clarity, remembered that moment.

Sitting in the lecture hall, the disruption when a girl with glasses and a hoodie had approached me. My friends laughing.

"Wait," I called after her. "I can explain."

"You keep following me, Oliver Frost," she yelled, "and I'm shoving a Christmas tree up your ass."

CHAPTER 72

"This is cozy," my dad said gamely as my brother and I dragged the sofa through the front door of the small apartment I had rented. Because it was Christmas and everyone was catering to tourists, things were expensive and inventory was low. Come New Year, I would have more opportunities to find a new house for my family.

The Moi Cheaters app had been getting a lot of press on talk shows and morning shows, and Elsa and I had been busy over the last couple of days retooling the website, buying more server space, reconfiguring the app so that we had advertising space, and, of course, hiring.

Alumni were coming out of the woodwork wanting to work for me. My dad had filled the small office space Elsa and I rented with garland and Christmas trees. My mother passive-aggressively cooked food for everyone. She still was not speaking to me.

We also had to work on the personal finance app. With New Year's two weeks away, we needed the app to be ready for everyone's resolutions to get their financial houses in order.

"Mom, do you want the TV on this wall so you can see it from the kitchen?"

"Does anyone know where this TV should go?" my mom asked dramatically. "Maybe the person who solves everyone's problems can figure it out?"

"Mom, I'm sorry," I apologized for the tenth time. "I didn't mean anything I wrote. I love you. You're an amazing mom."

She sniffed and helped Gran arrange the garden clippings along a shelf under the window.

The bank wouldn't budge on letting me pay off the loans. Now that I didn't just have to repay the debt but essentially buy all the land, it would be way more money than I could justify taking out a loan for, especially considering I wasn't going to develop it, just move my family back into a rundown cottage.

"Why don't I build us some bunk beds," my dad said with overdone cheerfulness as he stomped through the apartment in heavy boots.

"Guess we're still all going to be rooming together," I told Elsa and Dove.

"Probably will have to fit Azalea in with us, too," Gran said grimly, "since there's only two bedrooms."

"You can share the pull-out sofa with me," my brother suggested.

Azalea punched him in the arm. "As if I'm staying in this dump. I met another single mother at the Christmas story hour. She just messaged me on Facebook that she was looking for a roommate. She runs an in-home daycare and needs another set of hands."

"Oh," my mother said in shock. "You're moving out?"

"Talk about a Christmas miracle," Gran muttered.

"I'm twenty-five, Mom. I think it's time for me to go. I'm going to work part-time at Girl Meets Fig."

My parents hugged her.

"We're so proud of you," my mom said, choking up. "My daughter's all grown up, getting a job, and moving out."

"We'll miss you and Dove and the babies," my dad added.

Dove scowled. I knew exactly who was going to be watching all those kids.

"Dove can't come," Azalea stated.

"She can't?" we all chorused.

"There isn't enough room for her in the house. So she has to live here with you all."

"You can't just dump her here. You have to have someone sign power of attorney documents," I argued.

"Dove knows how to forge my signature," Azalea said, picking up her screaming kids and her suitcase.

"She'll come back for you," my dad assured Dove. "She just needs some space."

I wasn't so sure.

My mom was suddenly much more chipper than she had been the last few days.

"I can't wait to see Deborah's face when I tell her Azalea's finally moved out!"

My mother looked less sure of herself once we were standing inside Deborah's impeccable home. It was a tastefully redone old Victorian with soaring ceilings and a huge Christmas tree in the living room.

Deborah's annual Christmas party was packed. It spilled out into the manicured backyard with a fire pit and a swimming pool that I had taken Dove to that summer for a pool party.

"She has such a lovely home," my mom said with a wistful sigh.

"And so many bathrooms," Dove whispered.

Deborah had done things the right™ way—attended college; married her college sweetheart, who had a high-paying tech job; had children at a respectable age; and was involved with the PTA.

"Her spinach and artichoke dip isn't as good as yours," I said to my mom.

"Then why are you eating so much of it?" she hissed under her breath.

Why? Because I still wasn't over Oliver.

I had been so spent after he bailed me out of jail that I hadn't even been able to cry.

After all that energy I'd spent obsessing about him, fantasizing about confronting him, what had I really expected? That, like breaking an evil witch's curse, he would suddenly remember me and beg me to take him back?

Oliver was indifferent. He seemed to care more about how the whole situation made him look than how it had made me feel.

Deborah and her husband posed under the mistletoe and kissed to cheers from the partygoers.

"Sarah," Deborah exclaimed when she saw my mom. "I'm so glad you were able to unchain yourself from the stove and come party! You work too hard. At our age, we should be enjoying the fruits of our labor and patting ourselves on the back for putting in the work to achieve so much success in life."

What a cunt.

My mother squared her shoulders. "This is a lovely party, Deborah, and we're so glad you thought to invite us."

"James couldn't make it?" Deborah asked with an exaggerated sad face. "Too bad. He should find an office job and stop playing Christmas tree farmer. I thought your son was going to take over that hobby business anyway."

"Jimmy is still working out what he wants to do in life."

"He has such great role models. I'm sure he'll figure it out eventually." Deborah pulled her daughter over.

Stacey gave Dove a snotty look.

"Stacey here isn't sure if she wants to go to NASA space camp this summer or do horseback-riding camp. It's so difficult today for kids to find a path that suits them. Dove, do you know what summer camp you're going to?"

Dove looked down at her boots, which were my old ones, scuffed and stained. I made a mental note to buy her some new ones once I had a better handle on the burn rate at my app companies.

"Dove doesn't go to camp," Stacey said snidely. "She stays at home on her family's farm and does manual labor. Harvesting crops and things like that."

"What a sweetheart. Dove is such a simple, small-town girl, just like her grandmother. Adorable."

"I thought you all lost that land," Deborah's husband said.

"You did?" Deborah asked in mock shock, even though the whole town knew about our land. "What happened?"

"You gotta be careful with leveraging property," her husband said tipsily, taking a sip of his spiked punch. "People think living off the land is all sunshine and rainbows, but you really have to have a mind for finance."

"Her poor husband never went to college. He wouldn't know." Deborah grabbed her husband's arm. "Why don't you get with him and help him out, honey? Even though my husband is a high-level project manager at Svensson PharmaTech, he's also very good with budgeting, finances, and investment," Debora told my mom.

My mother was seething. "We're fine, thank you."

Deborah gave a fake laugh. "Are you? Oh dear, you're not homeless, are you? I know, I'm going to organize a casserole train for you and a charity drive. We small-town folk have to stick together and take care of our neediest."

"I don't need your charity," my mother exploded. "I don't need your snide comments or your judgment about my life or all the gossip you spread about my children. My daughter is more successful than your daughter will ever be, especially if you're shelling out money for camps instead of having her work at a real tech company like Dove will be doing with Noelle this semester."

She is? Okay.

"Azalea is working at a tech company?" Deborah's husband asked in shock. "Good for her."

"Azalea has moved out and is going to be working. Though," my mother said hotly, "we're very proud of her. Her and Noelle. It's really something special to have a Harvard graduate in the family. Not to mention she just got awarded *Shark Tank* money for her businesses."

"Series A funding, Mom, but I appreciate the enthusiasm."

"Series A funding," my mom said forcefully. "Eighty million dollars. She runs her own company, and she's going to be on *Good Morning America* tomorrow to talk about her app. It's called Moi Cheaters, and you better be a little more discreet when you go down to the firehouse to flirt and drop off food because you could end up on the front page."

Deborah gave an indignant screech.

"Thank you for inviting us, but we really must be going. Noelle is very busy. Also," my mother added as she grabbed Dove's hand, "you need more salt and less mayonnaise in the spinach and artichoke dip. It's bland and runny."

I bit back laughter as we exited the party, triumphant warriors in the latest battle of small-town mean girls.

"Oh my god," my mother cried when we were back outside. "I should have just kept my mouth shut. I know Deborah and her friends are in there gossiping about me, calling me crazy."

"So what?" I said. "Let them talk shit."

"You were awesome!" Dove crowed. "Can I really come work for you, Noelle?"

"Since your grandma already announced it at Deborah's party, you better start taking a coding crash course now."

"Oh, gosh, I am so sorry, Noelle," my mom said. "I'm sorry I was a bad mom and grandma."

"Stop apologizing," I insisted. "I should apologize to you. I didn't mean anything I said the other day. You are a great mom, and I wouldn't trade you for anyone." I hugged her.

"Don't lie to me. I drink too much, and I never finished high school."

"You're slightly above average, then. But then, so are we." My mom pulled Dove into the hug too.

After a moment, Mom asked, "What are we going to do about Christmas?"

"Order Chinese and watch movies?" I suggested.

"We need to do more than that."

"Yeah, this might be the last Christmas Noelle has before she goes to jail," Dove said dryly.

"Goddamn it," my mother swore. "I completely forgot to yell at you about burning down that park!"

CHAPTER 73

Oliver

"Hold that thought," Greg said as his phone rang.

Tristan and I waited as he took the call.

"Yes, we understand there's quite a lot of interest in investment opportunities with the Moi Cheaters app."

Are you fucking kidding me? Tristan mouthed at me.

"We will have to review the array of investors and decide who we would want to partner with. We'll be in touch." Greg hung up. "Continue," he said to us.

"To conclude," I said, "in light of recent events and our inability to purchase the Christmas tree farm, we would like to proceed with the purchase of the expo site for the factory."

Outside the glass walls of the conference room, an impromptu Christmas party was going on. People were sipping wine and eating appetizers while watching a business news program. The announcers were singing the praises of Svensson Investment and the Moi Cheaters app and predicting when it would achieve unicorn status—in other words, be valued at a billion dollars.

The program played a few clips from Noelle's *Good Morning America* appearance. She looked like a polished yet fun tech millionaire.

She could have been my wife if I hadn't blown it.

"You're lucky," Greg stated, tapping his pen on the leather portfolio open on the table. "If your sister hadn't brought in that Moi Cheaters app, I would have mounted your head on top of my Christmas tree."

Tristan grimaced.

"As it stands," Greg said, "we'll put up the money for the expo site purchase. Since it's currently in the hands of the city development authority, they will give us a deal to take a Superfund site off their hands."

"While we're waiting for the toxins to be cleaned out of the site, you can help push the Moi Cheaters app to unicorn status," Belle added.

"I think that's a little below our pay grade," I said in disbelief.

"No," Greg said slowly, "babysitting you and holding your hand while you flail around trying to start a business is below my pay grade. Svensson Investment has early investor status in an app that's about to make an obscene amount of money. It's all hands on deck. You don't like it? You should have done a better job of land acquisition."

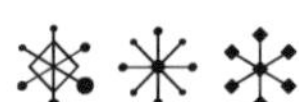

"That went better than it could have," Tristan said as we waited in the bank lobby for our appointment.

To start the process of petitioning to purchase the expo site, we had to have signed paperwork from the bank to show we had enough cash to complete the purchase as well as a plan and funds in place to clean up all the toxins.

"Thank God Noelle created that app and has a hard-on for revenge."

The Ring camera video of her burning down the park was making the rounds on social media. That had added gasoline to the fire and started a rumor that I was the reason she had invented Moi Cheaters. Social media portrayed her as a woman scorned. According to my sister, Noelle was getting a hundred thousand new sign-ups a day.

"I never should have listened to you," I said bitterly.

"I'm sure she'll come around," Tristan said as the secretary waved us into our account manager's office.

"She's paid off the Christmas tree farm, and she's running the hot new app. You just have to make a nice apology, and I bet she'll take you back."

The memories of how angry and hurt she was surfaced. "I think I blew my shot."

"Did I hear you all were still interested in the Christmas tree farm?" the banker asked when we sat down across from him.

Most of the bank employees were only pretending to work and were instead counting down excitedly for the Christmas holiday.

"I thought Noelle paid that off," I said, pausing as I handed over the paperwork to him.

"Oh no, because you both cut off the engagement, the hold was removed, and the property has now been foreclosed on."

"Why didn't you let her buy it back?" I demanded.

He shrugged. "We offered, but she said it was too expensive."

I frowned. If Noelle was pumping all her funding into scaling up her apps, then I supposed she wouldn't have the cash on hand to afford it.

"So we can purchase it?" Tristan asked in excitement.

"What about your California investors?" I asked, dubious.

"There seemed to have been a miscommunication issue. They didn't understand that they could not just build a mall there, that we have rules around zoning, and no, you could not just bribe a city official, even if this is a small town."

"We're back, baby." Tristan pumped a fist. "How much?"

"Ten million."

"I'll give you five," I offered. "Cash."

"I'll submit your offer. You still have to go through the city for a zoning and land use review. They could deny your factory," the banker warned.

"I'm not putting a factory on it."

"You're not?" Tristan sounded appalled.

I ignored him. "I'm going to build a lodge and retreat on the Christmas tree farm instead."

Tristan perked up. "That sounds like a great idea. It will be a good hedge fund project."

"Actually, I already have a partner in mind," I told him. "But I'll put your name on the list."

CHAPTER 74

Noelle

"Only a woman wronged would come up with an app called Moi Cheaters," the morning anchorwoman said to me.

Wearing black skinny jeans, leather boots, and a high-end Christmas sweater, I tried not to shift awkwardly on the hard stool adjacent to her.

"Fortunately, no one cheated on me," I said, hoping I didn't sound robotic. "But I just can't stand cheating. My parents have been together for twenty-five years, and they still love each other just as much as they did the day they met."

"What a wonderful love story."

"Just to be clear," her cohost said, "you didn't burn down your ex's Christmas decorations and half a park because he was cheating?"

I grimaced.

"It was a little more complicated than that. We met in college. Hormones were high. Neither of us were acting all that mature."

"Have you given up on love? Because let me tell you, scrolling through this app has turned me off love," the anchor said to applause from the live audience. "I might just go adopt another cat."

"I—" I paused. "I was never really the girl who dreamed about her wedding. I always wanted to be the rational one, the one who was above it all. But then, when I did actually fall in love?" I shrugged helplessly. "It's better than bourbon hot chocolate. What can I say? The thing is, I don't want to give some guy my heart carefully wrapped under a Christmas tree just so he can try to exchange it for a gift card, you know?"

"Amen."

The hosts turned back to the camera.

"While many people are looking for love this holiday season, those of us in the know are looking for revenge. Get the most addicting app in your Christmas stocking. Thank you, Noelle."

It was dark and snowing when I finally closed my laptop. I had been up for almost twenty-four hours straight by then.

But we had hired a ton of new people and booked advertising deals.

Christmas music drifted down the narrow street. The new office was a few streets away from the Christmas market.

I pulled my coat around me against the cold and stepped out onto the sidewalk.

Now that I didn't have to sling coffee or dance to sell Christmas trees, part of me did want to wander through the Christmas market and soak up the holiday atmosphere.

A children's chorus sang softly and sweetly on the stage in the center of the town square. Couples wandering arm in arm basked in the holiday lights. Happy families explored the Christmas market, making last-minute purchases.

It was magical.

My heart lifted. I breathed in the air, smoky from hickory fires, sharp with the scent of snow and pine.

"Noelle?"

Oliver stood there, framed by the softly falling snow. He gave me a wary smile.

"Out soaking up some Christmas cheer? Letting the Whos from Whoville teach you about the true meaning of the holiday? Or are you just finding something to burn down?"

My lip caught in my teeth as I tried not to laugh.

"Too soon?" His mouth quirked.

"You and your Christmas obsession," I said, pursing my lips.

"You can't call it an obsession when it's Christmas Eve," he said.

"It is?" I said in shock. "I completely lost track."

"Merry Christmas."

We stood there awkwardly.

He took a deep breath.

"I was going to come see you earlier, but my sister-in-law just had a baby, and I went to go visit."

"That's awesome," I said, sincerely meaning it.

"I'm finally an uncle."

"Let me tell you," I said. "Nieces and nephews will drive you crazy."

"But in a good way, I hope."

"No, in the worst way." I smirked.

He took another breath. "I need to explain myself."

"No you don't," I said unhappily. "I clearly read something into a situation that wasn't there. I trusted you, and I shouldn't have. I loved you, and I shouldn't have done that either. Clearly, you and I were never meant to be together."

He stepped toward me.

"Noelle, back then—really, my whole college career—I was a wreck. My sister, who had raised me, disappeared. I blamed myself. I was anxious and lonely. I didn't know where she was. I thought she had abandoned me. I thought she hated me because my parents had forced her to take care of me and raise me. I started drinking. So much. Way too much. All the time. I don't know how I managed to graduate. I don't remember half of what I did during college." He closed his eyes and looked away.

My heart hurt for him.

"That's not an excuse for how I treated you, how I hurt you."

I stepped toward him and laid a gloved hand on his arm.

"I know. But I appreciate the explanation."

"I remember that day in the lecture hall. It was an evening class. I was with people I couldn't stand who also had terrible parents but didn't have the benefit of having a caring older sister. I had already started my daily ritual of drinking myself blackout drunk. Then you were there, with your big hopeful eyes and your sweatshirt. It had a corgi in a Harvard scarf on it."

He smiled sadly, like it had happened only yesterday.

"You seemed so wholesome and sweet. Those people I was with—they just started in on you. They liked to flaunt their wealth because they didn't have anything else—no loving family, and honestly, even their friends didn't like them. They were lonely, empty people."

"To me, they had always seemed on top of the world. Guess you never really know what's going on in someone's life," I said softly.

"I didn't want you to get sucked in, into the drinking and the partying and the credit card debt and the loneliness and self-loathing. You seemed too nice, too good. You didn't belong with someone like me. Someone who got blackout drunk every night and paid off people when he destroyed their property. That moment was a wakeup call for me. I realized my choices were so bad that I couldn't trust myself with a nice girl like you and changes had to be made."

He sighed and looked out over the Christmas market.

"I started buckling down, getting serious. I dropped that friend group, stopped drinking so much, read self-help books, and started making better choices. I wanted to be a better person so that I didn't have to be afraid I would ruin someone else's life."

He gave me a sad smile.

"I moved to a small town and learned to appreciate the little things. I met a nice girl. And I still managed to ruin her life. Guess people don't really change after all."

His gray eyes met mine. "I see why you hate Christmas, Noelle—the fakeness of it, people trying to prop up façades of themselves to keep from ruining the holiday."

He handed me a large brown shopping bag.

"For your family, and there's something for you too."

I took the bag automatically. "Oliver..."

"Merry Christmas, Noelle."

He turned and walked away, disappearing into the crowd.

I reeled.

I had been important to him?

You severely misread the situation.

"Wait!" I yelled.

"Noelle." Dove ran up and threw her arms around me. She had been clingy the last couple of days.

Azalea had not come back for her daughter.

There had been a screaming fight at the lawyer's office. She had accused Dove and me of conspiring against her to ruin her life. Then she had stormed off.

Dove had seemed sad and resigned when I signed the papers. She was even more upset when Azalea started making thinly veiled Facebook posts about ungrateful children, starting over with younger children, and how horrible tween girls were.

"Did you finish your Christmas shopping?" she asked me, pointing at the bag.

Shit.

I had not done a lick of Christmas shopping.

"Uh—" I looked around in a panic.

I had always judged the people who waited to the last minute to shop for Christmas. Now I had joined their ranks.

"Just have to get one thing," I said hastily to Dove. "Wait here."

A nearby stall was selling Christmas-themed puzzles.

I'll order Chinese food and have a whole family game night thing, I decided, *and buy some Amazon gift cards online for my siblings and Dove.* I had half a bottle of vodka stashed in my bag that had been left over from the company Christmas party. I would give that to Gran.

Lamest Christmas ever.

"All done," I said, returning to my impatient niece.

"Dad and Uncle Jimmy are almost done selling Christmas trees. Elsa said they were selling out. Do you think my mom has a Christmas tree?"

I hugged her.

"Don't be sad. After all the tourists leave, I'm going to find us an amazing place to live. You'll have your own room. We can decorate it."

"I guess."

"I promise," I said, turning her to face me. "I will always be here for you."

With my arms wrapped around her, we walked through the snow flurries to the Christmas tree lot.

"We saved one last one," Elsa called when she saw us.

She had left work early after our impromptu office Christmas party catered by my mom.

"That is a sickly little Christmas tree," I said.

"We can name him Tiny Tim," Elsa joked.

"Why did you cut down one so small, James?" my mom chided when the tree was inside the apartment. It barely came up to my chin. We set it up so that it was flanked by the stockings my mom had hung up over the TV.

"Gran backed up over it," Elsa said with a grimace. "Had to get some value out of it."

"It's the perfect size for the apartment," Gran insisted.

The cat crept out from her hiding place under the sofa and cautiously sniffed the little tree.

I pulled out the wrapped presents from the bag Oliver had given me and began arranging them under the small tree.

"You didn't have to buy all that," my mom chastised. "You're already paying for this apartment. Save your money."

"I actually only bought this one," I said, shaking the wrapped puzzle box. "These others are from Oliver."

"Oliver?"

My parents were shocked.

"There's one for me," Dove said in amazement.

Now that she didn't have to babysit three babies, she was calmer and less bratty, though maybe she was a little depressed.

Aren't we all?

"Don't get too excited," Gran said. "He probably gave us all coal for Christmas."

"I hope he got my mom coal," Dove said with a scowl.

"You know what?" I said. "Why don't we open Oliver's now?"

Dove's eyes lit up.

Normally, Christmas morning was a big to-do at the Wynter house. There were speeches and special foods, and we had to find all the "clues" Santa had left when he'd visited. We wore matching pajamas and took family photos. It was my mom's favorite holiday, and we all tried to be on our best behavior to make sure she was happy.

My mother poured wine into a Santa-shaped coffee mug. "You know what? Why not? Go ahead and open them."

Dove tore into her present. "Oh my god," she said, clapping both hands over her mouth. "It's the deluxe Hello Kitty makeup set. It's sold out everywhere, literally everywhere."

"Make sure you write Mr. Frost a very nice thank-you note," my mom reminded her.

"Especially considering Noelle went full-on trash panda on his house," Gran said as she opened her present.

"Hot diggity!" She proudly held up the bottle of bourbon. "Aged twenty-five years."

"You need to have a refined palate for that." My mother sniffed.

My dad opened his small box.

"It's a keychain," he said happily, "and it's got a little truck on it. Aw, this looks like my truck from high school. Did you know you and your siblings were conceived there?" He and my mom hugged me. My brother was out spending Christmas Eve with his daughter, so I was the one who had to suffer that reminder alone.

"Yes, and every time I finally forget it, you always remind me."

"I hope the new landowners adopt it; maybe they can fix it up." My dad had tears in his eyes.

A note fell out of the box.

Dove held up the note and read it aloud. "'Since I didn't receive an angry call from you, I think it's safe to assume you didn't know I borrowed your truck. It's parked outside, waiting for you. I cleaned it up a bit. Hope you don't mind. It runs like a dream, by the way.'"

We all crowded to the window and looked out over the snowy street.

"Oh my gosh!" My dad was ecstatic. "That's my truck. There it is."

My mother's gift was a painting of what looked like a ski retreat in the mountains surrounded by old-growth pine trees.

The sign on the front read Wynter Lodge & Restaurant.

"Huh," my mom said. "That's strange. I wonder where he found this painting."

My gift was a single flat envelope. I carefully removed the wrapping paper. My mom liked to reuse it. Inside was a stapled set of documents.

I scanned them in confusion then disbelief. "This is our property. He bought it back."

There was a snowman Post-it note on the last page.

You should build your mom's lodge and restaurant on this property. Let me know if you need an investor.

"It's a Christmas miracle!" my dad whooped. "Merry Christmas! Merry Christmas!"

The rest of my family jumped around yelling, "Merry Christmas."

"Come on, Noelle," my mom cajoled. "Where's your Christmas spirit?"

Grinning in spite of myself, I tipped back my head. "Merry Christmas!"

"Too bad you let that man slip through your fingers," Gran remarked.

"More like took a sledgehammer to that relationship," my mom said with a laugh while my dad raced around handing out coats and hats, trying to herd us to the door for a joyride in his truck.

"Good thing you're already a grandmother," Gran told her as my mom tied a scarf around her neck. "Noelle's too hard on men."

"Give him another chance," Dove begged me.

"I can't," I said, bitterly. "I destroyed his house, ruined his Christmas, and told him I hated him. He's never going to forgive me. I threw away the best thing that ever happened to me."

"Nothing a good casserole can't fix," my mother insisted. "And a little Christmas magic."

"But the car," my dad pleaded as my mother grabbed her apron.

CHAPTER 75

Oliver

I couldn't stop staring at the picture of my niece. She had her mom's shock of dark hair and my brother's icy blue eyes.

I was an uncle. It seemed like a Christmas miracle.

Eve Frost. Born on Christmas Eve.

Though I was ecstatic, I felt a desperate longing in my bones. I wanted that. I could have had it with Noelle, if I hadn't been such a terrible person.

I didn't want to go into the house. It wasn't just the torn-up Christmas decorations that made it depressing—it was the big emptiness, the dark loneliness.

Motion caught my eye, and I glanced at Mrs. Horvat's house. She and her husband were gawking at me through the window.

"Guess it's just you and me for Christmas," I told Max and turned off the car.

The dog bounded around through the snow.

The lights from the large Christmas tree shone through the window, dappling the snow with multicolored shimmers.

"A Christmas tree?" I said, doing a double take. "I thought Noelle burned that?"

The front door opened, and her family streamed out while I looked on in disbelief.

"Just wanted to let you know I tossed out some of those casseroles people brought over here," Noelle's mom called, a big smile on her face. "Mrs. Roberts makes a whole batch of zucchini casserole in the summer and freezes them to hand out throughout the year. It's watery as all get out, and it smells atrocious. I did you a favor. Also, I made you some fish casserole because I knew it was your favorite and a breakfast casserole and a Christmas casserole. That's my specialty. Don't forget there are Christmas cookies and a pan of cinnamon buns. They're rising in the bottom oven. You can bake them in the morning. Yes, I saw Dot gave you some, and they're perfectly fine to serve if you have family over that you don't like."

I grinned.

"Thanks, Mrs. Wynter."

"I told you, that's my mother-in-law. That's the least we could do after your lovely Christmas gifts," Noelle's mother said, giving me a big hug and a kiss on the cheek. "I think I will be taking you up on your investment offer. Of course you can come eat whenever you like."

Her father pulled me into a big bear hug and squeezed me tight. "You're the real St. Nick. Merry Christmas! Hope you like the new tree. It's the best one yet."

Dove gave me a shy hug, and Gran toasted me with a glass of whiskey and drained it.

"Don't take the man's tableware," Noelle's mom scolded and handed me the empty glass.

"Don't you want to stay for a drink or something?" I asked them, trying not to sound like I was begging.

"We have to go pick up Noelle's brother," Sarah said. "Apparently, our granddaughter has had enough of Santa Claus for one evening. Merry Christmas!"

I waved to her family then stomped up the steps to get the snow off my shoes.

Inside, the house glowed with warmth. The whole place smelled like Christmas cookies. A fire crackled in the hearth, and new, fresh-smelling garland decorated with strings of cranberries graced the doorways and the stair banister. In the dining room, the place settings were back, albeit slightly scorched and chipped.

A huge Christmas tree towered over everything. Instead of the perfectly curated glass ornaments and small white LED lights, it was strung with big colorful vintage Christmas lights, popcorn strings, paper snowflakes, and gingerbread people on ribbons. Hand-knitted Christmas stockings hung up at the mantel.

It was a perfectly cozy family Christmas scene—minus the family, of course.

I desperately wished my siblings were there, but they were all in Manhattan with Owen and Holly. I had planned on joining them tomorrow, but maybe I would go back tonight.

It seemed like such a shame to waste all the Wynters' hard work, though.

Still, the loneliness was crushing me.

In the kitchen, someone started cursing.

"Noelle?" I said in shock as I walked in.

"Ah," she said, turning around. "Hi. Merry Christmas."

"You did all of this?"

"I had a number of little elves that liberally helped themselves to your wet bar and also might have snooped in your underwear drawer."

"You can touch my underwear whenever you want."

She gave me a crooked smile.

"Well, it was Gran, sooo... I am currently washing everything she touched."

"Oh, so that's why you're still here."

"I mean, I can leave..." she said, twisting her apron strings.

"No," I said. "I just thought—"

"It's not that. I—"

"Sorry," I said. "I didn't mean to interrupt. Go ahead."

She tugged at the sleeves of her sweater.

"Thank you for telling me about what happened that night in the lecture hall," she said finally. "I didn't know that you were going through all of that."

"I'm sorry I hurt you."

"I'm sorry I stalked you for a year."

"You were stalking me?"

"Not like outside of your house, staring into your windows," she said with an awkward laugh. "Well, not until this December, anyway."

"Holy shit, that wasn't a raccoon. You were watching me change clothes."

She covered her face with her hands. "I was obsessed with you and creepy, and now I'm in your house again uninvited. Also, I spied on you and your siblings."

"I knew someone was out there. I wasn't crazy."

"I am a terrible person!" she wailed.

"If you insist on breaking into my house, it's better when you're leaving food and not destroying my stuff," I said with a quirk of my mouth.

She made a face. "I'm sorry about that."

I crossed my arms. "I'm not that angry; I deserved it. And I already told the police I wasn't pressing charges against you. Also, apparently the money they made posting the viral video of you getting blasted by the fire hose is more than enough to pay for the fire damage at the park, so you're not going to jail."

"Oh my gosh."

"I'm going to ask your grandmother to knit that scene into a sweater for me."

"Worst Christmas ever."

I laughed. Then we were silent again.

"Thank you for my Christmas present," she whispered. "I love it."

"Actually," I admitted, walking into the living room and grabbing a small box, "that was an apology present. This was going to be your Christmas present."

She took the box from me and shook it.

I winced. "It's fragile."

Noelle laughed and carefully undid the wrapping paper.

"Aww," she cooed. "It's so cute!"

The Christmas ornament had two little glass corgis in a Santa and a Mrs. Claus outfit, connected by a heart.

"This is too pure. Merry Christmas." She hung it on the tree.

I wanted to kiss her. I loved her so much.

"I failed to do my Christmas shopping in a timely manner, so I might just have to give you a blow job instead," she said brightly.

"I can tie a ribbon on it."

"You don't have to," I said in a strained voice. I wanted her more than anything.

"What if I want to?" Noelle said simply.

"You don't hate me?"

"No," she said. "Maybe it's obsession or I'm just horny. But it feels a lot like I still love you."

"I love you more."

"I loved you longer," she replied.

"I'm sorry I didn't remember and I hurt you."

"It sounds like you were hurting too," she replied, her eyes searching mine. "And honestly, what's the point of Christmas if you can't extend a little grace?"

I leaned down hesitantly and brushed our lips together.

She threw her arms around the back of my neck and kissed me hard.

"Better than I remembered," she said against my mouth. "Now get on the couch and let me give you your Christmas present."

Her embrace was everything I desired. But soon I wanted more. I started hiking that sweater up and over her head, and she raised her arms to let me strip her of it. Then she was clawing at me, too, and I stripped off my shirt to the side. Running her hands over my bare chest, she smiled like someone about to get everything they wanted on Christmas morning.

My own slacks slid down my legs, and she eagerly looked up at me. She licked her lips, pulling aside my boxer-briefs and revealing my cock. I was already hard at the thought of her.

She dropped to her knees, and my cock jumped with anticipation. A gentle finger ran down my length. A shuddering warmth followed her touch. She jerked me a bit before batting at the head of my cock with some playful licks. She puckered up her lips before beginning to take me between them, so unbelievably tight for me, going inch by inch down her throat. Fuck, she was so damn good at this.

With a playful jumbling of my balls in her hand, she started to suck me.

I pulled away from her.

"Don't like your Christmas present?"

"As much as I love you sucking my cock, Noelle, right now I need to fuck you."

She looked up at me wide-eyed.

I slid my hands down her waist as she peeled off the black skinny jeans, revealing her curves.

I grabbed her around the waist and set her on the oversized ottoman. Then I slid her soaking wet panties down and threw them on the rug. She moaned as I buried my face in the V between her legs, licking and teasing the slit.

I couldn't wait for the bedroom.

My body pressed against hers, her tits rubbing against my chest—everything was so electric. I kissed her deeply, my tongue twisting into hers. I ran my hand down between us and went to her pussy, feeling how ready it was for me. I rubbed her gently, letting her shudder and gasp against me.

All the noises she made, the little moans and whimpers, were driving me crazy. I needed to fuck her. I stopped only to snatch a condom out of my pocket and put it on.

She was flat on the ottoman, her hips in the air, pussy wet and ready for my cock. I guided myself to her tight opening and thrust myself in, taking all of her and feeling her heat close around me.

She ground against me. She wanted it fast, rough, and dirty. Every thrust sent a blissful shiver through her, and she rolled her hips against me with each of those thrusts. Every penetration brought us closer, both to orgasm and to one another.

We were wild and insatiable, and we threw ourselves fully into the pleasure of the other. The rising tide between us was growing so fast. She cried out wilder and louder.

Soon, though, we couldn't resist one another anymore. I held out a little longer, wanting to hold her on the edge a moment more. But then she was screaming for me, her entire body trembling around me from the hard and furious fucking.

I felt the powerful release pulse through me as I let myself go, wrapping my arms around her and letting orgasm overwhelm me as it had done her.

"I love you," I whispered, holding her tight. It had gotten quiet enough that she had to have heard it, no question.

"And I love you," she whispered back.

We lay there in one another's arms for a time, which I hoped would last for the rest of our lives.

"Hey, Oliver," she said, kissing my jaw. "I think we need to go pay your parents a little surprise visit."

"My dad is going to be so pissed when he wakes up and sees that in the front yard," I whispered as Noelle and I jogged down the street back to my car.

The giant metal reindeer stood to attention front and center in the middle of my parents' perfect lawn.

"I would kill for a video."

I leaned over and pressed a kiss on her mouth. She wrapped her arms around my neck as I twirled her around in the falling snow. It was the perfect Christmas Eve with the woman of my dreams.

"Ready to go sit by a fire and watch a Christmas movie?" I asked her.

"Uh, no."

"Come on, you're supposed to learn the true meaning of Christmas after you steal everyone's presents," I teased.

She stuck her tongue out at me.

"I have! And there's nothing more traditional on Christmas Eve than last-minute shopping."

CHAPTER 76

Noelle

Oliver's sister-in-law and brother were waiting on his front porch when we pulled up. The sun was just rising, sparkling over the freshly fallen snow, a perfect start to a Christmas morning. Before our Christmas sabotage mission, Oliver and I had bought a trunkful of food that I was going to cook up for his brother and sister-in-law and their new baby.

The one thing I hadn't been able to find at the store was an eel. It wasn't Christmas without eel pie. Fortunately, I was able to swap a box of cookies for one with a farmer down the road who raised them illegally in his barn.

Oliver's brother Owen looked a little shell-shocked. A fluffy husky-looking dog bounced at his feet and kept rising on his hind legs to sniff at his coat.

"I thought you just had a baby," I said to Holly. "What are you doing here?"

"I'm starving," she said as Oliver unlocked the front door. "I heard there was casserole. I really need some casserole. God, your house smells amazing. Oh, look! You redecorated," Holly exclaimed as she maneuvered her way toward the kitchen.

Owen carefully removed his coat to reveal a very tiny baby strapped to his large chest, drooling on his expensive suit.

"It was the craziest thing I've ever seen," Owen said to his brother in a low voice.

I left them and started playing hostess. Holly was in the kitchen, going to town on my mom's fish casserole. I dumped the eel in the large sink and pulled out a sparkling water for her. She chugged it down.

"Do you need to lie down?" I asked in concern.

"God, no. Can I have some hot chocolate?"

"Coming right up."

I did not make hot chocolate from a packet. My recipe was cocoa powder, a little cinnamon, whole milk, and maple syrup stirred slowly. I was whisking on the stove when the doorbell rang.

"Merry Christmas," my mother called.

My parents, accompanied by Dove, trucked boxes into the kitchen.

"Noelle, I'm going to help you cook for Oliver's sister-in-law," my mother said. "We're going to make her some food you can take with you when you visit."

"She's already cooking," Dove argued.

"Extra food never hurt anyone." My mom shushed her.

"Did you make this casserole?" Holly asked, mouth half-full when she saw my mom.

"Noelle and I did." My mother beamed.

"I love you," Holly said, wrapping her arms around her. Then she gave me a hug and sniffed the hot chocolate appreciatively.

Owen came into the kitchen. The baby was awake and blinking on his chest.

"Oh my gosh," my mother said, looking between Holly and the baby.

"*You* just had a baby. Don't you want to sit down on the couch?"

"I heard someone say 'eel pie,'" she said.

"Look at those little feet. How adorable," my mother said softly, making a gooey face at the baby. "She's so much cuter than Noelle was. And look at those blue eyes!"

"Gee, thanks, Mom."

As much as I wanted to hold the baby, it didn't look like her father was ever letting her go.

I linked my arm with Oliver's, and we strolled out into the living room. "Your house seems a lot happier filled with people."

He leaned down to kiss me.

"You mean our house. If you want it," he said when my face fell. "You don't have to move in with me. I just thought..."

"I do," I said. "But..." I chewed on my lip. "My sister just dumped Dove on me. Signed papers and everything. I sort of promised her we would find a house so she could have her own room."

"Dove can move in here," Oliver said automatically. "There are more than enough bedrooms."

"Here in this beautiful house? Are you sure?"

"All I want for Christmas is you." He leaned in to kiss me softly.

"And an eleven-year-old?" I raised an eyebrow.

"Family is important, Noelle, and as a newly minted uncle, I insist that the niece of the woman I love will not be out on the street."

We found Dove snapping photos of the garland-draped curving staircase.

"Do you want to go upstairs and pick out your new room?" I asked her.

Her eyes bugged out in confusion.

"Wait. What?" she screamed.

"If we are going to be living together," I warned her, "I need it to not be like the set of a Nickelodeon show."

Oliver laughed.

"I can live with you here, Aunt Noelle? Really? No joke?"

I nodded and grinned.

She screamed again. "Oh my god, Stacey's going to be so jealous."

I shook my head as she raced up the stairs. "You sure you want this?"

Oliver swung me around and kissed me. "An instant family? Of course."

"More like instant drama."

"Have you met my brothers?"

"Speaking of..." I pointed.

Several men with Oliver's coloring knocked on the windows.

"Merry Christmas!" they chorused when we welcomed them inside.

"Man, what is that amazing smell?" one of them asked.

"Not for you," Oliver joked as the Frost brothers and their girlfriends all piled into the kitchen.

"I thought we were all going to Manhattan?" Oliver's brother said, confused.

"Holly said there was food here," Chloe said, "so we just came here instead."

"Besides," Jonathan added, "there's nothing like a small-town Christmas."

Introductions were made. Oliver had a lot of siblings and future sisters-in-law.

"Holy shit!" Jack laughed at his phone. "Remember Sam? His parents live across the street from our parents. He texted me and said someone left a giant penis statue in Mom and Dad's front yard. He said they're freaking out and his mom has taken to the Facebook group to complain."

"Gee," Oliver said, rocking back on his heels, "that sounds very upsetting."

He and I snickered.

Morticia took off her dark glasses, gazed at the eels in the sink, and gave me an approving nod. Then she pulled out a large cleaver.

The doorbell rang again.

"We brought the turkey," Gran hollered.

My little nieces ran into the living room, followed by my brother with a huge bird.

"Oh my god, you all can't just crash Oliver's party. You have to wait on the porch." I tried to shoo them all outside.

"It's fine," Oliver assured me. "It's Christmas."

One of his brothers turned on a Christmas movie on the TV for the kids.

My brother started talking to Owen about the joys of fatherhood.

I resisted rolling my eyes.

"I brought the puzzle for them to do," Gran said, waving it at me, "to keep your brother and dad busy while we cook."

"Oh my god, Noelle," my mother chastised me, "you bought this?"

I took a good hard look at the cover on the puzzle box and bit back a curse. I had just grabbed the first puzzle I saw at the stall. It had been dark in the Christmas market.

"Okay, we are not making that puzzle."

"Fa la la!" Merrie, Matt's girlfriend, who also happened to be a year above me in high school, waggled her eyebrows. "Oh yes we are. Someone get me some extra rum for my eggnog."

The puzzle box had a picture of a very ripped and well-endowed man with long flowing hair. He wore black boots, a belt, and a Santa hat, and he was posed suggestively in front of a castle. The text on the puzzle read Merry Christmas, Ladies!

"You know," Matt said dryly, "I always wondered how those stalls at the Christmas market made enough money to stay in business."

"Sex sells," his girlfriend said cheerfully.

"No shit. That puzzle was freaking expensive."

"Noelle, I need rosemary from the garden," my mother called from the kitchen.

"I'll have to go back to the cottage and grab some," I told her, giving the hot chocolate another stir. I shoved out of the way several dogs who seemed much too interested in the turkey she was stuffing.

"I'll come do the roast beef when I get back," I added, opening drawers, looking for a pair of kitchen shears.

"We have goose, too, so you need to make some k*nödel*," my mom said happily.

My mother was born to be a homemaker. Now that she had access to a top-of-the-line kitchen, she was going all out. Deborah had nothing on my mom.

"There are some in the greenhouse outside, I think," Olivier said, ushering me out into the snowy, quiet garden.

I brushed the snow off the door handle. The greenhouse was warm and protected against the chill. Some enterprising decorator had even turned this small glass building into a Christmas wonderland.

"Mistletoe," Oliver said, pointing up at the vine on a tree. He leaned in and kissed me.

"Merry Christmas, Noelle. I love you."

"I love you," I whispered.

"You have made this the best Christmas ever."

"Resting grinch face and all?" I teased.

"Please." He smirked at me. "You so love Christmas."

"Fine, guilty as charged." I stuck out my tongue. "But I think I might need you to give me a live-action remake of that Christmas puzzle just to make extra sure I've maxed out my Christmas cheer!"

The End

GRINCH Please!

A
SHORT
HOLIDAY
ROMANTIC COMEDY

CHAPTER 1

Noelle

The diamond ring sparkled on my finger. No, not that finger—on my right hand. I'd kept the giant snowflake diamond ring.

Sure, some girls might think wearing that ring would remind them of a time in their relationship they didn't fondly remember.

But my family had survived by being frugal. I canned my own food, shopped at thrift stores, and reused an item until it couldn't be reused anymore, at which point it was to be set with loving care in a large pile of similar items, just in case it might be useful one day.

My momma did not raise me to throw out a very pricy diamond ring. That thing would be with me on my deathbed, along with all the charging cables I couldn't get rid of...

I straightened the last wreath in the window of the brand-new Wynter Retreat Lodge, Restaurant, and Spa that was opening just in time for the Christmas season.

"Happy Black Friday." I waved to Elsa, who was back in town from visiting her brothers.

"Okay, so check this out. I have been trying a new recipe for spiked hot chocolate," she said, thrusting a thermos at me.

I took a sip. "Wow, that is strong."

"Right? Your mom was saying she wanted a signature drink to serve at the restaurant."

"This will certainly put everyone in a festive spirit."

"The place is looking great," Elsa marveled.

The lodge was built to look like a log cabin constructed from huge heavy timbers—but upscale, of course. We were trying to attract people from Manhattan to come have glam winter weekends in the woods. Huge glass windows let in as much of the winter daylight as possible. A fire burned merrily in the two stone fireplaces that flanked either end of the large great room. They were big enough for me to stand in.

Gran was stirring a big pot of spiked cider in one of the fireplaces.

"Oh, Elsa," my mother called, hurrying through the lodge.

This was her baby, her dream. But now that it was almost a reality—well, I had inherited my anxious tendencies honestly.

My mom gave Elsa a big hug. "You're so sweet. You didn't have to come. I know you and Noelle have to work. You're so busy with your company. Oh, I baked pinwheel cookies for your employees."

"I thought these were for the opening?" I said as my mother shoved a huge box of cookies at me.

"I don't think anyone's coming," she said, dropping her voice.

"Um, Mom, the entire freaking town is going to be on your doorstep tomorrow. Don't you worry."

"That's just the grand opening party." My mother waved me away. "But I have barely gotten any interest. We're not going to have any customers."

"Noelle said you guys were all booked up." Elsa reached in the box for a cookie.

"Who knows if they're going to show up?" my mother said dramatically. "That app Noelle made says that up to fifty percent of people don't show up to claim a hotel booking, so you should overbook. But I haven't been able to overbook that much."

I frowned. "My app said that?" The app was designed to support small businesses and trawl the internet for facts and tidbits related to the app owner's industry. But those were just meant to be factoids. You weren't supposed to base real business decisions on the pop-ups.

"It's going to be fine, Mom," I assured her. "But stop overbooking people. This isn't a Marriott with four hundred rooms. You only have twenty-five."

"I have thirty rooms booked for tomorrow," she said.

"Oh my god." I started freaking out. "What if everyone shows up?"

"Your app said they wouldn't," my mother shrieked.

"Let's all just remain calm," my brother said.

"Oh, look at him. Doesn't he look handsome in his uniform?" my mother called.

My brother was the bellhop. Carrying suitcases up and down stairs and driving the van to the train station to pick up guests worked well with his video gaming schedule.

He saluted me.

"Merry Christmas!" He snagged a cookie out of the box. "Gran, hit me up!"

Gran sloshed a generous helping of cider into his mug.

"Guests aren't arriving until tomorrow. Guests aren't arriving until tomorrow," my mother muttered to herself.

"Jimmy, the door," Azalea yelled to my brother from the front desk.

Yep, this was a family affair. Well, for everyone except me.

"Bet you're glad this isn't your Christmas circus," Elsa whispered to me and passed me a cookie.

Because I had a real company. And I lived with Oliver in his very nice house. Without my family.

Even though I, too, was living out my dream, a part of me wished I was still under one roof with my family, working at the lodge.

The top half of a very large Christmas tree slowly maneuvered into the great hall, guided by my father and Oliver.

"Is that what he had you come over here to do?" I asked Oliver. "Dad, Oliver is busy. You said you wanted him to look at your electrical system, not do manual labor."

My father gave me a sheepish smile. "Just wanted to include him in the Christmas traditions."

I smiled at Oliver and mouthed, *Sorry*.

He gave me a strained smile and leaned over to plant a sadly chaste kiss on me. Then he turned his attention to trying to rotate the fifteen-foot-tall Christmas tree so that it stood proudly in the double height space.

My shoulders slumped.

"Did something happen with one of his siblings?" Elsa asked me in a low voice. "I thought he loved Christmas. He should be hopped up on those Yuletide vibes."

I stuffed a cookie in my mouth.

"I'm not sure," I admitted. "He's been a little cold the last few weeks. Whenever I ask him, he just says he's dealing with a lot, what with trying to do the cleanup at the old country expo site and dealing with the railroad and the Department of Defense. But he's still cheery with Max."

The corgi raced around the living room, giving kisses to my nieces and nephews.

Dove, now that she didn't have to be the de facto babysitter or live full-time in a crowded house with my sister, had a much more generous and easygoing personality.

"Why don't you do couples counseling?"

"I don't want to rock the boat," I admitted to Elsa. "I have to keep the peace for Dove. She's finally starting to act like a human being and not a feral parrot."

"Maybe that's why Oliver is so cold."

I shook my head. "He was always nice to Dove, and she worships the ground he walks on. The only person he's weird with is me. Maybe he's waiting until after Christmas to break up with me."

"No way." Elsa shook her head.

"That's what some guys do. They think it's easier because then they don't have the guilt of ruining their girlfriend's or wife's holiday."

I didn't know if I could keep it together over the entire month of December with the possibility of a New Year's resolution breakup hanging over my head.

"Do you think he's cheating?"

"I don't know," I admitted bitterly. "He's been cagey with his phone lately, but maybe I'm paranoid and seeing things that aren't there. I have on occasion been known to do that."

"When was the last time you, you know?"

"Not lately." I dropped my voice. "I ordered a sexy outfit to, you know, try to add a little spice to the Christmas punch, so to speak. Problem is that Dove's still on Thanksgiving break 'til Monday, and she has been clingy lately."

"Leave it to your best-friend cousin," Elsa promised. "I will get her out of the house, then you can remind him who has the best tits this side of the Hudson River."

I gave her a small smile.

I wasn't sure.

But I had to do something. Otherwise, this was my last Christmas with Oliver.

CHAPTER 2

Oliver

"Are you serious?" I hissed to Noelle's father, flabbergasted he could do such a thing.

"I'm just so excited you're proposing tomorrow."

Noelle's mom was jumping up and down.

"Dove," I began.

"You didn't tell me!" she cried. I shushed her.

"If you had told me first, I would have kept it secret. This man became a grandfather before age thirty. He completely failed the marshmallow test. You can't entrust him with your secrets."

"She's right," James said solemnly. "You never should have told me. Guilty as charged."

"This is so exciting. We can have a grand opening and an engagement party," Sarah gushed.

"I'll make a sign," James said.

"A sign for what?" Azalea, Noelle's sister, asked, scowling as she stuck her head into the small manager's office.

Dove went cold when she saw her mom.

When Noelle had moved Dove in, I was happy to have her. But I had sort of thought that with some space, Azalea might start missing her eldest daughter and make moves to repair the relationship. But she missed therapy appointments, wouldn't do FaceTime calls, and hadn't even given the girl a birthday present. I didn't want to judge, because she'd had her as a young teenager, but still.

You of all people should know that sometimes you just can't repair the damage to the parent-child relationship and it's best for everyone to go their separate ways.

"You need to help Grandma decorate the tree," Azalea said sharply to Dove, "and stop making all that noise."

"You're never around. I don't have to listen to you." Dove was defiant.

"Dove, let me just talk to your mother. Then I'll come out and help you decorate. How about that?"

Azalea crossed her arms as we waited for the rest of the family to leave the office.

"So, either Noelle's pregnant or you're getting engaged—or both, I take it," she said, tone surly.

"Door number two," I replied.

"Huh. Guess you want to evict Dove now so you can have your own children. You better talk to my mother because I don't have room for her in the place I'm renting."

"No, no," I assured her. "The house is Dove's home too. I have no intention of kicking her out. In fact," I said, hoping Azalea would receive my request well, "I wanted to ask you if I could adopt Dove. Well, Noelle and me. If you would be okay with that. Eventually," I added because Azalea's expression was dark.

"So you think I'm a bad mother?" she shot at me.

Yes.

"Of course not," I said smoothly, slipping into the tone I used to deal with particularly irate investors.

"Yes you do," Azalea hissed. "Do you know how much I sacrificed to have that girl? I got pregnant at fourteen, and her father just ran out. Went back to fucking Denmark or wherever the hell he was from. Goddamn foreign exchange students. You think I wanted her?"

No, which is why I offered to adopt her.

"All she did was cry. And my mom would make me come rock her. I had to miss parties. I didn't go to prom. I couldn't find a decent man after that, and it was all because of Dove. She ruined my life. She owes me."

Damn.

"Forget I said anything," I told her. "I was just floating an idea. I thought it might make things easier for you."

"Easier for Dove, you mean," Azalea said darkly. "She made me miserable. She doesn't get to be happy."

"We can just continue on as normal."

"Yikes," Tristan said as we drove down the snowy country road out to the expo site. "And I thought my mom was fucked up."

"This whole situation is fucked."

"Did her dad tell you he wasn't going to bless your proposal?" Tristan asked.

"Exactly the opposite. He was so excited he told the rest of her family, and they all decided the proposal was happening tomorrow, at the grand opening."

Tristan started snickering.

"This is a crisis; it's not funny," I snapped.

"Just tell them you were planning on proposing on Christmas morning."

"They will spill the secret long before then. I wanted this to be a surprise. It has to be perfect to make up for the last proposal disaster," I said.

"You don't have the ring," he reminded me.

I planned events well in advance. It was my thing.

The ring was supposed to be here weeks ago, but the local artisan I'd hired to make it was running late.

"She swears she's going to get it to me by the end of the day," I told Tristan.

"Noelle's going to love the design," he assured me.

"Who knows what the ring even looks like at this point? This is why I wanted to have it in hand at least six weeks before, just in case it was terrible and I needed to postpone."

The artisan was a highly creative person and had sent me a steady barrage of text messages with cryptic pictures, scrawled sketches, and design-change whims over the last few weeks. I had no idea what the ring would look like.

"She can't not love it. It's got a huge diamond on it that you specifically sourced for her. Just get everyone drunk beforehand, and it will go perfectly."

But it wouldn't go at all if I didn't have the ring.

CHAPTER 3

Noelle

After waving off Elsa, Dove, and Max later that afternoon to go explore the Christmas market, I paced around the living room, waiting for my sexy surprise shipment to show up.

In a nod to my Christmas-loathing past, I'd ordered a sexy Grinch costume. I'd also made Oliver a roast beef with cheesy mashed potatoes, green beans, and lots of gravy and a cranberry loaf ring.

But first, we were going to get a little workout in.

"He's probably just stressed," I told myself as I paced around in front of the Christmas tree my dad had dropped off with me earlier. "You're being paranoid and crazy."

But I couldn't get over how he kept hiding his phone from me whenever it went off. What was the reasonable explanation for that?

"Give him a good orgasm and a nice meal, and he'll forget all about whoever he's having an affair with… Oh my god, he's having an affair." I started hyperventilating.

The doorbell rang, shocking me out of the oncoming hysterics.

"I need a signature," the harried postal worker said, handing me a stack of Christmas catalogs and mail along with a very large box.

"Merry Christmas," I called and shut the door. Then I headed up to the master bedroom. There was a very large mirror in the master closet. I quickly stripped off my clothes and tried on the outfit.

I had taken to wearing a thong, just in case Oliver decided he was in the mood. Then I could whip off my clothes and be like, "Ass and titties!" But he hadn't, and so I suffered with the butt floss.

"He won't be thinking about anything but sex when I surprise him with this," I said gleefully. It had been a while for me, and I was practically drooling thinking about his cock.

But my hoo-ha shriveled up and died when I lifted the sexy outfit out of the box.

"What in the fuck is this?" I shrieked. I pawed through the packing paper in the box, hoping this was a joke, that they had accidentally put someone else's order in with mine.

"This doesn't look like the picture on the website at all," I said in shock.

It was a Grinch costume, and I supposed someone might have thought it was sexy. It was literally a sexy Grinch costume. Like, it was the fur suit and pot belly of a Grinch with a bra and panties sewn on.

I slipped it on and took a few photos to show Elsa.

Elsa: *Um, WTF is that?*
Elsa: *Did you kill a deer?*
Elsa: *Holy shit, are you preggo?*
Noelle: *It came preloaded with a foam pot belly.*
Noelle: *WTF am I supposed to do now???*
Noelle: *This was supposed to be my plan to win Oliver back and rekindle our Christmas romance.*
Noelle: *I look like a Christmas serial killer.*
Elsa: *Did it come with the creepy long fingers?*

It did, in fact. And a giant candy cane whip. I slipped on the gloves and did a few sexy poses in the mirror for Elsa.

"Looking sexy," I told my reflection, then stripped off the suit and stood there in my thong.

What the hell was I going to do now?

"Noelle?" Oliver's deep voice called from the bedroom.

Santa's balls.

I hid the green furry suit in the box and hastily stuffed it behind the suitcases in the closet.

"I, um..." I said, walking out and surreptitiously setting my phone down on the dresser. "Merry Christmas?"

"What were you—"

I did a little jig, shaking my breasts for him and capturing his attention and ideally making him forget about asking me what I was doing in the closet.

"Hey, Noelle," he said, following the bouncing tits.

I did a little strut over to the bed, shaking my ass too. We would have to pivot from the original plan.

I bounced off the mattress, looking his way, spreading my legs. I licked my finger and ran it down my form, heaving my breasts out. My finger came down to my thong and ran it over to the perimeter.

His attention on me was rock solid. I had an absolutely captive audience.

"Why don't you take off that suit and join me over here?"

I rubbed myself a bit. It was enough to get the fire really roaring down there, even if it was nowhere near as good as Oliver's touch.

I blew him a kiss, watching as his eyes widened and he was riveted by each and every little thing I was doing.

I wasn't really much of a performer, but I needed him to still want me, still love me.

His shirt was off, revealing those washboard abs and broad chest I wanted to rake my nails down.

I threw my ass back toward him, feeling it jiggle for him. "We're doing something a little bit different tonight, Oliver. Spice it up." I winked at him. "I want you to come down my chimney, Oliver."

I threw my other Amazon order on the bed: Christmas-themed lube.

Oliver cursed as he stripped off the rest of his clothes. Then he was beside me on the bed. His touch ignited my body with warmth, and his hands went up and down my curves.

He kissed me hard, his large hands kneading my tits then slipping down and stroking my dripping wet pussy. I was half-gone already thinking about him inside me.

He positioned me on the bed, spreading my legs. He pulled the lacy thong down and tossed it on the floor.

Then his mouth was on my pussy, teasing me, licking me into a frenzy.

"I want your cock," I begged as his tongue twirled around my clit.

He inserted two fingers in my opening, stroking me while he licked me.

Before I knew it, I was coming. Like I said, it had been a while.

It wasn't enough, though.

"Fuck me," I panted.

His cock throbbed against my ass cheeks as he positioned himself behind me on all fours.

The cap popped off the lube. Then he was spreading my ass with one hand and inserting two fingers in me. I moaned at the sensation, my thighs trembling from desire.

He teased me with his cock for a moment then slowly pushed in. I gasped as I tightened around his thick cock.

Oliver held me tight as he let me adjust to his girth, giving me a moment. But this was not my first time, and I knew what I liked.

"Take me," I begged in a throaty voice.

He pulled out then pushed in again. I let out a low moan. Then, he started to fuck me. His cock slid out of my ass and in, the weird yet pleasant symphony of sensations hitting me and overrunning me with bliss. I panted, but as long as I didn't feel pain, he didn't stop. At a steady, solid pace, he kept up the pressure, stroke after stroke of him fucking my ass.

As I moaned for him, Oliver became bolder, taking me faster. I rubbed my ass against him, begging him to go deeper, faster. His arms wrapped around me as he took me from behind, holding my breasts, pinching the nipples, driving me crazy.

One hand gripped my hip tightly, and the other trailed over my curves, sliding between my legs, rubbing my aching clit. It wasn't long until I was lost in him, screaming to him, utter orgasm wracking my body and making itself all I could feel.

That was all he needed to crest over the edge, filling me with his hot come.

"God," I gasped, "that was so fucking hot."

He pressed sloppy kisses along my jaw. Being in his arms felt right, like how it used to be.

"I love you," he murmured.

"I love you too."

Maybe sex does cure all ills.

I felt in love and connected.

Until his phone chimed.

He rolled over, clearly blocking me from view with his body.

I felt heartbroken.

He was cheating.

"I have to go," he said, not looking at me.

He swung his legs over the side of the bed and quickly dressed.

Oliver didn't even give me a kiss goodbye.

"I made dinner," I said to the empty room.

I sat having a pity picnic in front of the unlit fireplace, alternating between stuffing myself with mashed potatoes and bourbon.

"This is why I hate Christmas." I sniffled to myself.

A shadowy figure appeared in the window.

I peered blearily, set down my whiskey, and stumbled over there.

"Are you the Ghost of Christmas Past?" I asked when I opened it.

"Get it together. It's still November," Azalea snapped at me.

"Come inside," I slurred, grabbing at her.

"Stop it. Are you drunk? It's not even seven o'clock. I'm telling Mom," my sister huffed.

"Nooooo!"

"God, and people think I'm a bad mother."

I hiccupped. "You're not a bad mother. I mean, sometimes you are, but there's worse out there. You have a job, and Kayleigh gets smiley faces in daycare."

Azalea had a pained look on her face. "I'm okay with the littles, but I'm a terrible mother to Dove. She hates me."

The words sobered me up.

"No she doesn't," I said. "She's just disappointed."

Azalea looked upset. "I can't be her mom. I never could. You, Mom, and Gran did more for her than I ever did. I can't even pretend to be one of those hardworking single moms who were forced to neglect their kid because they were out working three jobs. That wasn't me."

"There's always tomorrow," I said. "You can always do better."

"She's what, twelve? I think the ship is quickly sailing. I just..." She crossed her arms. "I never wanted her. I didn't want to be a mother."

"Then why..."

"I got caught up in it. I thought it would make me special. I was getting all this attention. Everyone wanted to talk to me in school. The principal, even the Danish consul, came and talked to me. I was famous. People were throwing me baby showers. It was like I was about to join this exclusive club. And then the baby showed up and after a month, people just weren't interested anymore. Then I was just a failure. The teen-mom daughter of a teen mom. Dove cried all the time. She didn't even like me."

"She was a baby. They cry."

"All I could think about when I saw her was how much she had ruined my life," Azalea said, tears filling her eyes.

I looked at her through the open window, an invisible barrier between us. My heart ached for my sister.

"And you," she continued, looking away, "you always judged me, rubbing your success in my face. It was so aggravating how much you and Dove connected. How much she liked you over me. I kept going after men who I thought would be able to take care of me, give me a nice life and a nice house, be a good father for Dove, but they were all complete shit."

"Guys suck," I said sympathetically.

"Not Oliver."

"No," I told her bitterly, "he sucks too."

"God, you are so spoiled and entitled. Grow up. He's perfect. You get everything you want, then you complain about it."

"No I don't," I argued.

"Yes you do," Azalea yelled. "It's not fair. Everyone likes you more than me. You're better than me. I'm a failure, and all of you hate me. Especially you. You hate what I did to Dove."

"Azalea." I stuck my head out of the window, the winter wind stinging my eyes. "I don't hate you. You're my big sister. We're family. I will always be in your corner. Always.

I love you. Anyone gives you trouble or talks shit about you, I will personally go over to their house and set their Christmas tree on fire."

Azalea gave me a small smile.

I made grabbing motions with my hands. She stepped up to me, and I gave her a big hug.

"I know you had a long way to climb, and I respect you for it." I put my hands on her shoulders. "Don't sell yourself short. You're the manager at the greatest boutique lodge, restaurant, and spa in the state of New York. And you make a mean jar of jam."

She rolled her eyes. "Mom's been cooking nonstop for the past week. I don't know what we're going to do with all the food."

"Have a kickass party!" I whooped.

Azalea and I grinned at each other.

"Do you want to adopt her?" she asked abruptly.

"Who?"

"Dove, moron. Do you want to be her mom? I mean, you basically have been."

"I can take care of her if you don't want to," I said carefully.

"No." She shook her head. "Are you yearning to be her mother?"

"Yeah," I said. "I love her. She's the Rudolph to my Santa."

"Okay," Azalea said, jaw set. "You can be who she needs better than I can. I'm sure you can get a fancy-pants lawyer to figure it all out."

She turned abruptly. "See you tomorrow."

I stood in the window with my nose numb, not quite processing what had just happened.

"Azalea," I called, "do you want some Christmas cookies?"

But my sister had already disappeared into the snowy darkness.

CHAPTER 4

Noelle

I took a deep breath once I was outside in the cold winter evening.

Why was I even wasting my time getting this ring?

Noelle had been taking pictures in the closet. She was sending them to someone. She must have been, based on how guilty she was acting when she exited the closet. Clearly, she was hiding something from me.

She was probably going to send them to you, the rational part of my brain said.

Except I had heard the noise the phone made when it sent a text message.

The message hadn't gone to me.

My fists clenched as I thought about our lovemaking earlier.

She felt so right. So perfect.

I loved her so much.

But did she love me?

Maybe I needed to call off the proposal.

At least until I figured out who she was sending those photos to.

The jewelry artisan was an older woman with crazy curly hair interwoven with feathers and beads.

Celestia was dancing and humming to herself when I approached the park bench. The light was low, though her face was lit up by a burning bunch of sage.

My eyes watered.

"Come in," she said, wafting the smoke at me. "Come into my shop."

I stepped up to the park bench.

You wanted to hire someone local, because Noelle would appreciate money staying in her community, I reminded myself. Though I wished I had just gone with a high-end Parisian designer like my brother had done with his girlfriend's engagement ring.

"So, how does the ring look?" I asked.

The artist ignored me and continued to sway. "Do you hear the spirits? The closer we get to the winter solstice, the brighter their voices."

I literally did not have the patience.

"Yes, they sound lovely. I'm sure you're busy, and I don't want to keep you. Would you like cash for the remainder of the balance or credit card?"

"My preferred method of payment is silver ingots blessed by a Celtic goddess."

"I have a silver credit card," I offered, thumbing through my wallet.

She pressed her hands together and took out her phone. "Close enough."

I waited impatiently while she tried and failed to get the card reader to work.

"I can take a look if you want," I said delicately.

"All this modern technology," Celestia said dramatically and flopped down on the bench.

I swiped the card, and the payment went through.

"Success," I said.

She was asleep on the bench.

"Ma'am?"

She snored.

"Ma'am, the ring?"

She woke up with a start. "It's the spirits."

"*The ring.*"

"The ring..." She pulled a small wooden box out of her pocket and presented it to me with a curtsy. "For your lovely bride."

Finally.

I opened the box... and tried to keep the horror off my face when I saw what was inside.

"This..." I said slowly, "was not what we originally discussed."

I couldn't propose to Noelle with this ring. It was hideous.

The original design had been a large diamond in the center surrounded by an even dusting of rubies and emeralds on the band.

This new ring design was lopsided, with the bear-cut diamond sitting on jutting pieces of silver, not at all the delicate swirls I had imagined. The emerald and rubies looked like they had been clumped on.

"I was moved by my intuition," the artisan said as she danced away into the night. "You're welcome."

"What the fuck? I cannot propose to Noelle with this," I said as I trudged back toward the Christmas market. I didn't know what I was looking for.

I needed another ring.

As if I could find a five-million-dollar diamond in a small-town Christmas market.

"Just go home," I told myself. "If she's sending pictures to someone else, maybe this is a sign from the universe that you need to rethink your plans for spending the rest of your life with Noelle."

CHAPTER 5

Noelle

We're overbooked!" my mother whisper-screamed when she saw me.

She dragged me down a side hallway into the manager's office.

"I told her not to overbook," Azalea said accusingly, "but Mom said you told her to."

"I didn't."

"The app said it," my mom insisted. "Now everyone is here."

"We're going to have to pay to have people moved to another hotel," Azalea snapped at me, arms crossed. "This is your fault. You need to pay for it. Mom's business shouldn't have to pay for your mistakes."

Fuck my life.

"Sure," I said, "fine."

Who cared about guests when the love of your life was cheating on you?

"Let's just make sure there isn't anyone super important that we absolutely cannot boot." I scanned the guest list then relaxed. Four of the rooms were booked for Oliver's siblings.

"These people are going." I circled the Frosts' names.

"You can't kick them out. They're family." My mother was scandalized.

"Uh, yes I can," I said, scowling at the Frost name. "Especially if they're that cheater's family. They can go live in his cheating fucking house."

Then I burst into tears.

My mom and sister looked at me like I was insane.

My mother squirmed.

"Don't you dare," Azalea said to her.

Azalea marched outside and came back in with a fistful of snow, which she stuffed down the back of my dress.

I screamed.

"Get it together," she scolded me. "We have half the town showing up in fifteen minutes, not to mention our guests. You cannot come apart."

"My life is over," I wailed.

Azalea pinched my arm.

"Ow." I rubbed it.

"Go deal with the Frosts," she ordered. "Then make sure Dad isn't giving away free Christmas trees to people. Jimmy's supposed to be picking up the first round of guests at the train station. Mom, all your food needs to be out on the tables. Go water down whatever alcoholic grog Gran has bubbling in the fireplace. We're not running a charity here. Speeches are at five, then two more hours of revelry, then everyone needs to be out. This isn't a frat house. We want our guests to feel comfortable. Don't fuck this up," Azalea warned us.

I saluted. "Yes, ma'am."

Everyone was laughing and having a wonderful time at the party as I meandered through the guests. My mom was aglow as all her friends and neighbors congratulated her on the beautiful building and the amazing food.

Elsa's older brothers had come in for the grand opening. They were all huddled on the opposite side of the yard, glaring daggers at the Frost brothers.

Nothing like Christmas to bring the drama.

I was back to my bartending roots, passing out drinks.

Oliver was with his family. His brothers were whispering angrily to him and pointing in my general vicinity.

Fuckers.

I had ignored him when I'd told his siblings that we were overbooked and asked if they could pretty please stay at their brother's house.

In my defense, Oliver hadn't been exactly warm and inviting to me either.

I didn't know what to do. I was supposed to adopt Dove, but now we might be kicked out of Oliver's house. It had been her home for the last year. For the first time in her life, she'd had her own room. I didn't know what it would do to her to have to pack up and leave.

"No sexy outfit?"

I almost spilled the drinks in surprise.

"Oh," I said when I saw Oliver.

He seemed crushed by my lackluster response.

"This is supposed to be a classy establishment."

His jaw clenched. He looked away then turned back to me.

"Then what were you taking photos of?" he asked in a rush. "I heard you when I went into the bedroom. You were taking pictures and texting someone and—"

My face felt hot.

"Nothing," I sputtered.

"And now you're lying to me," he growled. "Just tell me who he is."

This motherfucker.

"I'm not lying," I screeched then lowered my voice. "I'm not a cheater."

"Then who were you texting?"

Did I want to be right, or did I want to utterly humiliate myself?

Please. I was a middle child. I lived to win.

I whipped out my phone, scrolled to the text message to Elsa, and slapped the phone in his hand.

Oliver made a horrified face.

"Is this for the pageant?" he asked finally.

"What pageant?"

"The town is having a new annual pageant about how you stole Christmas and burned down the town." A smile played around his mouth.

"First off, mister, it was one fucking tree and some garland. And," I amended, "a bench and a gazebo. But that gazebo was haunted anyway, so who cares? Thirdly—"

"That's not a word."

"Third-fucking-ly. None of that is enough material for a Christmas pageant. I bought this for you to surprise you because you seemed stressed, and I thought this would help you, you know, blow off some steam."

"You wanted me to have sex with you in that?" Oliver asked, looking like he wanted to be anywhere but here having this conversation.

"God, no. Especially not since you're texting some other woman and sneaking off and—"

The microphone screeched.

I crossed my arms, and we turned to face the stage.

My dad was so excited he was bouncing up and down like a five-year-old.

"Thank you," he said in a rush.

Olivier stood next to me, jaw clenched again.

"My lovely wife, Sarah," my dad said, beaming at my mom, "is the best hostess, best cook, and best mother in town. She has poured her heart and soul into letting her light of creativity and hospitality shine in Harrogate. This beautiful building is a reflection of her creativity, grace, and ambition. I love you so much, honey. Congratulations."

My mom hugged him.

My dad still looked like he was about to pop. He stood next to Mom, grinning maniacally as she began to thank the architects, contractors, and townspeople.

When my mother finished her speech, my dad practically screamed out, "Noelle's getting engaged."

"It's supposed to be a surprise, James," my mother said through gritted teeth.

"I know, and I tried to keep it a surprise, but I'm just so excited."

"Well, come up and do your proposal, Oliver." My mom motioned to him.

"I'm not marrying you if you're cheating on me," I said stubbornly.

"I wasn't cheating on you," Oliver yelled. "I was trying to buy you a ring."

"Oh. But I already have one." I held up my hand.

"I'm not proposing to you with that," he scoffed.

"Propose, propose, propose!" the crowd chanted drunkenly.

"Here," Oliver said, handing me his phone.

There were like a thousand messages between him and the jeweler.

"Oh. Oh! This is a pretty ring," I said. "Oops! I guess I wasn't supposed to see that. I'm sorry my parents ruined the surprise, and I'm sorry I was ungrateful."

"I wanted to make it special for you. It was supposed to be on Christmas Eve," he admitted.

"I like early Christmas presents."

Oliver winced. "The ring does not look like that picture, so I need to find you a new one."

"Propose!"

"Ask her to marry you!" the crowd called.

"I'll love whatever you pick out," I assured him. "Even if it's made out of cookies. Actually, especially if it's made out of cookies. But seriously." I gazed up at him. "I love you, and I want to spend the rest of my life with you. I don't care about the ring. I just want you. Will you marry me, Oliver?"

He gazed at me adoringly. Then he pulled out a box and got down on one knee.

"Noelle, when you first dumped elf vomit all over me, you said you hated Christmas. But it's clear that you're no grinch. You deeply value your community, your relationship with your family, and your friends. You make your town a better place, and you make me a better man. Christmas only comes once a year, but I want to spend every Christmas with you."

He smirked.

"Also, you're the only woman I know that can make a green furry suit look damn sexy." He grinned. "Will you marry me, Noelle, and do me the honor of being my wife?"

He took my hand and slid an enormous ring on it.

His smile looked a little pained as I held the ring up to the light.

"Oh my gosh!" I started laughing and crying.

"I can find you a different one."

I leaned down and kissed him.

"It's the scene from *The Grinch*!" I said in excitement. "This is the mountain. This is Whoville. The diamond is all the snow. This is so cool. How did you even come up with this design?" I slipped it off to admire it more closely. "And it's even engraved with a quote from the story. I love it! It's perfect."

"Come up for pictures," my dad called. "Free Christmas trees for—"

"No," Azalea barked, as Oliver helped me up onto the steps of the lodge.

My sister was there, waiting with her hands on Dove's shoulders.

"Oliver has one more big announcement," she said to my father.

"Another announcement?" The microphone screeched.

I was confused.

Azalea and Oliver exchanged a look. Oliver took the microphone.

"Dove," he said, "since Noelle and I are getting married, I wanted to ask if you'd like to be part of the family too. Officially."

Dove's mouth dropped open.

I started crying.

Thank you, I mouthed to Azalea.

She nodded.

Dove ran into my arms, and I hugged her to me.

"I love you so much, Dove, and I love you too," I said to Oliver.

My fiancé hugged us.

"Best Christmas ever," Dove said happily.

"Totally the best Christmas ever."

"Spike that eggnog!" Gran called. "Drinks are on Oliver." She dumped several bottles of rum into a giant vat of eggnog.

"Oh Lord. They're never going to leave."

"Merry Christmas to all," Gran called, "and to all a good 'nog!"

The End

Jam-Sandwich Christmas Cookies

Ingredients

3 large eggs
3/4 cup sugar
1 cup European unsalted butter
2 teaspoons vanilla extract
4 cups all-purpose flour
1 teaspoon baking powder
1 (12-ounce) jar raspberry jam
Confectioners' sugar, for garnish

Instructions

1. Gather the ingredients. Preheat oven to 375 F.
2. In a large bowl, beat the eggs and sugar with a hand mixer until light and foamy, about 5 minutes.
3. Melt the butter and let cool slightly. When cooled to room temperature, add it slowly to the egg-sugar mixture with the vanilla, mixing constantly.
4. Whisk together flour and baking powder; slowly add it to the egg mixture to create a firm dough.
5. Roll out the dough to 1/8-inch thick on parchment-lined baking pans and cut with a round cutter.

6. Use a small cookie cutter in a fun shape to cut out a hole in the center of half of the cookies and remove scraps.
7. Bake about 8 minutes. Remove from oven and cool completely.
8. Re-roll scraps and repeat.
9. Sprinkle the cookies with holes with confectioners' sugar. Spread cookies without holes with a raspberry jam. Press together jam-filled cookie with holed-out cookies to form a sandwich.
10. These make a great gift!

Acknowledgements

A big thank you to Red Adept Editing for editing and proofreading.

And finally a big thank you to all the readers! I had a great time writing this hilarious book! Please try not to choke on your wine while reading!!!

About the Author

If you like steamy romantic comedy novels with a creative streak, then I'm your girl!

Architect by day, writer by night, I love matcha green tea, chocolate, and books! So many books…

Sign up for my mailing list to get special bonus content, free books, giveaways, and more!

http://alinajacobs.com/mailinglist.html

Made in the USA
Monee, IL
20 November 2023